The Best American Mystery Stories 2020

GUEST EDITORS OF
THE BEST AMERICAN MYSTERY STORIES

The Best American Mystery Stories™ 2020

Edited and with an Introduction
by **C. J. Box**

Otto Penzler, Series Editor

MARINER BOOKS

HOUGHTON MIFFLIN HARCOURT

BOSTON • NEW YORK   2020

hmhbooks.com

ISSN 1094-8384 (print)   ISSN 2573-3907 (e-book)
ISBN 978-1-328-63610-2 (print)   ISBN 978-1-328-63612-6 (e-book)
ISBN 978-0-358-39459-4 (audio)

Printed in the United States of America
DOC 10 9 8 7 6 5 4 3 2 1

These stories are works of fiction. Names, characters, places, and incidents are products of the authors' imagination or are used fictitiously. Any resemblance to actual events, locales, or persons, living or dead, is entirely coincidental.

Contents

Foreword

ANOTHER YEAR, ANOTHER EDITION of *The Best American Mystery Stories*. Just as each year presents surprises and memorable moments, so does each volume in this prestigious series. It has been my privilege to be the series editor for all twenty-four annual volumes of these monuments to excellence in the realm of the mystery short story.

Writing a good mystery story is no small thing. Many of the novelists I've worked with over the years have claimed that it's harder to produce a good short story, where every word must count so heavily, than to have the expansive luxury of telling the story over scores of thousands of words.

John Dickson Carr, the greatest writer of impossible crime stories who ever concocted a locked-room puzzle, claimed that the natural form of the traditional mystery is not the novel but the short story. It is not uncommon, he pointed out, for a detective story to revolve around a single incident, with a single clue, which can be discovered, divulged, and have its significance explained within a few pages. The rest is embellishment.

While it is redundant for me to write it again, since I have already done so in each of the previous twenty-three volumes of this series, it falls into the category of fair warning to state that many people regard a "mystery" as a detective story. I regard the detective story as one subgenre of a much more inclusive literary form, which I define as any short work of fiction in which a crime (usually murder, as the stakes are highest when a human life is being taken), or the threat of a crime (creating suspense), is central to the theme or the plot.

While I love good puzzles and tales of pure ratiocination, few of these are written today, as the mystery genre has evolved (for better or worse, depending on your point of view) into a more character-driven form of literature, with more emphasis on the "why" of a crime's commission than the "who" or the "how." The line between mystery fiction and general fiction has become more and more blurred in recent years, producing fewer memorable traditional detective stories but more significant literature.

As is true every year, I could not have perused the 1,500–2,000 mystery stories that were published and examined last year, and much of the heavy lifting was done by my invaluable colleague, the longtime editor Michele Slung. She is able to read, evaluate, and commit to seemingly lifelong memory a staggering percentage of those stories, culling those that clearly do not belong on a short list—or a long one either, for that matter. She examines twice as many stories as that to determine if they have mystery or criminal content, which is frequently impossible to know merely by reading the title.

The same standards have pertained to every one of the volumes in this important series. The best writing makes it into the book. Fame, friendship, original venue, reputation, subject—none of it matters. It isn't only the qualification of being the best writer that will earn a spot on the table of contents; it also must be the best story.

After Michele has gathered the stories to be seriously considered, I read the harvested crop, passing along the best fifty (or at least those I liked best, which I like to think is the same thing) to the guest editor, who selects the twenty that are then reprinted, with the other thirty being listed in an honor roll as "Other Distinguished Mystery Stories."

Sincere thanks are due to this year's guest editor, C. J. Box, the number-one *New York Times* bestselling author of twenty-seven novels, including the Joe Pickett series. He has won the Edgar Allan Poe Award for Best Novel (*Blue Heaven,* 2009) as well as an Anthony, a Macavity, a Gumshoe, two Barrys, and the 2010 Reading the West Book Award for fiction. His novels have been translated into thirty languages, and over 10 million copies of his books have been sold in the U.S. and abroad.

This is an appropriate time to thank the previous guest editors, who have done so much to make this prestigious series such a resounding success: Robert B. Parker, Sue Grafton, Ed McBain, Donald E. Westlake, Lawrence Block, James Ellroy, Michael Connelly, Nelson DeMille, Joyce Carol Oates, Scott Turow, Carl Hiaasen, George Pelecanos, Jeffery Deaver, Lee Child, Harlan Coben, Robert Crais, Lisa Scottoline, Laura Lippman, James Patterson, Elizabeth George, John Sandford, Louise Penny, and Jonathan Lethem.

While Michele and I engage in a relentless quest to locate and read every mystery/crime/suspense story published, I live in terror that I will miss a worthy story, so if you are an author, editor, or publisher, or care about one, please feel free to send a book, magazine, or tearsheet to me c/o The Mysterious Bookshop, 58 Warren Street, New York, NY 10007. If it first appeared electronically, you must submit a hard copy. It is vital to include the author's contact information. No unpublished material will be considered, for what should be obvious reasons. No material will be returned. No critical analysis will be offered, nor an explanation of why a story wasn't selected. If you distrust the postal service, please enclose a self-addressed, stamped postcard.

To be eligible, a story must have been written by an American or a Canadian and first published in an American or Canadian publication in the calendar year 2020. The earlier in the year I receive the story, the more fondly I regard it. If it is published near the end of the year, that can't be helped, so please get it to me as quickly as possible. For reasons known only to the dunderheads who wait until Christmas week to submit a story published the previous spring, holding eligible stories for months before submitting them occurs every year, causing murderous thoughts while I read a stack of stories while my friends are trimming the Christmas tree or otherwise celebrating the holiday season. It had better be a damned good story if you do this.

Because of the very tight production schedule for this book, the absolute firm deadline is December 31. If the story arrives one day later, it will not be read. This is neither whimsical nor arbitrary, but absolutely necessary in order to meet publishing schedules. Sorry.

O.P.

Introduction

SEVERAL YEARS AGO I published a collection of my short stories (including a couple of new ones) under the title *Shots Fired: Tales from Joe Pickett Country*. Although I knew my editor wasn't wild about the idea and a majority of regular readers would prefer a new Joe Pickett or Cassie Dewell novel, the collection did well and I'm quite proud of it. When I want to gift a book to someone who isn't familiar with my work, I give that person *Shots Fired*.

What did surprise me (and, to be honest, disappoint me as well) were the number of folks I met along the trail who said things like "Sorry—I don't read short stories," or, worse, "I hate short stories. I prefer the real thing." The real thing, of course, meaning full-length novels.

I tried to gently persuade the former commenters to give them a try. Short stories done well, I told them, can pack a punch like no other form of writing. A few of the people agreed to give them a read.

As for the "I hate short stories" people, I shot them on the spot and stepped over their bodies (after a final double tap) to engage with more pleasant people. Of course, this is a lie.

For years now, the brilliant and legendary Otto Penzler has devoted thousands of hours of his time to studiously reading short mystery stories that appeared the year before in anthologies, collections, and specialty publications. Of those he read last year, he winnowed them down to his fifty favorites and then sent them to me. Having had the real pleasure of reading those works, I think he got it exactly right, and selecting the final twenty was no easy task.

For over a century in America, short stories were a staple of both literary and mainstream magazines and periodicals. Great and popular short story writers were well known and valued, as they should have been. I think that's one reason why this country has such a long tradition of excellent short stories and short story authors.

But things changed. Just try to find a short story in a popular magazine today.

Nevertheless, Otto has kept the flame alight.

And it's an honor for me to have been asked to write this introduction.

I remember when I found out that a short story of mine had been selected to appear in the 2017 volume of this series. The story was called "Power Wagon," and the anthology was edited by John Sandford. I was absolutely—and maybe disproportionately—thrilled. It's a badge of honor as well as a validation that's hard to put into words. I would venture to say that the authors included here will feel the same way.

I'll confess right here that crafting a good short story is much harder than writing a full-length novel. Not all of the short stories I've written are the same quality, damn it. The length and breadth of novels leaves you room to adjust, to fill in, to take a couple of side trips, and all is forgiven in the end. It's the difference between stringing a series of dissimilar pearls on a string and calling it a necklace and being the oyster who creates a single perfect pearl. This volume contains twenty perfect pearls.

It's strange how the whims of popular culture go. Albums used to be the thing for music lovers. Now it's hit singles. These stories are hit singles, literary version.

Take, for example, John Sandford's brilliant little gem "Girl with an Ax." How can anyone who loves the genre not want to read *that?* It begins: "The girl with the ax got off the bus at the corner of Santa Monica Boulevard and Gower Street and started walking the superheated eleven blocks down Gower to Waring Avenue, where she lived by herself in a four-hundred-square-foot bungalow with an air conditioner designed and manufactured by cretins." I love everything about that opening, and it only gets better from there. It's a wonderful story that can only be described as "Sandfordian."

I made notes and bullet points next to some of the selections so

I'd remember which ones to read a second time later. On a few of the stories, I underlined sentences I *wish* I'd written.

An unscientific smattering of notes includes:

- "On Little Terry Road" by Tom Franklin: ". . . the room so cold he could see the captions of his breath." The story itself: Desperate. Very, very dark.
- "Security" by Jeffery Deaver: A political hit job like no other, ever.
- "Nightbound" by Wallace Stroby: Breathless, action-packed, great sense of place.
- "Home Movie" by Jerry M. Burger: An entire life in five reels of 8mm film.
- "Deportees" by the master James Lee Burke: Evocative, haunting. "She was a beautiful woman and had a regal manner, but she was also crazy and had undergone electroshock treatments and had been placed in the asylum in Wichita Falls."
- "See Humble and Die" by Richard Helms: "She looked like someone had wrapped a refrigerator."
- "Pretzel Logic" by dbschlosser: Clipped, severed, sharp dialogue. A terrific scheme.
- "Second Cousins" by Michael Cebula: Noirish, featuring a woman named Toola. Cool twist ending. I cannot *not* read a story with a character named Toola.
- "Shanty Falls" by Doug Crandell: Dark and mesmerizing. Haunting.
- "Rhonda and Clyde" by John M. Floyd: With a setting in my home state of Wyoming, this is a mini-symphony of misdirection.

And those are just a few of the notes I made on the selections here. The rest are just as tantalizing.

Since you're reading this introduction and holding this book in your hands, it means you don't hate short stories. Good for you. It means you can live. It also means you have a special appreciation for this form. For that reason, I can safely say that authors, editors, and fellow short story readers hoist a toast in your honor.

Thank you.

C. J. Box

The Best American Mystery Stories 2020

PAMELA BLACKWOOD

Justice

FROM *Alfred Hitchcock Mystery Magazine*

HE HAD NOT been able to sleep, as usual. Even after a day that had started before sunup and ended in the dark as well, a day that had pitted his muscles against five hundred tons of soil, or so it seemed. Judging from the dull ache in his lower back, the soil had won. He had twisted into every position imaginable in bed to ease the pain, curled in like a spider and straightened out flat like a board, and nothing had helped. He had even considered waking Callie and having her walk on his back like she did sometimes when it was knotting up on him, but it seemed a selfish thing to do, like recalling an angel from heaven to earth. In the long run, it would have made no difference anyway. It was the state of his bed, not his back, that kept him awake for hours each night. No matter how he twisted and turned and shifted, half of his bed was still empty.

He finally left it, pulled on clothes, and made his way to the door without even lighting a candle. The faint glow from the dying fire gave him enough light to find the heavy wooden bolt, and he lifted it and opened the cabin door without making a sound. Once outside, seated on the stone stoop and breathing in the night air, he felt better. He was in the outside world now, the world of infinity. Hannah's new world.

He looked toward heaven, where the preacher said she was, and then looked east, where he knew for a fact she was, at least the part of her he had known on earth. If she were coming home, some evil voice whispered, this is where she would appear to him, stepping out of the forest just beyond the corncrib. Tonight, with his back throbbing, his muscles taut with exhaustion, and his brain unable to rest, William gave in to the wickedness, and his mind set to work. Hannah was coming home again.

She would find her way out of the grave somehow. That was not his concern. Once freed, she would shake off the soil (for his mind insisted on this grisly detail, proof of the evil in it) and start for home. She would walk the three miles from the cemetery, unaffected by the darkness and the cold, her bare feet treading on sticks, and soon she would reach the edge of the forest, where the senseless separation would end.

At this point in the fantasy, the details varied. Sometimes she was holding the baby boy who had died with her, cradling him to her chest against the chill of night and smiling because they'd been blessed with another child. Other times she was alone as she stepped from the forest, always pausing a moment beside the corn-crib to catch William's eye, always smiling at the joy of reunion. Then she would come quickly to him and the nightmare would be over.

Some nights William could see her there as clearly as the creamy moon above. He knew it was evil, twisted thinking to imagine her back in a body no longer fit to house a soul, but most nights he couldn't help himself. Tonight he found, with some irritation, that he had the opposite problem. He could not lose himself in the fantasy due to a riot of barking dogs.

He had not given much thought to the racket at first. Since he'd taken to sitting on the stoop at night and thinking about Hannah, he had grown accustomed to hearing dogs barking all around him, at treed possums or the full moon or at some specter of their own creation. It was the lone barkers that he loved, the lonely call into the night of one creature facing the universe, alone. He thought to them across the pine forests and the freshly turned earth, *Yes, you're right, that's exactly how it feels,* and it seemed to him that at least in that, he had some company.

Tonight was different. The barking was closer, maybe a quarter mile down the road, and it was savage. He held his mind still for a moment and listened. This time it was no midnight loner but what sounded like several hounds working themselves into a frenzy. What made it queer was that's how it had started, just a few moments after he'd seated himself on the stoop. Not with the usual traveling frenzy that either grew or diminished in volume according to the movements of some prey, but a sudden outburst, beginning and continuing in one spot. William thought he was catching voices mingled in with the barking when he heard a sound coming from inside the cabin. Pushing the door behind him open, he heard disembodied sobs, growing louder as Callie made her way down from the sleeping loft.

He pushed himself up from the stoop, brushed his hands together and then against his breeches. When he called Callie's name, the sobbing grew louder and he could hear her bare feet, slapping on each step, hurrying to get to him. Fearful that she would stumble in the dark, he went inside and met her halfway up. Scooping her up into his arms, he returned to the stoop.

It was not a nightmare this time, although they had been common enough since her mother had died. This time he could see the problem right away. In one hand she was clutching a hair ribbon. One of the pigtails he had so inexpertly braided a few hours earlier had come undone.

After waiting through the necessary tears and drama, he took the pink ribbon from Callie, set her on her feet, and turned her around. Working more by feel than sight, he began the task of re-braiding.

His hands, rough and clumsy as a hound dog's paws, were chilly, and the fine dark hair kept slipping from his fingers. When his handiwork dissolved for the third time, he gave up. No hands would work that were chilled such as his and no eyes in such poor light. Five minutes in front of the fire, after a bit of stoking, and the task would be done. Getting to his feet, he watched Callie sit on the stoop and cross her arms.

"Let's go in," he said, and held one hand down for her to grasp. "Papa's hands won't work in the cold."

"No," she said simply, and drew her knees up under her arms. It was her new way, since her mother had died. Not defiance so much as a courtesy, informing him of how things were going to be. William, who never would have tolerated such behavior six weeks earlier, sat back down and put his hands under his armpits.

Immediately Callie jumped up and ran to the well in the center of the yard. He called her name, knowing all the while that it was a useless exercise, then got up and followed her across the swept ground, keeping an eye that the white nightgown stayed on the outside of the circular rock wall that surrounded the well. When he caught up with her, she had hunkered down in front of it. He sat down beside her.

"Look," she called, and one slender arm flew out from the huddle of nightgown and disordered hair and pointed to the sky. "There's the dipper," she shouted, and danced the shape of it in the air with her finger.

"That's right," William said, and deciding that he could at least keep her warm even if he couldn't control her, he stretched out his legs and pulled her onto his lap.

"But there's no water," she said, as if her heart would break, and William sensed the beginning of a storm of vexation over this notion. He had discovered that the only way out of these dark fits of anger was a quick distraction.

"Callie," he said in a loud whisper. He ducked his head and looked from left to right and then at her as if he knew a marvelous secret that no one else must hear. Seeing her eyes open wide, he knew the trick had worked.

"What?" she whispered, and he felt her face turn up to his.

"You hear those dogs? Those barkers down the road a bit?"

She nodded her head, enthralled.

"You know what's making 'em go on and on like that?"

She shook her head, lips parted and eyes unblinking, all past traumas forgotten. William had no idea what was coming next, but he had learned to improvise like never before in the last few weeks.

"Well," he said, and looking up to the sky, it came to him. He turned Callie outward and lifted her face toward the stars.

"You see that star up there," he asked, and aimed her head toward the North Star. At that moment the barking grew to a fever pitch and William imagined that he heard a man shout. But it was all around him now, every dog on every homestead alerted to something in the night, and William, in the cacophony, could hardly be sure of what he heard. He looked back down when he felt Callie tugging on his sleeve.

"I see it," she said, slightly piqued, and William knew he was in danger of losing ground if he didn't hurry on.

"That's the North Star," he said. "But it's part of something else too. That star makes up part of a bear up there in the sky. That's what my daddy, your granddaddy, told me when I was little like you and that's what's got those dogs all keyed up. They're barking after that bear up yonder and there's nothing more they can do than bark."

"I don't see any bear," Callie said, and stood up, stepping to the left and to the right and all the while squinting upward. "I don't see a bear," she said again, her voice smaller this time and closer to tears. William pulled her back on his lap.

"It's a dipper too," he added in desperation, and ran his finger along the trail of stars that made up the Little Dipper. "See there?" he said, trying to cover her with his coat. Her bare feet were ice, even through his trouser leg.

"Where?" she shouted, and William ran his finger along the sky trail again, pulling his coat closer around her when she threatened to burst out of it.

Please let her see it, he implored, and finally she saw something, because her head started banging against his chest in an enthusiastic nod.

At that moment the barking stopped, as suddenly and inexplicably as it had begun.

William looked away from the sky, stared into the darkness, and wondered at the oddness of it. Callie began pulling on one of his shirt buttons.

"What's his name?" she asked, giving all her attention to the button, twisting and turning it and plucking it with her fingers.

"Stop that, Callie," William said, sharper than he meant to because he'd be more likely to traipse across the moon than be able to sew a button back onto a shirt.

"It pushes," she said in a high-pitched whine, and William opened his shirt where the button was digging into her head and felt a rush of pleasure at the brush of her soft hair against his bare chest. For now, at least, he still had her and her little sister and he would move heaven and earth and hell to keep them alive. Thinking that perhaps the night air was not the best thing for Callie, he decided to begin the process of putting her back to bed. He savored the touch of her for another moment and then hugged her and set her on her feet.

"What's his name?" she insisted, stomping one ice foot into the earth and pointing toward the sky.

"Virgil," William said, thinking of his father's name and then thinking faster still. "And he has ordered most of these dogs down here to hush up and go to sleep. You hear how those closer ones have gone quiet?"

Dogs were still barking in the distance all around them, but William was hoping that for once Callie would not examine the statement for absolute truth.

"They've gone quiet as church mice, haven't they?" he hurried on, taking her hand. "Most of them, anyway. They know it's bedtime for dogs and children. And old Virgil up there, he'd like to see them all go to sleep, all dogs and children as well. Think you can oblige him?"

Some miracle of five-year-old logic stepped in, and Callie nodded. William smiled and counted it as a victory. It was one of the precious few he'd had since being thrust into the uncharted mystery land of children, with scant provisions and no map. He was making his way, but slowly.

They had turned to go into the cabin when he heard it.

A pair of riders were coming down the road, pushing their horses until the sound of hooves hitting dirt filled the night. He heard them coming, heard the desperate clomping pass his property, and heard the sound echo off the trees as the riders pressed on into the distance. Any minute he expected an abrupt end to the sound, as pushing a horse like that in the dark was a fool's game, asking for a misstep that meant death for horse and rider.

In another moment it was as if the sound had never existed. The hoofbeats that had dominated the dark had faded and then were gone as quickly as they had come, returning the night to the barking dogs.

William felt Callie's arms tighten around him and looked down to find her sobbing quietly onto his breeches. When he tried to kneel down, she pressed her face even harder against his thighs.

"What is it, Callie?" he asked, stroking her hair and wondering if he'd ever be any better at this, at the whys and hows of tending children.

She mumbled something but it was garbled by sobs. He bent his head closer and asked her to repeat it.

"Reaper," she whispered, and he knew in an instant what was in her mind. *Like a thief in the night,* the preacher had spoken over her mother's coffin, *the Grim Reaper comes and takes what he will and then is gone, but our Heavenly Father* . . . William had shut his mind to the rest, having no patience for a justification of Hannah's death.

"No, Callie," he said down to her. "That's just a couple of men on horses, riding down the road in a hurry. That wasn't the Grim Reaper. That was just men like Papa. There is no Grim Reaper." *Just as there is no Heavenly Father,* his mind continued.

They're lying about all of it, but another corner of his mind recoiled in fear at that and still another corner mocked him and said, *Speak it aloud and see for yourself.*

"There is no Grim Reaper," he repeated. "Now let's fix your hair and then maybe I'll tell you a story." She moved her head, which he took for a nod. Lifting her up into his arms, he walked back to the stoop.

No Grim Reaper, the mocker in his head screamed, and William thought back to the mocker, *That's right.* Even so, he shuddered when he saw the cabin door standing slightly ajar, even while knowing that was surely the way he and Callie had left it.

Drying tears he had quickly become adept at, through lots of practice. In order for them to survive, he had also learned to put something like a meal on the table twice a day, on dishes that had at least been scraped clean of the previous meal. Every garment they owned had been washed at least once since Hannah had died, and he was able to keep the girls at least a stage away from filthy. Hair, it seemed, would be his undoing.

He had started the hair-washing ordeal on the next afternoon, suffering through tears at each stage, from the wetting down to the scrubbing with soap, through the futile attempt at combing out the pair of ravaged birds' nests. Louisa, who shed silent tears in the company of her thumb, had been bad enough. But when Callie had shrieked at every slight pull of the comb, he had given up and placed them both in front of the fire with their dolls until their hair was completely dry. In this decision, even shrieks were powerless against him. He would not risk them getting chilled and then fevered or worse.

Now, getting them ready to go to the tavern, he wondered what Hannah would think of her oldest daughter going out into the world looking like a miniature madwoman, her hair hanging about in tangled clumps. *If you cared, you shouldn't have left me,* he thought, and then wondered at his own sanity. Settling the girls in front of him on the horse, he dismissed the issue as irrelevant. He would have to carry on whether sane or insane, so why even bother to consider it? Nudging Gus gently forward toward the road, he worried over another matter entirely—would the girls be quiet long enough for him to get a swallow of gin and a scrap of adult companionship. At this moment in his life, after five days of working alone, it was all he wanted.

Last time out they had not. Louisa had fretted at the loud men hurting her ears, Callie had seen a witch on the ride over and clung to William's leg the rest of the evening. Tonight, if they could be still at the same time for a slim half hour, he had promised to buy them each a new hair ribbon at the dry goods store. Bribery, he had discovered, was even better than diversion.

Once there, he set them on the floor in the corner of the tavern with two dolls and a bag of marbles and got himself a glass of gin. Taking a chair at a nearby table, he nodded a greeting to one of his neighbors.

"So you still haven't found anybody," Josh Miller said by way of greeting.

"Not looking," William said, stretching his legs out under the table and leaning back. It felt good to sit down, good to be warm, good to have a drink in his hand and a neighborly body to drink it with. "I don't need anybody," he continued, and then took a drink of gin to wash his throat clean of the lie.

"Seems like you do," Josh said, looking pointedly into the corner at Callie's matted hair. When William looked daggers at him, he just shook his head. "A man can be too stubborn sometimes, seems like to me. Besides, those two little ones need something better than you to look at."

"Can't argue with that one," William said, and looked over the other patrons in the tavern. The place was crowded with men and boys, with a stray female here and there. One over near the keg seemed to be the centerpiece of a small throng of boys who were vying for her attention with lively words and gestures.

William saw them all as potential murderers, for surely one would win her heart and vent his passion on her until she died. That was the way of the world.

"It's no use thinking about that one," Josh said. "Unless you can drop ten years off your body and twenty off your thinking. I doubt she'd be satisfied to tend children, but she might know of—"

"I thought I said, pretty clear, that I wasn't looking," William said. "I reckon she'll die soon enough without coming around me. I've killed one already, seems like that's enough for a while."

"You stupid fool," Josh said with feeling but no malice. "If you figure on calling yourself a murderer, I reckon that little baby boy is a killer too. Killed his mama and himself. You reckon that's the way of it, Will?"

"I reckon some folks need to tend to their own business and keep out of mine. Don't you have another subject, Josh?"

"As a matter of fact, I do," Josh said. "Talking about killing, there was a killing over near your place last night. Ben Pierce was riding early this morning down the Raleigh Road and nearly stumbled over poor old Johnny Grant lying sprawled out beside the road with his throat cut. Been robbed, it looked like. You know that pouch of money he always wore around his neck?"

"Yep," William said, fighting a numbness that was starting at the tips of his fingers and working up.

"Well, that was gone, and you know he never went nowhere without it, even wore it to bed, they say. That was gone and his old daddy's pocket watch was gone and that locket that had his mama's likeness, they took that off him too. I don't reckon he had much more than that, being an idiot and all. And you know them dogs he always kept running around at his feet?"

William nodded.

"Caught one of 'em with a knife. Ben carried that one home but figured the other one must have got away or crawled off to die, since it wasn't around nowhere. A damn shame, is what it is. You hear anything at your place last night?"

"Yep. Dogs barking, pitching a fit—late, after ten o'clock. Then a couple of horses running full chisel a few minutes later. I reckon I heard the whole thing." He had gotten up from his bed to look for peace, to be with Hannah, and had heard a murder. A tiny ember that had been smoldering in his brain sprang to life. "Who do you reckon would kill an idiot boy like that?"

Josh looked at him and tipped his head toward the circle of young people across the room.

William let the gesture lie. "Could have been anybody. Lots of folks knew Johnny took that road home from the sawmill every night. Being the way he was, he'd be easy pickin's. A stranger could have done it, would have known once he had a word or two with the boy that he wasn't right in the head."

"Could have, but didn't," Josh said, and with the words came a chill that William sensed in spite of the flames at the tavern's hearth and the bursts of laughter and easy talk that hummed around them.

"So what are you saying, Josh?" William asked, and then was distracted by Louisa tugging on his sleeve. Her doll, she explained, had suffered a hurt leg when Callie had deliberately dropped her from a dangerous height. William took out his handkerchief and dried Louisa's tears and then wrapped the doll leg, glancing at Josh and at the rag leg he was tending and then across the room where he'd seen Josh look. Finishing the job, he handed Louisa the doll and told her to run along, but instead she climbed into his lap and lay against him, sucking her thumb and stroking the wounded doll.

"You're saying it's somebody we know," William continued when Josh showed no sign of answering his question. "You're saying it's somebody in this taproom, if I'm reading you right."

"You see that group over yonder?" Josh asked, and dipped his head in their direction again. "Wendell Pike, Jimmy Galton, Eddie Bishop, and all them boys around Mary Ann Graves?"

"I see 'em," William said. "I'd be blind and deaf not to, the way they've been cutting up all night."

"Well, I been watching them, both before you got here and since. They been cutting up all right, trying to impress that girl, mainly with fancy talk. But some of that fancy talk, a lot of it, I'd say, has centered around Eddie and Wendell and something Eddie keeps bringing out and dangling around to show everybody. I got a good look at it once, when I went out back. It's a watch."

"Lots of folks have watches, Josh."

"That's so. But what's so dang funny about that one? He's showing it off like a square nickel."

"Could be new to him. Could be his daddy's or his granddaddy's or he just bought it himself."

"It's new to him, all right. Newly filched off of Johnny Grant's body. You know and I know that his daddy, being both a drunkard and poor as Job's turkey, didn't buy that boy no new watch to show off like that."

"Maybe the boy bought it himself. He works at the sawmill, doesn't he?"

"He turns up at the sawmill now and again and Wendell's daddy might give him a day or two of work if he has it, but that's hardly enough to go buying a fancy watch when your daddy barely makes enough to keep his own body and soul together, let alone his children's. That's Johnny's watch, I'd bet my head on it."

"Rather than bet your head, why not talk to the sheriff?" William said. He felt Louisa flinch in his lap when the group in the corner burst into laughter. When she put both fists over her ears and began to whimper, he knew his time at the tavern was almost over.

"I intend to tell him," Josh said. "Trouble is, that'll likely be the end of it. Like you said, lots of folks have watches, and who's around to testify to that one being Johnny's? The boy didn't have no family and hardly any friends. Just them two dogs, and they're good as gone too."

"He went to the sawmill nearly every day of his life," William said. "Some of them must have known him."

"He did do that. He was a pest they tried to run off, and when he came back, they ignored him best they could."

"Still, some of them must have seen that watch."

"'Course they did. That's why they figured on robbing him. They saw the watch and they saw the money pouch and then went through the poor boy's pockets after they'd finished their handiwork on him and took his mama's locket as well. It's just a wonder they didn't open his mouth and check for gold teeth."

"So tell the sheriff," William said, and set Louisa down on her feet. Finishing the last of his gin, he gestured to Callie, who studiously ignored him. "That Grant boy is entitled to justice same as any man under this roof. More so, since he was soft in the head and couldn't defend himself."

"I agree with you, friend," Josh said, and after one long last look, he turned his back on the group of young people. "And I will talk to Clayton about it. But the fact is, Wendell Pike's daddy owns the sawmill and Eddie's his best friend and Johnny Grant was just an idiot boy who had nothing and no ties and nobody's going to care much that he's gone. I reckon he'll find justice in the end, like the rest of us. Trouble is, he's going to have to wait till then to get it. Till then, he's just dead and that's the end of it."

"That's never the end of it, Josh," William said, adding a goodbye before going to the corner to gather Callie and an ever-widening circle of marbles.

Never the end of it, he thought again when Louisa woke up a few nights later crying for her mama and inconsolable. He would have preferred a knife in the ribs to the child's pitiful cries, but there was no one to give it to him, so he simply held her until she went back to sleep, a rough and clumsy substitute for someone who had been silken and soft and warm. He slept no more that night but went about the cabin waiting for dawn, from the hearth to the stoop to the stairs, there to listen for the girls' soft breathing. Place made no difference now, for everywhere was the same—a place without Hannah.

Finally seeing the sky lightening in the east, he made himself think about the coming day. He had chores to do. He had turned the soil in both cornfields but not yet put in the first seed. March was creeping into April and he had not planted a salad garden. He would work on that, turn the old bed near the cabin, work in some leaves and manure, and get the soil ready to set in seed. He could do that; in fact, had to. In spite of his soul rending in two, they still had to eat. The salad garden was nearby, so he could watch the girls playing around the cabin, maybe even set Callie to work with a spade, helping him. With a plan in mind, he turned to breakfast.

The plan worked for half the morning and then went sour. The girls played house on the stoop, bringing out dishes and pans and the churn, and things went well until Callie appeared in the doorway with an armful of linen. Picturing himself washing bedsheets for days, William put a stop to that and set off a string of misbehavior that climaxed with one arm being torn off Louisa's doll when his back was turned, a crisis no amount of lemon drops could set right. Putting his plow in the toolshed, he rinsed his hands and spent a half hour working with needle and thread. After finally re-attaching the severed limb, he hitched up the horse, tidied both girls and himself, and set off down the road for the Methodist church. It was time to visit Mama.

Tying up in front of the church, he lifted the girls out of the wagon and watched them run around to the back as if their mother would be there waiting to welcome them to a picnic or a game of jacks. Instead there would be silence and a stone and that would be their mother for the rest of their lives. William walked around

the church slowly, dreading the sight of the stone and the mound
of earth, always dreading it, as if each time he saw these terrible
objects, Hannah was lost to him anew. Coming to the corner, he
braced himself and moved quickly, wanting to get it over with, to
let the gouge in his soul bleed a little more until perhaps, one day,
it would begin to heal.

He was surprised to find the girls talking not to their mother,
as they usually did, but to Henry Cobb. The man was standing on
Hannah's grave, shirtsleeves rolled up, leaning on his shovel. As
William reached them, he heard Callie imploring the gravedigger
to start lifting the dirt off her mama.

"Hush, Callie," he said, pulling her up to hold against him. "I'm
sorry to see you back at work so soon after just laying Matt Avery to
rest last week."

"Yes, sir," Henry said, and lifting his shovel in the air, he plunged
it into the earth that was Hannah's grave. William winced slightly,
as if the action could hurt her. Turning his mind from his own
foolishness, he set Callie down and nodded toward a freshly turned
plot in the far corner of the burial ground.

"Who'd you put way down yonder, Henry, in that swampy ground
down there? Water stands like the devil there when we get a rainy
spell."

"Yep, I know," Henry said, reaching around for a flask hanging
from his belt. He took a long drink and sighed with satisfaction. "It
was that idiot boy that got himself killed over near your place, the
one with them dogs."

"That was a week ago," William said, and smelling whiskey fumes
coming from the man, he reckoned that was what it took to do such
a job as covering people with earth. "He's just now getting buried?"

"Yep. Nobody claimed him, nor any interest in him. Some of the
women laid him out for a day or two and waited, but no one turned
up to see him or take him, and you can't wait forever, not with it
warming up soon. Millie came by a while ago and we said some
words over him and then I got to work."

"But why'd you put him down there, Henry, away from all the
folks and in that soggy ground?"

"What's the difference?" the gravedigger said, and shrugged. He
took a cloth sack off his belt and pulled a piece of cornbread out
of it. "Been a long time since breakfast," he said, and started eating, dropping crumbs on the ground around him. "Nobody'll be

coming to see him, so nobody's going to get their feet wet. What's
the use of wasting good space on a boy like that, as long as he's
put down good and proper like everybody else? Sorry, William," he
said, and stepped away from Hannah's grave with his johnnycake.
"I didn't mean no disrespect. Guess I forgot myself for a minute."

"Guess you did," William said, wanting to knock the man flat to
the ground with his fist. Instead he took the shovel away from Callie, who had started scraping it across the raw earth, and handed it
back to the gravedigger. "If it's all the same to you, Henry, the girls
and I would like to visit with their mama for a bit."

"Sure enough, Will," the man said, and shoving the rest of the
corn cake into his mouth, he threw the shovel over his shoulder
and headed for a fat pine tree at the edge of the cemetery.

William kicked the crumbs off the grave and told the girls it was
time to say a prayer for their mama and go. Callie questioned the
haste of it and Louisa whined. William had in fact planned to stay
longer, but the gravedigger was sitting under the old pine watching
them, and William felt the intrusion keenly.

After speaking his own empty words to the sky, he waited while
the girls each spoke a prayer, with Callie's being a jumble of lamen-
tations and requests addressed to God and her mama in turn, and
Louisa's a suggestion that Mama come down for a visit. William
tried to listen to the phrases like he always did, to see what was
in each girl's heart, but his mind kept slipping away, to the fresh
mound of earth in the swampy ground that no one would be coming to visit.

It started a few days later, without William even realizing anything
had begun. He had not left the farm for several days, doing man's
work in the daytime, woman's work in the evening, and the devil's
work at night, sitting on the stoop and longing for Hannah to come
back to him. Sleep, which had become a matter of three or four
hours a night, was something he longed for during the day, when
it was impossible. So it had been with a foggy brain that he had
gone to the feed and seed store and bought exactly half as much
corn seed as he needed for his southern and most productive corn-
field. Getting the girls ready for another trip to town to buy more,
he wondered if they were even safe with him as a caretaker. Perhaps he would confuse Louisa for a barrel of pickles and leave her
standing beside the counter in the store or forget he had children

altogether and ride off with a couple of feed sacks in their places. Nothing anymore would surprise him.

For this reason he spoke to the girls quietly after lifting them from the wagon in front of the store, asking them to remain in his sight at all times and to hold hands and never lose sight of each other. Even Callie was sobered by something in his demeanor, and the two followed William into the seed store like a pair of tiny ghosts and stood quietly behind him, moving as he did and never uttering a sound. And so it was that William, who had been living a life of nothing but distraction for weeks, was able to take note of his surroundings in the seed store. And what he noted was that the man leaning on the far end of the counter, waiting for his order to be filled, was Eddie Bishop.

William could not have sworn it was the Bishop boy; he had never spoken to him that he could recall and had no more than a nodding acquaintance with his father. On getting closer, however, he saw what he needed to see. An old scar, running from the boy's left ear to his upper lip, marked him as Eddie Bishop, the Eddie Bishop who had gotten his face half cut off in a drunken brawl one night after work.

Sending Callie and Louisa over to warm themselves by the stove, William walked down to the end of the counter where Eddie stood.

"Morning, Eddie," he said. The boy looked at him briefly before returning his attention to the door of the storeroom.

"Morning," he muttered almost inaudibly, dropping one arm onto the countertop and stretching to see as far into the back as he could. After a moment or two, he fell back on his heels and began drumming his fingers on the countertop.

"I was wondering what the time is, Eddie," William said, not bothering to conceal the chain of his own watch. "Would you happen to have the time?"

"What?" Eddie asked. He stopped drumming his nails on the glass and stared at William as if he'd asked for a ride to the moon.

"The time," William repeated, putting his hands into his pockets in such a way as to leave the watch chain draped over the flesh of his arm. "I know you've got yourself a new watch. I saw it the other night at the tavern. I was wondering if you could give me the time."

"What's wrong with your watch?" Eddie asked, turning to face him for the first time.

"Not a thing," William said, and in that moment they locked

eyes and William knew he had achieved his purpose, which was to do nothing more than needle the boy, to nudge him into a state of unease.

"The time, Eddie," William said again. "I really need to know the time."

Eddie scowled and looked away, then fumbled at his pants pocket and pulled out a watch. "Half past eleven," he said, fumbling again to replace it and nearly missing the pocket when the storekeeper suddenly appeared with his order. The boy slung the two feed sacks over his shoulders and left the store without giving William another glance.

Walking to the other end of the counter to place his own order, William counted the first skirmish as his, although the victory had no practical merit in the course of the war.

Two more days passed, and in those days William tended the children and worked to keep up with his chores but no longer as a sleepwalker stumbling through an endless succession of hours. The tiny flame in his brain that had sparked to life on hearing of the murder now bore a steady light, neither flickering nor dancing but glowing brighter and stronger with each passing day. On the third day he determined it was time, or well past time, to talk to the sheriff. The boy had already been dead for two weeks and William had heard nothing more about it.

He dropped the girls off at Lottie Calvin's place, partly because she had been pestering him for weeks to accept some help and partly because he did not want them to hear his conversation with the sheriff. Louisa screamed as if she was being thrown to the devil and Callie attached herself to his leg, but he had to let them out of his sight sometime, so he passed them over to Lottie, waited till she had hold of them, and left. There was nothing for it but to close his heart as best he could, though Louisa's screams echoed in his brain all the way to the county jail.

He had known the sheriff would be hard to nail down and it took three more stops before he found Sheriff Clayton Burwell engaged in a game of horseshoes behind the gristmill. Even though prodded by his own impatience, he knew better than to interrupt the game. Hoping the man he needed the ear of would win, he watched and waited until Arnold Morgan got two ringers in a row and Sheriff Burwell was undeniably defeated. Without giving the man a chance to engage in the usual banter, William stepped up to him and asked for a word.

"Sure, Will, what's on your mind?" Burwell asked, rubbing his palms against his trouser legs and then lifting a tankard that sat on the ground beside them. "That was a stinker, wasn't it? Two back-to-back and by Arnold Morgan."

"Rotten luck," William said, and then rushed on while the man was taking a drink. "I was wondering, Clayton, what's been done about that Grant boy's killing. It happened near my place, you know, close enough for me to hear the whole thing."

Burwell exhaled with satisfaction and shook his head. "That was a bad thing, killing a half-wit boy like that: cutting his throat like a hog and leaving him laying in the road to bleed to death. Some folks are too damn mean to live and that's the truth."

"And?" William prompted and waited, but the sheriff was deeply engaged in slaking his thirst and dismissing his horseshoe opponents with a wave and a few acid remarks. When it seemed as if he had forgotten the subject altogether, William brought it up again.

"Have you gotten anybody for it yet?" he asked. "Josh Miller told me he was going to talk to you about it—about what he knew. Or what he thought he knew."

"He did," the sheriff said, and collecting the horseshoes from the far stake, he walked over to the back of the mill and hung them on a nail. "I listened to him and I thanked him."

"And?" William said again, wondering if the man was thick. "What came of it? What are you doing about Eddie Bishop?"

"I rode over to the sawmill one day when he was working. I asked him if he had anything whatsoever to do with the killing of Johnny Grant. He said no, or I believe it was, hell no. I asked him if he'd gotten himself a new watch recently, that someone had seen him with one the day after the killing and it looked mighty suspicious, and I wanted to know the truth. He said he had got a new watch recently and not that it was any of my damned business, but Wendell Pike gave it to him because it seems Wendell was figuring on getting himself a new one and didn't need it anymore. Not that it was any of my damned business, I believe he added in case I missed it the first time."

"And?"

"And what, Will?"

"What did you do then? What else did you ask him?"

"I asked him nothing else. Told him he could do with a damned sight more respect for the law and left. What more was there for me to ask him?"

"Ask him if you could see the watch, see if it looked like Johnny's."

"I don't know what Johnny's watch looked like. Do you?"

"No, but somebody must have seen it, somebody at that sawmill or some neighbor. Or a shopkeeper, maybe."

"Will, I'll tell you what I told Josh Miller. That boy had no living relatives. The only neighbor that cared a whit about him was old lady Cox who lives in that shack down the road from him, and she's blind as a bat and couldn't tell a pocket watch from a wagon wheel. I think it's an act of pure evil what was done to that boy—a gentle soul like that—but without a witness, without something to link a man to the killing beyond a bunch of guesswork and just plain talk, there's not a thing I can do about it. You got anything to add? Josh said you heard the whole thing happen. You hear Eddie Bishop's voice? Or Wendell Pike's? Hear Johnny yell out their names or anybody else's?"

"No. I heard voices, but—"

"But they could have been anybody's. The dogs were barking up a storm, you said that yourself. I got no reason to hang any crime on Eddie Bishop because he's got himself a new pocket watch. There's nobody to say it was Johnny's, and frankly, Will, like I told you, nobody gives a tinker's damn that the boy's gone, beyond the awful meanness of it. I'm sorry, but that's just the way it is. The only way the Bishop boy's got any chance of being brought up for that killing is if someone finds the money pouch or that locket in his possession, and you can be damned sure nobody's going to, not at this point. Or, even more unlikely, if he confesses. Or, best of all, if Johnny Grant rises up out of the grave and points a finger at Eddie and says, *That's the one who cut my throat.* The boy's off scot-free, Will, and there's not a thing for it, not a thing."

"Maybe not," Will said. He thanked the sheriff for his time and determined to himself that there must be a thing for it, that he would find the thing for it, and the thing he found would bring that dead boy justice.

It was the first thing that had made sense in weeks.

*

The sheriff had given him no satisfaction but several ideas. Find the money pouch and locket. This had no realistic value, since Eddie Bishop, although rough, was not stupid and would know these two things would link him to the crime. The sheriff's favored option, Johnny rising up from the grave, was also not worth wasting a thought on, although with his newfound fantasy of Hannah doing the same, it was hard for William not to picture this, picture the boy coming forth from the earth and finding justice for himself.

A confession seemed only slightly more possible. Any man who would do such a deed would not have to worry with being pricked by a conscience. Either he had none or a conscience so twisted that his only notion of good and evil involved injustice to himself. William thought and thought, he thought while covering seeds, while chopping wood and combing hair and collecting eggs. He thought of Johnny Grant and the boy's naive trust and how it had probably helped to kill him, and he thought of Eddie Bishop and his meanness and greed, which would probably kill him one day but hadn't yet. He had taken everything the Grant boy had in the world, even his dogs, at least one of which had been cut for pure meanness, and he had taken his mama's locket, which had been taken for greed. Done everything, Josh Miller had said, but open up the boy's mouth and . . .

William, as though suddenly bewitched, put the egg in his hand back into the nest and sat back on his heels in the floor of the chicken coop. Gold teeth. If the boy had had them, the killers would want them. But only if they thought they were there.

The new plan, conceived in an instant after weeks of pondering, was as obvious as it was frightful. William faulted himself for not thinking of it the same night Josh had spoken the words, for not going home at once for the shovel and rope. The trouble was, then as now, he would need some help.

He had not had much use for the preacher since Hannah had died. The man, who had no wife to miss and no children to raise alone, had asked William to accept the unacceptable. The idea that Hannah was in heaven did not warm William's bed at night, nor dry her daughters' tears. To the girls, William spoke of Hannah being in a better place; to himself, he only knew of a stone and six feet of earth.

He had spoken to no one about his thoughts, for they were

surely blasphemous, and as bitter as he was, there were still the girls to think about, their place in the community and their future, for who would want to bring into the fold of their family the daughter of a blasphemer? The few remarks he had made, sentiments that had leaked out after several mugs of rum, had been to Josh, who had suggested, stupidly, that he speak his mind to the Reverend Brown. At the time, William had likened that notion to thrusting a scalded hand into the fire. Now he had a real use for the man. What he was planning was against the law and was on church property. More importantly, he needed another pair of eyes and ears to make the scheme work, a pair of eyes and ears that carried the weight of moral authority behind them. Who better, if he could be convinced of the sanity of the scheme, than the Reverend Brown?

For several more days William went about his farm work, rehearsing and carrying out the plan in his mind, flinching at the open horror of it but at the same time reveling in the idea that it might work and the boy might ultimately rest in peace.

He made inquiries of his more pious neighbors about when the preacher's circuit would bring him their way, about where he'd be staying and how long. Finding this out, he did what he had to do. Come the Reverend Brown's Sunday, William scrubbed the girls the night before, dressed them in their cleanest dresses, suffered through the purgatory of hair combing, and went to church.

The service lasted two hours and consumed most of his patience, the socializing with friends and neighbors the rest. He had spent half an hour watching the girls gather bluets for their mother's grave by the time most all of the wagons had gone, finally giving him a chance to speak to the minister privately. He had originally thought to invite the man home for a meal, but Callie and Louisa were terrified of him and William did not want to start a series of nightmares that might go on for weeks. Instead he requested a private meeting for later that night, around nine if it was possible, as he had already arranged to leave the girls with a neighbor and his need to speak with the reverend was urgent.

After laying out his request, William willed the preacher to accept it. If he did not, if he balked or as much as hemmed and hawed, William planned to plead an immediate need for spiritual guidance, for salvation from hell, for anything that would draw the man to the church at nine o'clock.

He was relieved when the Reverend Brown immediately agreed

to the meeting. Figuring he was chalking up sins fast enough without lying to a man of God, William gathered up the girls and left the churchyard quickly, before the preacher had a chance to ask him what it was about.

The girls had cried again at being left, and William wondered at the condition of his own heart that he felt simple sadness for this instead of agony, that his newfound craving for justice had grown stronger than his need to spare his children pain. He had assured them they were needed to keep Aunt Lottie company, kissed them both, and left. Riding to the church, rehearsing his upcoming speech in his head, he felt something akin to excitement. The emotion was so foreign, he wondered again at his own sanity.

Tying up at the church, he tilted his watch into the moonlight to check the time. He had thirty minutes to spend with Hannah before the minister arrived. Lighting the candle he'd tucked into his saddlebag, he walked around to the back of the church and found the stone he had carved weeks ago with the girls' wilted wildflowers lying atop it. It was the first time he had been alone with Hannah since she had gone.

He stood for a moment, then knelt down; not, he assured God, to display any piety, but in order to be closer to Hannah. He had intended to send his thoughts to wherever she was, to commune with her even if the communication was only one way. But after a few minutes the ache to touch her was so great he grew weary of fighting it. Touching his fingers to his lips and then to the earth above her, he left the burying ground and walked back around to the front of the church.

If God was inside, William had no desire to be, so he put the candle out and settled on the front stoop to wait for the preacher.

When the man finally arrived, William stood up and led the way into the tiny sanctuary. Using the church's tinderbox, he relit the candle, set it on top of the stove, and settled on the first bench. Impatiently he listened through the Reverend Brown's small talk, waited while the man settled down beside him and placed a tattered Bible on the pew between them. The sight of it loosened William's tongue.

"You can put that book away, Reverend, because we won't be needing it. Although you might take issue with that after hearing me out."

"If you don't mind," the minister said, "I'll leave it between us. Even if you've got no use for it, I might. And it's not impossible it could help you, William."

Damn Josh Miller and his flapping tongue, William thought, but he didn't plan to argue, at least not that particular point. He bore on to the business he'd come for.

"Reverend, I don't know if you've heard, but a boy was murdered here a couple of weeks ago, an idiot boy named Johnny Grant."

The Reverend Brown nodded. "I heard about the fact of it happening. I didn't hear much more than that."

"Well, I heard the whole thing happen," William said, and again in his mind he heard the dogs barking and barking and then silent. "The ones that did it slashed his throat, stole his money pouch and his mama's locket and his pocket watch, and cut his dogs. They did that last just for meanness. Then left the boy there in the road to die alone, bleed to death while his dogs bled with him, one beside him and one off somewhere else. He lived alone and he died alone with not even a dog to comfort him. And the ones who did that to him walked away and are going about their business while that boy lies back of the church in swampy ground that butts up against the woods. Dead for all time and nobody thinking much of it but what an awful shame it was and what a meanness. But what can anybody do about it without some kind of proof saying who did it?"

"Does anyone know anything at all?"

"It was done by Eddie Bishop," William said, "with some help, I believe, from Wendell Pike. Eddie was showing off a new watch soon after it happened and cutting up with Wendell like they were big bugs, and you know Wendell thinks he is one, what with his daddy owning the sawmill. I think they just got tired of Johnny hanging around and the two of them cooked up a scheme to get rid of him and line their pockets at the same time. I want them to pay for that. The Grant boy had nothing in life. The least he deserves is justice in death and I aim to get it for him. Don't tell me about the great reward he's receiving in heaven or the better place he's in right now, about how we should envy him. Right now he's under six feet of swamp ground."

William waited for recriminations, lectures, even a sermonette on his impiety, but the Reverend Brown simply looked at him for a moment. In the candlelight, William could read nothing in the man's face except fatigue. Suddenly the preacher seemed more human than divine and William felt some of his own hostility drain away.

"I need your help, Reverend," he said, and when the Reverend Brown nodded and said, "Go on," William took a deep breath and explained his scheme in full.

Again the preacher was silent for several moments. When he reached down for the Bible, William stiffened in his seat.

"If you've got a bone to pick with me, Reverend, I'd rather hear it from you than from that book there. With all due respect, I've not had much use for it since Hannah died, and I don't see how it could help with what's facing us here. If you can't see your way clear to help me, I'll do it alone. But I intend on doing it, one way or the other."

"On the contrary, William," the Reverend Brown said, and tilting his Bible toward the candlelight, he flipped its pages quickly at first and then slowly and then one at a time until he'd found the thing he was looking for. Running one finger down the page, he stopped near the middle and looked up at William. "Of course I'm going to help you. Do you think I don't want murderers brought to justice? I'll help you, but it'll have to be soon. I can't stay past Thursday night or I won't make it to Calvary Springs by Saturday afternoon. You'll have to get things in motion quickly and pray they go as you need them to. It's so outlandish it just might work."

"It'll work, Reverend. I intend to be sure of that." William stood, impatient to get back to the girls. "You got all the details straight for your part, times and everything?"

"Yes, I think so."

"Good. Then I'll do what I have to do tomorrow night, and come Tuesday night we'll see if we can't get that confession that Burwell needs." William took up his candle and was ready to leave the church when politeness forced him to acknowledge that the Reverend Brown was still sitting with his fingers on a passage of scripture. "You got something under your finger there, Reverend, before we set off for home?"

"I do," the minister said, "and I want you to remember this on Monday night, when you're standing behind the church, ready to start on the boy's grave. Remember that you won't be alone."

The sanctuary was quiet for a moment as the Reverend Brown found his place, and then the words came softly into the silence, filling the room as if God himself were speaking.

"The Lord killeth, and maketh alive; he bringeth down to the grave"—here the preacher looked him straight in the eye—"and he bringeth up."

William nodded, acknowledging the man's point so he'd close his Bible and go home.

The plan would be carried out in three parts. The first part, and undeniably the hardest, would have to be completed on Monday night. That would be the setting of the trap. On Tuesday morning there would be the bait to cast about, and on Tuesday night the prey would be ensnared by their own greed, if everything went according to plan. Or if anything went according to plan, William had to admit to himself.

He spent Monday going over the details of the evening that lay before him. In addition to spinach seeds to sow, there was a considerable amount of wash to be done. Jabbing down on the garments in the washtub with a hoe handle, William considered what tools he'd need for his evening's work. A shovel, certainly. A lantern to see what he was doing. An ax and a clawhammer because he didn't know if the boy had been buried in a coffin or a winding sheet. A pint of rum to keep his nerves steady and keep his hands moving. Rope to pull the body up and a feed sack to move it in.

What to do with the boy's body in the interim had been a thorny problem, but the Reverend Brown had finally suggested that he himself could find a few hours on Monday afternoon to leave his parishioners on the pretext of needing a time of private prayer.

Then, a few hundred feet into the forest surrounding the cemetery, he would dig the boy a temporary resting place. The prayer story, he assured William, would be no lie. He would surely be praying with every shovelful of earth that justice would be visited on the living and the dead. The new grave would be flagged with a strip of white cloth and William prayed the preacher would remember this detail. He had no desire to stumble around in the dark dragging a dead man in need of a grave.

He made the girls a special supper of buckwheat cakes dredged in molasses, and as darkness fell, he told them a story about how lonely Aunt Lottie would be tonight if they didn't come again, and how she said she would make gingerbread and keep it warm near the fire just for them. He had told Lottie only that he was feeling the need to make frequent trips to the church. Assuming his need was of a spiritual nature, she was happy to tend to the girls. *Let her think what she will,* William thought. When Callie asked him about the tools he was assembling in the wagon before they left, he told her he would be digging potatoes and hoped she would forget his answer before she had a chance to tell Lottie that he was digging potatoes in April in a churchyard.

He left them on the warmth of Lottie's hearth, without tears this time, a fact he was grateful for. As soon as he was a good half mile from Lottie's place, he stopped the wagon and reached under the seat for the jug of rum he'd stowed there. His nerves, which had been none too steady all day, were beginning to work on his hands, making them tremble a bit as he thought of the job he'd cut out for himself. He had shoveled tons of soil without a thought, but now it would be a delicate operation, else he could harm the boy further, a thought that sickened him. He held the jug in his hands, waited for the first swallow to settle, then took another drink. That would be all for a while. He could not afford to get drunk, at least not until his evening's work was done.

Pulling up in front of the church, he was relieved to find it dark and silent—no late-night parishioners seeking guidance such as Lottie imagined him to be. He waited in front of the building for a moment to be sure no one was coming down the road from either direction, then got down from the wagon and took hold of the reins. With the lantern held high in one hand, he led Gus around to the rear of the church and pulled the wagon up as close behind the back wall as he could get it. Any late-night traveler riding by must see nothing but a dark church and an empty graveyard.

Tying Gus to a pine at the corner of the building, he took the tools and feed sack and carried them down to the boy's grave. Coming back to the wagon, he picked up the jug and finally the lantern, which he turned down to a flame the size of a feather tip.

He stopped at Hannah's grave for a moment and wondered if she knew what he was about to do and if she knew, did she approve. But he could feel nothing of her tonight, only the darkness and isolation of the place, and he wondered if his nerve would hold out for the duration of the task.

Bidding her farewell for now, he lifted the lantern and the rum and walked downhill to the soggy ground where Johnny Grant lay buried and where Johnny Grant would soon not lie buried, courtesy of William and his shovel.

Taking another drink before he began, he wiped his mouth on his sleeve and put the jug down close by. Then he picked up the shovel and set to work.

He rose late the next morning and, after a breakfast of bread, butter, and coffee, went to work on the second part of his plan. Today he would cast the bait. This could involve one stop or many, depending on how long it took him to find his prey. He hoped it would only involve one stop — the sawmill where Eddie Bishop was known to show up on occasion and work. No matter what, William intended to keep hunting the boy until he found him.

He had left the girls at Lottie's overnight and stopped by to see them and to spin another lie to Lottie. His conscience, which had lain dormant for weeks, had begun to prick him, but the lying would soon be done. The plan would come to its conclusion tonight, either to success or failure. Either the prey would take the bait or not, either the boys would both come or not, either the words of confession would be spoken or not. He challenged God to make it happen while dismissing the hope that he would. He had once beseeched God to stop Hannah's bleeding and beseeching had proved useless. He doubted a challenge would go much further, but it was the closest he could get to prayer.

His first stop, at the sawmill, came to nothing. Wendell Pike's father was just finishing up a small order and had not needed extra manpower. Eddie Bishop, if he had come, had not been needed and had not stayed. William thanked the man, said he'd consider the price for boards they'd discussed, and left, marveling at the ease with which he was concocting and delivering lies.

He tried the gristmill next, with no luck, and then the tannery, in case Eddie or Wendell was passing time there and jawing with some of the other boys, and then the store, where he was told Eddie had come and gone after doing some business. Everywhere someone would listen, William spun his tale, the one he wanted spread around until it would be impossible for Eddie Bishop and Wendell Pike not to hear it, even if they didn't hear it from him. Figuring he could never be so lucky as to find Eddie or Wendell at the tavern, William went in anyway to get himself a drink and spread his bait around a bit more. When he found Eddie Bishop inside, kneeling over a game of marbles, William made a tentative pact with God to reconsider his new faithlessness.

Having found his prey, he looked about for a suitable ear to hear his tale. The tavern was not thickly crowded, with it being the middle of a working day, but there were a few men like himself, slaking their thirst before or after attending to business, and a group of ne'er-do-wells over in the corner with Eddie, some engaged in and some watching the game in progress. William ran himself a mug of rum, took a chair at a table as close to the marble group as possible, and began speaking with great drama to a man he had never seen before in his life.

"Traveler?" he asked, turning his chair so his voice would be projected into the marble corner.

The stranger nodded. "Passing through on my way to Charleston."

"You wouldn't be Johnny Grant's uncle, then."

"Never heard of him," the stranger said. "My name's Davis."

"Oh," William said, and held out his hand to the man. "Will Gibson's the name. Glad to make your acquaintance, Mr. Davis. Not that I'm trying to meddle in your business, but we're expecting a visitor to the neighborhood and I thought you might be him, seeing as how I didn't know you. Pretty important man coming here, as I understand it. Coming here to do a sorrowful thing, though."

"Is that right?" Davis said, and William could see he had aroused the man's interest, as he had hoped to. "And what would that be, if you don't mind telling it."

"Don't mind a bit, seeing as how everybody will know it sooner or later. This gentleman who's coming here, Beau Grant's his name, he had a nephew here name of Johnny Grant, who was robbed and killed a couple of weeks ago. Cut down in the road just like a dog and left to bleed to death. The poor boy didn't have his right mind and didn't have any relations here, so he was buried in a soggy old grave behind the New Hope Methodist Church and we all thought that was the end of it. But that was before his Uncle Beau got wind of what happened."

Davis sat up lazily in his chair and scowled at William. "If the boy didn't have any relations, then who told his uncle?"

"Well," William said, thinking fast and cursing the stranger Davis for being so quick-witted, "one of the women of the church, who knew about this uncle, she sent him a letter about it. And just the other day she got one back."

William looked over to the marble corner and saw Eddie had

lost his turn and had moved back a bit from the group. Judging from his intense frown, William assumed he was concentrating on something other than marbles.

The stranger nodded as if that were the close of the subject and swilled his drink. William continued as if he'd been asked for more.

"Seems like this uncle, Beau Grant, is a wealthy man and didn't like the notion of his blood kin being cut up and left to die and then buried in swamp ground. He's a good man, this uncle is, because he hardly knew the boy and knows he didn't have a thing to his name hardly except what the thieves took off him, and of course that's gone. Not a thing left on the face of this earth but that row of gold teeth in his mouth," William said. "After all," he added, and chuckled, "what thief would have thought of opening up a boy's mouth and plucking out his gold teeth, even if they would bring a pretty penny?"

The stranger was looking at him as if he were daft, but William plowed on, rewarded by Eddie's rapt attention. The boy was now clearly paying no mind to the marble game in front of him.

"So what Beau Grant's fixing to do is only because he wants the boy to rest in peace in a nice place and near to one relative at least. He's expected sometime tomorrow, and he's going to dig that boy up and take him back to his own home and put him in the family burying ground up where he lives near Richmond. Coming all this way to carry that boy to a proper grave, that's a good man."

Davis nodded in agreement. "Train? Ugly work to carry a body that far any other way."

"Horse and wagon," William said without thinking, then quickly set out to cover his mistake. "He is a rich man; in fact, he paid for those teeth, but he wants to keep the boy in his hands and under his care all the way. Feels like he's suffered enough at the hands of strangers. So tonight will likely be the last night that poor boy will spend in his grave behind the church, God rest his soul. His uncle will have him up by tomorrow night and on his way back home." William spoke the word *tonight* a little louder than the rest and hoped the gears would start turning in Eddie's head.

"Well, he's a better man than I am," Davis said, and finished his drink. "I can't say I'd be real eager to dig up a body that's been put down for weeks and tote it a couple of hundred miles with me on the back of a wagon. A grave's a grave, regardless of where it is. Why go to the trouble, especially since he hardly knew the boy?"

"It's just the kind of man he is," William said, and rushed to finish his speech because the stranger was brushing off his coat and pushing back his chair. "And it won't be that much trouble, not with the kind of spring we've had. It'll take some time, that's true, but the earth's neither crusty dry nor heavy sodden. 'Course where the boy is, the soil's damp all the time and it would be a lot quicker job for two men than one. But I expect Mr. Grant can get some help if he needs it. Good luck to you, sir," he finished, and stood up himself. "I hope your business goes well in Charleston."

Mr. Davis nodded in response and made his way out of the tavern. William walked over to the keg, ran himself another rum, and sat back down at the table. He could not have asked for the second part of the plan to run more smoothly. The bait had been cast and he just had to wait and see if the fish were biting.

He stretched his legs out under the table and leaned back in the chair, sipping at the rum and watching Eddie reenter the marble game. It was with great satisfaction that William saw him lose his turn right off.

The hours before dusk had to be filled, so he filled them with his daughters, playing games and telling stories between the chores that could not be postponed. Finally, when the shadows were slanting long and narrow, he told them another story about how Aunt Lottie would need them for just one more night, and then she'd be all right on her own, and they could sleep in their own beds at home once again. He dropped them off with little fanfare, except for Lottie's questions, which he pretended not to hear. Tomorrow he would tell her everything. Tonight he had nothing on his mind but capturing his prey. Again the church was dark and the churchyard empty when he got there. Riding around to the back, he dismounted, shouldered his shotgun, and scanned the woods that surrounded the small burial ground. If the Reverend Brown had gotten there first, he had hidden himself well. William saw nothing but tree trunks and undergrowth dissolving into blackness.

He led Gus into the woods on one side, and after tying up to a sturdy persimmon tree, he stepped back into the clearing. Following along the edge of the woods, he turned to look where Hannah lay but dared not stop because the cover of darkness was complete, and his prey would be eager for their treasure. Stepping back into the forest just behind the boy's grave, he squinted and finally, some twenty feet in, caught sight of a glint of metal. Stepping another yard sideways, he saw a faint glow emanating from behind a large tree trunk. Moving forward as quietly as he could, he walked in toward the light and found the Reverend Brown sitting cross-legged beside an ancient oak tree, his Bible open on his lap. Next to him, hidden from direct view by the massive trunk, a kerosene lantern was glowing. Sitting beside that, wedged upright into the oak leaves, was a silver flask.

"Didn't know you were a drinking man, Reverend," William said, settling down on the ground across the lantern from him. "Hope I haven't driven you to it, with this scheme of mine. You're a good man to help me."

"You haven't driven me to anything, William. I drink hot coffee even when I'm not spending a night in the woods trying to catch two killers. I just hope we won't be needing that." He nodded toward the shotgun over William's shoulder. "And call me Mark, if you don't mind. Seems like we're going to be here too long to stand on formalities."

William was struck dumb for a moment and then extended his hand as if he'd just met the man. "I never figured on you having a first name somehow. Stupid of me."

"That's all right," the preacher said, and offered his hand in return. "Lots of folks feel that way. Coffee?" he asked, and lifted the flask.

"Don't mind if I do," William said, and took a drink. It was perfect, lukewarm and strong. "How long have you been here, Mark?" He said the name only with difficulty, as if breaching a taboo.

"I got here just before dark and checked inside the church to make sure it was empty. Found this spot and got settled in about a half hour ago. I expect we've got a long night ahead of us. You got the boy . . . up all right?"

"Yep," William said, remembering the soft resistance of the shovel tip when it met flesh. "The poor soul was put down in a sheet, not even a decent coffin."

"That's a shame, but made your work last night easier. You find the new spot all right?"

"I found it," William said, remembering himself pulling the boy's body behind him, his handkerchief up to his nose. "Don't you suppose we ought to turn that light down, Reverend—Mark, in case one of them is sharp-eyed and looks this way?"

"There'll be time enough for that. We're liable to be here a couple of hours before they come and I'd planned on doing a little studying. We hear anybody coming, we can put it out in a second. You couldn't see it from the back of the church, could you? I couldn't when I looked."

"No," William admitted. "And I reckon we'll hear them long before they could see us."

The Reverend Mark Brown nodded and they said a few more things and then the preacher looked back down to his Bible. William moved back and leaned against a tree trunk. He closed his eyes, better to hear any hoofbeats in the distance, but all he heard was a chorus of spring peepers filling the night air with their singing.

He had not realized his own fatigue. Coming out of a restless sleep, he checked his watch and found that an hour and a half had passed. The sight of the minister still bent over the Bible in his lap gave William such a feeling of annoyance that he had to look elsewhere. Stretching out flat, his fingers interlocked under his head, he gazed up into the overhead limbs. After a few moments, his eyes got used to the dark and he searched out star patterns in the sky. He tried to find Virgil the sky bear but could only see scattered stars against a backdrop of eternal blackness.

And yards away from him, Hannah lay under the earth, just as isolated as any star overhead, her coffin nailed shut tight, another world of eternal darkness. Knowing the preacher was still reading, wasting the light of a lantern to study the meaningless ancient words, William felt his blood begin to run a little faster, his mind become a little sharper. He sat up and stretched his legs.

"Mark," he said, still with difficulty because the existence of a Christian name made the man harder to hold at arm's length.

The preacher stopped reading and looked over at him. "Yes?"

"How old are you?"

He closed the Bible, leaving a twig to hold his place. "Twenty-four."

"You don't have a wife, do you? Or children?"

The younger man smiled. "Hard to have one without the other."

"But you don't have either."

"No, I don't. Hope to, someday."

"You hope to," William repeated, feeling that some blister in his soul was about to burst and it would kill him if it did and kill him if it didn't. The preacher's face was earnest, interested, innocent of life as it really was. William knew now his goal was to erase that look on the younger man's face and replace it with one that reflected life on earth.

"So," William continued, pausing briefly as they both heard a horse coming down the road. The hoofbeats rose and then fell away into the night. After a moment the spring peepers, who had hushed for the disturbance, started their chorus again.

"So," William repeated, "you don't have a wife. If you did, would you love her?"

"I hope so," the younger man said, and laid the Bible on the ground beside him. "That is the main idea on entering into marriage, I think. At least, in most cases." His tone was still conversational, jocular; it was a lighthearted chat with a parishioner.

Around them the forest was teeming with life, with the singing of frogs and the stealthy movements of animals who lived their lives after dark and crept about the forest floor unseen. Even the treetops swayed gently in the night breezes, stoic and silent but alive nonetheless, the stream of life flowing into them from the dark earth below. This was the land of the living.

Twenty feet away was the land of the dead, where Hannah lay, now and forever.

"Ever see anybody bleed to death, Reverend Brown?" William said abruptly, and felt a rush of pleasure as the complacent face on the man of God melted away.

"I can't say that I have," he answered. "I've been at the bedside of the dying—"

"Ever seen someone you love bleed to death, regardless of what you did, ever watched the life seep out of them until their heart stopped and they lay staring at you, cold and dead? Ever put them away in the ground, Reverend, under six feet of earth and left them there and gone home alone?"

The minister's face was somber now. William feared the man would reach for the Bible and start flipping pages, but he didn't.

"No, I haven't, William. I've lost loved ones, of course. Who hasn't?"

"Of course," William said, but in truth he had no mind for other folks' loved ones at the moment. "I'll tell you something, Reverend. I do appreciate you trying to help me catch these boys. I don't know if they'll even come or not, but at least we did what we could and maybe the Grant boy can rest in peace knowing that. But I can't say I want the Almighty here too, in the form of that book you keep reading. I don't have much use for the book or its subject."

William felt a strange sense of liberation, as if he had just had words with God himself, expressing an anger that had existed since time began. He waited for the preacher to sermonize, but the blasted man just kept looking at him, waiting. William decided to give him what he was waiting for.

"You said at Hannah's funeral that we'd see her again. Well, it doesn't make me feel any better that I'll see her in fifty years or ten years. I want to see her tonight. I want to see her now." He stopped and thought of her just thirty yards away and forever beyond his grasp, and the cruelty of it enraged him. "Can you show me," he said, nearly choking on his own anger, "can you show me one verse in that damned Bible of yours that justifies a mother being taken from two daughters who need her? One reason that makes sense, why God allowed her to bleed to death when he could have spared her?" By the last sentence he was shouting. He couldn't help himself.

"No, I can't, William," the preacher said. "There's absolutely nothing in the Bible to make sense of it, and no one could truthfully say that there is."

William waited for the next part, for the list of *buts*—but our Heavenly Father knows what's best; but we have to rely on faith alone; but Hannah was called by God to be an angel; but we'll all understand one day. Instead the minister was finished. A fountain of rage that had been building for weeks and would have erupted if the man had said more suddenly eased off and dissipated. William slumped against a tree trunk and took a deep breath. The blister had burst at last and had not killed him.

He was still catching his breath when they heard more hoof-beats. The minister held up one hand for silence as the animals slowed and then stopped in front of the church. Around them the spring peepers abruptly fell silent.

"It's them all right," Mark whispered into the darkness. He had extinguished the lantern on hearing the horses being led around to the back of the church.

Lying low, silent and motionless, they heard intermittent talking and a loud nervous giggle coming from behind the church. After a pause of several moments, a light sprang to life near the building. While William watched, it diminished slightly and then began moving from the back of the church to the lower end of the cemetery.

"They've got a lantern," he whispered from where he lay stretched on his belly. "They just turned it down because they don't want to be seen back there at work. I did the same thing when I dug the boy up last night."

Finally the lantern stopped moving and appeared to hover in the air for several moments. Then they set it down and William heard the sound he had been hoping for since a row of shiny gold teeth had popped into his mind like a dream. They were digging in the earth, lifting the soil away from a boy they had robbed once and now a corpse that they hoped to rob again. William smiled.

A half hour passed and then another and William thought his soul would burst from the flesh, he was so impatient for the final scene to begin. At last, when the boys were waist deep, he whispered to the preacher, "Let's move up now. They're about halfway down and concentrating on the dirt under their feet. They're not going to look up for another half hour at least. I'll go first and find us a good spot. When you hear me stop, count to ten slow, then feel your way up till you find me."

William moved forward on his hands and knees, putting his weight down silently like a cat stalking his prey. He stopped once, when they did, and waited for them to rest. After a moment he realized he might be missing just the thing he'd come to hear and so began moving forward again, an inch at a time. By the time he had gotten close enough to understand their words, they had taken up the shovels and gone back to work.

In a few minutes the Reverend Brown came up beside him, shaking and kissing the heel of his palm. "Sweetgum balls," he whispered when William glanced at him. "How much deeper do you guess they'll go before they start wondering?"

"We've got another good half hour of waiting time, I'd say. Settle down and get comfortable. Go to sleep if you want to. I'll nudge you if they start getting peevish."

"I'd just as soon keep my eyes open, William. Have you noticed those rifles they've got at the edge of that hole they're working in?"

"Sure," William said, patting the stock of his shotgun. "I'm ready for 'em," he added, and then fell silent and watched as the diggers went deeper and deeper, their breath now tearing in and out of their lungs like fire. They spoke little, and when they did, the words were muffled by the thrusting and pulling of shovels.

"William," Mark whispered after a bit, "you think we'll be able to hear them from here? I can't understand a word they're saying."

"We're gonna have to," William said, "because we can't risk getting any closer. I don't think we'll have a problem once they get back on the surface and Eddie's temper gets fired up."

The Reverend Brown nodded and the ground crackled as he shifted his position. Still they watched as the diggers went down into the ground, until at last they were watching shovelfuls of soil flying up from a gaping hole in the earth. When one of the boys scrambled up and out and took the lantern back into the pit with him, William gripped the preacher's arm.

"Get your ears ready, Mark. I reckon they've gone far enough now to start expecting their reward."

For fifteen minutes there was nothing but an unearthly glow from the grave and random scrapings and William knew they were checking for substance beneath the soil. There was some indistinct mumbling, then more soil came flying out of the open hole, and more scraping, and finally Wendell Pike's head and the lantern appeared at the edge of the pit. In a moment the rest of him followed, hoisted up by Eddie. When Eddie followed and thrust his shovel into the ground like a spear, William held his breath.

"How far down do you reckon they put him?" Wendell said, and his voice had a nervous edge to it that William relished. "We musta gone six feet by now."

"Yeah, we've gone six feet," Eddie said, stalking around the grave but looking at Wendell. "We went six feet pretty damn quick seems like to me. That dirt lifted up mighty easy, like it's been lifted up before, lately. What do you guess, Wendell?"

"What the hell are you talking about?" Wendell answered, turning with Eddie as he paced back and forth. "Of course it was lifted easy. He ain't been put down but a couple of weeks."

"You know damn good and well what I'm talking about," Eddie said, his voice rising a few notches. Good, William thought, his temper was already outstripping his caution.

"All I know," Wendell said, "is I just spent half the night digging up an empty hole in the ground. How do you even know this is where they put him?"

"'Cause this is the only grave in the swamp ground. You see another one, Wendell? And you're the one who walked right down here to it, even though I was carrying the lantern. You knew where it was right off, didn't you? You musta done it this afternoon, musta gone straight from your place after I told you about it. I reckon it didn't matter if you got caught 'cause your big old daddy would get you out of it."

"Done what?" Wendell said, getting in Eddie's face and shouting. "Done what?"

"You know what," Eddie said, and jerking his shovel out of the earth, he slung it into the field of headstones that stood as mute witnesses to his fury. "You came out here already this afternoon and dug him up and knocked them teeth out of his head and probably already traded 'em off. Then let me come out tonight and dig at an empty hole for two hours."

"You're crazy," Wendell shot back, and the shouting began in earnest. "I never been out here before in my life, but you thought the idea up, so maybe it was you that dug him up, then was too scared to admit it and tried to blame it on me. How stupid do you think I am?"

"How stupid do you think I am?" Eddie yelled back in his face.

"Stupid enough to miss half a dozen gold teeth in a dead man's mouth."

"Like you didn't?"

"I'm not the one who had their hands on him, am I, Eddie? I'm not the one who killed him."

"You reckon I opened his mouth and looked in after I finished him?" Eddie shouted, pushing Wendell backward into the dirt pile.

William sat up at once, his fingers closing over the shotgun beside him.

"At last, thank the good Lord," the Reverend Mark Brown said aloud, getting stiffly to his feet. "You ready to end this, William?"

"I am," William said. "Thank the good Lord, at last."

JERRY M. BURGER

Home Movie

FROM *The Briar Cliff Review*

ELAINE THREADS THE Super 8mm film through the projector, connects the loose end to the return reel, and closes the panel door. She turns the control knob to Play, and the dimly lit room is suddenly cast in silver and gray hues as images of men and women flutter onto the screen.

"Reel One," she says aloud to no one. "The Birthday Party."

She sees a version of herself from decades earlier sitting at her old dining table, hair permed to flip away from her face, an effort that she knew even then fell pathetically short of the intended Farrah Fawcett look. Neighbors dressed in 1977 fashion — tight blouses, wide lapels, oversized glasses — dart silently in and out of the picture. The old projector sounds as if it's grinding the film; worn sprockets cause an occasional stutter and jump. Everyone is aware of the camera. They squint and smile, some wave. Dan Carpenter, who would die two years later from stomach cancer, sticks his face close to the lens with an exaggerated expression that is supposed to look as if he is having a great time but that always strikes Elaine as an omen of tragedy.

The camera zooms to a cake adorned with a forest of pink and white candles. It's her twenty-eighth birthday. Nathan made all the arrangements and extended the invitations before he told her. By design, too late to talk him out of it or to call the whole thing off. There are two ashtrays on the table, and no one seems to mind that several guests are smoking. As she recalls, she was one of the few nonsmokers in the neighborhood.

The quality of the photography is awful. At any other gathering,

Elaine would have been in charge of the camera. She was the one with the talent and the training. The behind-the-scenes person, the one never pictured in the photo. But that day Bruce had insisted. She was the guest of honor, he said. He would take care of recording the event. Unfortunately, her bighearted next-door neighbor was oblivious to his limited skills. There is no sense of framing, no point of entry for the eye. Full body shots are taken when torsos would have worked better, poses are held so long people signal "cut" with their hands. Clueless Bruce. She wonders if he had his suspicions even then, three months before he came to see her.

Elaine tastes her bourbon, swirls the ice, and takes another sip before setting the glass down on the TV tray next to the projector. Nathan is about to make his appearance on the screen.

Her husband enters the kitchen with his usual broad smile. He shakes a few hands and hugs the women. His eyes are set too far apart and his forehead is too large for him to be considered handsome, but he engages everyone with a confidence that belies his physical appearance. On the right edge of the screen, the red sleeve of a woman's dress moves in and out of the picture. A few seconds later, Samantha steps into the middle of the frame. Her bright red dress, flawless and radiant, instantly captures the scene. Her long dark hair is expensively styled, the hem of her dress two inches higher than women her age wore them back then. She is a woman in control. Every glance, every gesture, is calculated and perfect. Elaine had been wary of her from the start, from the day Samantha and Bruce moved next door. Elaine's first observation: boob job. Apparent to all the women in the neighborhood, even if Nathan and some of the husbands disagreed. Weren't boobs that size supposed to bounce when you walk?

Nathan reenters the scene. His face brightens when he sees Samantha, and he mouths words that Elaine has come to read as "Don't you look nice." He raises his eyebrows and grins at Samantha's reply, as if she has said something delightful or, more likely, a tad racy. Always the master flirt. Before Nathan has a chance to respond, the camera spins to a chubby woman entering the room with a large wrapped package in her arms. Elaine doesn't remember the woman's name.

The screen turns white, the room brightens. The dangling end of the film slaps against the back of the projector with each rotation of the reel. *Whamp, whamp, whamp.* Three minutes, the length of a home movie back then. Elaine rewinds the film. While the projector whirs, she lights a cigarette.

"Reel Two," she announces. "The Backyard Barbecue." This time she is behind the camera, and so it's just the three of them on the screen—Nathan, Samantha, and Bruce. Samantha had insisted that Elaine and Nathan come over to celebrate Bruce's promotion. *My husband, a vice president! Can you believe it?* What's not to believe? It's the kind of thing that happens to women like Samantha. Elaine had known them all her life, had studied them from afar. Vacations in Europe, ballet lessons, clothes from stores Elaine felt uncomfortable just walking through. Of course Samantha went to a private all-girls college. Of course she never had to work. Of course heads turn when she enters a room. *What a lucky guy that Bruce is!* Even Nathan had uttered those exact words.

It's the middle of summer, and the harsh outdoor light makes her job as photographer a challenge. Although few would ever notice, Elaine always took the task seriously, even when relying on something as rudimentary as a home movie camera. Her first camera had come to her by chance when she was ten. An old Kodak box model her father found when going through his mother's belongings. Did Elaine want it? It seemed disrespectful to say no. Her first roll of black-and-white prints had consisted largely of family members smiling on cue with either the sun in their eyes or shadows across their faces. But the last picture on that roll, taken quickly so that she could run the film to the drugstore, captured something Elaine had never seen. Her father, an endless source of comfort and reassurance, unaware of her presence, gazing at his feet, shoulders slumped and weary, as if beaten down by a powerful foe. The image changed forever the way she saw not only her father but everyone. In that moment she understood in a way a younger child cannot the dark underside of being, the weight of hidden burdens. It also was the moment she discovered the power of the camera. For years she spent every cent she earned buying and developing film. Then came a better camera, subscriptions to photography magazines, two years as photo editor of her high school newspaper, a professional camera, her own darkroom in the garage, and a bachelor's degree in art with an emphasis in photography. Those were the days she could always be found with a Nikon

strapped around her neck, engaging the world through the lens of
her camera.

On the screen Bruce stands next to the Weber, spatula held
high to greet his arriving guests. Nathan hands him a beer, and the
two men pose for the camera with their bottles, chests expanded
as if mocking but also somehow validating their masculinity. It's
too small a gathering for Elaine to blend unnoticed into the background; capturing candid moments is next to impossible. But there
is much to see if one knows where to look. The outdoor light accen-
tuates the deepening lines around Nathan's eyes. When he turns
his back, a flash of sunlight reflects off his newly formed bald spot.
Bruce pauses for the briefest part of a moment before returning
to his work at the barbecue, considering and dismissing a thought
he never puts into words. The strap of Samantha's pink bra peeks
out from under her thin blouse in almost every scene. But the most
striking revelation that day—what Elaine had succeeded in capturing with the movie camera—is the nonchalant way Bruce manages
to act around his wife. So different from the visibly shaken man
who had knocked on her door a week earlier. *Nathan's not here,* she
had told him. He knew that; it was her he wanted to see. Maybe
Samantha had said something. Maybe Elaine saw something he was
missing. Twice he broke into tears while laying out all the reasons
he was certain his wife was having an affair. *No kidding,* she had
wanted to say. *If any woman's fooling around, it's Samantha.* But she
held her tongue. She said all the right things.

Everyone sits down to eat. Elaine has positioned the camera just
above the lip of the table, with place settings in the foreground and
the swimming pool in the background. Bruce and Samantha have
the only pool in the neighborhood. Their casual backyard dishes
are more expensive than any dishware Elaine owns.

After the visit from Bruce, Elaine also had to act as if nothing
was amiss. She forced herself to greet and smile and make eye contact with Samantha the way she always had, all the while playing
out delicious scenarios in her head. In one, Bruce crashes through
the door of a cheap motel room and catches Samantha and her
lover in the act. It's a seedy, rundown place, utterly without dignity,
which adds to the humiliation. Samantha bursts into tears, begging
for a second chance, promising in an obviously insincere manner
that it will never happen again. Bruce leaves her. Then the lover

disappears—it was never anything more than physical. And for once in her life Samantha knows the pain of rejection.

The final few seconds of the reel are especially good from a photographer's point of view. Samantha is standing in her rose garden, her features softened by late afternoon shadows, perfectly framed with Nathan and Bruce on either side. There's no mistaking the confidence in her eyes, the sense of ease and poise, while all the time pretending to be unaware of the men's attention. The shot is impressive, especially considering that there were no second chances back then. What you shot was what you got. No erasing, no do-overs.

Try as he might, Nathan never fully appreciated her love of photography. He called it her hobby, referred to her pictures as "snapshots." Efforts to explain the art of it went nowhere. She went to exhibits by herself, bought the occasional book of photographs that she kept on her side of the bed. What was so hard to understand? A photo exhibit is a peek into another person's world. To know a photographer's work is to know the photographer. Each picture screams out, "This is me. This is what I see."

Elaine refills her drink. She thinks it's her second, but it might be the third. "Reel Three," she says. "Thanksgiving with the Neighbors."

Suddenly her old living room is on the screen. The horrible green couch, the stark white walls. Samantha and Bruce are just taking off their coats. Still together several months after Bruce revealed his suspicions to Elaine. It was Nathan's idea to invite them. Neither couple had kids. Why not spend the day with our friends? Why cook a big meal for just the two of us? But, Elaine would like to know, where is it written that friendship is the default option between next-door neighbors? Aren't you supposed to choose your friends? Still, as always, she played her part. She chatted with Samantha across their adjacent driveways as often and with as much enthusiasm as required. Anyone listening to Samantha's side of the conversations would assume they were the closest of friends— *my girl, sweetie, hon.* She invited Elaine to go shopping with her and to stop by sometime for coffee. An occasional cup of coffee Elaine could tolerate. Shopping with Samantha was never going to happen.

Nathan said they were lucky to have such good neighbors.

Then again, her husband saw good fortune everywhere. They were blessed to have their home, their health, their jobs. She should be thankful she's married to an accountant, someone who would never be out of work. In fact, for reasons she kept to herself, Elaine did consider herself lucky. What no one knew—what someone like Samantha could never imagine—was that when Elaine met Nathan their junior year in college, she had been on only two dates her entire life. And, truth be told, both were more like an evening with a friend than a date. Those old movies and TV shows where teenage girls gossip about boyfriends and spend weeks getting ready for the prom don't apply to everyone. Some girls are shy and awkward and plain. But no one seems to notice them.

Now Samantha is in the kitchen—Elaine's kitchen—helping with the last-minute preparations for the big holiday meal. It's what the girls do while the men talk football and cars. *Just tell me how I can help, dear. Anything at all.* Samantha cuts mushrooms for the salad, pulls some plates from the cupboard. Just enough to fulfill her obligation.

Elaine tested him once. Starting a few weeks after she lost her virginity in Nathan's dorm room one Saturday afternoon when his roommate was out of town. She complained when he wore wrinkled shirts, criticized his friends, groused when something annoyed her. He saw her with unwashed hair, without makeup. She came as close to showing him her real self as she dared. And, to her surprise and relief, he stayed. He even started ironing his shirts.

They were married two months after graduation. Nathan had job offers waiting; she took a series of temporary positions. The plan had always been to open her own studio. Family portraits and weddings would pay the bills, but there would also be time for creative work. She could exhibit her photography in her own gallery adjacent to the studio. It all seemed entirely plausible, and Nathan was supportive. But that was before. Before two cars, furniture, and a mortgage barely within reach of their paychecks. A studio? How would they pay for the space, the equipment, the advertising, and all the overhead? Maybe someday, when things were more settled. As Nathan would say, they were doing fine. And there was nothing wrong with being a receptionist in an insurance office.

The reel ends with the predictable shot of Nathan carving the turkey. The table is set with their wedding china, tiny flames flicker atop new candles. The camera keeps rolling while everyone takes a moment to say grace. Two young couples enjoying each other's company on a day set aside to give thanks. How appropriate, Elaine thinks, that she is not in the picture. Exactly what did she have to be thankful for? That she had one more week before everything fell apart? That for a few more days she could still believe in the fairy tale? She stares at the image of Samantha—eyes closed and head bowed devoutly—until the scene mercifully comes to an end.

"Reel Four," Elaine bellows. Her tone is defiant. Anyone who doesn't want to watch doesn't have to. "The Plot Thickens."

On the screen, more neighbors. Some of them the same as in Reel One. They are gathered in her den, a decorated tree perched in the background. Most years they didn't bother with a tree, but Nathan said they couldn't host a Christmas party without one. The lights are low, the images darker than in the earlier films. Deliberately so. The camera moves boldly, some might say belligerently, from person to person. She gets right in people's faces. You want to be in the movie? How's this? How do you like it now? The smiles are forced, the expressions pained. The discomfort palpable.

The blinders had come off a few weeks earlier, the Thursday Elaine had come home in the middle of the day with what surely were early signs of the flu. She called Nathan at the office. She needed some over-the-counter medicines; they didn't even have aspirin in the house. But Nathan wasn't in. She called a little later. Still not in, and they didn't know where he was or when he would return. So reluctantly she phoned the only person she knew who didn't have a daytime job. But Samantha wasn't home. She tried both numbers off and on the rest of the afternoon. About a quarter after 5:00, she saw Samantha pull into her driveway. Then, before she could pick up the phone, Nathan drove up in his car.

The movie shifts to the kitchen. Elaine leans forward. On the screen before her, a conversation between Samantha and Nathan. Just a friendly chat, nothing suspicious. It takes a trained eye. The two neighbors are standing farther apart than one would expect. Only by a few inches, but noticeable and revealing. Nathan seems uncharacteristically self-conscious. He thinks about each movement, his gestures are awkward and unnatural. He laughs too readily and exaggerates his expressions. An actor too aware of the audience. Samantha is better, but her usual air of self-assurance is missing. She is stiff, formal. She glances about, eyeing nearby guests instead of the other way around.

Everything had quickly fallen into place, the unraveling as predictable as a movie plot. It was all there. The hint of perfume, the excuses, even the long dark hair on the jacket. Then there was Nathan's out-of-place defensiveness, the obvious lies. *I was seeing clients. I see clients, you know.* And the late meetings that often coincided with Samantha's comings and goings.

You deny the facts as long as possible. The eye willfully follows the magician's misdirection. But at some point it all collapses, leaving everything exposed and indisputable right before your eyes. Each of Nathan's desperate efforts becomes more evident and more insulting than the last. An expensive dinner for no reason. Compliments for routine things. *You look wonderful in that dress. Is it new?* What little respect he must have for your intelligence. Are you supposed to be flattered? Blinded by all the attention? Oblivious to the forced passion, the empty smiles?

How long can this go on?

We think we know ourselves. We rely on our principles, values, and character to guide us. But you might be surprised. We may all be capable of things we never imagined possible. We may all harbor longings and passions no more available to us than the inner worlds of the people who surround us.

There are times you have to act, when continuing the pretense is unbearable. Sometimes choices narrow to a single path. And you know even at the time that there will forever be a before and an after.

"Reel Five," Elaine says, barely above a whisper. Or maybe she doesn't say it at all. She starts the projector.

Nathan and Bruce are working on the backyard fence that separates the properties. The winter weather has taken its toll. Their breath clouds in the chilly air, hammers rhythmically pound nails into new posts. Men's work. Nathan correctly guessed that it would do Bruce some good. At this point it's been more than eight weeks since anyone has seen Samantha.

Bruce is a broken man. Although only a few months have passed, he looks as if he has aged five years since the last reel. Everything about him seems drab—his cotton work shirt, his complexion, his once-glistening eyes. He needs a haircut. Nathan has become his pillar of support. He checks on Bruce daily, invites him to dinner at least once a week.

The rumors were rampant. Who had Samantha run away with? Every neighbor had a theory about this man or that. Margie from across the street was certain she saw Samantha at a downtown restaurant having lunch with a blond man in a blue blazer the very afternoon she disappeared. Another story placed Samantha and a mysterious but, as always, very handsome man in the lobby of a nearby Hilton. The police weren't buying any of it. Why would she leave everything behind—clothes, jewelry, money? No note, no phone call. No use of her credit cards or bank account. The investigation went on for months. For a while it was all anyone could talk about.

You can't get over how something so consequential could be so easy. *Let's have lunch. Followed by a little Christmas shopping.* How could Samantha resist? Even at the time you half expected a moment of doubt would arrive, a sudden jolt of conscience that would force you to reevaluate. But it never came.

Bruce would sell the house later that year and move out of state. He sent a card the first Christmas, promised to visit but never did. They lost contact with him after that. There was a what-ever-happened-to story in the newspaper on the tenth anniversary of Samantha's disappearance. And that was it.

The movie ends. Elaine turns off the projector, switches on the nearby lamp. She lifts her glass to find nothing but an amber ring at the bottom. As always, she reaches for the yellowed envelope sitting on the table, the same place she found it almost exactly one year after filming the boys mending the fence. The once-bright stationery has faded into uneven shades of gray. The single sheet of paper, cracking at the folds, is held together with discolored cellophane tape. She has long ago memorized every word and each detail of Nathan's simple handwriting, even the spaces between words. Still, she starts from the beginning, reading each line slowly, pausing at key words and phrases.

. . . leaving you . . . most difficult decision of my life . . . will always care for you.

She reaches the last paragraph, absentmindedly lifts and then sets down her empty glass before continuing.

I'm moving to St. Louis with Connie Wilkerson. You probably don't remember Connie. She worked as a temp in my office three summers ago. Please understand that this is not a sudden impulse kind of thing. Connie and I have been involved romantically for nearly three years. For what it's worth, this has been my only infidelity. Connie and I love each other very much.

There was never a sense of triumph, only a moment of relief that it was over. For years she waited for her punishment, for the start in the middle of the night, the crushing guilt. Eventually she settled into a blunted state of acceptance, resisting the pull of either shame or self-pity. She seeks no forgiveness, doesn't feel she needs any. Sometimes options disappear. At some point the script is written. You are only the actor.

She returns the projector to the hall closet, places it on the shelf next to the cameras she has not touched in years. She no longer believes in the magic of photography. A painter creates with brushes and oils, a photographer merely records with lenses and light. Of course, you have your tools and your tricks. You can draw the eye, freeze a moment, highlight, obscure, grab that split second when a guard is let down. But in the end, we see only what we are prepared to see.

She places the scruffy yellow boxes into the worn leather case and sets them next to the projector. She will watch the movies again. Maybe next week. Maybe in a few months. There is something comforting in the never-changing images unfolding in their predetermined sequence, a reassurance that comes from knowing that, perhaps like one's fate, no alternative endings are possible.

JAMES LEE BURKE

Deportees

FROM *The Strand Magazine*

PEOPLE THINK THE Dust Bowl ended with the 1930s. It didn't
in Yoakum, Texas. I remember how cold and brittle and sharp the
air was at eight in the morning six days after Pearl Harbor when
my mother and I arrived at Grandfather's paintless, pitiful home
in our old coupe with the hand-crank windshield, but I remember even more the way the dust was piled as smooth as cinnamon
against the smokehouse and barn and windmill tank, and how the
sun was a dull silver disk and the sky an ink wash and the pecan
trees bare and black like they'd been scorched in a fire.

The first thing Mother did when we entered the house was sit
down at Grandfather's piano, which he had bought from a saloon
in San Antonio, and play "Clair de Lune." She was a beautiful
woman and had a regal manner, but she was also crazy and had
undergone electroshock treatments and had been placed in the
asylum in Wichita Falls. The edges of the wood grips on Grandfather's revolver were cut with nine notches he had tried to sand out
of existence with a nail file. It worked about as well as the electroshock treatments did on my mother.

"How you doin', Buster Brown?" he said.

"That's not my name, Grandfather," I said.

"That's right, stand up for yourself, Aaron," he said. "But you
ought to get you a little dog named Tige."

You didn't win with Grandfather. Even in old age he still stood
six foot six. When he was a Texas Ranger he knocked John Wesley
Hardin out of his saddle and kicked him in the face, and for good

measure nailed chains on him in the bed of a wagon and threw him in the county jail and poured a slop bucket on his head.

He was sitting by the fireplace, his face warm and yellow as a candle in the light. "Y'all come to he'p me put up the Christmas tree?"

"Yes, sir."

He knew better. My father had disappeared again. My mother kept playing "Clair de Lune," an expression on her face like the shadows rain makes running down a window.

Grandfather got up and went into the kitchen and lifted a tin sheet of biscuits off the woodstove. The biscuits were brown and crusty and oozing with melting butter. The sky was dark, dirty with smoke, and I could see flashes in the clouds and hear the rumble of thunder that gave no rain. I thought I saw people rush past the barn, gripping their belongings against their chests, their clothes streaming in the wind, their faces pinched as though raindrops were stinging their skin, although I knew there was neither rain nor hail inside the wind, only dust.

"There's Mexicans running across the lot, Grandfather," I said.

"They're wets. Don't pay them no mind."

He smiled when he said it. But I knew he didn't mean anything mean or racial. In hard times you don't share your secrets and you sure don't borrow trouble.

"A woman was nursing a baby and running at the same time, Grandfather."

He scraped the biscuits into a galvanized bucket, then slid a sliced-up ham onto the biscuits and draped a checkered napkin over the top and hefted the bucket by the bail. "Let's go, Buster Brown."

We didn't need books to learn about the history of our state. It was always at the ends of our fingertips. It was even in the eyes of my crazy mother, who often seemed to take flight and travel back in time, for good or bad, mostly for bad. How about this? In 1914 an old woman outside Yoakum told my mother this story. When the old woman was a girl, two dozen mounted men with weapons tied to their saddles rode into the yard and asked if they could have breakfast. The girl and her parents started a fire under a Dutch oven and boiled coffee and cooked meat for the riders, all of whom spoke little. Their leader was a lantern-jawed man with soulful brown eyes and oiled, thick hair that hung on his cheeks. After a while he rested his knife and fork over his plate. "Why are you looking at us in such a peculiar way, little girl?" he asked.

"We don't often see people who wear animal hides instead of clothes," she replied.

"Back in Tennessee buckskin is considered right smart fashion. You and your folks have been mighty kind. One day you can tell your grandchildren you fixed breakfast for Davy Crockett and his Tennessee volunteers on their way to San Antonio de Bexar to give ole Santa Anna the fight of his life."

I loved my mother. She stuck up for poor whites and people of color, and was generous to a fault with the little money we had. But I avoided looking into her eyes and the memories from her own life that were buried there. The same with my father. He was an educated and genteel man from South Louisiana who went over the top five times in what he called the Great War. He was an extremely intelligent and perceptive man, and consequently doomed to a life of emotional and intellectual loneliness. Mother's depression and frigidity did not help, and I thought it no wonder my father's most loyal companions had become his beer at the icehouse and the whiskey he hid in the garage.

"What are you studying on?" Grandfather said.

"Why do you call the Mexicans wets?"

"Good question. You could walk across the Rio Grande on your hands. We're going outside. Find you a hat in the hall. That wind has no mercy."

He was right. It was dry and full of grit and as cold and mean and ugly as a witch's broom. We ran for the barn. There must have been eight or nine Mexicans sitting in the straw, and maybe more back in the darkness. The chickens were trying to hide in the loft. I don't think I ever saw people as hungry or lean. The baby I saw sucking at its mother's breast looked made of sticks and a hank of skin and hair. Grandfather passed out the ham and biscuits and went out to the windmill and unhitched the chain and used a clean syrup can to catch the water under the pipe that fed the stock tank.

When he returned, he passed the syrup can among the Mexicans and told them he would get them more water when the can was done. The wind was puffing under the roof, straining the tin roof against the beams and storm latches. From outside I could hear the sound of a car engine and metal rattling and bouncing. Grandfather put his eye to a crack in the door. He spoke without taking his eye from the crack. "Aaron," he said.

"Yes, sir?" I replied, aware of the change in his voice and the fact he had used my christened name.

"Keep these people inside. Don't open the door. Not for any reason."

"What's wrong, Grandfather?"

He slipped a shovel loose from a barrel of tools. "I try to avoid confrontations with white trash, but sometimes they don't give you no selection."

He pushed open the door and stepped out into the cold. I felt a solitary raindrop strike my eyeball, as bright and hard as a chip of glass. Then Grandfather shut the door. I squinted through the crack and saw him approach a Model T Ford in the middle of a dry streambed that led down to the river. A tall man as thin as a lizard stepped out on the ground, his tie lifting in the wind, his suit flattening against his body. He had a long, unshaved face and tubular nose, shadowed by a John B. Stetson hat. He had to shout to be heard. "Fixing to take a shit in the woods, Mr. Holland?"

"I don't abide profanity on my property, Mr. Watts."

"I'm here out of respect. I'm also here to avoid trouble."

"I have no idea what you're talking about, Mr. Watts. I'm sure the failing is mine."

The man named Watts looked at Mother's car and at the dust on the running boards and the swaths of it on the windshield. The wind flapped his coat back, exposing the brass star on his belt and the holster and sidearm on his hip. "Miss Wynona is visiting?"

"What's the nature of your visit, Mr. Watts?"

"We think there's infiltrators coming up from the border."

"Infiltrators?"

"To be specific, Japs."

"The Japs are fixing to bomb Yoakum, Texas?" Grandfather said. "That's what you're saying?"

Mr. Watts's face made me think of soil erosion. His eyes were as flat and black as watermelon seeds under his hat brim. "I never spoke badly of you, Mr. Holland. I know what whiskey can do. There's a seat in our church anytime you want it."

"I know your preacher well. I saw him at a cross-burning once.

He was setting fire to the cross. I was writing down license numbers."

"Jesus didn't choose to be born a colored man. There wasn't any on the Ark, either."

"I got a theory on some of that," Grandfather said. "Know why God made certain kinds of white people?"

"No, and I'm not interested. I been sent out here by federal authorities."

"He was sending a message to the nigras about the superiority of white intelligence."

The wind gusted, rattling the blades on the windmill. Mr. Watts gazed at the barn door. "You calving early this year?"

"My cows were gone in '31. My grandson and I were gathering up some eggs."

"You wouldn't go upside my head with that shovel if I looked inside your barn, would you?"

"No, sir. But I'd file charges against you if you did it without a warrant."

"I see. Tell your daughter hello for me," Mr. Watts said. He turned his face so it caught the light. He winked, a grin at the corner of his mouth.

I saw Grandfather's right hand twitch, as though stung by a bee. "Come back here," he said.

Mr. Watts drove back down the streambed, the tires of his Model T rolling over fat white rocks that were webbed with algae and that crackled loudly when they were heavily pressed one against the other.

We fed the Mexicans and went back in the house. It had a second story and dormers, but it was a tinderbox and creaked with the wind and had bat and squirrel pellets all over the attic. At one time Grandfather had owned five farms and ranches, one of them on the green waters of the Guadalupe River outside Victoria. But his love of cards and liquor and outlaw women created numerous graves that had no marker and children who had no father.

He never got religion, at least not in the ordinary sense. I also doubted if he dwelled long on the men he shot, since most of them were killers and not worth the dirt it took to bury them. The children he had abandoned were another matter. He could not ignore

the despair in my mother's face when the afternoon sun began
to slip below the horizon and evening shadows dropped like wild
animals from the trees and crept across the yard in order to devour
her heart. In those moments there was no way to shake the terror
from her face.

She found a substitute for her father when she was seventeen, but
no one was ever sure who. There were many soldiers in town, and
also traveling salesmen. Some said her lover died in the Meuse-Ar-
gonne offensive. Whoever he was, he disappeared from her life
and she quit high school and went to Houston. Three months later
she returned and picked cotton with the darkies, and later went
to night school and learned shorthand. For the rest of her life the
one subject she would never discuss was abortion and would leave
a room if anyone alluded to it.

After Mr. Watts had gone and Grandfather and I came back into
the house, Mother kept staring at the barn and the trail of white
rocks in the gulley that used to be a streambed. Her skin was still
clear and youthful, her amber hair thick and full of lights, piled
on her head like a 1920s woman would wear it. Her dress was pa-
per-thin, printed with tiny red roses, and washed almost colorless.
"What's going to become of the Mexicans?" she said.

"I know a man in Victoria who's hiring," Grandfather said. "He
can pick them up tonight."

"There's an enormous hypocrisy about all this," she said.

"In what way?" he said.

"In good times we bring them in by the truckload. When there's
drought, the Mexicans are the devil's creation."

He watched her eyes and the way they followed the streambed
through the trees down to the river. "Was it Watts?"

She turned her glare upon him. "I have no dealings with Mr.
Watts. I suggest you don't either."

"If it was him, Wynona, I need to know."

She sat down at the piano and began to play "Malagueña," by
Ernesto Lecuona. She played and played and played, hitting the
keys harder and harder, until Grandfather stuffed his fingers in his
ears and walked out of the room. Then she stopped and stared at
me. "Get your coat," she said.

"Where we going?"

"To town."

"To the matinee?" I said.

"We're going to buy some milk."

We walked past Grandfather in the kitchen. He was at the window, his back to us, framed in the gray light, his right hand opening and closing at his side, as though he were squeezing a rubber ball, the knuckles ridging.

Mother and I drove down a dirt road into the county seat and parked at a grocery store on a side street, next to an icehouse and a cinder-block building where chickens were butchered. It was Saturday and both the grocery store and the icehouse were crowded. She pressed a nickel into my palm. "Go get you a Grapette, Aaron, but drink it in the car," she said.

"Yes, ma'am. Are we breaking the law?"

"Who told you such a thing?"

I picked at my hands. "It's the way we're acting."

I said *we* instead of *you.* She kissed me on the head. "You're a good boy. Don't be speaking bad of yourself or me either."

I went inside the icehouse and pulled a Grapette from the cold box and paid at the counter. Through the side windows I could see the rear lot of the slaughterhouse and a sloping rivulet of feathers and chicken guts that had merged and congealed with the runoff from the ice-maker.

The men around me were bundled up and drinking beer and smoking or chewing tobacco, their clothes sour with the odor that sweat makes when it's trapped inside wool. They were talking about the American sailors who had been drowned inside the *Arizona,* a subdued anger as thick as spit in their throats.

"What you doin' in here, little fellow?" said a voice behind me.

I looked up at the silhouette of Mr. Watts. "Drinking a Grapette," I said. "But I'm supposed to drink it in the car."

"Where's your mama at?"

"The grocery store," I said. "Across the street," I added, not knowing why.

"Getting y'all a mess of eats, is she?"

"Not really," I replied. "Grandfather gets by on the preserves he puts up in the fall."

"Bet she's buying milk. Right or wrong?"

I knew somehow he had bested me and caused me to give up a secret, but I wasn't sure how or what. He smiled down at me and stuck a long, thin cigar in his mouth, then took a kitchen match from his shirt pocket and scratched it on the butt of his revolver. He puffed on the cigar, his eyes hazy, and fitted his hand like a starfish on my head and worked his palm and fingers in my hair. "You don't like that? If so, just say. Don't be giving adults mean looks."

I went back across the street with my Grapette and climbed into my mother's car. I felt dirty all over. She came out of the store with a big grocery bag clutched against her chest. She set it on the seat between us. Inside it were three sweaty bottles of milk and two cartons of Cream of Wheat.

"What's wrong, Aaron?"

"Nothing."

She hadn't started the car. She twisted around and looked through the rear window. Mr. Watts was crossing the street, his Stetson slanted sideways, his cigar poked back in his jaw. "Did that man say something or do something to you?" she said.

"He put his hand on my head, like he was wiping it on me."

She looked straight ahead, her face tight. She started to turn the ignition, her hand shaking on the keys. The keys fell to the floor. She reached under the seat and pulled out a leather quirt. "Stay in the car."

She opened the door and stepped outside, her hair blowing, her profile cut out of tin.

"You haven't changed," Mr. Watts said, tipping his hat. "As fresh as the dew, no matter the season."

"You touched my son?"

"I don't know rightly what you mean by *touched*."

"Don't you put on airs with me," she said.

"I thought we were friends."

She slashed the quirt across his face and laid open his cheek.

"Lord, woman, you flat cut loose, don't you?" he said. He pressed the back of his wrist against the cut and looked at the smear of blood on his skin. "Warn me next time and I'll stay out of your way."

She began to thrash him, raining blows down on his head and shoulders, weeping at her own rage and impotence and shame while two men grabbed her by the arms and dragged her back on the sidewalk, easing the quirt out of her hand.

"It's all right, everybody," Mr. Watts said to the onlookers. "Miss Wynona is distraught. She didn't mean no harm."

People patted him on the back and shook his hand and told him what a kind and Christian man he was. I ran to my mother and hugged her around the waist, as though we were the only two people on earth.

The man from Victoria who was supposed to pick up the Mexicans never arrived. Mother fed the Mexicans and Grandfather cussed out the man from Victoria on the phone. "You're going to he'p the war effort by not hiring wets?" he said. "I got a better way for you to serve your country. Shoot yourself."

The sun went down and so did the glow of lights from town that sometimes reflected on the bottoms of the clouds. In the general store at the crossroads the radio with the tiny yellow dial broadcast stories about the Japanese dropping parachutes loaded with incendiary devices into our forests and grasslands. There were also reports of pamphlets that floated out of the sky and burst into flame when children picked them up. Street mobs were attacking Japanese businesses in Los Angeles.

Grandfather put on his canvas coat and tied on his wide-brimmed hat with a scarf and walked his fences with a lantern, out of fear not of the Japanese but of the evil potential of Mr. Watts, or maybe in bitter recognition that his era had passed and the injury he had done to his family could not be undone and the moral failure that characterized his life had poisoned everything he touched and saw.

That night I helped Mother and Grandfather in the barn with the Mexicans. She gave her greatest care to the woman breastfeeding her infant and held it in her arms while the mother used the outhouse. The Mexicans were a sad lot, their skin as gray as the fields, their faces like mud masks, their clothes and hair sprinkled with bits of hay that had turned yellow.

Back in the kitchen Grandfather told me the Mexicans had crossed the Rio Grande far south of us, then had been betrayed by an illegal contractor who was supposed to drive them to San Antonio.

"He took their money and left them with the clothes on their backs," he said.

"What's going to happen to them?" I asked.

"They'll get caught and sent back. The government calls them 'deportees.'"

"That little baby is mighty thin," I said.

"Your mother worries me."

"Sir?"

"I let her down," he said. "She blames herself for something that wasn't her fault."

"She never speaks bad of you, Grandfather. Not ever."

"Past is past. Wait here." He went into the living room and picked up a deep cardboard box from behind the couch and carried it back into the kitchen. I heard scraping sounds inside the cardboard.

"I got this from a lady friend of mine. Take a peek."

The pup could have walked right off a Buster Brown promotion in a shoe-store window—chunky as a fireplug, his brown eyes as round and big as quarters, his stub of a tail swishing against the box.

I picked him up and breathed his clean puppy smell and felt his tongue on my face. "He looks just like Tige."

"I declare, you and him make quite a pair."

Two weeks went by, then Wake Island fell and supposedly a Japanese submarine fired artillery shells into a California oil field. Some of the Mexicans went away on their own, single men who hopped a freight or women without children looking for work as cooks and cleaning maids. A half dozen stayed with us, including the woman with the infant. Her name was Maria; her child's was Jesus. Her husband had died of a snake bite in Coahuila, just before they crossed the river into Texas.

As we entered the new year, Grandfather incrementally gave jobs to the remaining Mexicans so their visibility would grow a little each day, until a passerby might think they had always been with us, patching the barn roof, washing clothes on the porch, burning tumbleweeds in the ditches, harrowing a field for the spring. I don't know what he paid them. I'm sure it wasn't much, if anything, for he had very little money. But the Mexicans didn't seem to mind. My mother bought baby clothes for Jesus and started teaching Maria English. Toward the end of January Mother received a postcard from my father. He said he was returning to Houston and hoped she and I would rejoin him in our little ivy-covered brick bungalow on Hawthorne Street.

"We're going home, aren't we, Mother?" I said.

"I suspect," she said. "Directly, anyway."

"What's *directly* mean?"

"It means *directly*."

She twisted her fingers idly in my hair, her gaze just this side of madness.

Two days later we drove to town with Grandfather. He had never learned to drive a car and always looked upon a ride in a car as a treat. We parked at the open market by the train depot and got out. I had forgotten my bad experience with Mr. Watts, as though it were a bad dream that fell apart in the daylight. A locomotive with a caboose and only two passenger cars on it had pulled into the station, the engine hissing steam. Mother was browsing through some open-air clothes racks and Grandfather was buying a piece of cactus candy from a booth when we saw Mr. Watts ten feet away, eating caramel corn from a paper sack while he watched us.

"Good morning," he said. He was wearing a black suit with a silver shirt and a vest and a string tie. "A friend of yours on the train would like to say hello."

"Tell him to get off the train and do it," Grandfather replied.

"Maybe him and some others don't want to draw attention."

The shades were drawn on all the passenger windows in the train. "They're celebrities?" Grandfather said.

"Maybe one of them was there when Bonnie Parker and Clyde Barrow got it," Mr. Watts said. "Know who that might be?"

"You're talking about Frank Hamer?"

"He didn't give his name. He just said he knowed you."

"Which car is he in?"

"The second behind the engine."

Grandfather took me by the hand and we walked past the caboose to the first passenger car. It was the dark green of an olive. "Let's see what's going on, Buster Brown." He swung me up on the steel steps.

The passenger seats had been removed from the car and replaced with benches, a pickle barrel, and a table that had smoked fish and several half-empty bottles of Hires root beer on it. There was a potbelly stove in one corner. Five men in suits and slouch or cowboy hats were sitting on the benches. Two of them wore mustaches. All of them were unshaved and looked like they had slept in their clothes. All of them were armed.

"One of you wanted to see me?" Grandfather said.

A tall man stood up. His mustache was jet-black and drooped to his collar. "I always wanted to meet you. I heard you slept with the girlfriend of the Sundance Kid." He grinned.

"You must have me mixed up with somebody else," Grandfather said. "Number two, I got my grandson with me."

"Excuse me," the man said.

"Y'all Pinkertons?" Grandfather said.

"Friends of the railroad."

"One of y'all saw Bonnie and Clyde get it?"

"*I* did," said the same man.

Grandfather studied his face. "No, you didn't," he said. "I know every man who was there."

"I got pictures. But I won't argue."

"What do you fellows want?"

"We think there's some Chinamen coming through here with the wetbacks. Except they're not Chinamen."

"They're Japs?" Grandfather said. My hand was still inside his. It felt hard and moist and callused and yet gentle.

"Would that surprise you?" the tall man said.

"Stay clear of me. That includes my family and workers."

"We don't call the shots. The railroad is going to be carrying a lot of soldiers through here."

"I understand that and I don't need to hear any more," Grandfather said. "You got my message."

"You really knew the Sundance Kid?"

"Yes, I did. He was a moron who breathed through his mouth a lot. Are y'all going to make trouble for me?"

"That's up to you, Mr. Holland."

"Son, you don't know what trouble is," Grandfather said.

One of the other men set his Hires root beer on the table. In the silence the sound made my face jerk.

I was too little to understand adult cruelty. Like most children, I thought adults possessed all the power they needed and hence had no reason to be cruel. So I was not equipped to comprehend the events that happened three days later when Mr. Watts's Model T drove up the dry streambed, followed by a big khaki-colored truck with a canvas top on the back.

Mr. Watts and the man with the mustache got out by the barn. The truck made a circle into the field behind the windmill and hcrdcd three Mexican men toward the house. No, I didn't say that right. The men hung their heads and walked with the docility of animals going up a slaughter chute. Maria was squeezing out the wash with a hand-crank roller on the back porch, her baby in a bassinet made from an orange crate. Three of the men from the train car jumped off the back of the truck, rifles in their hands. Mother came out the screen door wearing a man's suit coat, her face disjointed, the way it did before one of her spells came on.

"What do you think you're doing?" she said.

"The Mexican woman and the child are illegals," a man with a chin beard said.

"You have no proof of that."

"We don't need it, lady."

"Don't you dare put your hand on her," Mother said. "Did you hear me?"

"Ma'am, don't mix in it or we'll have to take you too."

"That's what you think," she said.

"Step back, please," the man said.

"Hold on there, Ed," Mr. Watts called, walking toward us. "I'll handle this."

"You will handle nothing," Mother said.

"Get your father out here," Mr. Watts said.

"He's in town," she said. "If he was here, you'd be dead."

"Well, we'll have to do our job without him, won't we, Wynona?"

"You will not address me by my first name."

Mr. Watts turned to the other men. "Load them up, the female and the baby first. Search the barn and the loft. Look in the outhouse as well, and then in the main house."

"You don't have the authority to do this," Mother said.

"I'm head constable," Mr. Watts said. "These men are contract law officers working for the government. Now you stand aside or I'll arrest you myself."

"Like hell you will," she said.

Mr. Watts looked at the windmill spinning and the dust blowing out of the fields. His eyes were bright and small under the brim of his hat. He bit the corner of his lip. "Cuff her and keep her here till we're gone," he said.

And that's what they did, with her arms pulled behind her, her throat corded with veins. The child began crying in the orange crate, his little chest and fists shaking with the effort. Minutes later

Maria looked back at us from under the canvas top on the truck, her body rocking with the movement of the bed, her face small and frightened inside the scarf tied on her head.

Mr. Watts started toward his Model T, then returned to the porch. "Stop yelling," he said to my mother. "Don't you tell lies to your father about me, either. Goddamnit, shut up! They're just deportees."

That night Mother sat in her room upstairs by herself while in the kitchen I told Grandfather what had happened. He was quiet a long time. The wind was up, the sky black, and through the window I could see sparks twisting from the ventilation pipe on the smokehouse.

"Did she strike Mr. Watts?" he said.

"No, sir."

"You're sure?"

"Yes, sir."

"Did they put their hands on Miss Maria?"

"One man held her while another man carried the crate to the truck."

"The man with the mustache from the train, the one who was talking about the Sundance Kid, what was his part in all this?"

"He told me he was sorry. He said to tell you that. He acted afraid."

"Ask your mother to come down here, please."

"What for, Grandfather?" I rarely questioned what Grandfather said. But this time I was truly scared. For all of us.

"I need her to drive me to town. You'll have to come with us. I don't want you here by yourself."

"What are we doing, Grandfather?"

"That's up to other people."

I got my mother from upstairs. Grandfather had already put on his canvas coat. His revolver and gun belt and holster were on the table, the belt wrapped around the holster, the leather loops stuffed with brass cartridges.

"Don't do this, Daddy," Mother said.

"He's the man who caused you all that pain, Wynona," Grandfather said. "Now he's doing it again."

"I do not think about him anymore," she said. "He has nothing to do with my life."

"Will you drive me to town? I can saddle Blue. But it's fixing to rain."

"It might rain in your prayers, but that's the only place you're going to see it," she said.

"Either h'ep me or I'll get my slicker."

We climbed into the car and drove to town. I could see flickers of light on the horizon, like a string of firecrackers popping on the rim of the earth.

The saloon was a leftover from the nineteenth century, the ceiling plated with stamped tin, the bar outfitted with a brass foot rail and cuspidors. Not far away some of the pens that marked the exact inception spot of the Chisholm Trail were still standing. Mother parked at an angle to the elevated concrete sidewalk and cut the engine. The window of the saloon was gray with dust, a solitary bulb burning inside. Through the windshield I could see men tipping tin cups in a bucket of beer and playing poker dice at the bar.

"We'll wait here," Mother said.

Grandfather got out on the passenger side, his gun belt looped on his shoulder, the revolver hanging under his armpit. "I want Aaron to see this," he said.

"See what?" my mother asked.

"That our family doesn't tolerate abuse."

She half opened the driver's door and stood partially in the street and looked across the car roof at him. She wasn't wearing a coat, and her flesh was prickled with cold, her amber hair wild and beautiful. "I made my choices. Now, leave well enough alone, Daddy."

Grandfather looked down at me. "We do it our way, don't we, Buster Brown? Come along now and don't pay your mother no mind. She knows I'm right."

I put my hand in his and walked with him into the saloon. I thought I smelled rain. I was sure I did. The way it smells in the spring. Like a great gold-green world full of pure oxygen and mist and sunshine and new beginnings. The bell rang above the door. A half-dozen men turned and stared at us. Mr. Watts shook the dice in a leather cup and slung the dice along the bar. "Wrong address, Mr. Holland," he said.

"What'd y'all do with Maria and her baby and the rest of my Mexicans?" Grandfather said.

"They're your property, are they?" Mr. Watts said.

Mother came inside and closed the door behind her, the bell tinkling again. The smell of rain went away and the air became close and laced with a masculine odor and a burned stench from the woodstove. A man in a mackinaw bent over and spat a stream of tobacco juice in a cuspidor. Grandfather let go of my hand and approached Mr. Watts. "Say you're sorry."

"To who?" Mr. Watts said.

"My daughter."

"For what?"

"What you did."

"I have nothing to apologize for." Mr. Watts reached around for his tin cup and accidentally knocked it over. "Give me a towel over here," he said to the bartender.

"Forget the towel," Grandfather said. "Look at me."

"I will not do anything you say." Mr. Watts pointed his chin in the air, like a prideful child.

The man with the drooping jet-black mustache was three feet from Mr. Watts. "We ain't part of this, Captain Holland."

"Then stand aside," Grandfather said.

"You're not really gonna do this, are you?" said the man with the mustache. "You're a smarter man than that, right?"

Grandfather picked me up and put me in Mother's arms. "Go sit by the stove, Wynona."

"Please, Daddy," she said.

"Do as I ask."

She walked with me to the rear of the saloon and sat down in a rocking chair. She kept me on her lap, her arms folded across my chest. I could feel her heart beating against my back, her breath on my neck.

Mr. Watts was staring at Grandfather, his hands by his side, as though he didn't know where to put them. "This needs to stop. We're all white men here. We're all on the same side. There's a war on."

"Apologize and we'll be gone."

Mr. Watts looked sick. The contract lawmen around him moved slowly away from the bar.

"You cain't walk in here and shoot a constable," Mr. Watts said.

"Give me your word you'll bring Maria and her baby back to our house."

"They're already on their way to a processing station in Laredo," Mr. Watts said.

"Then you'd better go get them," Grandfather said.

Mr. Watts's bottom lip was trembling, as though he were about to cry. With time I would learn that his desperation was even greater than I thought. He had reached that moment of fear and humiliation when a man is willing to take whatever measure is necessary to avoid the shame and self-loathing that follows a public display of cowardice.

"You were a drunkard back then, Mr. Holland," he said. "Half the time you were in a blackout. That's why they took your badge. It wasn't me caused the problem with your daughter."

"What?"

"Ask her. I brought her home from the movies. A week later she told me what you did. You were drunk and you put the blocks to her."

He could hardly get the last sentence out. Grandfather shook his gun belt from his arm and curled his hand around the handle of the revolver as the belt and cartridges struck the floor. He cocked the hammer.

"Tell him, Wynona," Mr. Watts said.

"He's lying, Daddy," she said.

"Bring a Bible out here," Mr. Watts said. "I'll put my hand on it."

"Is he telling the truth, Wynona?" Grandfather said.

"How many times were you so drunk you couldn't remember what planet you were on?" Mr. Watts said. "Down in Mexico in 1916. You didn't do that with Pancho Villa's señoritas?"

"You close your mouth, you vile man," Mother said.

Grandfather's eyes were pale blue, lidless, empty of feeling or thought, as though his soul had taken flight. I saw him swallow, then he eased down the hammer on the revolver and picked up his gun belt and replaced the revolver in its holster. "We're leaving now," he said. "Come on, Aaron."

"He's a liar, Daddy."

"I don't know what I did back then. I never will. I killed people in Mexico who have no faces. There's a whole year I cain't remember."

We went out the door and into the night. The wind was howling, the clouds huge and crawling with electricity. I sat in the front seat of the car with my mother. Grandfather was hunched in the back, like a caged animal, his eyes tunnels of sorrow.

Grandfather finalized our defeat that night when he went into the barn with a lantern and returned with a bottle that had a cork in it and no label. He carried the bottle into his bedroom and sat on the side of the bed and pulled the cork and tilted the bottle to his mouth. My mother took me upstairs and told me to put on my pajamas and lie down. Then she put Tige in bed with me and sat down beside me and looked into my face. "Pay no attention to what you saw or heard in the saloon, Aaron," she said. "Grandfather is a good man and would never intentionally do harm to his family."

"What was Mr. Watts saying?"

"Never listen to people like Mr. Watts. Their words are like locusts in the wind. I have to run an errand in town now. Don't worry if Grandfather gets drunk. He'll be all right in the morning."

"What kind of errand?"

"I know someone who might be able to help Maria and Jesus," she said. "He's a federal judge."

I looked at her eyes. They were clear. "It's too late to go to town," I said.

She stroked my hair, then clicked off the light and went down the stairs and out the front door. Through the window I could see the beams of her headlights bouncing on the fence posts and fields along our road.

I woke to sunlight and the sound of rain ticking on the dormers and people's voices downstairs. I got up and put on my blue jeans and went to the head of the stairs. I could see Grandfather talking to the sheriff and a deputy and a man in a suit with a stethoscope hanging from his neck. I did not see my mother. I walked down the stairs, still in my pajamas, Tige running in front of me, his nails clicking on the wood, his rump waddling on each step.

"We need to look at it, Hack," the sheriff said. "Hackberry" was Grandfather's first name.

"Big waste of time, if you ask me," Grandfather said.

"You know the position I'm in, Hack," the sheriff said. He wore a white beard and was almost as big as Grandfather. "Just bring it out here, will you?"

"Whatever you want," Grandfather said.

He went into the hallway and returned holding his holstered revolver, the belt wrapped around it. The sheriff took it from him and he slipped the revolver from the holster and half cocked the hammer, then opened the loading gate and rotated the cylinder. "Smells and looks like you just cleaned and oiled it."

"A couple of days ago, I did."

"When did you start loading with six rounds instead of leaving an empty chamber?"

"Since I stopped toting it," Grandfather said.

"I'll keep this for a while, if you don't mind."

"You're going to run ballistics on it?"

"I ain't got any ballistics to run. The rounds never slowed down and are probably halfway to San Antonio."

The sheriff shucked the rounds from the cylinder one by one and dropped them in his coat pocket and stuck the pistol back in the holster and handed it to his deputy. The only sound in the room was the creak of the wind.

"So we're done here?" Grandfather said.

"It was the way he went out that bothers me," the sheriff said.

"A bullet is a bullet," Grandfather said.

"Watts got one through the mouth and one that took off most of his penis," the sheriff said. "What kind of shooter is apt to do that, Hack?"

"I guess somebody who was a bad shot or pretty mad."

"Let me restate that," the sheriff said. "Which gender is inclined to do that?"

"It's a mystery to me," Grandfather said.

My mother walked from the kitchen into the hallway. "The coffee is ready if you gentlemen care to sit down," she said.

The sheriff looked at his deputy and the man with the stethoscope and at Grandfather. "I think that would be fine, Miss Wynona," he said. "Are you feeling okay today?"

"Why wouldn't I be?" she said.

"I know what you mean," the sheriff said.

In April of 1942 Jimmy Doolittle bombed Tokyo and crash-landed his B-25s on the Chinese mainland. In reprisal for the help given to his crews by Chinese peasants, the Japanese murdered 250,000 civilians. Maria and Jesus were brought back to Grandfather's place, and Mother and Tige and I rejoined my father in our little brick home on Hawthorne Street in Houston. That summer, after the Battle of the Coral Sea, the war turned around at Midway, and we knew that in all probability the light of civilization had been saved. It was a grand time to be around. Anyone who says otherwise doesn't know what he's talking about.

MICHAEL CEBULA

Second Cousins

FROM *Ellery Queen Mystery Magazine*

"COULD YOU EVER kill a man?"

That's how she said it, that's how she laid it on me, us two in bed and it so early in the morning that I hadn't even had my first cigarette. Of course, I could guess who she was talking about.

I took my time, which is my way, and before I could respond, Toola turned and propped herself up on her elbows, looked me over, and answered herself.

"You could do it," she said.

I knew how she came to that conclusion, or thought I did. I've got that lean and hungry look, one you're born with, one that persists even on a full belly, and it's enough to make people assume you'll do anything for a dollar; it makes them think they can ask you something like that and you'll stick your hand out and say, "How much?" without ever wondering *How come?* Didn't even matter that she knew I was a deputy and had the badge to prove it. The color of your eyes and the set of your mouth determine your destiny as much as anything else. Well, that and your family.

"That's quite a question," I said, "for so early in the morning. I don't know."

"Now you're going modest on me?"

"When wasn't I modest before?"

Instead of answering, Toola turned again and lay on her back and stared at the ceiling, her old and much-abused mattress squeaking and protesting like it'd been shot. The box fan on her bureau did nothing to cool the room down, and sweat lingered on her chest like some kind of slick icing. Toola claimed she was thirty-one, her license said thirty-six, and sometimes when she'd smile you'd swear twenty-five. She had long black hair and soft white skin and was good-looking in all the ways you'd expect, but what caught me first was she had the greenest eyes I'd ever seen. She told me later they were contacts.

Now I pawed at the nightstand beside me but couldn't find my cigarettes. I was feeling about half starved, but even after all our times together I still didn't know if Toola could cook, only that she wasn't the type of woman you asked to make you breakfast. My head was aching and I wanted to sink back down into that bed, but I could already hear the combine running over the soybean field across the road. That meant somebody could have seen my patrol car out front. I hardly had the energy for it, but I swung my legs over the bed and looked around for my clothes. My clothes and my cigarettes.

Toola said, "You ever think of leaving here, Danny?"

"Can I put my pants on first?"

"They're in the kitchen. Under the table, next to your boots."

"In the kitchen, under the table. How did they—never mind."

"What I meant is, you ever think of just hitting the road? Getting in your car and driving until you leave everyone behind and find someplace better than all this?"

I gave up looking for my cigarettes and walked to the door. Toola hadn't moved a muscle. You never could guess what that girl might say next. But I always liked hearing her talk.

"No place is all that different," I said. "Not in any way that counts."

"Lord," she said. "Don't tell me that."

I left Toola where she was, and where she was likely to remain for as long as the sun was up, and walked outside to the porch. My patrol car was out front, surrounded by a mess of chickens, but I'd locked the doors the night before so I wasn't too worried about them stealing it even though they moved with the nervous jitter of a money-hungry band of tweakers. It was hot already and humid, the kind of air you don't walk in as much as swim through, and I wasn't much looking forward to my shift, even before you considered my hangover.

Me and Toola had been visiting each other several nights a week for the last six months, and while that had its benefits it was costing me sleep, especially sleep in my own bed. That's one of those prices you pay that looks different in the daylight than it did the night before. Which isn't the same as saying you regret it. Toola was the kind of woman that was hard to get out of your mind.

I could still hear that combine, but I couldn't see it. Couldn't see any other cars or houses, for that matter, only woods and soybean fields. Probably only two or three people passed by Toola's house in a given day, but leaving my cruiser out front was sloppy. I knew Toola sold weed, and she knew I knew she sold weed, and we never talked about it. My job was to stop criminals from hurting people, and Toola never hurt anybody, was the way I figured it. Now, the sheriff, he might have seen this different. Which was why I kept my mouth shut about Toola.

I stopped at home long enough to grab a shower and a clean uniform and eat a plate of eggs and potatoes, that tired bachelor meal, one served at my place as much as three times a day. After a while on your own, you start to wonder how many men get married just to improve the menu. When I finished, I radioed dispatch to say I was going straight to patrol. Nobody cared. They never do once you earn their trust.

There's country roads here in Ohio that you can roam for miles without seeing anything other than soybeans and field corn, copses of trees and maybe a stray barn. It's enough to drive you crazy with loneliness or thrill you with the illusion of freedom, depending on your mood. I picked one of those roads at random and set to it. My inclination that morning was to lay low and let that hangover burn off. I pulled two people over for speeding and let them both off with a warning. I never give tickets unless I have to, even though I'm mostly convinced that anyone driving slower than me is an idiot and everyone else is a maniac.

It turned out that second driver was some distant acquaintance of my father's, and he went on for so long at his surprise at finding me on this side of the law that I thought for a moment of giving him a ticket after all, but in the end I just stone-faced him and gave curt, unhelpful answers to his questions about my father's current whereabouts and he drove off mad like somehow I was the jerk in all of this. There's some people you just can't do favors for.

It was on about noon by then, and I was thinking of heading into town for lunch when I saw them: brief black skid marks shooting off the road not far in front of me. I don't know why exactly they caught my eye. Maybe you drive these roads enough, day after day, you notice anything new. Or maybe I saw them because that's how it was always meant to be. Either way, I stopped my cruiser along the side of the road, got out, and looked down the hill, over the grass field and into the woods. It wouldn't have been visible if you were driving past, singing along to Waylon or Johnny Cash, but standing where I was and looking close, you could just make out the back of a steel-gray Cadillac Eldorado sitting silent between two fat buckeye trees.

I froze for a moment. That car was as familiar to me as my own name.

I walked back to my cruiser and looked down the road both ways. Still empty. I drove down the road about a mile, then backed into a small dirt trail that led away from the road and into the field corn. Anybody that passed by and saw my cruiser would figure I was taking a snooze.

I slipped down the trail into the woods and backtracked toward the Cadillac. By the time I got there I was sweating hard and about ate up by mosquitos. The window was down, the flies were buzzing, and the smell was awful. I looked inside. One dead, gunshot, the same man I expected.

This was bad. Really bad. And not just for the usual reasons either.

I spent a few more minutes looking in and around the car, then headed back to my vehicle. But I didn't call it in to the sheriff. I wasn't that stupid.

My half-brother, C.T., lived outside of town in a beat-up piney-wood cabin surrounded by overgrown and dying ash trees. He was as good a place as any to start. I about wore out my knuckles knocking on his front door before he finally answered.

"What in the world?" he said, blinking in the harsh sunshine, his wet eyes shining liquor-slick.

"Too early for you?" I said, with as much false cheer as I could muster.

C.T. didn't move from the doorway. He looked at my patrol car, then back at me. "Depends what you're here for."

C.T. sold weed, pills, and powder. And probably a whole lot of other illegal substances too. But he would have been reluctant to talk to me even if all he hawked were steak knives or newspaper subscriptions. Me and C.T. had never been friendly, even when we were kids.

"Why don't you invite me in first," I said.

"Is it gonna be that kind of conversation?"

"It might could be."

C.T. sighed and turned and walked back inside, which was as much of an invitation as I was likely to get. However you are picturing the inside of C.T.'s house is pretty much how it looked. There were too many empty beer cans and whiskey bottles to count and enough dirty dishes laying around that I had to take a minute to clear a space on the couch to sit down.

C.T. sat across from me in a ripped and faded easy chair, sipping a two-liter bottle of orange soda. He had the kind of thick long blond hair that you knew would last forever, and he wore the casual and wrinkled clothes of someone who never punched a clock. Me, I spent all day in uniform, and though I was barely thirty, my own hair was starting to retreat in a way that told me it would disappear slowly and then all at once like clear-cut timber. One night Toola had run her hands through what still remained and told me she thought bald men were sexy. I hadn't yet decided how I felt about that.

"What'd you spike that soda with?" I said.

"Nothing you could handle." C.T. took another sip. "What is it you're wanting?"

"Haven't seen you in a while," I said. "Thought it might be good to hear what you've been up to lately."

"Same as always, man. Just trying to find me a pretty girl, you know, one that's got legs as long as a Monday."

"And a skirt as short as the weekend?"

"It's not as funny if you steal the punch line," he said.

"How about you try being a little more specific."

C.T. slunk back in his chair like a sulky child. "Is this a cops talk or a family talk?"

He always said it like that, *cops,* just so he could turn it into a four-letter word. It was unspoken between us, but we had a kind of silent agreement that I wouldn't ever bust C.T. and in return he would give me a little information from time to time. It never amounted to much; the rare solid piece of info was always aimed at some new enemy of his and was more gossip than anything else, but so far it had suited us both fine.

"Let's make this one a law-enforcement conversation," I said. "The kind where I hear enough good intel that I lose interest in searching your pickup to see what I might find."

"Man, you don't have to put it so harsh as that," C.T. said. He leaned farther back in his chair, stared at the ceiling, and rubbed his mouth. "Okay, let me think on that for a minute. What would Deputy Dan like to know, what would Deputy Dan like to know. Well, how about Lowell Adams is selling pills out of that new bait shop of his."

"Not anymore. He got popped two days ago."

"Shoot, really?"

I couldn't tell if C.T. really didn't know or was just feeding me stale information. He wouldn't help me if he didn't have to.

"Yes, really," I said. "You got something worthwhile or not?"

"Now, just hold on," C.T. said. "Don't get so agitated. Give me a second to keep on thinking." After a moment he grinned. "You hear Laurie DelMarr's stepping out on Horace?"

"Why you telling me that for?"

"Man, I'm telling everybody," C.T. cackled. "You imagine what's going to happen when Horace finds out?"

I stood up. "It's a shame you don't know anything good," I said. "Looks like I'm going to have to search that truck of yours after all. The barn too."

"C'mon, man, if I don't know, how can I tell you? I'm just small-time now; it's not like the glory days, you know? I do a little business and it's hardly enough to pay my rent."

"Believe it or not, I've heard sadder stories than that, C.T. How about you join the rest of us and get a real job?"

"Hey, man, I look for work, like, every week."

That was a lie. C.T. would rather have a crooked quarter than a straight dollar.

"If times are so tough," I told him, "you ought to go work for Selby Cluxton."

I said that to needle him, and also to throw out a little bait. But C.T. didn't even nibble at the hook.

"Can't see myself ever getting so desperate as that," he said.

It wasn't the answer I was hoping for. I looked around the room, at a loss for what to do next. C.T.'s place always depressed me, probably because it looked no different from the series of dumps we'd lived in growing up. Neither one of us spoke. I needed to figure out if he knew anything about the dead man in the Cadillac without letting him know what I'd found. I was about to press C.T. again when something caught my eye.

On the windowsill, next to two dead flies, was a half-empty pack of Chesterfield cigarettes. I walked over and picked it up with my pen, the way I'd seen actors on television do. Only one man around here smoked these.

"This mean what I think it means?" I said.

"Daddy always did have particular tastes. He come on over the other day, must have left them on accident once we got to drinking."

"He's back?" I said. "Since when?"

C.T. kicked his feet up on top of the wobbly coffee table and grinned. Did I mention he was taller than me too?

"Aren't you supposed to know Daddy's back?" he said. "Being the law and all?"

"We don't keep track of all his comings and goings. He doesn't rate that highly, not anymore."

"Maybe not to the rest of them. But to you?"

C.T. was enjoying this a little too much. "All I'm asking is how long he's been back," I said. "And what you've been up to."

"He's been back, say, two-three weeks. He didn't come calling till last week, though, wanted me to help him move some new furniture to where he's staying now."

"Should I be checking reports of armed robberies at furniture stores?"

"Nah, he bought it. It's all legit."

"Is that a fact?"

C.T. shrugged. "He's going legit. For real."

I shook my head. "You believe that?"

C.T. leaned forward, still grinning. "You can't even say his name. You know what that tells people?"

"Is it better or worse than what it tells them when a grown man calls his father 'Daddy'?"

C.T.'s smile dropped as quick and final as a man in a noose. "There's no call for that kind of talk," he said. "Listen, you want to search my property, then try and get a warrant. Until then, maybe you ought to get going, so I can get my beauty sleep."

"It's lunchtime."

"You keep your hours and I'll keep mine."

"What's he planning to do, now that he's back?"

"If he told me, and you know that's an if, how could I ever tell you?"

And there it was. So much for turning legit.

"I expect he's wanting to take back what was his," I said.

"Look at that," said C.T. "And people say you're not smart enough to make sheriff."

I kept the Chesterfields, even though they're not my brand. In fact, just the sight of them on the seat next to me turned my stomach. On the way back to town, I stopped at a gas station to buy my own. While I was there, just to check, I used the pay phone to call C.T. His line was busy. Two guesses who he was talking to.

My father, the man C.T. called "Daddy" and I called Lionel, had run the drug game in this county and the ones surrounding it for most of my life. He did until recently, that is, due to a two-year stretch he'd served in the penitentiary for beating the tar out of a mouthy college boy who was filled with more whiskey courage than good sense. Lionel had been released six months ago, and then he'd just gone and disappeared without so much as spending a single night in the one town he'd ever called home. Nobody knew where he went, though I had my guesses.

The beating he laid on that college boy, the beatings he used to lay on me, all the drugs he sold, and all the dirt he did to stay on top, none of that is what broke us up. No, only one crime of his really mattered to me. When I was six, my mother disappeared. Ran away, if you asked Lionel. Which, for lack of proof to the contrary, is what ended up in the official report. I know, because I've seen it. It was all lies. Problem is, there's what you know is the truth and there's what you can prove, and they're only about as related as second cousins.

It's embarrassing to admit, but Lionel was the reason I was a deputy. Before I was big enough to hold a gun there was some stupid notion in my mind as a kid of arresting him, leading him off in handcuffs. Not for what I knew he did to my mother—that case was long since ice cold—but for dealing, or beatings, or any of the other evils he did every day. That's kid stuff, those fantasies, and I never told anyone about it, just kept it alive in my heart. Except then once I finally convinced the county to hire me, I was immediately taken off any case that might relate to him. Conflict of interest, they said; what would the voters think, relying on a son to investigate his father? It was funny, in a way.

When Lionel was released from prison a few months back and then disappeared himself, people figured he didn't come back because they thought he couldn't. See, Lionel never had a true second in command, unless you count C.T. It wasn't my father's way to share one bit of power. And when he was sent away to serve that two-year stretch, C.T. was in no position to hold on to what Lionel had built. It just wasn't in him.

So in Lionel's absence, a foulmouthed and filthy-minded creep nobody much liked named Selby Cluxton rose up and took everything over. Selby had always been a fat and greedy low-level dealer held down by my father, most likely because Lionel knew the threat he could become. But once Lionel was gone, there was nobody stopping him. Toola worked for Selby. Most everybody that sold pills, weed, or powder around here did.

Creep though he was, it said something about Selby that people would think he could keep Lionel from coming back. But it said more about how quick people are to forget. Because I knew Lionel wasn't scared of Selby or scared of coming back. Lionel wasn't afraid of anything, because nothing in his life had shown him he ever had reason to be. I knew Lionel wasn't avoiding Selby, he was only out of state for a little bit, repairing the relationships he needed to keep him with a steady supply of drugs to sell. He'd be back sooner or later to take over again.

And if people had a little more information, if they knew what I knew, then they'd start to believe that time was now. After all, it was Selby Cluxton that was laying dead in that Cadillac.

The sheriff's station might have been impressive when they built it fifty years ago, but I doubt it. All I knew for sure was that now it was a squat, faded red-brick building that was too hot in the summer, too cold in the winter, and looked like something God had squished with his thumb. I stayed away as much as I could, but I didn't have that option now.

Inside the station Billy Price was reading the newspaper, his long legs kicked up on his desk, looking as thin and limp as a string hanging from a balloon. Billy had a deputy's star and the title that came with it, but he was seldom allowed to carry a gun or go out in the field. Only the sheriff knew why that was, but everyone acquainted with Billy agreed that it was probably a good idea anyway.

Now Billy looked me over lazily and yawned. "Where you been at all day?"

"Keeping the world safe from outlaws and Methodists," I said.

Billy laughed, a little too hard. He always did, as if he wanted to prove he could recognize a joke. You'd be surprised who gets hired for jobs that nobody particularly wants.

"The sheriff in?" I asked. I was feeling anxious. If I was going to do anything on Selby Cluxton's murder, I had to hustle. There was only so much time before the Cadillac would get discovered. Somebody skipping work to go fishing or poach deer would find it sooner or later. And then they'd box me out and there'd be nothing I could do. Before that happened, I wanted to grease the skids that pointed to Lionel. Give them a head start, so to speak. And I needed to do all this without telling anybody about that dead body.

"Sheriff's in his office," Billy said, nodding toward the back. "Same as always."

Sheriff Gutherie was in fact in his office, hidden behind three tall stacks of paperwork on his desk. The sheriff was a good man, as far as that went, but he seemed constantly vexed, like a man who had to spend each day trying to shovel another hundred pounds of garbage into a ten-pound bag. There was a rumor every year that he was going to retire, and those rumors were getting stronger now.

"Okay," he said, after hearing what C.T. told me, "your father's back." He shrugged. "Probably was going to happen sooner or later."

I glanced at the door like I didn't want to be overheard. "What worries me is, he's not exactly the type to take to rehabilitation."

"You're probably right on that. But we can't arrest a man for what he might do."

It was a weird feeling, not reporting the murder. But there was no other way.

"We can follow him," I said. "That'd help keep him on the straight and narrow."

"How am I going to do that? And who am I supposed to do it with?"

"What about Billy?"

"Deputy Price is good right where he is, sitting at his desk reading the paper cover to cover every day. We shouldn't strain that brain of his with anything more difficult."

The way the sheriff folded his hands across his gut and leaned back in his chair, I knew he had made his decision and I had lost. But I had to play my role anyway.

"I'm just worried it's only a matter of time," I said. "Before he's back to doing his dirt."

"And then we'll investigate it when he does. Look, I appreciate you telling me this, I know it's hard for you and you only want to keep him out of trouble. But we can hardly deal with the crimes that have happened, let alone the ones that haven't yet."

The sheriff set a chaw in his lip and scooted the tallest pile of paperwork closer to him. His way of saying goodbye. There wouldn't be any tail on Lionel, and that would make my job that much tougher. For a second my nerves got to me and I wondered if the sheriff could be in Lionel's pocket. But the sheriff was cautious and responsible to a fault, the kind of man who gets more pleasure from reserving his cemetery plot than buying a new pickup. The sheriff wouldn't take a dirty dollar, I didn't think.

He looked up from his work, as if surprised to still find me there. I stepped out, like a scolded child, and shut his door. I stood for a moment in the empty hallway, thinking.

That Lionel killed Selby Cluxton would make sense to everybody; they wouldn't need a calculator to add it all up. The problem was, guesswork would be all they had, and that wasn't near enough to convict anybody, let alone someone as slick as Lionel. Five decades of committing every crime you could imagine and the only time the jury got to say guilty was when he beat that college boy, and that was only because an off-duty highway patrolman drinking in the corner of the bar happened to see it all. Unless you got that kind of luck, you need confessions, physical evidence, eyewitnesses.

For now I had none of that. And with no tail on him, Lionel would be free to go and do as he pleased. But that didn't mean I was quitting.

On my way out of the station, I rapped my knuckles on Billy's desk to wake him up.

"Come with me, deputy," I said. "You just got a new assignment."

Billy was nervous, and that's without me even mentioning the murder. I explained it to him again.

"All I'm asking is, back my play," I told him. We were sitting in Billy's borrowed cruiser in the empty parking lot of a bankrupt lumberyard, while my patrol car idled a few feet away. "There's no risk in it for you. It works, you get all the credit. If it doesn't, nobody will ever hear about it."

"Yeah, but—"

"You want to get out in the field more than once a month? You want to carry a gun without asking permission? Then you got to give the sheriff a reason to believe in you."

"Yeah, but—"

"Besides, Joe might not be sheriff much longer. Who knows who the next sheriff might be. Doing this would go a long way in impressing whoever that is. And look, this won't sweat you any. You see something, you call for backup. You don't, you go on home. It's gonna be easy as shelling peas. You used to do that for your mama, right?"

Billy laughed, too hard again. It didn't give me a good feeling, but there was nothing that could be done now. All I could do was hope that the next time I saw Billy he'd be accepting handshakes and backslaps from the rest of the department, not tightening the noose around my neck.

I got out and tapped the hood and Billy drove off. It was time for me to go find Lionel.

The new girl that lived with my father was glassy-eyed and talked real slow, like her mouth had a limp. I call her a girl, but she must have been twenty, standing in the doorway looking thin as a promise and wearing only an old white T-shirt. She saw my badge and set her mouth and you could almost see her trying to remember her line.

"Lionel?" she said. "Lionel's not here."

"Don't worry," I told her. "He trained me to say the same thing five years before you were ever born." Then I edged past her into the house.

I figured if Lionel was back in town and wanting to lay low, he'd head to this hunting cabin north of town that he'd bought a decade before. My guess was right.

Lionel was sitting at the kitchen table working over a pen and paper, next to a pile of safety-deposit keys. When I came in he looked up for only a moment, then he went back to work as if I'd arrived a few minutes early for an appointment instead of this being the first time we'd seen each other since the morning the judge handed him a two-year stretch.

The funny thing about that day was, everybody in the courtroom expected him to get at least five years. But then, for reasons nobody knew but I could guess at, the judge dismissed the most serious charges and gave him the minimum. The prosecutor looked like he'd just learned that his wife had run away with the local preacher and took the dog too, but I could have told him it wasn't personal, he was just another in a long line of men to get rolled by my father.

Now I set my hat on the kitchen table, sat down, and wiped my face. "Boy, it's hot out," I said. "If we don't get any rain soon, the trees will start bribing the dogs."

Lionel kept working. "You come to talk about the weather?"

"Not exactly," I said.

Lionel looked the same as ever. Broad shoulders sticking out from underneath a cut-off black Harley T-shirt, long white hair in a ragged ponytail, and pale blue eyes that always seemed to look right through you. He had a few more tattoos than before, but that was all. He was still bigger than me, and showed no sign of slowing down.

A small fan pointing at Lionel was the only sound in the room. He continued to ignore me. I realized I was chewing my nails and I wiped my hand across my leg, disgusted with myself. How long could you live with a man that you knew killed your mother? A day? A week? I did twelve years. And leaving home doesn't fix anything.

I nodded toward the front room. "What's this one's name?"

"Who, Keely?"

"Yeah, Keely. You tell her she's only the latest in a series?"

"I don't know that that would surprise her."

"She be surprised to know how the other ones fared?"

Lionel kept working. "That's a better question for her than me," he said. "If you're really wanting to know, then you ought to hustle on in there and ask, because if I meet my guess there'll be no talking to her in another twenty minutes."

"Guess that's what it takes to keep them when you're more than twice their age."

"No, but it does save a lot of time and hassle." Lionel got up, stuck the keys in his pockets, and shoved the papers in a drawer. "Speaking of hassle, looks like you're still as much of one as ever. I see you haven't lost your taste for judging people."

"I come by my self-righteousness honestly, through prayer and hard work."

Lionel leaned back against the kitchen counter and looked at me, his eyes running over me cold and flat, completely at ease, like a rattlesnake sunning itself on a rock.

"That's why you never accomplished anything," he said. "Too busy making jokes. What you never learned about women is, they're as disposable as socks—when they get too old or worn out, or hell, you just get sick of them, there's no use keeping them around. Now, tell me what you're here for or get the hell out."

I wanted to slug him then, but that would have ruined everything. I get a smart mouth sometimes, but Lionel always held the trump card. I took a breath, tapped my hat against the table, and tried to appear relaxed. I had to be careful. Lionel was slick, too slick for me to see every move. I had to keep things simple, not try to prove the whole case right here.

"How long you been in town for?"

Lionel shrugged, like the question bored him. "Maybe a week."

That didn't square with what C.T. told me, but I expected the lie. I didn't know when Selby Cluxton was murdered, but by the looks of him, it had been within the last few days. Before I went too far, before I got more people involved, I had to know for sure that Lionel didn't have a card hidden up his sleeve, some airtight lie that put him out of town.

"What have you been doing since you been back?" I said.

"Fixing this cabin up, what do you think? C.T. was supposed to take care of things, but turns out he's not as reliable as I'd expected."

"That's all you been doing, just playing handyman?"

"C.T. and Keely and me, we been here all day every day working."

So C.T. and Keely would be Lionel's alibi. Everybody knew they'd repeat whatever lie he taught them.

"Nobody's seen you for six months," I said. "People thought you were gone for good."

Lionel grinned. "Damn, son, almost sounds like you wished I stayed away."

"Wouldn't have cried any. Especially since I know what you're planning."

"That right?" Lionel shrugged. "Plenty of people thought they had me all figured out. But I'm still around and they're not."

That was true. And it worried me.

"I know what you're planning," I said. "It's not hard to figure. But I'm giving you a chance. Clear out, tonight, leave town and don't come back. This county is closed to you."

"Closed to me. This county I've run longer than you've been alive." Lionel shook his head. "What is it about you that's always made you so eager to spit into the wind?"

"There's going to be a raid on all your stash spots tomorrow. Starting with the loft in C.T.'s barn. You're done here. I'm giving you a chance to run instead of going back to prison for a longer stretch than two years. Don't screw it up."

"And why would you be telling me this for?"

"Because you're my father."

Lionel laughed. "You develop a lot of love for your daddy while he was gone?"

"No. But I aim to be sheriff of this county. And I can't do that with a jailbird father in prison for dope."

"You think they'd elect you anyway? All them voters know your blood."

"I'd like to take my chances. And they're a damn sight better if you're a million miles from here."

Lionel thought that over for a moment, then sat back down. His hands looked like something you'd see in a zoo, and he cracked his knuckles one by one. Those hands could hit you hard enough to shake your life loose. I knew it, because I'd seen it.

Suddenly his hand shot out and I jerked back. But Lionel was only reaching for my hat.

His lips smiled but his eyes stayed lethal. I hated myself for flinching like that. He set my hat on his head, then took it off and tossed it back on the table.

"When, exactly?"

"They plan to hit you in the morning, at dawn," I said, trying to act more relaxed than I felt. "When they figure you'll be asleep. That means you got to leave tonight."

Lionel sighed and waved his hand, dismissing me. "All right, then," he told me. "You've said your piece. For all the good it will do."

I didn't know if I'd accomplished anything, but I'd given it a shot. I stood to go as Keely walked in. She tried to slip past the table to the sink, but Lionel grabbed her by the hip and made her sit on his lap. In the soft kitchen light, I could see a dim yellow bruise shining under her left eye like an ignored caution signal.

"Look at her," Lionel said. He grabbed her face and turned it toward me. "Bet you can't remember, but she's just the spitting image of your mother."

Lionel wouldn't run. But he wouldn't sit still and lose all his dope either, and working to save his product would tie him up for a bit. If I was lucky, that was enough time to put me a half step ahead of him. But something told me that was as likely as finding a box of day-old sunshine.

I rolled my window down and lit a cigarette, cruising empty backcountry roads as the sun began to set. Growing up, on hot summer days we'd jump off the highest cliffs we could find into cold spring quarries. And every time I did it, there was a feeling halfway down that everything was moving too fast and I couldn't quite believe how I'd put myself in that position. That's how I felt now. I needed to talk to Toola.

I caught her just as she was locking up the house, on her way out for the night. We sat on the porch swing together, listening to the crickets and watching the chickens hunt them in the stiff yellow grass.

"You been out playing hero?" she said.

"Do I look like any kind of hero to you?"

She grinned. "Sometimes salt looks like sugar."

Could I trust Toola? was the question. Sometimes I think your feelings mostly lead you into bad places, especially when you've spent your whole life alone and searching. But then, you never know if those feelings are worth anything unless you try.

"Selby Cluxton is dead," I said.

Toola's eyes went wide and she quit trying to light her cigarette and just looked at me.

"I found him, this afternoon. Off of Paint Creek Road. You're the only one I've told, but the sheriff will find out soon enough."

Toola looked confused. "How come you didn't tell the sheriff?"

"People will be smart enough to guess my father did it," I said. "But they won't be smart enough to prove it. Not without some help. I want to make sure they can, but I need time to do it. I don't want him to wiggle out of this one."

I waited to see how Toola would take that, but she was smart and a big girl; she had to be to survive the way she had. She didn't even blink.

"Lionel's back," she said.

"He's back," I said. "Look, there's a lot going on and I'm not sure how it's all going to play out. Why I'm telling you is, you ought to lay low for a while, until things die down. I don't think you're in any danger, but better safe than sorry."

"I got people expecting me. Customers. I don't know if—"

"They can wait a day or two. It won't kill them any. This thing with Selby, it's going to shake up a lot of people, there's no telling how they'll react. Or what Lionel will do."

Toola stood up and stuffed the pack of cigarettes in her jeans. It wasn't in her nature to rely on anybody. "Shoot, if it's that bad, maybe I ought to leave town," she said.

"It's not so bad as that yet," I said. "And if it ever is, then I'll be there running right behind you. But for now, go stay at your mother's old place. Nothing bad will happen there."

Toola paused and looked away. I stood up, sweating and nervous. How does a woman decide to trust a man? Why would they ever? The moment stretched. Then, finally, Toola nodded. That's all, just nodded one time. I knew enough about her experience with men to know that even that much was harder than it seemed. I just hoped I wasn't going to be the next man to let her down.

Toola packed quick and went on her way, and for a moment I felt about as alone as I ever had in my life. I wanted to stay at the house with all its reminders of her, but that made me feel weak and anyway it was too far from the action. So instead I drove back to that bankrupt lumberyard where me and Billy had met a few hours before.

It was full dark now and my mouth was dry. My brain was working on overdrive but not in a good way. Things were in motion and there was nothing for me to do now but wait. That gave me too much time to think and worry, remembering all that I knew of my father.

I kept thinking of a dealer named Donald Ray Wallace the most. One time, years ago, when I was little, Donald Ray got tired of working for my father. In fact, he got so tired that he went to the police station up in Harris County and offered to set my father up, wear a wire and get him on tape making a big heroin buy. The cop up there told Donald Ray that was a good idea, the cop told him to go about his business as usual and he'd call him when the warrants and such were in place. A few days later the cop told Donald Ray to meet him out at the Milk Creek mines, that he'd give him his instructions and wire him up there. Except when Donald Ray drove out to those old abandoned mines the cop wasn't there. Only Lionel was. And nobody ever saw Donald Ray again.

Lionel didn't live on luck, is my point. He was smarter and meaner and willing to do more than anybody I'd ever met. He had to be, to stay on top as long as he had. Nothing I'd ever done in my life could compare.

Was Billy Price leading me to the same fate as Donald Ray? Were there men like that cop in Harris County working in my department? Was there something I was missing? I couldn't say. But there's times in life that the world calls you to shoot your shot, and this was it for me.

My radio cackled to life. Billy was calling me in.

I put my flashers on and floored the gas, running red lights and passing every car in my way. Before long town was far behind me. Heat lightning shot across the sky, but everything else was black. Miles rolled past just that quick, then I turned off Cross Creek Road and headed into the woods down a ragged dirt track that I hadn't seen in more than twenty years.

How many times in your life do you know that you're approaching a moment that will change everything in your world, either for the good or for the bad? That old feeling, falling quickly through space and wondering how I put myself in that position, came over me again. My heart was pounding, thinking of Donald Ray Wallace, my mother, of all the times Lionel had come out on top. I crested that last big hill and saw cherry lights from patrol cars—one, two, three, four in all. I prayed Billy Price had come through.

I parked on the perimeter and got out of my cruiser, with my holster unbuckled and my hand by my gun. As if that would help me. Billy came running up, like he'd been waiting for me.

"It was exactly how you said it'd be," he told me. "Just exactly."

His eyes shone wide and his smile too, like some kind of game-show winner. My heart tripped a little, in a good way. But I kept my hand near my gun all the same.

"Tell me," I said.

"I sat up on that hill like you told me and on about midnight here comes your father with the other two, and they start unloading product off their truck into that bunker." Billy motioned to the other deputies working somewhere behind him. "I got dispatch to call up a couple of the guys real quiet, and we ambushed them as they came out of the bunker for the last time. We got all of them, the girl, C.T., and your father. It was just as simple as you said it'd be."

Billy couldn't keep the smile off his face. I let out a shaky breath and buckled my holster. I don't think Billy saw me. He was in his own world now.

"You know what to tell everybody from here on out?" Any screwups could still kill me.

"Oh, sure, that's the easiest part," Billy said. "I'm gonna write it up how you told me to. On my way home, I see some jerk swerving all over and I go after him. I lose him in these hills but then I see some lights off in the distance and decide to investigate. That's when I see your father and that girl and C.T. unloading a bunch of dope into that old bomb shelter."

Billy laid it out like a hard-won war story, and in time, with enough retellings, I knew he'd come to believe it too. Seeing Billy so confident and sure, seeing the flashing lights and the deputies securing the scene, I tingled, beginning to wonder for the first time if maybe everything really would work out. The bomb shelter was Lionel's oldest, most secret warehouse. I had come here once, as a child, when Lionel had to unload product in some kind of emergency. I kept that secret in my mind for years, protecting it like a precious inheritance. I didn't know where his other stash spots were, not anymore, but I had a hunch that he'd move it all here if he was worried about a raid. It looked like I was right.

"Listen," Billy said. "I appreciate you bringing this to me. I know it wasn't easy on you, it being your father and all."

I shrugged, kept my face blank, and retreated to the safety of cliché. If nothing else, I know my role. "What's right is right. People can't sell dope in this county. I just don't want anybody knowing I was behind my own daddy getting locked up."

Billy nodded, looking sympathetic, then he pointed to a patrol car underneath an ancient blue spruce tree. "He's sitting right there, if you want to talk to him."

I thought about that for a second, then decided I did.

Lionel sat in the back of the patrol car, looking angry but in control. The deputy standing watch nodded and wandered off a respectable distance. I leaned over Lionel's window, took in the scene surrounding us for a moment, then looked inside and locked eyes with him. Seeing my father handcuffed in the back of a patrol car and knowing I put him there, it felt like the enormous weight that had been crushing my chest and my heart for most of my life had started to lift just a little.

"Thought you were leaving town," I said.

"I don't expect that's exactly true."

"No," I told him, "it isn't."

Lionel leaned back, looking comfortable, but that didn't bother me as much as I'd have thought it would. It was all out there in the open between us now.

"I got two sons, and each one is dumber than the next," Lionel said.

"Is that a fact?"

Lionel shook his head. "You must think this will make you sheriff. You're so dumb you can't see that Keely and C.T. will tell everyone those are their drugs." He shrugged. "This is nothing, this will be just a parole violation for me. I'll do six months at most."

"Is that a fact?" I said again.

Lionel nodded. "None of this will stick to me. It never does."

I looked at him and smiled. And my smile got wider and wider, so wide that it felt like my face would crack. And my father looked at me, really looked at me, for maybe the first time in his life. And when he did, I leaned in close and whispered in a voice as clear and cleansing as a mountain creek: "Old man, it's not the drugs you should be worried about."

I left Billy to his paperwork and the slaps on the back. He didn't know it yet, but he'd be getting a lot more of both soon. Who knew, maybe before I was done Billy would be the next sheriff, him the deputy nobody much trusted with a gun.

As for me, there wasn't much else to do. Just the last two dangerous parts.

First I went back to the Cadillac and Selby Cluxton's body one more time. Nobody saw me. I mean, Lord, I hope not. Then, when I was done there, I went looking for Toola.

I found her at her mother's old house, like she said she would be, sitting on the front porch steps, as if she had been waiting for me all night. She wasn't wearing makeup or any colored contacts now, and her eyes were a soft blue-gray. She looked more beautiful than I could ever remember.

"They caught Lionel moving a mess of drugs," I said. "He's on ice now. He will be for at least a couple months. It's awful hard to buy judges or intimidate witnesses from prison, even for Lionel. And that's all the time we'll need."

"Need for what?"

Toola looked at me for a second, waiting for an answer, and I felt that tingle again, that belief that it was all going to work out. Then I put her necklace in her hand, the necklace I found ripped and broken beneath the driver's seat of Selby Cluxton's Cadillac yesterday morning. I didn't know for certain why she shot that disgusting creep or why her necklace would be ripped and lost right there. There's a danger in letting your mind run wild. And there's a danger too in asking for explanations.

"Tomorrow morning you need to go to the sheriff's station and ask for Deputy Price," I said. "Tell him that Selby Cluxton is missing and you haven't seen him for a couple days. And that the last thing he said was, he was going to meet with Lionel to settle a disagreement."

I took a deep breath and kept going.

"If they don't find Selby in a couple days, I'll make an anonymous call. I'll tell them about seeing Selby's Cadillac off of Paint Creek Road. They won't find anything of yours there, I made sure of that. But they'll find Lionel's pack of Chesterfields on the dash. I made sure of that too."

Toola looked at me and she didn't nod or say anything. There wasn't a need to, not anymore. But after a moment she smiled.

Because to answer Toola's question, I still didn't know if I was the type of person who could kill a man. But I knew for certain now that I could send a man to prison for a crime he didn't commit. I could do that if it meant getting revenge for the woman I had always loved. And if it meant protecting the woman, I believed I was starting to. Lionel would learn that about me soon enough, but he wouldn't be able to complain. That's the way the world works, after all. Like he taught me years ago, what the truth is and what you can prove, they're only second cousins.

The Surrogate Initiative

FROM *Alfred Hitchcock Mystery Magazine*

CASSANDRA HOWARD WALKED around the small band of protesters gathered across the street from the courthouse. The hand-
written signs they raised read JURIES ARE HUMAN! and MY PEER
IS NOT A DROID!

The Frank Murphy Hall of Justice in downtown Detroit was a
rectangular cement monolith, its brutal bulk squatting over nearly
an entire city block on St. Antoine Street. Every time she visited the
Third Judicial Circuit Court, Cassandra was reminded of an enormous mausoleum built to endure centuries.

She climbed the steps and entered the courthouse. She swiped
her hand under the yellow UR? reader that registered the I-AM chip
implanted at the base of her right thumb before passing through
the softly humming maze of body scanners. Security drones hovered in the lobby, running facial identification checks on the crowd
as Cassandra crossed to the elevators.

The chief judge's chambers were on the sixth floor.

As the elevator doors whisked shut, Cassandra recognized a colleague crossing the lobby. Forrest Latham walked with his hands
in his pockets and his head tilted to the side as if he were considering an entertaining thought. His stride was slow and leisurely.
He carried the air of a bemused man who had nowhere to be anytime soon and for whom everything came easy. Cassandra found
his charm and confidence to be as annoying as it was attractive.
In graduate school at Carnegie Mellon, he once asked her to dinner, but she had lied out of nervousness and told him she didn't
date white men. He hadn't approached her again, but she'd felt

self-conscious around him ever since. She knew he had been re-cruited to work on the Surrogate program—there were, after all, only so many AI psychologists—but what was he doing in Detroit?

Cassandra closed her eyes briefly as she realized Forrest was likely the consultant for the prosecution.

"Terrific," she muttered.

Then she inhaled deeply and exhaled. It would be fine. She hadn't had time for a relationship in school and she certainly didn't have time for one now. She would put it out of her mind. *Focus,* she thought. She had more important concerns. The newly formed Federal Association of Court Management wanted to start implementing the Jury Surrogate system nationally within eigh-teen months, but everything hinged on this and the other pilot programs in St. Louis, San Diego, Charlotte, Boston, and Seattle succeeding.

Judge Cameron O'Connor was outside his chambers with Jessica Blick, one of the assistant prosecuting attorneys assigned to the ini-tiative. Blick was a short white woman with closely clipped red hair gelled to sharp peaks so that at the right angle it looked as if small flames flickered atop her head. The distinctive hairstyle along with her explosive temper tagged her with the nickname "Firecracker," though no one used the name in her presence.

"Ms. Howard," welcomed O'Connor, whose deep, resonant voice reflected his ego but belied his stature; he resembled a cherub in black robes. Broken capillaries marked his full nose and flushed cheeks.

"Judge O'Connor," said Cassandra, shaking hands. "Ms. Blick."

"We're just waiting for—"

"I thought that was you," called a voice from down the hall. Cas-sandra turned. Forrest came toward them, dressed in khakis and a blue suit coat, carrying a coffee in one hand and a leather lap-top satchel in the other. He grinned widely. His blond hair was strewn across his forehead and his beard needed a trim. "How are you?" he asked as he leaned in to kiss Cassandra on the cheek. She smelled chicory coffee and cinnamon on his breath.

"I'm good," she said. "How're you?"

"Great," said Forrest, still smiling. "It's good to see you again."

"I'm surprised," said Cassandra. "I thought you'd be working out of D.C."

"Nah, headquarters is boring," said Forrest. "I wanted to be in the field. This is great that we'll be working together."

"Not exactly working together, Mr. Latham," interjected Judge O'Connor. "Ms. Howard is advising the defense. You're advising the prosecution." He introduced Blick and then said, "Mr. Cervantez is waiting for us in my chambers. Shall we?"

Forrest bowed and waved the women ahead of him with a grin. He directed a wink at Cassandra.

The walnut-paneled walls of the chief judge's chambers were decorated with pictures of him posing with politicians and celebrities dating back twenty years. One shelf held awards from dozens of organizations, both local and national; another shelf held editions of the two books he had written, on the Sixth Amendment and juries (he was inclined to present guests with autographed copies). A third shelf held biographies of Winston Churchill (whom O'Connor was fond of quoting) and framed pictures of his family.

A slender man with thinning dark hair, a silvering goatee, and black-framed glasses turned from the bookshelf as O'Connor and the others entered. Cassandra noticed his ears were disproportionately long and his brown suit was ill-fitted, perhaps a size too large. She put him in his late fifties.

"Mr. Cervantez, this is Cassandra Howard from Real Thought Analytics," said O'Connor. "She'll be your jury consultant for the trial."

"I'm looking forward to working with you," said Cassandra as she crossed the room to shake Cervantez's hand.

"So you're to blame for this miscarriage of justice," he said, his hands remaining in his pockets.

"In small part," said Cassandra with a slight smile. "In very small part." She had become practiced in absorbing outrage and blowback over the Surrogate technology. People were resistant to change, and she had learned to put off any attempts at reasonable persuasion until emotional temperatures cooled. Cervantez was clearly still hot.

"Never mind him, Ms. Howard," said O'Connor. "He'll come around. Lawrence, behave yourself."

"But Judge, this is preposterous." Cervantez brushed past Cassandra. "A robot jury? How have we come to this?"

"They're not robots," said Forrest.

"Artificial intelligence then, whatever," said Cervantez.

"We call it replicate consciousness, actually," said Cassandra gently. "There's a marked difference."

"Artificial intelligence implies independent sentience," said Forrest. "The Surrogate program employs technology designed to replicate a specific consciousness." He grinned broadly.

Cervantez stared at Forrest a moment before turning back to O'Connor. "I have real problems with this whole idea, Judge."

"I know you do," said O'Connor, taking a seat behind his desk. "And you're not alone by a long shot, but the ABA and even the ACLU have both agreed to take a wait-and-see approach with the pilot program. So that's what we're here for. To show it can work."

"I understand this is the first live case?" asked Blick.

"Yes," said O'Connor. "Other actual cases will begin soon in the other pilot courts, but we are the first, and you should know I intend to stay first. I won't tolerate any delays. Jury selection starts day after tomorrow."

"Day after tomorrow?" Cervantez threw his hands in the air. "Judge, that is way too soon. How can you expect us to be ready for voir dire in a day and a half?"

"Relax, Larry," said Blick. "You've had two months to prepare your case. And you know as well as I do this isn't the one to go to the wall for."

Cassandra sensed the assistant prosecutor was keen on the prospect of being at the forefront of a technological—and legal—revolution, which meant Forrest was likely to encounter far less contention from her than it appeared Cassandra was going to get from Cervantez.

"So my client gets to be the victim of us working out the bugs," said Cervantez. "Terrific. How is that remotely fair?"

"Your client signed off on it, Mr. Cervantez," said O'Connor. "She's waived her right to procedural due process. Everything was explained to her."

"She's a khem addict, Your Honor. She'll sign anything for a fix. I have to say for the record that this is an outrage. I've been a public defense attorney for over twenty years and I've never seen anything this grievous."

"Mr. Cervantez, you can spare me the rhetoric. We're not in the courtroom yet."

"But Judge, how is this even constitutional?"

"Ah," said O'Connor. "That is yet to be determined. But there's certainly a legitimate path to constitutionality. The court recognized legal constructs as having the same rights as persons in *Citizens United,* and *Greene v. Osbourne* found sufficient digital data could be used to construct a personal value system and ascertain intent. The concept of a surrogate jury is just building on the evolving definition of *person* in a technological age. Welcome to the future, Mr. Cervantez. Kicking and screaming as you may choose."

The Full Belly was two blocks from the Hall of Justice down Clinton Street. The judge had strongly encouraged Cassandra and Cervantez to have lunch together. Unmanned electric cars traveled the streets at uniform speeds and distance. Drones flew between the buildings as though through canyons, delivering packages, auditing pedestrian traffic, and carrying air boards advertising insurance or pharmaceuticals.

"You know where this all started?" asked Cervantez as he and Cassandra stopped at the corner of Clinton and Beaubien to wait for the LED-lit walkway across the street to turn from red to green.

Cassandra spread her hands in question.

"When they replaced umps behind the plate with those pitch monitors," said Cervantez with disgust.

"They work," said Cassandra. "No one argues balls and strikes anymore."

"Exactly," said Cervantez. "Took away all nuance. We keep wanting everything to be black and white, but everything isn't black and white. Like the strike zone, there are edges. Humans understand edges are not clear-cut."

"Which is why people make mistakes," said Cassandra.

"Yep, they do," said Cervantez. "But isn't that what they say? To err is human. What if that ability is humanity's defining asset? We've spent thousands of years trying to eradicate human error. What if when we finally stamp it out for good, *poof!* No more humanity."

"That's probably a ways off," said Cassandra.

The walkway lit up green and they started to cross.

"Might be closer than you think," said Cervantez.

The restaurant was crowded with other court employees. At the order counter, Cassandra swiped her hand over the UR? reader and the vegetarian options were displayed on the menu screen in the countertop.

"Hello, Cassandra," said the menu. "What would you like for lunch?"

She ordered the grilled tempeh sandwich with avocado, roasted red peppers, and sprouts on ciabatta bread.

"Good choice, Cassandra," said the menu. "Enjoy."

Beside her, Cervantez ordered the BLT platter.

"This sandwich has 1,094 milligrams of sodium, Lawrence, which will exceed your personal recommended daily allowance," said the menu. "Perhaps you would like to omit the bacon or make another choice?"

"It's not a BLT without bacon," said Cervantez. "And no, I do not want to make another choice." He turned to Cassandra. "I hate it when it tries to tell me what to eat."

"It's just giving good advice," said Cassandra. "Too much sodium's not healthy for you."

"So I've been told," said Cervantez. "But it's my call."

"Your health insurance company may think otherwise," said Cassandra.

"Yeah, yeah," said Cervantez. "I know. So my insurance rate just ticked up. But a BLT is worth it."

They found a table along a back wall. Cervantez bit into his sandwich. "Mmm," he said. "Good bacon." He wiped at his goatee with a napkin. "All right. I guess we're doing this. So, jury consultant, tell me how the hell this works."

"You have an aunt?" began Cassandra.

"I have many."

"Well, pick one."

"My tía Mayra. Salt of the earth."

"Okay, picture your tía Mayra. Imagine all you know about her. Her likes, her dislikes. Her tendencies and quirks. Her experiences, her worldview. Technology now allows us to render all of those traits and qualities digitally." Cassandra concentrated on keeping her voice clinical, despite her enthusiasm for the revolutionary work. "Over the past decade, building on personality tests such as the Enneagram model or the Myers-Briggs Type Indicator, which we now recognize as primitive but at the time was highly influential, personality psychologists have developed a comprehensive—I'll call it a questionnaire—that assembles an individual's personality with such accuracy that we can extrapolate decisions and judgments the person would make in real-life situations."

"Uh-huh," said Cervantez. "My tía Mayra in a computer."

"Essentially, yes," said Cassandra, having forgotten her food. "Personality neuroscience has mapped the six major personality traits to regions of the brain. That's the foundation. Through a simple MRI we can identify the building blocks of an individual's personality."

Over the next half hour, Cassandra explained how through using intensive Likert-scale surveys, personality mapping, and inclusive mining of personal data from e-life platforms, Real Thought Analytics had developed the Surrogate program.

"As an early application of the technology, jury duty is particularly apt," she said. "Think of it. Almost everyone hates jury duty. No one has the time. Juries are costly, cumbersome, inefficient, and unreliable. The Surrogate system fixes all of that. We can employ a person's surrogate easily and without hassle. What's more —and this is critical—we're able to modify individual surrogates to compensate for biases and prejudices. Surrogates finally allow for an impartial jury in a way never possible before."

"By *impartial* you mean *emotionless*," said Cervantez, folding his napkin.

"Objective," clarified Cassandra.

"So much for a jury of your peers." Cervantez stood up.

"No," said Cassandra. "This is exactly a jury of your peers. Don't you see? Just with all the hate, suspicion, and prejudices stripped out."

"But also all empathy, compassion, and mercy, right?" asked Cervantez. "Hate to tell you, Ms. Howard, but my ability to access those emotions in jurors is often the only shot I have at an effective defense." He leaned toward her and lowered his voice. "Because, unfortunately, a good number of my clients are guilty." He pulled back, his voice returning to regular volume. "Come on."

"Where are we going?" Cassandra grabbed her purse.

"To see the human being your surrogate jury is going to judge."

The County Detention Facility, a cement box the color of sand perched on squat posts, was a short walk back up Clinton, across from the Hall of Justice. A tunnel under the street connected the two buildings, making it easier to transport inmates to and from trial. Drone perches hung from every side of the building like hornets' nests. Cervantez ushered Cassandra through the security checkpoints. Her short heels clopped on the industrial gray tiles of the beige-painted hallway as a guard led them to the attorney meeting room. The air smelled of an unpleasant combination of urine, body odor, disinfectant, floor wax, and mold.

"Here you go," said the guard, unlocking a cell door. "You'll all fit if you squeeze in."

The tiny space was featureless except for a brown metal table and two chipped metal chairs bolted to the cement-block wall. Ammie Moore sat on one of the chairs, spastically kicking her crossed leg and knocking the silver tracking bracelet around her wrist against the tabletop. Cassandra thought the young white girl looked small and thin in the yellow jumpsuit. She was probably in her mid-twenties. Her unwashed blond hair hung in strands and her skin was blotchy with a red rash. She blinked erratically and her lips twitched, evidence, along with the rash, of regular khem use.

"Hey, Ammie," said Cervantez, taking the other chair. "How you doing? This is Cassandra Howard. She's going to be helping with the case."

"You got a little something?" asked Ammie, ignoring Cassandra. Her voice was pleading.

Cervantez shook his head. "You know I don't, Ammie. You've been getting your script, though, right?"

Ammie snorted. "Yeah. I been getting it. But it's only enough to keep me from throwing myself out a goddamn window. Can't you get them to up it? Even a little?"

"I'll talk to the doctor when I leave." Cervantez reached into his briefcase and withdrew an e-folder carrying links to the case files. "Do you remember digistamping an agreement to take part in a pilot jury program, Ammie?"

"I don't know, maybe," said Ammie. "It sounded cool."

"Well, I wish you hadn't done that. Because now I have to defend you in front of a jury I have no experience with. And we already had plenty stacked against us. I want to encourage you one more time to consider a plea deal."

"But I didn't kill that guy." Ammie's soft voice rose. "I ain't saying I did it when I didn't. I've done plenty of other stuff, but not this."

"I know," said Cervantez, "but with the evidence the state has, I'm not certain I can convince a jury—any jury—that you're innocent. You're looking at life without parole. You know that, right?"

Cassandra had read the case file, and Cervantez was not exaggerating the strength of evidence against Ammie. The girl faced a felony murder charge for stabbing a man to death in his car while parked in a weedy lot behind a boarded-up muffler and tire shop on the west side. It was a burned-out area with few security cameras and where police drones rarely flew, so dealers and prostitutes favored it. Investigators found her blood on the passenger seat, her left shoe outside the vehicle, and she admitted the man had picked her up on a corner she worked.

Ammie stared into her lap, picking at her palm.

"You've got to give me something to work with, Ammie," said Cervantez. "You told the police he started slapping you and that you were able to get away and run off. But if you tell me that you weren't able to get away, then I can argue self-defense. You see?"

Ammie considered Cervantez. She darted her eyes over Cassandra.

Cassandra saw haunted fear in the young girl's face. She knew from the case file that Ammie had run away from an abusive, alcoholic father at sixteen and had been on the streets ever since. It could not have been an easy life, and the look in her eyes made it clear it had been a life lacking warmth, love, value, or security, all of which Cassandra had known. The girl had been routed for rough days and a bad end.

"You a lawyer?" Ammie asked.

"No," said Cassandra. "I'm a psychologist."

"I thought of being a psychologist back when I was little," said Ammie. She smiled briefly at the memory. "Didn't quite work out, though. You think you can help me?"

"We'd like to," said Cassandra. "But you need to tell Mr. Cervantez what really happened. You don't have to be scared."

Ammie chewed her lip and rubbed her arms. She looked down. "What if it was C-Jack who done it?"

"Who's C-Jack?" asked Cervantez.

"My boyfriend. He looks out for me."

"You mean your pimp," said Cervantez. "Okay, I'm listening."

Ammie hesitated and then let the story out in a rush. "The guy goes off like I said, slapping me and yelling that he was going to kill me, and suddenly the door jerked open and C-Jack was pulling me out and the next thing I know he's in the car stabbing the guy and so I just took off. I didn't look back either. Not once."

"Ammie," said Cervantez, his voice registering bewilderment, "why didn't you tell this to the police?"

"I was scared C-Jack'd kill me if I told."

The girl's tone of trauma and timidity gripped Cassandra. "No one's going to hurt you," she said, surprised by the vehemence in her voice.

Cervantez scrambled for his note recorder. "This is good," he said. "This is a proper defense."

Cassandra exited the detention center a half hour later. Cervantez had other clients to see. They'd agreed to meet the next day for her to show him the complete Surrogate system. The setting sun reflected in orange rays from the windows of the surrounding buildings as she walked to the corner to hail an autocab home.

"Hey, Cassie," a voice called from behind her. She turned to see Forrest jogging to catch up with her. "I forgot how fast a walker you are."

"One of the benefits of being tall," said Cassandra.

"How'd it go today?"

"Better than I expected."

He searched her face to gauge the level of truth behind her words, a habit she found unsettling and annoying.

"Great," he said. "I want to hear all about it. Let's get a drink."

"I can't," said Cassandra. "I need to get home. My dad's waiting."

"One drink," said Forrest. He blasted her with his strongest smile. "Please?"

Cassandra laughed. "You think that smile can get you anywhere, don't you?"

Forrest shrugged. "It has so far. I'm told it's the dimples."

"I believe it," said Cassandra. "I, however, am immune to their appeal."

"And I believe that," said Forrest. "It's probably why I find you so inscrutable."

"Inscrutable? I'm hardly inscrutable."

"Oh, but you are," said Forrest, searching her face again. "Cassandra Howard. One big mystery. Unfathomable. Elusive and remote."

"Are you done?"

"For now," said Forrest. "Hey, has Powell called you yet?"

"No," said Cassandra. "I'm sending him my status report tonight. Why?"

"No reason. I just know he's wound up for this to go smoothly."

"Powell is always wound up," said Cassandra, who had once described the project head of the Surrogate system at Real Thought
Analytics as the Dr. Frankenstein of the artificial intelligence industry.

"I know," said Forrest. "He's just worried we're going to screw
something up."

"I'm not going to screw anything up," said Cassandra. She waved
for an autocab. "Are you?"

"That is not my plan," said Forrest, and he grinned.

The streetlights were on when Cassandra arrived home. The
house where she grew up was a brick American Foursquare near
Holbrook and Woodward, walking distance from the Little Rock
Baptist Church, where as a child she had worshipped on Sunday
mornings with her father. She climbed the cement steps to the pil-
lared front porch that spanned the front of the house where when
she was little she had dressed dolls and built cities of connecting
plastic blocks on cool autumn evenings while her father rocked on
the porch swing, grading papers. She raised her hand to where the
doorbell used to be so that the home security eye could scan her
I-AM chip.

"Welcome home, Cassandra," intoned the system as it unlocked
the door.

Inside, she thanked the hospice nurse for staying late and went
to check on her sleeping father. The monitors beside the hospital
bed flickered green and red in the shadowed room. She checked
the cat's bowl before making a dinner of acorn squash, tofu, and
sautéed collard greens. She checked e-mails and reviewed project
updates while she ate. It was quiet enough for her to hear the sub-
tle creaks and groans the boards of the house made as they struggled with age. After she cleaned up, she returned upstairs to her
father's room.

Jarius Howard had been diagnosed with advanced colon cancer in April. Doctors told him he would likely be dead before the
year was out. He had two months to go to beat their prognosis, but
his energy and determination to show them up had dropped off

sharply in recent weeks and he had grown less interested in living simply to prove fools wrong.

"Did you feed Baedeker?" he asked Cassandra when she came in.

"Yes, Daddy, I fed Baedeker. Your beloved cat is not losing any weight."

"Unlike me, you mean." He chuckled and coughed.

"Stop that," said Cassandra. She sat beside the bed and took her Apple iGlass from her bag and rested it in her lap. She took her father's emaciated wrist and scanned his I-AM bracelet to check his vitals.

"Everything looks pretty good," she said.

"Must be why I feel so energetic," he said with a weak smile.

Her father had been a professor of philosophy at Wayne State University for thirty years and had raised Cassandra alone after her mother died, when she was ten. He had often taken her to the university to sit in on his lectures when he couldn't find someone to watch her, and she had sat in the back of the class listening to his strong, confident voice while she drew picture after picture of her mother.

Cassandra put on a pair of wireless connec-specs and blinked twice to open her father's identity folder on the iGlass.

"More questions?" asked her father.

"Only a few."

"What are you going to do with all this information you've been gathering, anyway?"

"It's just for work," she said.

"Mmm-hm. You work too much."

"I enjoy it."

"You should enjoy some life, too," said Jarius.

"I do, Daddy," said Cassandra. She tapped the iGlass and adjusted the spectacles. "You ready?"

"Fire away."

"I would never break the law, no matter how minor. Strongly disagree, disagree, agree, strongly agree?"

"Oooh," said Jarius. "A question about gray areas. I like the tricky ones."

"The key breakthrough was when the developers were able to quantify reasonable doubt," explained Cassandra. She and Cervantez were alone in a conference room on the twelfth floor of the Hall of Justice. They had blocked out the entire afternoon for Cassandra to walk the criminal defense attorney through the Surrogate system.

"So no more 'shadow of a doubt,' eh?" said Cervantez. He was scanning the digibinder Cassandra gave him on the system.

"Well, not exactly," admitted Cassandra, "but close. Using an interlaced algorithm, the system is able to attribute value to physical evidence, testimony, and other facts, and then weigh it as any human juror would do. If the calculation exceeds the equivalent of reasonable doubt—"

"Guilty," said Cervantez, rapping the table.

"Yes."

"What if they're wrong?"

"They haven't been yet."

Developers had presented Surrogate juries with tens of thousands of case studies from the past decade and the system had demonstrated a verdict variance with the human juries of 3.1 percent.

"What is that? A verdict variance?" asked Cervantez.

"It means that for every one thousand trials, the Surrogate system reached a different verdict from the human jury in thirty cases," explained Cassandra. "In each of those cases, our independent investigative department, working with the Department of Justice, determined that the Surrogate jury had likely reached the correct verdict. The human juries were wrong."

Cervantez pushed back his chair and walked to the window. He looked out over the city. "I don't understand how we've come to this. Machines judging people."

"They're not machines," said Cassandra. "They are replicate human consciousnesses."

"They are machines," said Cervantez, turning away from the window, his voice rising. "What do they know about guilt? Innocence? Human compassion? Not a damn thing. They're just electrical impulses!"

"So are humans," said Cassandra.

"Like hell they are," said Cervantez, turning back to the window. "I don't believe that."

"Believe this then, counselor," said Cassandra evenly. "It's estimated that more than twelve thousand people are wrongfully convicted each year. With refinement, the Surrogate system has the potential to reduce that number to zero in time. Isn't that something you can work for? How many of your clients who were innocent are sitting in a prison cell right now? It may not be many, but it's too many, and I know you believe that."

Cervantez looked to the ceiling as if searching for a message scrawled on the white paint above him and sighed. "Fine," he said, walking back to the table and picking up the digibinder. "What else do I need to know?"

"Let me show you the HD holograms," said Cassandra. Cervantez rolled his eyes.

The avatars were purely aesthetic, she explained as she clicked a controller. Twelve light forms slowly solidified across the table from Cervantez: seven women and five men. In short order, with the exception of an errant shimmer of light, the images appeared corporeal. Each hologram was an accurate representation of the Surrogate juror, created from a multitude of photographs collected from e-life platforms.

"The thought is that eventually holograms will be unnecessary," said Cassandra, "but we discovered attorneys in the beta stages were more comfortable arguing before avatars. Go on, give it a try."

Cervantez stared at her, his lips pursed cynically. Then he rubbed a hand over his head, inhaled deeply, and exhaled. He shot a look at the twelve avatars and stood up slowly.

"Ladies and gentlemen of the jury," he began. "You now know that Ammie Moore did not kill Russell Lipke—a violent, perverse man who was soliciting sex from vulnerable young women on street corners. After hearing all the evidence and testimony in this case, you now know she didn't do it. How do you know? Simple." Cervantez stopped pacing and turned to look directly at the avatars. "She told you she didn't. She told you under oath in vivid detail how Russell Lipke started attacking her in the car and how she desperately struggled to get away, accounting for his skin cells found under her fingernails. She told you how he struck her across the mouth, breaking her lip and accounting for her blood found on the car seat. She described how the car door suddenly flew open and Charles Jackson, her 'boyfriend,' pulled her from the car and then in a rage proceeded to stab Russell Lipke to death. She told you through sobs and tears how she ran off, scared out of her mind, and never looked back. That's the truth. That's what happened."

Cervantez paused and shook his head at the tale's tragedy before continuing.

"Now I know the prosecution says, 'Then why didn't she tell the police that's what happened when they first questioned her?' But what did Ammie say when I asked her that question? You remember. She was afraid Charles Jackson would kill her. And do you know why you can believe she feared for her life? Because here is a woman who has been physically and emotionally abused since she was a child. We know her father beat her until she was old enough to run away. And we know Charles Jackson beat her to keep her on that corner so he could get his payday. Ladies and gentlemen, here is a woman who has suffered at the hands of every man in her life. The very men who were supposed to take care of her and protect her. And how did she respond to all these men who raised their fists against her? Did she stab them to death? No. Shoot them? No. She ran. Just like she did this time. She ran." Cervantez leaned over the table and looked pointedly at each avatar. "And that is why I know you will find her not guilty. Because you know she didn't do it."

In the silence that followed, Cassandra clapped slowly and softly. "That's a pretty good closing argument," she said.

Cervantez snorted. "It would be. If your surrogate jury gave a damn."

It was late before Cassandra deemed Cervantez sufficiently prepared for jury selection the next morning and let him leave for home. His righteous indignation had not eased with his understanding of the system, but he had committed to learning how it worked, she had to give him that. She was gathering her equipment together when Judge O'Connor entered the conference room. It was the first time she'd seen him out of his judicial robes.

"How are things going, Ms. Howard?" he asked.

"Very well," said Cassandra. "I think we're ready for tomorrow."

"Glad to hear it." O'Connor picked up the hologram control and examined it. "And Mr. Cervantez? He's cooperating?"

"Absolutely," said Cassandra.

"Good, good," said O'Connor. "Maybe I shouldn't share this, but he was not my first choice. Strikes me as a bit of a pessimist. Reminds me of something Churchill once said: 'A pessimist sees the difficulty in every opportunity; an optimist sees the opportunity in every difficulty.' Are you an optimist or a pessimist, Ms. Howard?"

"I'm a realist, Judge," said Cassandra, stepping around his play of soft intimidation and taking the hologram control from his hand. She placed it in her case.

"Be sure to let me know if you run into any problems," said O'Connor. "I don't want any misunderstandings or antics to delay this trial."

"Of course not," said Cassandra. "We don't want one of the other pilot programs to move ahead of us, now do we?"

O'Connor considered her, smiling tightly, and she chastised herself for having possibly stepped over a line. Finally he said, "No, we don't. Do you know the first man to sign the Declaration of Independence, Ms. Howard?"

"That would be John Hancock."

"Yes, it would be. But I wager you don't know the second. Second never draws the same recognition as first does. First is history; second is merely trivia. I intend this case to be history. Everyone should be clear on that."

Cassandra snapped her case closed. "I don't think it's going to be a problem, Judge," she said.

"Good." O'Connor held the door for her. "It was Josiah Bartlett, by the way."

"I'm sorry?" said Cassandra.

"Josiah Bartlett was the second man to sign the Declaration of Independence."

"Is that right?" Cassandra passed through the doorway into the hall. "You learn something new every day."

Forrest pulsed Cassandra on her way home, again inviting her to get a drink. She pulsed back, again declining. At home, after feeding Baedeker and checking on her sleeping father, she spent time on her yoga, trying to clear her mind and focus on her center. Since middle school, when she reached her full height of five eleven, Cassandra had felt alien in her body, awkward and encumbered. She took up yoga in college as a way for her mind and body to relate. But tonight she was unable to fully close her mind down. Ammie's face stubbornly snapped into her consciousness and her timid voice repeated in Cassandra's ear.

When her father woke, she tried to get him to eat, but he complained that swallowing was painful. Instead they spent the evening with Cassandra asking him more questions. Jarius seemed to appreciate the short "strongly agree, agree, disagree, strongly disagree" answers. It was all he had energy for. In the quiet of the darkening room, it was just Cassandra's even-toned voice and her father's shallow breathing. Occasionally she had to ask him to repeat his answer and lean in to hear it. After a time she came to the end of the identity query.

"No more questions, Chickpea?" asked Jarius. He sounded wryly disappointed.

"No more questions," said Cassandra. "We're done. Why don't you get some rest?"

Jarius closed his eyes. He whispered something Cassandra couldn't understand.

"What's that, Daddy?" she asked.

But he was asleep, the cat curled beside him.

The HD hologram of a red-haired woman with oversized glasses rotated slowly in front of Judge O'Connor's bench.

"Ms. Renee Elder, fifty-two, works as a floral designer. Divorced with two children. Grew up in Grand Rapids, moved to Detroit to attend Wayne State University to study art education but didn't finish. On tab two you can see the various organizations she associates with, any volunteer activity, religious affiliations, and so on. And on tab three are her stances on a range of issues, from the death penalty to climate contamination." O'Connor looked up from reading the identity brief and addressed the attorneys. "Any objections?"

"None, Your Honor," said Cervantez.

At the next table, Assistant Prosecuting Attorney Jessica Blick leaned over to consult with Forrest.

"Your Honor," she said, "this juror would be acceptable if we modulated her emotional quotient as related to her oldest daughter's problems with drug addiction. The daughter's been in and out of rehab for several years."

"Mr. Cervantez?" asked O'Connor.

"I don't see what the daughter's experimenting with drugs has to do with Ms. Elder's suitability for this jury," said Cervantez. "In fact—"

"Mr. Cervantez," cautioned O'Connor.

The defense attorney sighed and looked at Cassandra, who was drilling down on the identity construct and calculating bias percentages. She whispered to Cervantez her recommendation and the attorney nodded.

"Your Honor, we would accept a modulation of thirty-five points to fall within the impartial range," he said.

"That wasn't so hard now, was it, Mr. Cervantez?" said O'Connor. "Does that sound acceptable to you, Ms. Blick?"

Forrest nodded and Blick said, "Yes, Your Honor."

"Good, that's what I like to see. Everyone working together," said O'Connor. "Then if there are no more objections we have juror number three." The hologram of the red-haired woman dissolved to be replaced by an older white man with a lean, shaved face and perfectly styled silver hair.

"Mr. Ian McMasters," said O'Connor.

Two hours later a jury had been selected, and O'Connor scheduled the trial to begin the following morning.

Cervantez leaned over and whispered to Cassandra, "I think somebody is anxious to start writing his next book."

Remote-controlled vid-drones whirred and hovered in the back of the courtroom like hummingbirds, streaming the trial live to subscription criminal justice channels.

Blick's first witness was Detective Darrell Foster, a square-jawed man with a closely trimmed Afro. The bailiff clipped a response sensor to the detective's right index finger and affixed a visceral patch below his left temple. A subcontractor had developed the advanced polygraph technology for Real Thought Analytics to interface with the Surrogates, who could judge the truthfulness of a witness's account through the extensive physiological feedback.

With Blick's guidance, Foster described the murder scene and the steps of the investigation that had led to the arrest of Ammie Moore. Throughout his testimony, he shot uncertain sideways glances at the avatars projected in the jury box. Under cross, Cervantez established that police had not found the knife used to kill Russell Lipke or any bloody clothes they could identify as belonging to the defendant.

"And finally, Detective Foster, I'm curious why you failed to interview Ammie Moore's boyfriend, Charles Jackson," said Cervantez.

"You mean her pimp?" asked the detective.

"Yes, a violent man known on the street as C-Jack."

Foster shrugged. "We couldn't find him."

"I see," said Cervantez. "Did you look very hard, Detective Foster, or had you already decided a poor drug addict nobody would believe was good enough?"

"Objection," said Blick.

"Withdrawn," said Cervantez. "No further questions, Your Honor."

When he returned to his seat, Cassandra leaned over to remind him the Surrogates would not be affected by inflammatory language.

"Old habits die hard," said Cervantez with a grin.

Ammie was dressed in a blue pantsuit that came from a wardrobe Cervantez had picked up over the years from thrift shops and kept in a closet in his office. He'd also gotten the doctor to up her dose of khem so that she didn't reveal telltale signs of withdrawal. With her hair brushed and wearing makeup, Ammie almost looked as if she could be an innocent college student. Cassandra told Cervantez the measures were unnecessary because the Surrogates would not assign any judgment based on a defendant's appearance, but Cervantez insisted; it was more for Ammie's dignity than the jury, he said.

The remaining witnesses included the medical examiner, who testified to the nature and angle of the more than a dozen stab wounds found on the victim, and an expert from the state crime lab, who established that trace evidence of blood and hair found on the passenger seat belonged to the defendant. It took time for the expert witnesses to become comfortable with the idea that they were freed from having to simplify technical descriptions into layman's terms, because the Surrogates had access to scientific portals that provided comprehensive glossaries. Once the ME and lab tech got the hang of it, they almost delighted in spouting industry acronyms and jargon.

At one point Cervantez stood and said, "Your Honor, I understand the witness does not have to simplify her testimony for this jury, and that's great, but if she could dumb it down for me, I'd appreciate it, because I have no idea what she just said."

Blick rested her case near the end of the day and O'Connor

adjourned court until morning. The media in the hallway was a roiling cluster of vid-porters, but Cassandra shook off shouted questions to make her way out of the Hall of Justice.

Jarius that night appeared weaker, more tired. He refused to eat again despite Cassandra's urging.

"Tell me about the trial," he said as Cassandra cleared the food tray. She sat by the bed and, as if reading him a story before sleep, told him all that had happened in court that day.

"Doesn't sound too good for that girl of yours," said Jarius at the end.

"No, it doesn't," said Cassandra.

"You think she did it?"

"It doesn't matter what I think," said Cassandra. "All that matters is what the jury thinks."

"I know," said Jarius, "but I want to know what you think."

Cassandra considered before answering. "I think she's innocent."

Jarius took her hand. "None of us is innocent, Chickpea," he said. "Not one of us."

Later, after she finished shaving him, he asked her to play the violin. He had always thrilled to hear her play, even when she was just learning and the screech of the instrument filled the house as she practiced. Later he would often cajole her into joining him in a duet while he plinked on the piano. She had begrudgingly obliged as a teenager, but now she held the memory of those musical evenings with great fondness.

"What would you like to hear?" she asked, unpacking the instrument.

"Surprise me," he said hoarsely.

She played "Autumn Leaves" and watched the smile on his gaunt face as he listened with eyes closed.

"Beautiful," he said.

"You've advised Ms. Moore she does not have to testify, correct, Mr. Cervantez?" asked O'Connor from the bench the next morning.

"Yes, Your Honor," said Cervantez. "She insists."

"Very well," said the judge. "Swear her in."

Ammie, dressed in the same blue pantsuit as the day before, took the witness stand. As the bailiff hooked her up to the polygraph interface, Cassandra sent her a tight smile of encouragement.

On direct, Cervantez led Ammie through a clear account of how it was C-Jack who'd murdered Russell Lipke. The girl surprised Cassandra with her self-possession. She was controlled when she told how Lipke started slapping her, splitting her lip.

"That must have hurt," said Cervantez.

Ammie shrugged. "It ain't the first time I was hit by a man. I been hit harder."

She only struggled with her composure when she recalled C-Jack attacking Lipke and hearing the man shout for help as she ran away.

"And you haven't seen C-Jack since?"

"No," said Ammie. "He's probably took off to Florida. He has family down there."

On cross, Blick appeared almost carnivorous in her eagerness to question Ammie. She asked Ammie to tell her story once more "to clarify a few details," but despite aggressive attacks and sly feints, Blick failed to snare Ammie in a contradiction or to uncover a crack in the story that the prosecution could exploit. Ammie followed Cervantez's instructions explicitly and offered no more details than necessary to answer Blick's question.

Blick's relentless interrogation came to a close two hours later, and Cassandra could tell from the pallor of frustration on the prosecutor's face that the Firecracker was displeased with not having exposed holes in Ammie's account.

Cassandra had prepared Cervantez for the speed with which the Surrogate jury would reach its verdict following closing arguments. Hours or days of deliberation were unnecessary. The program simply calculated the aggregate of the Surrogates' reasonable doubt total to determine the jury's decision.

Still, Cervantez grabbed Cassandra's hand in a startled reaction when, within seconds of O'Connor transmitting the jury instructions explaining the rules of law to the Surrogates, the judge received a response. O'Connor too seemed nonplussed by the swiftness of the determination.

He recovered by shooting a grin directly at a vid-drone and cracking to viewers, "Gives new meaning to 'rush to judgment,' doesn't it?" Then he cleared his throat and read from his bench screen, "In the case of the State of Michigan versus Ammie Moore, we the jury find Ammie Moore—" O'Connor paused for an appropriate dramatic beat before declaring, "Not guilty."

Cervantez sat upright and muttered an expletive of surprise. A hand covering her mouth, Ammie appeared uncertain whether to believe what she'd heard and looked with hesitant hope to Cervantez for confirmation.

"Ms. Moore," said O'Connor, "you have no further business with this court."

Cervantez smiled at Ammie. "You're a free woman," he said.

Cassandra stayed with Cervantez as he walked Ammie through the process of her release. Deputies scanned the recorded verdict, removed her tracking bracelet, and returned her I-AM tokens. Cervantez told her she could keep the pantsuit. In a side hall, away from the gaggle of vid-porters hoping to score an interview, the defense attorney shook Ammie's hand and wished her luck.

"I can just go?" asked Ammie.

"You can just go," said Cervantez. "It's over."

From the wariness in Ammie's eyes, Cassandra wasn't sure the girl believed that anything was ever over.

"What are you going to do now?" asked Cassandra.

"I don't know," said Ammie. "But I can tell you no man's ever going to hit me again."

She turned and headed to the door to the street. With evident doubt, she passed an I-AM token over the security scanner and exhaled relief when the door unlocked with a quiet click. She eased the door open and peered outside. She looked back at Cervantez and Cassandra, mumbled a quick "Thanks," and then slipped through the door, which snapped closed behind her.

"That," said Cervantez, "is real gratitude."

"She said thanks," said Cassandra.

"Oh, no, I know," said Cervantez. "It's the heartfelt appreciation from clients that keeps me in this job."

Cassandra laughed.

"I hear O'Connor has called a press conference," said Cervantez, turning to head back toward the lobby. "I hope he enjoys the attention while he can."

"What do you mean?" asked Cassandra.

"It's juries we're digitizing now," said Cervantez, "but don't kid yourself. It'll be judges next. And probably defense attorneys not long after."

Before Cassandra could voice a response, she was distracted by the sight of Blick and Forrest hurrying toward them. Blick walked with urgent short steps and Cassandra read concern on Forrest's face when he didn't smile at her as they neared.

"I just got a call that they found Charles Jackson," said Blick.

"Really?" said Cervantez. "They get a confession out of him?"

"They're good, but they're not that good," said Blick. "The man's dead."

"Dead? How?"

"Based on the knife they found still stuck in his ribs, they're guessing he was stabbed to death," said Blick. "They found him in a burned-out khem house over by the river. Looks like he may have been there a month or two."

"Huh," said Cervantez.

"Exactly," said Blick. "Where's Moore?"

Cervantez waved at the door. "Gone," he said.

Blick was unfazed. "Better get ready for round two," she told Cervantez as she turned away back down the hall. "It isn't going to go as well for you."

"Probably not," muttered Cervantez.

Cassandra's mind spun. She realized the implications of Blick's news immediately and understood now the serious tenor in Forrest's eyes.

"They believed her," she said, a hint of wonder in her voice.

Forrest nodded. "We better hope the problem was with the polygraph interface and not our calculations, or Powell is going to fry a circuit."

"What's wrong?" asked Cervantez.

"Ammie lied," said Cassandra.

"No," said Cervantez. "I'm shocked."

"You don't understand," said Forrest. "The Surrogates believed her. They're supposed to be able to accurately assess degrees of veracity, but they thought she was telling the truth."

"Maybe they aren't actually soulless then," said Cervantez. "Or she's one hell of a liar."

"This is no joke," snapped Forrest. "This could undermine confidence in the entire program and mean the end of our careers."

He turned to Cassandra. "I'm going to test the polygraph equipment first if you'll start looking at the data points—"

Cassandra received a pulse. It was the hospice nurse.

"I have to go," she said.

The room seemed larger without the hospital bed. Otherwise nothing had been moved. Jarius's books were still stacked on every available surface. A reproduction of Edmonia Lewis's famous sculpture *Forever Free* remained on its shelf below a Horace Pippin print of an African American family saying grace before a meal. One entire wall was covered in framed black-and-white photographs Jarius had taken of the city's neighborhoods over the decades. Despite being surrounded by her father's belongings, Cassandra felt the room swollen with absence.

The funeral was well attended, and she had been gratified to see so many of her father's colleagues and former students. She now sat in the quiet of the room, letting her thoughts whirl and settle. She had a conference call with Forrest and Powell scheduled in an hour to discuss Forrest's report that the polygraph readings had been distorted by unanticipated high levels of khem in the witness's system. Powell was furious with the oversight and was threatening to reassign Cassandra and Forrest if they couldn't come up with a work-around.

Nothing had been heard or seen of Ammie Moore since she walked out of the courthouse, and Cassandra was able to admit she hoped the girl had gone somewhere far away where she could live low and stay safe. There had been a flare of defiance in the girl's eyes at the end that led Cassandra to believe it was possible, though she knew Ammie's khem addiction gave her only an outside chance.

The silence of the house gathered around Cassandra as the shadows of evening lengthened. Baedeker wandered the upstairs rooms, unsettled and mewing questioningly. If Cassandra had felt isolated and apart at times as a child after her mother's death and later away from home as a Black student at Carnegie Mellon, she now experienced loneliness deeper even than she had dreaded since her father's diagnosis.

She couldn't abide it.

As Cassandra opened her iGlass to launch the Surrogate program, the home security system bell rang before announcing, "Forrest Latham is at the door."

Cassandra exhaled her frustration at the interruption. Forrest had attended her father's funeral, and she appreciated his concern and sympathy, but now his presence was just getting in the way.

"Doorman," she said, calling up the security system's audio. "Forrest, what is it?"

"I wanted to see you." Forrest's voice came from speakers wired into the room's molding.

"Our meeting with Powell isn't for another hour," said Cassandra.

"I wanted to see you before the meeting."

"I'm busy right now."

"Cassandra, please. It's important."

Cassandra sighed and snapped shut the iGlass. "Fine," she said. "I'll be there in a minute."

Even looking as if he hadn't slept in forty-eight hours, Cassandra couldn't deny Forrest carried a rumpled attractiveness. His tired eyes took in the living room as he unbuttoned his coat.

"So this is where you grew up," he said.

"This is it," said Cassandra. "What do you want?"

"How are you doing?" He studied her face with an incisive concern that made her uncomfortable.

"I'm fine, Forrest," she said. "What do you want? I have things to do."

He gave a short, rueful grin. "Ever the inscrutable Cassandra," he said. "Never letting anyone get too close."

"Forrest, I don't have time—"

"I know." He held up a hand. "I'm sorry. Listen, I know what you're doing, Cassandra, and you do not want to do it."

"Really? And what am I doing?"

"Come on, Cassie. This is serious."

"No, Forrest, what am I supposed to be doing? Tell me." Cassandra crossed her arms, waiting, presenting challenge and defiance, but she knew she was exposed and her mind was whirling to find plausible cover.

"I know you're running Surrogate off your home cluster, okay? I found the download time stamps when I was checking the analytics on the polygraph interface."

Cassandra started to protest, but Forrest cut her off.

"Don't," he said. "You covered your tracks pretty well, but if I found them in the audit logs, it's only a matter of time before Powell finds them. And he's going to trace the hack back to either you or me . . . and it wasn't me."

Cassandra stared at Forrest. She'd known the audit logs were a risk, but she took the chance, thinking no one would have cause to look. She saw only one out now.

"No one would have to know if you helped me scrub the audit file," she said.

Forrest shook his head. "I'd do a lot of things for you, Cassandra, but not that. You're jeopardizing everything. Your entire career."

"No one would know."

"Someone would eventually. And I'm not risking my career for you."

Cassandra turned away. "You should go then, Forrest."

"Look, I know you hacked Surrogate around the time of your father's diagnosis, and I understand why you did it, but your father wouldn't want this. You know that."

"You didn't know my father." She refused to cry, but she felt her throat constrict and it made her voice sound harsh. "You have no idea what he'd want."

"No, you're right. I didn't. But I do know he wouldn't want you to throw away everything you've worked so hard for. And you know it, too."

"I want you to go." She placed a hand on his shoulder to move him toward the door.

"Cassandra, please," begged Forrest. "Wipe Surrogate from your home cluster. You still have time to not completely ruin your life."

Cassandra's face was closed off, her mouth set firmly as she reached to open the door.

"It won't be him," said Forrest in a desperate rush. "It'll look like him and talk like him and think like him, but it won't be your father. You can't bring him back."

Cassandra inhaled sharply.

"I can try," she said.

"But at what cost?"

Cassandra closed her eyes and clenched her jaw to fight tears. "I would give anything to have him back," she said.

"I know," said Forrest softly. "But he wouldn't want you to."

"I don't want to be alone."

Forrest reached for her hand. "You don't have to be," he said.

Cassandra switched on the hologram projector in her father's room and linked it to the lone identity profile on her personal drive. Forrest watched from the doorway, his brow wrinkled in concentration and concern.

"One time," he'd agreed. "And then you wipe it."

Cassandra launched Surrogate and slowly a healthy-looking Jarius resolved in the center of the room. He smiled at Cassandra.

"How's my Chickpea?" he asked.

She dialed down the volume of his voice.

"I miss you, Daddy," she said.

Jarius laughed. "Aw, Chickpea," he said, "I'm right here."

And it seemed to Cassandra that he *was* there. The tenor of his voice. The cordy muscles in his arms. The slope of his shoulders. The way his brown eyes gazed at her with such tenderness. How his mouth was shaped as if he were ready to smile at any time. He *was* there. He was. She wanted to hug him, press her face into his shoulder and smell laundry soap in his shirt. But she knew, deeper than her perception of reality, that Forrest was right. The surrogate before her was only a remarkable representation of her father. It could not love her as Jarius had. She felt comforted by the sound of his voice and foolish for her willingness to be deluded.

"I have to say goodbye," she said.

Jarius nodded. "I know, Chickpea," he said. "It's the right thing to do."

"I love you so much," she said, and with the click of a key terminated the program before the surrogate could respond. Jarius blinked out.

"It's okay to cry," said Forrest gently from the doorway. "It's only human."

DOUG CRANDELL

Shanty Falls

FROM *Ellery Queen Mystery Magazine*

THE WALK TO the water was his usual routine, the waterfalls and
the smooth limestone his sanctuary and confession. As the morning sun rose, no matter the season or weather, for the last six years
David Holzer made the trek. It started with his usual 4 a.m. waking
up, two cups of coffee, black and sweet, at the kitchen table, slugged
back quickly, boots laced in the mudroom, and on to the porch for
a perfunctory review of the skies, measuring which trees could be
seen, poplars towering behind the barn, walnuts massive at the center of the yard, the fence line visible too if the morning didn't offer
a swell of fog. It wasn't his farm, only the house, bought outright
after an early retirement at fifty-five. It'd been a house he'd lived in
as a kid, but only briefly; his parents had moved all over the county,
sharecropping and barely making ends meet. The landlord at the
time was a man and his two college-aged sons, who laughed when
David and his parents had to pack up and move during a sunny fall
afternoon. One of the sons took a check from David's dad and pretended to be dribbling it like a basketball. "This thing's bouncing
just like the last two." More laughter, although the father tried to
act as if the boys should hush. David bought the house out of spite,
to prove to himself that he was safe, that money was no longer an
issue. His parents died in nursing homes with debt, and at night,
lying in bed, he could admit in the dark that he'd not let go of the
shame, that he took too much pleasure in knowing the landlord
had died early from a heart attack and that both sons were rich
but stupid, alone and addicted to painkillers, their reputations, if
not their actual lives, besmirched. On his morning walks, David

said a kind of prayer, to nature mostly, that he be forgiven his own reckless stupidity.

David took a step off the porch and into the cool morning, dew instantly wetting the cuffs of his pants. No one ever thought he was past sixty, and on the morning walks he could privately accept why that was the case. He took long strides and didn't have to think about breathing. He ate well, always had, never thinking about anything sweeter than the two teaspoons in his coffee each morning. Food bored him, or at least his interest in it was mainly connected to energy, proper health, daily seeing the pyramid in his mind from an elementary-school health textbook. He could do that still, see something on a page and recall it easily. He stepped over the hard maple trunk that had fallen during a storm last fall, then cut across the flat field where soybean stubble spread out like a million matchsticks over the two hundred acres that edged up to the forest. They'd be in the fields soon, within weeks. The river valley started here, the dark loam slipping toward the lowlands, where some of the richest soil had settled, coal black, and so fragrant David inhaled a few quick sniffs and smiled.

His running watch told him he was making better than usual time. Before long, even though he had to listen closely, the sounds of the falls grew closer with each step. The sun was still not up, but the silver and yellow lip of the bowl that surrounded the treetops seemed to pulse as it spread. David told people he could smell rocks, that Indiana limestone had a specific scent, like ice, or sand, which he also claimed had their own smells. His close friends, Simon and his ex-wife Cheryl and his daughter, shook their heads and laughed at David. He began a trot now, the hiking boots holding the soft spring mud, making them heavier.

He jogged through a bend and past a rounded stack of cobbled rock that'd been a foundation to an old milk house, then picked up the pace until he was on a path worn by people trying to explore the little caves tucked above on the brittle cliffs that had once been places of shelter for the Miami and Potawatomi tribes. He slowed his pace to a brisk walk and then stopped, listened for the waterfalls of Shanty. David pushed a button on his watch, and the milliseconds ceased their frantic tallying. He drank from a water bottle made of recycled aluminum. It had a filter so tap water could be used, but David filled the bottle from the already purified water he kept stacked high in the pantry. Through a tangle of red-bud-

ded branches he could see the water cascading off the flat layers
of rock, and always he recalled the first time he'd seen it as a kid,
exploring on his own and finding Shanty Falls before he knew its
name and believing he'd made a mammoth discovery.

David replaced the water bottle into its leather holster and took
a few more steps, looking up each time to fully take in the area.
He stopped abruptly before his mind could decipher the paleness
lying at the edge of the rippling waters. David looked behind him.
He crouched, stood, and crouched again, this time squinting. The
body was naked except for a pair of gym shorts. It was stocky. He
called out something he thought sounded like a question but was
not words. He stepped closer and looked behind him again, over
his shoulder and up toward the caves in the cliffs, now mostly out
of sight except for one of the larger ones, the opening crooked and
toothy, a yawning expanse of black. David pulled his phone from
the Patagonia khakis, glancing all around, then back at the screen.
The signal near the falls was almost always nonexistent, sporadic at
best. The 911 digits remained on the screen above the 00:00 that
would not advance by even one second. David stepped forward,
then back, but the service didn't change. He shoved the phone
back into his pants pocket. He walked backward for a few steps,
then sideways, before moving closer, stopping about forty feet from
where the body lay. He thought he smelled blood, maybe a whiff
of whiskey. It occurred to him to quickly take a few photos. The
camera on the phone ticked them off wildly. He hit Record and
narrated what he'd found, the time, what he was about to do. "I'm
approaching to assist if necessary. No cellular service. Will head
back toward house to get a signal and phone the authorities."

He took a deep breath and swallowed. "I'm coming to you," he
said, and the sound of his voice was like a stone dropping into the
water, hollow and rippling out through the bare trees. "I'm here to
help," he added, once again checking his surroundings, startling
just a bit when a squirrel leapt from limb to limb, the crack and
thump as though someone were jumping on him. His heartbeat
settled and he pushed on, not unafraid. At the edge of the water, he bent down and made sure his feet were planted firmly so
he could duck-walk the rest of the way. This close he could see
the chest rising and falling, slowly, with the kind of effort infants
use in fevers. He saw too now that the pale body was female, with
small swells around deep pink nipples. She moaned and turned

her head, and he saw her face was bruised, a gash over her right
eye, bleeding, the streaks of red giving way to a watery rose across
her cheeks. David recognized the facial features. She was a young
woman with Down syndrome, and he rushed to her, skidded across
the slick rocks and knelt beside the girl, and kept calling her *honey*
and stroking her short blond hair with one hand as he tried the
phone again with the other.

Her top lip was busted so severely the inside was nearly inverted,
swollen and twisted, looking like a wad of bubble gum was stuck to
her teeth. David placed his hand under her head and turned her
face toward him. "Shhh," he said. Her head lolled away from him,
and for a brief shock of a second, David feared her head would slip
from his grasp and smack onto the limestone. The water slightly
gurgling around them was pinkish, and colder now. He gently
placed her head back onto the rocks; David paused only briefly
before deciding on carrying her out of the falls and away from the
water. He put an arm under her short legs and the other behind
her neck and carefully rose, as if the earth might open up below
them. David took measured, planned steps forward, inspecting the
footholds so that each one was firm. The task seemed to help him
gather his air, and as he placed the girl down, he made sure to set
her in place like a doll, holding her torso to him so he could use
one hand to shuck off his jacket. He wrapped it around her, eased
her back, and folded her arms over, pulling the zipper up to her
chin, which was blue-green, like turquoise, with another gash right
in the center, red flesh filleted and parted.

David tried the phone again, but the bars were not there. He
looked around and brushed his hair back, scooted up next to the
girl. He placed two fingers at her pale throat; the heartbeat was
faint. She rolled her head toward his touch and said, "Daddy." The
word brought the pang of anguish it does for all true fathers; he
heard in it his own daughter's voice as the girl sputtered with a
cough and said again, "Daddy," this time with a weak plea.

"It's okay," he told her, taking off his denim shirt and placing it
over the jacket. "Honey, I don't have any cell service out here." His
words seemed to calm her and she stopped moving her head from
side to side. "I live a couple of miles away. I can run back and call
911 and I'll run as fast as I can back here." The girl was still, her
breathing slow and barely perceptible. David stood up, then knelt
again and leaned over her and whispered in her ear. "Hang on,

honey. I promise I'll be back." He gently touched her cheek and turned around and started to run.

In just a white undershirt, David sprinted back along the worn path, calculating the time it would take. He could walk the distance in just over twenty minutes; sprinting, he might shave off a quarter of the time, plus a few more minutes because he'd be able to get a signal once into one of the open fields. He rounded the bend where the rock foundation jutted out, then up along the sagging fence line. Blackbirds floated from the trees and mourning doves exploded out of the taupe fescue in the ditch. His lungs burned, and his eyes watered from the wind in his face. David thought then of Samantha, living in Chicago, a pediatric nurse, her mother a nurse too, the two of them living their lives as if men only weakened them, which was probably true. Samantha had told him over and over that taking a yearly CPR and first-aid course was just as important as his insistence on recycling, but during her last visit he'd waved her off again, saying he'd get around to it. He could see Sam at the girl's age, an awkward teenager, and the image of the little girl alone near Shanty Falls gave him more energy, and he pumped his arms and pushed the balls of his feet with force into the ground while his thighs ached and the image of the barns and the side of his house came into view in the distance. He stopped abruptly and pulled out his phone. The operator was clear and calm, the voice forgiving and hopeful. David swallowed and caught his breath. In one clean and concise rush he said, "I'm David Holzer. I live at 220 Pike Road, close to Shanty Falls. On my morning walk I found a girl. She's hurt badly. Please send an ambulance right away." The operator repeated the information and David confirmed it. "Hurry," he said, "she's lost a lot of blood." He put the phone back in his pocket and took a deep breath.

It occurred to him he could get back to the girl more quickly.

He sprinted toward the barn the Price brothers owned. They kept three ATVs inside, under tarps, for some reason only using them in the fall. He yanked off the dark green canvas and saw the keyholes empty. He searched the walls and found three sets of keys on an old hay hook. He put all three in the ATV ignitions. It'd been years since he'd ridden a motorcycle in college, but after a couple of false starts he found reverse with his foot, and was out of the barn and hitting second gear. At the edge of the woods he used his cell to call 911 again. "Tell the paramedics and police there are two

ATVs with keys in them in the barn." The operator told him they'd sent along a sheriff's SUV.

David zipped around the back of the farm and down the long stretch before the curvy footpath along the river bottom and caves. At the stone foundation, he stood slightly and kept driving, looking ahead, the smell of gas and oil somehow calming. His arms were cold and he said a short prayer in his head, asking that the girl be spared shock. He slowed down when he saw some movement, and something hard and cold froze in the center of his chest. As he shifted down to first gear, the ATV jerked and threw him forward a little, the wind now stronger and biting. He stopped completely and had to squint to make out a figure in the distance, shrouded some by low-lying bushes and several massive tree trunks that had fallen. He shut off the motor but kept his eyes on the person moving slowly in circles. "You there," yelled David, and he slid his phone from his pocket and damned himself for not bringing along the rifle he used to scare off foxes from his set of four hens. The figure kept pacing in circles. The motor on the ATV ticked as it cooled, like an old clock. In the far distance, the sirens wailed and receded, came back a little louder each time. David thought about just sitting it out, but he'd told the girl, no, promised her he'd be back. He climbed off the ATV and stood next to it. The voice of the girl, and Samantha's too, came rushing back into his mind. He heard them both calling him Daddy. David stepped forward and kept going, his stride long and heels thudding in the earth. "Hey, you there," he said, and David pointed in the person's direction. "Stay where you are," he commanded. David sniffed in deeply as the person finally heard him and stiffened, but only momentarily, before waving his arms and starting to jog in David's direction. "I said stay where you are!" David stopped too. At this distance, in the path, he could see the person was a young guy, barefoot but holding a pair of shoes like they might be precious or explosive. David stepped to the side of the path and could make out the girl's pale skin, about forty feet behind the guy. In David's absence she'd moved, still on her back, but legs positioned now as if preparing to do sit-ups, her feet planted on the cold ground, her knees shining like white saucers. "You know her?" asked David. The guy stood there like a surprised deer. "Tell me, son," said David, as he took steps forward. "You hear the sirens as well as I do. Better let me know what's happened here." The guy held on to the shoes, dangling at his side. David was within ten feet now, and could see the kid was familiar; he'd seen the face, the wide brown eyes and full mouth; he'd seen that face from the shoulders up before, but he couldn't place it. David stopped again. The sirens seemed to fade some now. "What's happened?" asked David.

The kid took a step forward, but David put out his hand. "Stay put."

The kid's mouth opened and he seemed as though the air had been knocked out of him. Finally he said, "I didn't mean to." He looked over his shoulder at the girl, who moaned.

David yelled, "I'm back, honey, just like I said. We're gonna get you out of here."

"She said she couldn't wait to tell everyone we were dating." The kid looked at the shoes, which David could see were expensive.

"Did you hurt that girl?" asked David, and he recognized in himself a palpable hatred for the kid, his spoiled face and styled haircut. He wore a wristwatch that gleamed even in the dull light of the gloomy forest. The thought surged in David, but the kid suddenly wore the expression of a child ashamed of its behavior. David took two more steps forward. The sirens looped back around and steadily grew closer, like a dream at daybreak, fading and at the same time rushing to be acknowledged.

"I didn't mean to hurt her," said the kid. He kept his shoes at his side, held away from his hip as if they were baby shoes about to be dipped into a bronze bath for keepsakes.

"But you did hurt her, son," said David. The morning turned sunny as a large cloud eased by, and the wind dropped back, the trees stilling and the only sound the falls, water cooing and the bare canopy warming. David walked the last few steps to the boy. "Have you seen what you've done to her?" he asked.

The kid started to sob, and for a moment it seemed he might pass out, but instead he collapsed into David's arms. From behind, David could hear voices, and the sound of an ATV motor immediately cut off. David held on to the kid and yelled over his shoulder, "She's just up ahead, to your right. Hurry, please hurry." A rush of bodies gave off the scent of soap and deodorant, the start of a shift. David allowed the kid to go limp in his arms. Overhead, the *thwack, thwack* of helicopter blades thumped like woofers in a jacked-up trunk of an annoying Monte Carlo. David pushed the kid's head to rest on his right shoulder, so he could see what they were doing with the girl. David caught the bright green flash of moss, the wet silver dullness of the limestone, and against those pulsing colors the pale legs of the girl, her feet bouncing each time they applied pressure to her chest. The helicopter hovered just over the treetops, the bare branches swaying, before it eased backward and rose, circled back to what David assumed would be his garden area, flat and wide open. The treetops now quietly undulated and lessened their movements. David noticed the kid's sandy-brown hair fluttered back into place, his scalp covered again. The paramedics barked instructions, sounding angry at their work, at what had been presented them. The kid sobbed into David's shoulder. Dogs brayed behind them, their barks hyper and insistent. David pushed the kid's head up, and it wobbled not unlike the girl's earlier. "You need to get yourself together, son."

The boy nodded. "Yes, sir," he said. The kid stepped back and let out a labored exhale. He still held the shoes in his right hand, his knuckles pink. "I didn't mean it."

Over his right shoulder David sensed three or four deputies. He heard the words "Back up" or "Step aside." He couldn't say for certain what they were instructing. The kid's eyes shifted into an awareness then, as David raised his hands and nodded for the kid to do the same. David thought of the pictures from his mother's Bible, the color ones where Jesus was arrested, the ones where his arms and hands were above him, palms nailed to an old wooden cross. "You best put those shoes down," said David, but the kid hesitated, glanced at them. "I don't want to get them dirty," he said as he let them slip from his hand. They landed on a mound of green moss. The kid raised his hands as David had, held them the same way.

Paramedics whisked the girl by them on a stretcher, her mouth covered in an inhalation bag, as the sheriff's deputies instructed through bullhorns for David and the kid to keep their hands up, to get to their knees, slowly. They both went down as if entering cold water, and as the kid's knees hit the ground, his exhaled breath was laced with the acrid stink of thrown-up liquor, so strong it made David hold his own breath. They were instructed to put their hands behind their heads. As someone gripped David's wrist and applied cuffs, he said out of the side of his mouth, "I'm the 911 caller." He watched as the kid was handcuffed and lifted from the kneeling position. They walked toward the black SUV, escorted by the deputies. One of the ATVs sat nearby. Two news vans were stuck in the wet muck of the field up toward the old fence line. They were put in separate cruisers. Now that David could see the deputy, he recognized her from the Chamber events. "Mr. Holzer," she said. He nodded, suddenly aware how tight his muscles were, the wracking pain in his head. "I've got to read you your rights," she added. The idea was nearly comical to David because of how surprised he was to hear these words, words he'd only heard in movies. The deputy smiled. "Only protocol, of course," she said. David listened as she began, and he looked out the window and into the other cruiser, where the kid sat with his arms behind him, using his head to motion toward David.

The sheriff's office smelled of burned microwave popcorn. David had always become mildly queasy from the smell, even when his mother had made it on the stove, the pulsating red coil like a planet from his science book. The stink of it reminded him of the kid's vomit breath. David sat back in the office chair; they'd put him in a conference room, offered him coffee and even snacks. He looked at his watch. It was almost noon. The female deputy appeared, balancing two cups of steaming coffee, not the Styrofoam kind from a drip pot but two large recycled containers with the stamp of the eco-green brewer that was constantly busy, opening two new sites near Midland University and putting the chain stores nearly out of business. "You like it black, double sugar?" she asked as she handed David the fibered cup, flecks of maroon in the cardboard ring meant to keep fingers from burning.

David nodded and rose, took the coffee carefully, as if it might detonate. "Thank you," he said, sitting back down. The deputy's name was Shelby, he remembered now, about four or five years younger than Samantha; she'd had a wicked jumper, if he recalled correctly.

Shelby sat down at the table, blowing over her coffee, and though he couldn't say why, it reminded David of how Samantha's mother had soothed her, soft and with determination, a kind of warriorlike reverence for lost sleep. "I suppose," she said, taking her cell phone from a holster and placing it on the desktop, "you've already realized he's saying he found her with your jacket on. That he's also saying that he was the one to find her, and that you showed up later, returning to the scene of the crime?" Shelby had shot three free throws in the 2004 regional playoffs, a technical foul, and she'd won the game, while Samantha had cheered the team on.

"And I'm assuming, Deputy, the physical evidence proves otherwise?" asked David as he swallowed a hot gulp of coffee he wished he'd cooled.

Shelby nodded, licked her lips, and tried to valiantly smile. "The girl is in ICU, a coma. Her vitals are all over the place. The blows to her head were enough to incite extreme swelling." Shelby turned down the mic at her shoulder when it squawked.

David nodded, held back the guttural instinct to stand and yell in opposition. "He as much as admitted to it before you guys got there. He said she was going to tell everyone they were dating." David looked as intensely as he could at the deputy. "The kid tried to kill her."

Shelby grimaced and placed her tall steaming cup of coffee onto the desk. "Maybe you recognized him. He's the point guard for Midland U.," she said, looking over her shoulder as sliding glass doors parted, then several drunk college students brayed and laughed as they were ushered into the processing areas.

"Stopped watching after Sam graduated," said David, as he too let his eyes follow the drunken college kids escorted to the mugshot area. The smell of burned popcorn receded, making it that much worse, faint and somehow slightly damp. David knew now why he'd recognized the kid, at least from the shoulders up, his player pic plastered everywhere on the state and local news feeds, a basketball star.

"My dad was the same way, Mr. Holzer," said Shelby. "He watched just so we'd have something to talk about on weekends." She leaned back in the office chair and put her arms behind her head; David reminded himself not to glance at her chest. She had the lean, muscular look of a young woman who liked to participate in Saturday biathlons. Shelby said, "His folks are rooted deeply. They give in the upper six figures to MU, they own three businesses in Rochester, plus the law offices, and there's a wing of the new hospital about to be named after them. Both are MBAs. And the father still practices law."

"Well, I'm a firm believer in our justice system to get things right about half the time," said David. "Of course, not in these cases." He drank his coffee in three deep gulps, his tongue burning, back of the throat too. He placed the cup on the desktop, sat back some, and posed a question. "Tell me, what's wrong with these kinds of kids?" He gestured with his head to some vague area in the middle of the room. "He was just as concerned about getting his goddamn expensive shoes dirty as he was about that poor little girl." David stood up and realized he was angrier than he'd thought; mostly, sitting there in the sheriff's station, he'd felt sad, worried, sick to his stomach, but now he was seething, because it seemed it wasn't a new story, every year some spoiled brat was profiled during the news, affluent, sports-minded, indulgent parents, and the judge complicit, people actually talking about how the offender's life shouldn't be ruined because of one mistake. They specifically said these words, and did so without a trace of self-doubt, as if they too could bash a little girl's face in, Down syndrome or not. "What am I not getting?" he asked with a smirk.

Shelby sat up straighter. "In this work," she said, pointing in the same general vicinity David had earlier, "you have to find a balance." She stood up now too. "I'm not the sole voice on callousness, Mr. Holzer, or how it comes about, why it seems to be growing." Shelby softened. "You likely saved her. And that's what I think about, I mean, when I'm doubting, after some awful crassness of youth, the middle-aged road rage, or the craven geriatrics," which she chuckled at, and seemed disappointed and slightly embarrassed that David hadn't responded with much more than a quick grin.

"You'll keep me posted, then?" asked David as he stepped back from the table, his hand on the doorknob.

"Well, since you're the only witness and the kid tried to implicate you, Mr. Holzer, I think you'll be seeing me quite a bit." She put out her hand and David shook it, warm and dry. He turned to leave, walked through a maze of cubicles, then past the interview rooms with glass windows to the ceiling and out a set of doors that were operated by a deputy who sat perched up in an elevated seating area.

Once David was outside, he stood and looked around from the top of the steps. Cars and news vans lined both sides of the street, two from Indianapolis and at least one he could tell was from Chicago. Crime had become an artsy endeavor now, the quirkier the better, serial stories on public radio shows, through podcasts popping up like fast-food franchises, and streaming series offering just as many takes, crime as sponsored by meal-delivery services, as biopsychosocial investigations. They liked crimes where someone was innocent, or just barely, the episodes building week by week on some new voice from the past, damning or confirming, but never enough to stop listeners and viewers from tuning in before the similarly inconclusive reveal. Crime was the new museum opening, the debut novel, the album everyone was talking about who had time to be purveyors of art in the episodic. David was cold in the cooler afternoon winds; March like a lion and all that. He took a few steps down the stairs and was nearly bowled over as reporters chased a haggard couple up the steps toward the sheriff's offices. The woman's face was red and swollen and the man kept his arm around her and sneered as he tried to usher his wife and himself closer to the entrance. Several deputies appeared and ordered the reporters back to the sidewalk. Shelby was taking the wife by the arm and helping her through the doors. David didn't know why he chose to wave at Shelby, but she had enough sense to only nod. She and the couple disappeared into the building. The kid and his goddamn stupid shoes, his haircut, and the way he cried near the waterfalls, as if he were trying out for a theater production, it all ran through David's mind as he realized he had no vehicle.

By nightfall the local affiliates all had slightly different still shots of Shanty Falls, silver water pouring over the serene white limestone, some of the poplar limbs within the frame, the soft green peat bulging up at the edge of the cold eddies. Names had been withheld, but then the girl's parents were in a Fort Wayne studio, dark bags under their eyes and faces twisted into a stolid anguish. David sipped tea and sat on the sofa with Bella, a border collie too old anymore to take on regular walks. The phone rang on the kitchen wall. He stood and Bella pretended she'd follow, but the fourteen years in her hips brought her back down with a sigh.

"Yes," David said into the phone.

"Dad," said Samantha. "Are you okay?" He could tell he was on speakerphone, that Linda was listening too.

"Fine, fine," he said, as the pale thighs and mangled face of the girl flashed into his head.

"Mom's listening."

"Hello, Linda," David said as he moved into the doorway so he could see Bella asleep on the couch.

"It's awful," said the two women, as if singing in rounds.

"Yes," said David, and he heard his daughter and ex-wife conferring in muted tones.

"Would you like us to come there? We could get flights and stay for a while." David thought he'd heard Sam shush her mother.

"No, I'm quite fine," said David. "It's a simple case, really. I suppose as time goes on I'll be asked to testify." He liked how that sounded, that he was doing the right thing, even waiting to do it, and these two women had seen him do otherwise far too often.

"We love you," said Sam, and her mother said it too. They sounded like they were tipsy on the wine they both loved so much.

"Same here," said David, and after a few more questions he hung up and returned to Bella, who was twitching in her sleep, running in her dreams, her paws moving like she was pedaling a bike.

David sat and watched the girl's parents crucified on television. They were putting their faces on a story that would last no longer than a twelve-hour cycle, rutted out by celebrity gossip and political polarization. He pointed the remote at the television and the room darkened. He put his arms under Bella's chest and belly and lifted her, carried her upstairs to her bed near his. In the dark of his bedroom, after he'd placed Bella into her bed, he thought of the kid, and how if he was given the chance, he'd punch him so hard the kid's fancy bangs would hang under his left ear.

Shelby knocked on the door, and Bella, up early for her, barked and growled, all the while her tail wagging, her tongue smiling as if she'd never had any company. David patted her head in his robe and opened the door.

"Mr. Holzer," said Shelby, holding two cups of coffee from the college campus store, Mean Bean. David held the door open as Shelby walked inside the mudroom and into the kitchen, where Bella was trying to show her old tricks, slow, but with real earnestness, black eyes flashing with the craven desire for attention.

Shelby smiled down at the dog. David shuffled to the table and slipped into one of the chairs, and Shelby did the same. "Wanted you to know," said Shelby, but she paused, then pushed a coffee toward David. "The kid's parents have gotten one of their high-profile friends to represent him. The district attorney says they're already concocting a defense that paints the girl as promiscuous, willing to do anything to be popular."

David took the top off the coffee and blew across the black surface. He sipped from the lip, then took another long gulp. He put the coffee in front of him as Bella whined until Shelby patted her head, then the dog sat, went fully down, and curled up next to Shelby's feet. "If I am recalling my law correctly," said David, "a young woman can't be beaten nearly to death even if she did want a homecoming date." David shook his head. "That kid will get what's coming to him."

Shelby raised her eyebrows, sipped from her cup. "I don't think it's best for the only witness to be making veiled threats, Mr. Holzer."

"All I'm saying is, if that kid walks away from this like the one in Milwaukee did, someone will take things into their own hands."

Shelby sat up straighter, cleared her throat. "So, what are you doing for your walk these days? Shanty will be closed for another few weeks until the scene is fully processed." David didn't respond; he knew his face was contorted, could feel the crease between his eyes ridged and tight. Shelby looked around the kitchen. "Just for inventory's sake, permit verification and all, you have any firearms, Mr. Holzer?"

David laughed, a quick burst of absurdity, followed by a deep inhale. "I don't like guns," he said. "Sam and her mother work in emergency care, remember." He paused and fiddled with the bottom of the coffee cup, picking at the peeling paper. "Seeing people's heads half gone kind of turns you off to the Second Amendment, Deputy." Shelby nodded, and started to stand up. David said, "Besides, I tend to think of retribution as something of an art form, you know, where creativity meets hatred."

Shelby stood by the table. She gave David a soft, determined smile. "There's an interesting legal interpretation of a person alluding to certain acts," said Shelby. "It's all about tone." She picked up her coffee and walked to the door while David remained seated. "Police officers in big cities even get training in narrative, so they can recognize irony and sarcasm, a simile and metaphor." She stood motionless as she turned the doorknob slowly. "It's where pragmatism meets incarceration." At the sound of the door clicking shut, Bella woke and looked at David and at the door, as if something should be done.

*

Days passed, and the television only spouted quick updates about
the girl, the kid, whose name David refused to commit to memory.
The two had met at a rally, the girl still in high school, a huge fan
of both Midland U. and the star point guard. At some point the kid
and the girl ended up in his Range Rover, with whiskey and wine.
David had to get out of the house or risk obsessing. He clicked a
leash on Bella, deciding a short walk wouldn't hurt her fourteen-
year-old bones. Out the back door and up against the sagging fence
line, saplings struggling in the row, contorting their growth toward
the sun and sky. David tried the syncopated breathing of his time
meditating. Bella sniffed and peed, even picked up the pace. Before long they'd made it to the edge of Shanty Falls, at least as far as
the yellow tape would allow. Bella lapped water from a silver rivulet,
the green moss around the edges like outdoor carpet. She plopped
down and panted with a gummy, grizzled smile. David surveyed
the entire area, even looking up above, where the branches held
fat red buds, some green shoots as bright as neon. The image of
his parents evicted from the house he now lived in — toting just a
few boxes and some clothes on hangers — reeled in his head. The
girl had been lifelined to a hospital in Cleveland, and both Sam
and her mother had said over the phone the trauma care provided
there was superior, a strange word, but their vernacular had long
ago taken on the spirit of recovery and accreditation. David stared
at the spot he thought he'd found her, but the area was different
now, the rocks somehow rearranged, the water itself falling more
slowly, the trickles at the limestone rim apparently gone. He sat
down next to Bella and stroked her head, and her eyes closed,
opened, and went completely shut as she let out a deep sigh. David
sat at the border of the waters and thought about what he might
be able to do, as blackbirds cawed overhead and the forest stilled
between surfs of breeze.

Shelby stopped by twice a week, and David welcomed her inside,
and their conversation inevitably turned toward the kid, the legal
wrangling, the certainty of David's deposition. His jacket, the one
he'd wrapped the girl in, had become part of the official evidence.
The girl's brain swelling had not changed, her condition remained
critical after nearly six weeks. Sam and her mother told David on
the evening phone calls that she'd likely have long-term impacts on
her activities of daily living.

At the kitchen table, David scrolled news headlines on a tablet. The kid's face flashed onto the screen. He'd been expecting the story so much that now, reading it, he could almost guess how it would go. The header was blocked and highlighted with a large question mark, asking readers to consider whether one mistake should doom the kid to losing the basketball scholarship, ruin his future. Stats—a near-perfect GPA and field goal and free-throw percentages—lined the edge of the text. The kid's attorney described the crime as an *incident,* one where two young people had each made ill-advised choices, ones that shouldn't permanently define them. David sat up in the chair and scrolled to the comments section below. There were hundreds of anonymous members fighting about who was to blame. One caught David's eye because Sam had once told him using all caps was like screaming. Pro Arts@ StarH2H: GIVE ME A BREAK! THE ASSHOLE NEARLY BEAT HER TO DEATH!!!!

Gunslinger@2ndAmend: CALM DOWN bleedy♥ AND TRY TO SEE IT FROM HIS SIDE OF THINGS! WE DON'T KNOW WHAT SHE DID! THESE KIDS SHOULD NEVER HAVE BEEN MAIN-STREAMED! MORE LIBTARD SOCIAL EXPERIMENTS AND LOOK WHAT HAPPENS!!!

Witnessing all the thumbs-up emoticons under the comment, David squeezed the edges of the tablet hard enough that the screen ebbed blue-green, like a microexplosion of plasma under the glass. He stood up and looked down at Bella, turned and started to call Sam, paused and thought briefly of phoning Shelby, even going for a run, but instead he sat back down and found the kid's address, synced it to his phone, searched online until he found three numbers, one for the kid's dad's law office, another connected to the address, and one more that seemed to be a cell-phone number. He put the tablet down gently and went upstairs.

Standing inside the closet, he chose a blue shirt, a dark brown jacket, and matching slacks, pulled on loafers he rarely wore anymore. In front of the mirror, he inspected the look. Did it represent a dependable person? Did he look like all he wanted to provide was a warning? Did the clothes communicate understanding? Some mercy? It had to be convincing.

He'd had the house renovated but kept a built-in chest of drawers his mother had loved while they'd rented the place. David pulled the top drawer open and reached under a stack of cardi-

gans. His fingers felt the chain, then the plastic piece. In grade
school he'd come home with the thing, a plastic butterfly shrunk
down in Mrs. LaSalle's toaster oven. David's mother wore it for one
whole year, then on special occasions, and finally left it in a box
of things from the hospice. He wrapped the chain around the yellowed plastic, the purple monarch almost occluded, and shoved it
into his pocket. He grabbed his keys and walked down the stairs to
the back door, pausing to check on Bella. He left the house at 4:10
p.m.

David stood by his car at the curb. The house was massive, ornate,
and easily worth five million. For a while he thought of just getting
back in the car and driving home, but something about how serene
and protected the black iron gates appeared, sturdy and attached
to the white stacks of limestone columns that rose fifteen feet into
the cool air, made David start toward them. A brief image of himself climbing the gates, clamoring and shaking the goddamn things
until the hinges unmoored, washed over his vision. He'd been
thinking on the drive about his folks, the last time he'd seen them
happy. They'd cobbled together enough money for a trip out West
to see Rushmore, the Grand Canyon, and Four Corners. They'd
taken pictures and wanted him to see the thick stack of them over
shit on a shingle and black, bitter coffee. Three years later both
were gone, both from cancer.
    He pressed the button on the intercom, and above his head an
LCD panel blinked on. A brown face flashed into existence. "Yes?"
the woman said, squinting into the camera. "*Sí?*" She held her
hands as if halfway through a magic trick.
    "I'd like to talk to the Schafers. I've got news." The woman
shrugged. "Tell them it's David Holzer from Shanty Falls." She
nodded slightly, then turned and disappeared down a massive hallway, a glimmering chandelier partially visible and a white bichon
frise standing motionless underneath it, the dog's dark, narrow
eyes buried in round coifed fur, staring up and into the camera.
David blinked, thinking it might be a stuffed toy, but then it took
two circus steps and barked, head thrown back, mouth moving but
muted. The kid had grown up behind these gates, a maid, a chef,
numerous vehicles, ATM cards, electronics, on-demand entertainment, indulgences, and then more. David watched a squirrel,
which in his current state of mind also seemed privileged, a red

and healthy tail mane, gourmet grains in shiny stainless-steel feeders, and its playground several acres of lush turf, with the perimeter buffeted by towering long-leaf pine, flat staircases of dogwood branches climbing into the ether, the boxwoods clipped into exact lines, long rectangles that bordered smooth slate stretching toward a circular fountain surrounded by squat Japanese maples.

David stared at the far-off slope of the property, and came to as the father stood within the span of camera. "Mr. Holzer, it's a pleasure. Corina is on her way to greet and welcome you to our home." The man smiled, his teeth as white as the dog, his eyes genuinely flickering with positivity; anything could be resolved, all it took was strategy and resources, solid logic, and, of course, friends, connections. "It'll take her a bit to get to you; we've been spending most of our days in the guest residence."

David said, "Thank you," not certain if he was supposed to push an intercom button.

The kid's dad kept talking. "It's nearly time for dinner, or at least an early one, can I have something prepared for you?"

David shook his head. "No, that's not necessary. I've only come with an update. I won't take up much of your time." David thought he heard the word *nonsense* as Corina opened the door and handed David a glass bottle of sparkling water and turned, motioned for him to follow her.

Inside the large home they trekked down pristine corridors, paintings on the walls as large as interstate signs and staff milling about. They passed a room set up with video equipment, sound systems, and lights and screens for professional headshots. David followed the woman through a massive kitchen onto a mason patio that dwarfed his own home. At the bottom of the mammoth steps sat a golf cart. Corina pointed to the passenger seat. "Sit."

They drove over acres of grass, the guesthouse in the distance and cool air lapping at both of their bangs. Finally the father came into view, standing in a circular driveway, hands in his pockets and his face wearing that same calm, positive smile. Corina killed the motor and hurried off the cart and toward a back entrance.

"Mr. Holzer," said the man. His handshake was all attorney, not lawyer, soft and assured, a winner all the time.

"Yes," said David. "Your son," he added, "is he home?"

"Why, yes," said the man, his smile fading only a little. "But let's go inside. Have a drink."

"I'd rather not," said David. "I'd like it if your son heard what I have to say." The attorney raised his chin, examined David, considered his eyes. "I assure you I'm only here to provide some information," said David.

The attorney glanced over his shoulder and back again at David. "Come on inside and I'll have Teresa bring him down." They walked into the house, the spring sun slipping behind the trees and the cold evening air descending.

Once in the living room, a flatscreen muted, a French movie playing with subtitles, David decided he'd come across the wrong way. "Actually, I'd love a white wine," he said. The attorney smiled and motioned for Corina.

They talked about weather. "I suppose you'll be glad when this is settled," said the attorney. He responded to David's silence. "I understand you're an avid hiker, to Shanty Falls, that is." Corina handed them both a white wine as the kid and his mother appeared at the edge of the room. The woman was small, even mousy, which surprised David.

"Yes?" she said as the kid looked at David as though he had no idea who he was. David knew what he was about to do wouldn't last long—maybe an hour? Two, before they called and found out the truth?

David stood, handed the wine to the attorney. "I'm afraid," said David, and he paused, looked to Corina standing in the foyer. "I've come to let you know that the girl is dead. She passed away a few hours ago." The mother put her hand to her stomach and slowly turned and walked away. The attorney rose and went to his son. They stood side by side.

"What's that now?" said the attorney. The kid looked at his father, both tall in the same way, hair alike too.

David put his hands in his pockets, felt the necklace he'd made his mother. "Yes, it's terribly sad, but I thought you should know. My ex-wife and daughter work in the ICU. She went into cardiac arrest and couldn't be revived." The lies felt like punches, and David followed the one-two combination with some gut shots. "The deputy also called." The attorney held his kid, the two tall handsome men stooped now, about to be knocked out. "They, of course, will now bring murder charges." The kid sobbed while the dad looked around, as if searching for something to hold them both up.

David stood silent for a while, then said, "I really shouldn't have come, but I thought you should know." The phone rang, and kept ringing. Corina held her hand over her mouth. David turned and walked to the door. "I'll drive myself back to my car," he said. The kid sobbed and then started crying like a small child, demanding his father "get Mommy, get Mommy."

On the golf cart, gliding over the soft hummocks, swallows dipped down and flashed up again. David hadn't expected he'd feel anything but sadness after he'd offered up the con, but he also hadn't anticipated the hatred he had for the kid, his parents. Near a gate that led around another, smaller fountain, he left the golf cart and walked toward his car at the curb. His phone vibrated in his pocket, clinking softly against the monarch under plastic. He pulled it out and answered. "Dad," said Sam. "What are you doing?"

David couldn't answer.

DAVID DEAN

The Duelist

FROM *Ellery Queen Mystery Magazine*

WITH JACKETS REMOVED and cravats undone, the two men faced each other in the sweltering heat of the new morning. The older man was tall and robust-looking, with curls and a large mustache, the younger of average height and delicate frame. Like a fiery eye, the distant sun rose above the sandbar they stood upon, revealing a desolate waste of scrub oak, sassafras trees, and driftwood, a shifting island that lay just beyond the reach of Mississippi law.

Having no excuse to remove their own outer clothing, the small gathering of spectators sweated and chafed. Most were also afflicted with hangovers, or remained actively drunk, which only added to their discomfort. One gentleman, whose straw hat had blown off crossing the Big Muddy, had passed out from the sun beating down on his bald pate. Now he lay, pale as a corpse, beneath the meager shade of a tenacious palmetto.

Myron Gill, his own dented top hat firmly settled on his large skull, predicted, "He'll have company soon enough," nodding at the unfortunate bald man. "Only he shan't be breathing." Tall and cadaverous, Myron's somber appearance belied his curious and gregarious nature.

Standing to his left, the small, portly stranger he addressed replied, "You wager it will be that boy?"

Even at the distance they stood, it was plain to see the pistol in the younger man's hand tremble from time to time.

"He has only minutes left on this earth, I fear," Myron declared, taking a moment to study his fellow spectator. Though he had crossed the river with all the other drunks, loafers, and gamblers from the tavern, Myron had not seen him before this morning. Small and neat, he had a certain fussiness of appearance, his cravat a frothy, if somewhat soiled, work of art, his clothing expensive. Myron's keen eye noted a slight fraying of the cuffs and lapels gone shiny with wear. This was a man who had seen better times. Beneath the shadow of the stranger's once-white plantation hat, Myron discerned he was dark-complexioned and brown-eyed, his black hair worn long, its oily locks cascading to his small, rounded shoulders.

"You are both satisfied with your weapons and that they have been properly primed and charged?" asked the referee loudly enough for the spectators to hear. He was a former senator, now retired to private life.

Nodding his head, the bigger man answered, "Yes, yes . . . Let's proceed—this heat is ghastly."

"Yes," the smaller agreed, glancing up at his challenger, his fair hair hanging in damp strings along his pale cheeks. "I'm satisfied."

"There is still time to rescind the challenge," the referee reminded the big man. "Mr. Forrester has made it clear on several occasions that he never meant to give offense. You both may withdraw from this with honor. You've only to say the word, Captain Noddy."

"He should've considered that before making his slanderous claims. May we continue?"

With a sympathetic glance at Forrester, the referee called out, "If there is nothing more to be said, then . . . gentlemen, turn and await my count."

At this command the spectators went silent, the hot wind riffling through the dry leaves the only sound.

"Perhaps he will only wound the boy," the man with the frayed cuffs ventured in a whisper. "Surely he is a sporting man?"

"He is not," Myron assured him. "The boy will die."

Turning their backs to one another, the duelists raised their pistols and took a measured step with each number called out. Upon the number ten being reached, there was a pause in the count.

The portly man with the frayed cuffs glanced at his fellow spectators. None appeared to be breathing.

"Turn and aim!" the retired senator commanded.

Pivoting smartly, the duelists lowered their pieces.

"Fire!"

At this crucial moment the weapon of the unfortunate Forrester once more shook in his grasp, sending the bullet that followed far wide of his opponent.

"Dear God," he managed to gasp before Captain Noddy's answering shot entered his skull through his left eye. Collapsing onto the hot sands, his limbs twitched convulsively for several moments before falling still.

The doctor who had been standing by knelt down in a perfunctory examination, though it was obvious to all that life was extinct.

"Dead . . ." the doctor confirmed with an exasperated gesture, adding, "What else?" Stalking off toward one of the beached rowboats that had transported them all, he cried, "I don't know why I'm here; the undertaker should attend these damned things, not me."

"As I said," Myron murmured.

"Yes . . . you did . . . you did indeed," the portly man agreed. Taking a pinch of snuff, he regarded the slender, pitiful corpse of Forrester and opined, "Why, I don't think he was much more than eighteen."

He offered the silver snuff case to Myron.

Shaking his head, Myron replied, "We'd best be off. This is a thirsty crew, and they won't hold the boats a moment longer than they must."

Turning toward the waiting vessels, the portly man remarked, "By God, Noddy is a fearsome marksman — that shot went exactly where he aimed it." Shaking his head, he added, "He could have spared that boy just as easily."

Minutes later they were rowing hard against the current for Natchez.

Sharing a table at one of the many gambling dens that lay at the foot of the Natchez bluffs, Myron remarked to his new companion, "Here's to another day's living," raising his glass on high.

"Yes, another day," the portly man rejoined. "It's never certain, is it?"

"We've seen clear evidence of that this morning."

"Another . . . ?" The portly man signaled the young boy running from table to table.

"You've been damned generous . . . mister . . . mister . . . Good heavens, have I forgot your name already?"

"Not at all, we've yet to exchange them. My name is LeClair . . . Darius LeClair, newly arrived from Mobile." He flipped the boy a coin and was rewarded with two more bourbons.

"A pleasure, Mr. LeClair."

"Please call me Darius; I'm not one to stand on ceremony."

"Darius . . . yes . . . a pleasure! I am Myron Gill, long a resident of this fine city."

"We are well met, sir, as I've never set foot here until last night, arriving by late coach. It was my good fortune to fall in with you this morning."

Setting his now half-empty glass next to his dented top hat, Myron mopped his formidable brow. "How then, might I ask, did you come to be amongst the dueling party?"

Smiling broadly, Darius answered, "Having come in for a nightcap, I found the saloon abuzz with nothing but talk of your Captain Horatio Noddy and his latest duel! The tales of his prowess described him as a modern Achilles—deadly and indestructible. When I saw a party was gathering to witness this Homeric figure's latest exploits, I simply joined them. Hence our fortuitous meeting this morning!"

"And were you satisfied with your hero?" Myron asked.

"Oh yes . . . quite satisfied. Truly he is a terrible opponent. Why anyone would agree to face him, I can't imagine. It would seem his reputation alone would preclude any sensible man from doing so."

"One would think so . . ." Myron began, distracted as a small party of men entered the saloon to hails and huzzahs. "You conjure the devil and he appears," he exclaimed in a whisper.

"Why, it is the man himself," Darius concurred.

Despite the crowded circumstances, a table was vacated for the hero and his entourage. Darius recognized the duelist's second, as well as several hangers-on from the sandbar.

Returning to his previous topic, Darius asked, "Why then *do* they do it, Myron?"

"Face him . . . Noddy . . . do you mean?"

"Exactly."

Myron took another pull from his whiskey glass. "Most were young fools from the country—like our fellow Forrester. They come into Natchez to negotiate loans, or arrange the sale of their cotton, et cetera . . . Being young, they usually find their way to 'The Bottoms,' as we have so colorfully named this delightful district of gambling dens, saloons, and whorehouses, to indulge their vices, as young men will."

Setting his now empty glass down onto the sticky tabletop, Myron leaned toward the smaller Darius and spoke in a confidential tone. "I suspect that that is why you are here, my new friend, to relieve some of these callow lads of their excess cash. Do I recognize a fellow gambler in you, sir?"

Smiling back, Darius answered, "You do, indeed, sir. Games of chance have been my stock in trade for many years." Running his hands down his shabby lapels, he added, "As you have perhaps inferred from my appearance, my luck has abandoned me of late, necessitating the need for me to remove myself from my beloved Mobile—hence my arrival in this Athens of the South."

"The truth be told," Myron responded with a sheepish grin, "I am not a native myself, but a son of Memphis, where, like you, I found my circumstances somewhat straitened by a series of poor decisions. But I have made my home here for many years now and feel confident to be your guide and adviser . . . and my first, and most urgent, advice to you would be to avoid that man at all cost." He tilted his head carefully in Captain Noddy's direction, adding, "At peril of your life."

"How have so many run afoul of this fearsome man?" Darius persisted.

"You may well ask—Noddy seems to wait for them like some great spider in his web. This latest *affaire d'honneur* resulted from the young bumpkin making the unfortunate claim that New Orleans was a more robust city than Natchez. It fell upon the sensitive ears of our captain as a slur upon the character of our upstanding citizens. He likened it to being accused of some form of communal slothfulness. The others whom he called out committed similar unforgivable, and fatal, remarks."

"And how many lives has our Captain Noddy deprived their owners of as of this latest duel?"

"I reckon our Mr. Forrester to have been number twelve."

"Number twelve . . ." Darius repeated, staring across the smoky, busy tavern at Noddy's jubilant table—several women of questionable character had joined his party, the laughter grown louder.

Waving the bar boy over, Darius tossed a few coins onto his platter and gave him some instructions. Within moments their whiskeys had been replenished, while a fresh round arrived at Captain Noddy's table.

As the two gamblers watched, Myron in puzzlement, Darius with a pleasant smile, the bar boy was quizzed as to the origins of the fresh drinks. With a grimy finger he indicated the correct table. Darius raised his glass as the captain and his followers turned to take in their benefactors. Seeing the scrutiny they had come under, Myron hastened to raise his own glass, spilling some down his sleeve.

The captain's handsome face creased ever so slightly in acknowledgment. If he actually smiled, it was concealed beneath his mustache.

As he was turning away once more, Darius called out, "A good and thorough killing today, Captain Noddy; that young whelp stood no chance! You surpassed him completely!"

The hubbub at the captain's table softened somewhat at this, and Noddy studied his new, and enthusiastic, supporter carefully for several moments before returning his attentions to the young women at hand.

"Don't say another—" Myron began hoarsely.

"Why, it was as if that young man had never fired a pistol before today, so outclassed was he!" Darius called over. "A memorable action, sir . . . memorable indeed!"

Noddy's table had now gone silent, while the rest of the tavern's occupants grew quieter by degrees, according to their level of inebriation.

"Have you listened to nothing I've said?" Myron whispered urgently. "Remember what you witnessed this morning!"

Pivoting his chair around to face Darius, Captain Noddy's dark eyes came to rest on the squat, pudgy man who seemed determined to gain his attention. "What did you mean by 'no chance'?" he asked across a tavern gone so quiet that his voice was audible to all.

Appearing flustered at the attention, Darius sputtered, "Oh . . . yes . . . that. I . . . I just meant that confronted with your superior marksmanship and experience . . . who *would* have any chance?" Darius chuckled, then went quiet himself.

"You're sure of that?" Noddy smiled just a little.

"Oh yes . . . of course," Darius agreed, speaking now to Noddy's back as he was dismissed once more, and over the growing sound of laughter running through the crowded room.

"With such unseasoned and raw candidates to cull from," he continued unexpectedly, "it must be a little like shooting fish in a barrel for someone like you, a man of your nerve and skill. That's all I meant." This time the room went silent before Darius finished speaking.

Noddy rose from his chair, his hand on the butt of a pistol snugged within the sash he wore round his narrow waist. "Do you mean to draw me out?" he asked. "Take care that I don't answer that call, or you may find yourself joining those boys you seem so concerned about!" Noddy cut a handsome figure, being tall and broad-shouldered, his clothes well cut, his tall black boots shining beneath the lamplight.

Like an aging and chastened schoolboy, Darius appeared to be studying something on the dirty floorboards. "Well . . . that *is* to my point," he resumed in a small voice. "Those boys, as you yourself just referred to them, were just that—hardly a fit challenge for a man of your stature. The last . . . Forrester, I believe was his name . . . could hardly hold on to his gun, he was so struck with terror—as he rightly should've been, having incurred your ire, Captain."

There was a titter of laughter from a dark, distant corner of the room, but Noddy silenced it with a glance.

"But are such opponents worthy of you, sir?" Darius went on. "I suggest not. I say you deserve better than a steady stream of country bumpkins to take practice upon."

"And are you suggesting that *you* might provide such a challenge?" Noddy asked.

Darius appeared lost in thought.

"I'm speaking to you, you little toad!"

Looking up at the enraged duelist, Darius replied in a shaky voice, "I never meant to offend you, Captain, in fact, my intentions were—"

"Then, by God, you shall," Noddy spat, cutting short Darius's reply. "My second will call upon you tomorrow . . . *if* you can still be found at that time."

A long pause followed this pronouncement.

"I pray I can muster the courage to remain, Captain," Darius answered at last, rising to cross the smoky room with uncertain tread. He offered his soft, tremulous hand to his opponent. "Darius Le-Clair, sir, of the Natchez Queen Hotel . . . at your service, I fear."

Noddy disdained taking it, and Darius added, "It is my under-standing that I will be your thirteenth challenge, Captain Noddy. If, after considering the significance of that number, you should wish to withdraw, I wouldn't object, I assure you."

"*You* wouldn't . . ." Noddy sputtered in fury. "The day after to-morrow I will kill you, sir, as soon as the sun rises." Snatching up his coat from the back of his chair, he stormed out the door.

"Oh dear Lord," Darius said aloud to the silent room, "that went badly."

The tavern erupted with laughter.

By the next day the talk of Natchez was all about the duel; rumors were rife throughout the town, and the local newspaper had even managed to include a completely fabricated version of the chal-lenge. The breathless article described the noble Captain Noddy defending the virtue of his young and innocent fiancée, who in reality did not exist, from the outrageous importuning of a grace-less foreigner (a description perhaps inspired by Darius LeClair's rather exotic name and swarthy appearance). It was hinted that Darius had killed a person of quality in France and been forced to flee the guillotine.

Embellishments and wishful thinking by the citizenry quickly followed, transforming the pudgy and unimposing Darius into a mysterious duelist newly arrived from the Continent. Within hours it was said that he had slain everyone from German princes to Italian counts and had come to the New World in order to find a challenge worthy of his deadly talents. For the first time in a de-cade, there was open discussion of a less than certain outcome for Captain Noddy. The stranger's much-bandied words had the ring of truth to them—who could deny, now that the subject had been broached, that Noddy's victims had all been young, feckless "bumpkins," as the European combatant had pointed out?

But even as this line of thought gained traction, more sober cit-izens reminded one and all of Noddy's undeniable and demon-strated marksmanship. Seeing the wisdom in this view, all but the most degraded of gamblers resisted making book against the hometown favorite. It took only a moment's reflection to envision the usual outcome to the fight ahead and foresee that a list of those betting against Noddy might also become a calling card for future challenges.

"Has his second called upon you?" Myron asked his new and suddenly famous companion. He stood in the doorway of Room 4 of the Natchez Queen Hotel, feeding the brim of his hat through his hands and feeling somehow responsible for the peril Darius faced.

"Oh yes," Darius replied. "I must say he was very formal and respectful about it all. He even gave me Noddy's calling card! Strange, isn't it—we assert our determination to kill one another, then present calling cards."

Myron stared at the bouquets festooning the small, shabby room. "My God," he whispered in awe, "you are a luminary!"

"None of the attached cards are signed." Darius laughed. "They wish me well while remaining safely anonymous."

Shutting the door behind him, Myron observed, "They wish to go on living—who can blame them?" Drawing closer, he added, "You still have until tomorrow, Darius. For God's sake, slip away tonight after dark! Believe me, in a week's time the whole sordid affair will be forgotten."

Sitting on the edge of his narrow bed, Darius indicated the only chair in the room for Myron. Pouring them each a whiskey from his flask, he said, "You see no chance for me?"

"Of course not—you're a gambler, not a duelist—you don't have the look of a killer about you at all," Myron answered, downing his drink.

"You don't believe the stories about me that have been circulating about town?"

"What . . . ? Of course not, you told me yourself that you're just here for the gaming."

"Yes, that is what I said," Darius confirmed.

Myron held out his glass for a refill, noting the steady hand that poured it. His mouth opened, then shut once more, then opened again. "Are you telling me that wasn't true?"

Darius looked back at him, saying nothing, his face unreadable.

"You . . ." Myron began, then tried again. "You can't be . . . you don't even carry a gun. How can you . . ." He stopped midsentence as Darius withdrew a slim mahogany case from his valise, opening it to reveal a pair of gleaming and expensive dueling pistols chased in silver. Myron leaned closer to read the engraved escutcheons on the grips.

"Perhaps I wasn't altogether truthful," Darius answered, snapping the case shut and returning it to his valise before Myron could make out the inscription.

"You . . ." Myron sputtered, taking in the expensive pistols, the implication of their possession, ". . . you . . . you're a *ringer,* by God!"

"Not so loud, if you please. The walls here are rather thin, I fear."

Myron began to laugh. "I never would've thought . . ."

"No," Darius replied, "of course not." Pouring them another round from his flask, he added, "There *is* something you could do for me, Myron."

"Yes," the bewildered gambler answered, catching Darius's tone and becoming serious. "What would that be?"

"That you place whatever money you can afford on me, and if you don't mind, place my wager as well." He stuffed a wad of bills into Myron's front coat pocket.

"We *could* make a deal of money," Myron replied, rubbing his long hands together like a fly. "A great deal, indeed!" Then, in a more worried tone, "Providing I can find a bookie to take our bets. That may prove a challenge."

"There's always someone to take your money," Darius assured him. "Perhaps if you whispered into the ear of a particularly hungry oddsmaker of what you've learned here . . ." He left the rest unsaid. "Now . . . if you don't mind, I have to ready myself for the Midsummer Ball this evening."

"You've been invited to the ball?" Myron stammered. "I've lived here for years now and never managed to snag an invitation. You are a wonder, sir!"

Laughing, Darius replied, "It seems that this year no ball will be complete without its mysterious European assassin."

Taking a brush from the dresser, he proceeded to clean the dust from the only coat he owned.

Watching the young ladies of Natchez glide through their graceful, complicated steps reminded Darius of how long it had been since he last attended such a genteel gathering.

Sipping from a crystal cup of rum punch, he reflected on those long-ago days when his world of privilege had been a thing taken for granted. It had only asked of him that he take his place each day; that he follow the prescribed steps, much like the young women he was watching. He had found himself unable to do so. There was inside him a difference. He could not think why it should be so, but neither could he resist its power. In time, despite his best efforts to disguise it, he was exposed and cast out.

Noticing some of the young ladies throwing glances at him as they spun round the ballroom, Darius raised his glass and smiled. Several tittered and whispered to their female friends as they swirled round the room. He was well aware that women did not find him attractive.

Darius observed the feminine spectacle before him like carnations of various colors drifting and spinning in the current of an invisible river. Though beautiful to behold, they failed to stir in him any passion. Rather, it was their male escorts that occasionally caught his eye and aroused his feelings—young men who, in his eyes, were every bit as beautiful as the women they squired round the dance floor . . . and far more forbidden.

A hubbub at the entrance to the ballroom put an end to Darius's reverie. Heads began to turn as the tall figure of Captain Horatio Noddy arrived for the dance. His handsome visage with its dark curls and mustache rose above the crowd.

Making his way through his admirers and well-wishers, Noddy stiffened upon seeing Darius. Taking up a cup of punch, he said, "I'm surprised to see you here, LeClair . . . if that really is your name." His entourage formed a semicircle behind their man, their ears pricked.

"I surprise myself sometimes." Darius smiled.

"Obviously the standards have been lowered to allow for foreign trash."

Noddy glanced to his followers for a reaction and was rewarded with sniggers from the young fops. He smiled then as well.

"It occurs to me, Captain," Darius replied, "that my invitation here betokens something altogether different from a lowering of standards. Rather it reveals a division in the ranks of your adoring public, sir—that there are some . . . perhaps many . . . who long to see your fall on the morrow."

Noddy's mouth fell open in disbelief at the brazenness of Darius's response.

"You goddamned rascal," he managed after a moment, thrusting a hand into his waistcoat.

Placing a restraining hand over Noddy's own, his second warned, "Captain . . . don't . . . Tomorrow will come soon enough."

"A hidden Derringer!" Darius exclaimed, a little louder than was necessary. "I'm surprised at you, Captain Noddy, that you should feel the need to go about secretly armed amongst your own people. Do you not feel safe?"

This time the titters arose from the gathering gentlemen and ladies of the ball attracted by the confrontation.

"How dare you, you . . . you prissy little bastard!" Noddy cried. "Do you call me a coward?"

The great room was now silent, the orchestra having ceased their play, the dancers like statues.

"Oh yes," Darius answered pleasantly, going all in. "Yes, I most certainly do—a damned . . . cowardly . . . murderer. I am not one of your farmboy victims, Captain, if in fact you really are a captain. Tomorrow you shall meet your better upon the field of honor . . . and this time honor *will* be satisfied—your murders atoned for in blood."

Throwing his drink to the floor to the accompaniment of feminine screams, Noddy lunged for Darius, but his second restrained him once more. "You damned scoundrel!" Noddy screamed at the little gambler. "I don't have to tolerate this!"

"It seems that you already have," Darius rejoined, while using his only clean handkerchief to pat the drops of liquor that had spattered his clothing. "However, I am done with you for now."

Straightening up from his task, he added, "But I *will* wait on you tomorrow at dawn . . . make no mistake about that. Now . . . I suggest you retire before disgracing yourself further."

Carefully selecting a brimming cup from the table, Darius brought it to his lips without spilling a drop . . . making sure as he did so that his gloved pinkie was daintily lifted.

This was received by the enraptured crowd with a round of polite applause as Noddy glared at them all.

Excusing himself with a slight bow, Darius walked away to join a game of Black Widow in an adjoining study, and within minutes was playing his hand as if he hadn't a care in the world; no challenge to his life come dawn.

Sitting so as to face the French doors thrown open to the ballroom, he was gratified to see that Noddy, in defiance, had remained and kept returning to the refreshments table. Each time he stared about as if daring anyone to challenge his right to another drink.

No one did, and after a while the members of his party gathered round him in entreaty. As he staggered and cursed they managed to lead him away into the night and his distant bed.

Rising, Darius bid the other players goodnight and retired to the Natchez Queen Hotel. There, in the darkness of his room, clutching the rosary given to him by his mother upon his confirmation, he prayed as he had not prayed in many, many years.

It was still dark the next morning when Darius was awakened by a tapping at his door. He opened it in his nightshirt to find Myron Gill awaiting him with a cup of chicory coffee and a beignet.

"With the compliments of management," he murmured while holding out the offerings.

"Breakfast for the condemned man . . . ?" Darius asked with a smile, taking the tray. "Do come in, Myron, and thank you." Sitting on the edge of his rumpled bed, he took a small bite of the one and a sip of the other. "Wonderful," he said around a mouthful of pastry.

"I've placed the money," Myron assured him. "The odds against us are rather phenomenal, as you might imagine."

"I should hope so," Darius replied.

"Seeing as how you are laying your life on the line for these potential riches, I guess the least I can do is offer to accompany you as your second—presuming you don't have one." Myron couldn't mask his apprehension at making such a bold offer, his long, pale face assuming an even more alarming pallor.

"That is kind of you, my new friend," Darius assured him, "but I think it best you stay out of Noddy's crosshairs, just in case things go badly."

Myron nodded a little too readily, then hastened to ask, "But who will act your second?"

"That was arranged with his man yesterday—the good captain, knowing me to be a stranger in these parts, has been kind enough to supply one."

"He what . . . ?" Myron blurted out, his face a mask of consternation. "You'll be relying on those intent on doing you harm, Darius! They are Noddy's creatures!" He took a breath, adding in a tone of relief, "At least you are supplied with your own weapon."

Darius appeared puzzled for a moment, then exclaimed, "Oh . . . those," nodding at the valise containing the dueling pistols. "Yes . . .

well . . . you see, I told Noddy's second that I would use whatever pistol they had on hand—the damn things are so tedious to clean afterward, and one gun is as good as the next, really . . ." He let the rest of the sentence hang in the air between them.

"I had not taken you for a madman until now," Myron replied. "I fear my few dollars have been wasted."

"I do hope that you're wrong, my friend, as I will pay a significantly higher price than you."

Brushing crumbs from the front of his nightshirt, Darius added, "I really should get dressed now, Myron. Will you cross over with me this morning?"

"Of course," Myron replied in a mournful tone. "Though I must say, I don't like your phrasing."

Closing the door softly behind him, Myron took a shaky pull from his flask, then went down to the lobby to await his reckless companion.

The sun rose on a tableau not unlike that over which it had risen two days before—the combatants stripped of their coats and hatless, a drunken assortment of dandies, gamblers, and barflies in attendance, Myron amongst them. On this occasion, however, he had carefully brushed the beaver fur of his well-worn top hat in deference to his brave, if foolish, friend.

Seeing that companion squared off against the tall, imposing Captain Noddy only served to renew his earlier apprehensions, as his champion appeared so diminished in his presence. The small, pudgy Darius, he thought, had more the appearance of a schoolmaster or scholar than a duelist as he squinted up at his deadly opponent. A dark lock of his greasy hair had fallen across one eye, and as Myron watched, Darius carefully secured the errant strand behind an ear, smoothing it with an almost feminine gesture. Several in the crowd tittered and made crude remarks concerning the manliness of Myron's new friend.

"Dear Lord . . ." he muttered.

With the rising of the sun the humidity thickened like gumbo, conjuring a mist from the surrounding river. Tendrils of it drifted across the shifting sandbar like ghosts of the recently slain.

As Myron looked on, the seconds presented Darius and Noddy with their weapons. Darius removed his from its case and held it awkwardly, as if it were too heavy for his grip. Noddy retrieved his own pistol without a glance and grasped it with a confidence born of long familiarity.

"Are your weapons met with your satisfaction?" the retired but much in demand senator called out.

"Yes," Captain Noddy answered promptly, but with hoarseness.

Darius continued to allow the pistol to dangle in his grasp without answering. After a moment he brought it up to his ear and gave it a little shake, as if he were straining to hear something within.

"Mr. LeClair?" the senator prompted.

"I wasn't aware the pistol would be brought to me loaded," Darius commented with a slight smile. "Is that the custom in these parts?"

This remark managed to confound the retired people's representative into silence, while causing a good deal of discussion amongst the gathered witnesses.

"What are you implying?" Noddy growled. "Do you think I would allow any tampering?"

Still smiling, Darius replied, "Of course not . . . surely you are above such flummery . . . and perhaps even incapable of plotting something so insidious as to squib the load of the pistol you were kind enough to supply me."

The crowd understood that a squib load was a skimping of sufficient gunpowder in order to create a misfire, and the murmur from them rose accordingly.

Noddy, hungover from the previous evening's ball, seemed to be turning Darius's words round in his clotted thoughts, attempting to define the insult hidden within.

"What are you saying?" was all he could manage.

"Just that, considering your current unfortunate disposition, perhaps someone concerned for your welfare might have acted on your behalf."

"How dare you, sir!" both seconds cried in unison, apprehending the charge could be leveled at either of them, they being Noddy partisans. "I will have—"

"Shut up!" their master commanded, and both men went silent. Still wrestling with Darius's line of reasoning, Noddy glared at the little man. "What do you mean by my 'unfortunate disposition'?" he enunciated.

"Why, my dear fellow," Darius began, throwing open his arms, the questionable gun wobbling about in his loose grasp. Several onlookers backed further away from the erratic muzzle of the firearm. "You're in a state! You've behaved heroically in spite of it, for which I commend you, but many of us witnessed you disgorging your previous evening's meal and refreshments upon arrival this morning. It has happened to the best of us—a night of dance and drink . . . perhaps a few too many, but understandable. Nerves, Captain, nerves! There's absolutely nothing worse than imbibing too much in order to soothe them. It never works!"

The sun, having risen higher over the sandbar, poured down its hellish heat like a molten god. Myron, and the rest, could see the truth of Darius's observations in the slight swaying that Noddy displayed, a tremor from time to time in the hand holding the pistol. The referee, the doctor, and the seconds, being closer still, could also discern his bloodshot eyes, the nervous licking of his chapped lips.

"I suggest," Darius continued, "that given your current condition, you be allowed to withdraw from the field if you so wish . . . honor intact."

The murmur from the crowd rose as the enormity of the insinuation sank into their collective consciousness—not only was their champion being labeled a drunk, but also a coward! None had ever experienced a duel in which the insults continued right up to the moment of truth. It was incredible and without precedent! A man could, in theory, die for any of the several slurs made by Darius, but in fact could only die once, which seemed unjust to many on the sandbar.

"Dear Lord," Myron repeated, stunned as well by the audacity of his boon companion.

"Until . . ." Darius held his free hand up to quieten the chatter, "until, that is, you have returned to yourself, Captain, and are once more a worthy opponent!"

"Your answer, sir," the senator intoned, as if he were overseeing a congressional debate.

"Goddamn you!" Noddy cried, switching his grip on his pistol and raising it above his head to club Darius. "I cannot bear another moment of this!"

"Stop, sir!" the senator demanded, having produced his own pistol in the proper manner, muzzle pointing at the potential recipient of its ball. "There will be no brawling under my watch!"

Lowering his weapon, Noddy complained, "It's insufferable . . . insufferable, I tell you!" He appeared to be near tears.

"Your answer, sir," the senator repeated.

"No . . ." Noddy replied, his whole demeanor one of distraction and anxiety, then again, "No."

Appearing unfazed by his opponent's disreputable behavior, Darius stated, "Very well, then . . . if you insist."

The mob, having hushed during this brief exchange, became instantly reanimated at its conclusion. The duel was on once more.

"However," Darius intoned, quieting the crowd yet again, "I wonder—since you have been good enough to supply me with both a gun and a second—whether we might exchange pistols? I only ask in order to satisfy any doubts that might exist following the outcome of this affair."

"You venomous little troll," Noddy spat, looking pale and sweat-soaked beneath the climbing sun. "You satanic imp . . ."

"Captain . . ." Darius's second began, then went silent.

Darius's eyes cut from the captain to the second, then back again.

Noddy's hand hovered over the proffered weapon and began to tremble.

"Is there a problem?" Darius asked.

Goaded, Noddy seized the pistol while thrusting his own at Darius. "Take it . . . take the damned thing!"

"Are we finally able to proceed?" the perspiring senator asked, both puzzled and alarmed at the transaction. Had Noddy refused the exchange, then under the circumstances, he would have ordered a close examination of the pistol. But since he did not, he could not do so without impugning the captain's honor.

"Seconds, step away!" he commanded. "Combatants, cock your pistols and stand back to back, weapons raised. When I begin the count, you will take a step with each number called out. When I cease the count at ten, you will stop and remain stationary until I command you to turn. Afterward I will instruct you both to take aim. Finally I will give the ultimate order to fire! Should either of you do so before that order is given, I will shoot you where you stand. Is all this firmly understood?"

Having assumed their back-to-back positions, both men nodded their comprehension.

"One!" the count began.

As the two men commenced their fateful march, it was evident to all that something was decidedly wrong with the avenger of Natchez. His gait, usually so decisive and measured, had become a hesitant, and increasingly mincing, shuffle. A pall of dread had fallen over him, draining the captain's handsome features of blood and setting the hand holding the pistol to spasm like a divining rod.

His diminutive opponent, however, appeared to have grown in stature during the runup to the duel — the plump and infuriating Darius now infused with a deadly dignity, a certitude that bode ill for the stricken Noddy.

"Ten," the senator completed the count.

Both men halted.

"Turn!"

Darius did so with smooth alacrity.

Noddy, with slumping shoulders, his booted feet dragging through the sand, followed suit.

"Aim . . ."

The dejected-looking captain's arm shot out and locked at the elbow. Darius did likewise.

Before the following and final command could be uttered, the explosion from the captain's gun sent his ball flying as a corresponding cry of outrage went up from the crowd.

Cognizant of his duty, the senator's own pistol rose to point at Noddy, and he cocked his piece preparatory to its execution.

"Hold!" a strong voice rang out. "The shot is mine!"

Almost forgotten in the shock of Noddy's violation, Darius still stood, his pistol still leveled at the now cowering Noddy. Behind Darius a large chunk of bark had been sheared away from a pine tree, leaving a raw white wound.

Wreathed in an acrid cloud of gun smoke, Noddy sank to his knees in the soft sand, letting go the damning pistol and holding up his left hand in front of his face, whether in fear or shame was anyone's guess.

"Don't," he moaned. "Please . . . don't."

"The right is yours, sir," the senator informed Darius, uncocking his own piece.

"Dear God . . . have mercy," Noddy pleaded, tears now streaming down his pale cheeks and soaking his drooping mustache.

Darius lowered his aim in acknowledgment of his opponent's new and abject posture, continuing to keep him within the cross-hairs, a finger movement away from death.

"You have killed twelve young men," Darius began, a heat present in his voice that had been wholly absent before. "All of them lamb to slaughter, all without experience, aptitude, or friends; each and every one dying for the sole purpose of stoking your vanity. Honor never entered into it—you murdered them all."

Darius took a deep, shuddering breath, then went on. "One of those young men . . . you damned butcher . . . was my brother!"

"I didn't know," Noddy sobbed. "Mercy . . . mercy," he pleaded.

"Shall I show mercy?" Darius called out to the spectators.

"No . . . Hell, no . . . Pull the trigger . . . Shoot!" they shouted back, enraged at their hero.

"It seems your former friends and countrymen wish me to kill you," Darius advised Noddy.

"Please . . . please . . . don't . . ."

"And I shall oblige them, you low dog."

The shot rang out, echoing across the river.

But when the smoke cleared it was plain to all that Darius had thrown wide his shot—Noddy still lived.

"Now you know how *they* felt—the terror . . . the loneliness," Darius informed the defeated Noddy. "*You,* I sentence to life. Rise and join your fellow citizens . . . if they'll have you."

Tossing his weapon into the sand in front of his opponent, Darius marched off to the boats, ignoring the congratulations of the thoroughly entertained bystanders. Myron hurried after him, and as they were rowed across the river once more, Darius studied the sluggish current in silence while squeezing his hands together to stop the tremors that had seized them.

Emptying the pockets of both his coat and waistcoat, Myron tossed wads of cash onto the narrow bed of Room 4.

"We've made a packet, Darius! By God, we've made a packet!" he cried.

"Everyone paid their debts, did they?" Darius asked, pouring them both a whiskey, his hands once more his own.

"They did so with enthusiasm—they feared the ire of the Continental duelist!"

"Is that so?" Darius responded with a slight smile, handing a brimming glass to his gambling partner, noting how flushed Myron's normally pallid cheeks had become. "What a passel of fools."

Myron raised his glass to Darius and they both took a sip of the liquor. Smacking his lips with relish, Myron asked, "Fools, Darius? What do you mean?"

"I've never in my life set foot in Europe," Darius replied. "Your local newspaperman has a vivid imagination and, thankfully, few scruples—I paid him well to conjure up that story."

Myron's wide mouth fell open a bit. "You paid him? Why?"

"Nor am I a duelist," Darius went on, ignoring the question. "Until today I'd never fired a weapon in anger, and I'm certainly no marksman. If I were, Horatio Noddy would be dead this moment instead of sneaking out of town with his tail between his legs." He refilled their glasses and sat down. "Did you see how wide of the mark my shot went? I couldn't have hit an elephant at that distance."

Still standing, the newly charged glass forgotten in his hand, Myron struggled to assimilate his partner's words. "What . . . you . . ." he sputtered, ". . . but . . . but . . . the *pistols!* What of your fine set of dueling pistols? I saw them!"

"Oh yes . . ." Darius squirmed a bit in the room's only chair. "*Those.* I came into their possession as a result of a poker game in Savannah. Handsome pieces, aren't they?" Grasping Myron's wrist, he said, "I do hope you can forgive my deceiving you, my friend. Your good faith . . . *and* wagers . . . went a long way toward enhancing my little fiction."

Remembering his glass, Myron took a moment to down its contents. "My God," he said, settling himself onto the edge of Darius's bed by degrees, "you might have been killed! You risked your life knowing full well that you stood no chance. I just don't understand."

"Oh, but I did, Myron . . . however slim, I stood a chance. That's our profession, isn't it? It was only a matter of sizing up my opponent, assessing his weaknesses. From all that I observed and you had told me of Noddy, I could see that his deadly career was based not on courage but careful selection. He trolled for victims, not challenges, selecting only the very young, who, by virtue of their age, were both inexperienced and volatile.

"Further, they had traveled alone and therefore had no seconds on hand. As no one in this virtuous town wished to act against the fearsome Captain Noddy, the only second that could be found for the stranger was one of Noddy's own entourage, who no doubt regaled him with tales of the captain's deadly prowess."

Catching his drift, Myron broke in, "And they squibbed the load of the youngsters' pistols, just as you insinuated today, insuring the captain's safety against a lucky shot!"

With a slight shrug, Darius answered, "Well . . . that's a possibility, perhaps. However, they did not do so to my pistol this morning. The one I exchanged with Captain Noddy—it was fully charged—I heard the ball whistle past my ear at a terrifying velocity. Still," he continued, "it did give the mighty captain pause when I suggested one of his people might have been secretly aiding his triumphs all along by doing so."

"Yes!" Myron exclaimed. "I saw it in his face! Clearly he dreaded exchanging weapons with you. You devil! You planted yet another terrible seed of doubt there!"

"And, not to put too fine a point upon it," Darius concluded, "it was Noddy's *thirteenth* duel—the unlucky number was his, not mine."

Myron's expression grew somber. "When all is said and done, Darius, you exhibited terrific courage today, or incomprehensible foolhardiness, I'm not sure which. But at the end of it all, you have achieved some measure of justice for your slain brother—Noddy is ruined! His new reputation will follow him like the stench of the grave."

Darius's expression softened. "As to that," he began in a quiet, tired voice, his eyes moistening, "I was not altogether truthful either. You see, the young man I sought to avenge was not, in fact . . . my brother. Rather, he was someone . . . a dear friend . . . that I loved as if he were . . . well . . . it's difficult to explain. Perhaps it will suffice to say that he was dear enough for me to die for. Do you understand?"

Though he found himself nodding in the affirmative, Myron was not entirely sure that he did. "A dear friend . . ." he murmured in reply.

"Yes," Darius agreed. "Dear enough for me to risk anything . . . anything at all."

Security

FROM *Odd Partners*

I

March 13

"The meeting's finished?"

"It is," Bil Sheering said into his mobile. He was sitting in his rental car, your basic Ford, though with a variation: he'd fried out the GPS so he couldn't be tracked.

"And you're happy with the pro?"

"I am," Bil said. The man on the other end of the line was Victor Brown, but there was no way in hell either of these two would utter their names aloud, despite the encryption. "We talked for close to a half hour. We're good."

"The payment terms acceptable?"

"Hundred thousand now, one-fifty when it's done. Hold on."

A customer walked out of Earl's and headed to a dinged and dusty pickup, not glancing Bil's way. The Silverado fired up and scattered gravel as it bounded onto the highway.

Another scan of the parking lot, crowded with trucks and cars but empty of people. The club, billed as an "exotic dance emporium," had been a good choice for the meeting. The clientele tended to focus on the stage, not on serious, furtive discussions going on in a booth in the back.

Another customer left, though he too turned away from Bil and vanished into the shadows.

Bil, of medium build, was in his forties, with trim brown hair

and a tanned complexion from hunting and fishing, mostly in a
down-and-dirty part of West Virginia. "Bil" had nothing to do with
"William." It was a nickname that originated from where he was
stationed in the service, near Biloxi, Mississippi. The moniker was
only a problem when he wrote it down, B-I-L, and people wondered
where the other L went.

"Just checking the lot," Bil said. "Clear now."

Victor: "So the pro's on board. That was the most important
thing. What're the next steps?"

"The occurrence will be on May six. That's two months for
training, picking the equipment. A vehicle that'll be helpful. Lotta
homework."

They were deep into euphemism. What *equipment* meant was rifle and ammunition. What *vehicle* meant was a car that would be
impossible to trace. And *occurrence* was a laughably tame name for
what would happen on that date.

There was silence for a moment. Victor broke it by asking, "You
are having doubts?" A moment later the man's slick voice continued, "You can back out, you want. But we take it a few steps further,
we can't."

But Bil hadn't been hesitating because of concerns; he'd just
been scanning the parking lot for prying eyes again. All was good.
He said firmly, "No doubts at all."

Victor muttered, "I'm just saying we're looking at a lotta shit and
a really big fan."

"This is what I do, my friend. The plan stands. We take this son
of a bitch out."

"Good, glad you feel that way. Just exercise extreme caution."

Bil hardly needed the warning; extreme caution was pretty
much the order of the day when the son of a bitch you were being
paid to take out was a candidate for president of the United States.

II

May 6

The Gun Shack was on Route 57, just outside Haleyville.

The owner of the well-worn establishment was a big man, tall
and ruddy, plump with fat rolls, and he wore a .45 Glock 30 on his

hip. He'd never been robbed, not in twenty-one years, but he was fully prepared—and half hoping—for the attempt.

Now, at 9:10 a.m., the shop was empty and the owner was having a second breakfast of coffee and a bear claw, enjoying the almond flavor almost as much as he enjoyed the aroma of Hoppe's Gun Cleaner and Pledge polish from the rifle stocks. He grabbed the remote and clicked on ESPN. Later in the day, when customers were present, hunting shows would be on. Which, he believed, goaded them into buying more ammunition than they ordinarily would have.

The door opened, setting off a chime, and the owner looked up to see a man enter. He checked to see if the fellow was armed—no open carry was allowed in the store, and concealed weapons had to stay concealed. But it was clear the guy wasn't carrying.

The man wasn't big, but his shaved head, bushy mustache—in a horseshoe shape, out of the Vietnam War era—and emotionless face made the owner wary. He wore camouflaged hunting gear—green and black—which was odd, since no game was in season at the moment.

The man looked around and then walked slowly to the counter behind which the owner stood. Unlike most patrons, he ignored the well-lit display case of dozens of beckoning sinister and shiny handguns. There wasn't a man in the world that came in here who didn't glance down with interest and admiration at a collection of firepower like this. Say a few words about the Sig, ask about the Desert Eagle.

Not this guy.

The owner's hand dropped to his side, where his pistol was.

The customer's eyes dropped too. Fast. He'd noted the gesture and wasn't the least bit intimidated. He looked back at the owner, who looked away, angry with himself for doing so.

"I called yesterday. You have Lapua rounds." An eerie monotone.

The owner hadn't taken the call. Maybe it'd been Stony.

"Yeah, we've got 'em."

"I'll take two boxes of twenty. Three-three-eights."

Hm. Big sale for ammo. They were expensive, top of the line. The owner walked to the far end of the shelves and retrieved the heavy boxes. The .338 Lapua rounds weren't the largest-caliber rifle bullets, but they were among the most powerful. The load of powder in the long casing could propel the slug accurately for a mile. People shooting rifles loaded with Lapuas for the first time were often unprepared for the punishing recoil and sometimes ended up with a "scope eye" bruise on their foreheads from the telescopic sight, a rite of passage among young soldiers.

Hunters tended not to shoot Lapuas—because they would blow most game to pieces. The highest-level competitive marksmen might fire them. But the main use was military; Lapua rounds were the bullet of choice for snipers. The owner believed the longest recorded sniper kill in history—more than a mile and a half—had been with a Lapua.

As he rang up the purchase the owner asked, "What's your rifle?" Lapuas are a type of bullet; they can be fired from a number of rifles.

"Couple different," he said.

"You compete?"

The man didn't answer. He looked at the register screen and handed over a prepaid debit card, the kind you buy at Walmart or Target.

The owner rang up the sale and handed the card back. "I never fired one. Hell of a kick, I hear."

Without a word, the sullen man grabbed his purchase and walked out.

Well, good day to you, too, buddy. The owner looked after the customer, who turned to the right outside the store, disappearing into the parking lot.

Funny, the owner thought. Why hadn't he parked in front of the gun shop, where seven empty spaces beckoned? There'd be no reason to park to the right, in front of Ames Drugs, which'd closed two years ago.

Odd duck . . .

But then he forgot about the guy, noting that a rerun of a recent Brewers game was on the dusty TV. He waddled to a stool, sat down, and chewed more of the pastry as he silently cheered a team that he knew was going to lose, five to zip, in an hour and a half.

Secret Service Special Agent Art Tomson eyed the entrance to the Pittstown Convention Center.

He stood, in his typical ramrod posture, beside his black Suburban SUV and scanned the expansive entryway of the massive building, which had been constructed in the 1980s. The trim man, of pale skin, wore a gray suit and white shirt with a dark blue tie (which looked normal, but the portion behind the collar was cut in half and sewn together with a single piece of thread, so that if an attacker grabbed it in a fight, the tie would break away).

Tomson took in the structure once more. It had been swept earlier and only authorized personnel were present, but the place was so huge and featured so many entrances that it would be a security challenge throughout the nine and a half hours Searcher would be at the center for the press conference and rally. You could never scan a national special security event too much.

Adding to the challenge was the matter that Searcher—former governor Paul Ebbett—was a minor candidate at this point, so the personal protection detail guarding him was relatively small. That would change, however, given his increasing groundswell of support. He was pulling ahead of the other three candidates in the primary contest. Tomson believed that the flamboyant, blunt, tell-it-like-it-is politician would in fact become the party's nominee. When that happened, a full detail would be assigned to nest around him. But until then Tomson would make do with his own federal staff of eight, supported by a number of officers from local law enforcement, as well as private security guards at the venues where Ebbett was speaking. In any case, whether there was a handful of men and women under him or scores, Tomson's level of vigilance never flagged. In the eighteen years he'd been with the Secret Service, now part of Homeland Security, not a single person he'd been assigned to protect had been killed or injured.

He tilted his head as he touched his earpiece and listened to a transmission. There was a belief that agents did this, the touching, which happened frequently, to activate the switch. Nope. The damn things—forever uncomfortable—just kept coming loose.

The message was that Searcher and his three SUVs had left the airport and were ten minutes away.

The candidate had just started to receive Secret Service protection, having only recently met the criteria for a security detail established by Homeland, Congress, and other government agencies. Among these standards were competing in primaries in at least ten states, running for a party that has garnered at least 10 percent of the popular vote, raising or committing at least $10 million in campaign funds, and, of course, publicly declaring your candidacy.

Besides the normal standards, one of the more significant factors in assigning Ebbett a detail was the reality that the man's brash statements and if-elected promises had made him extremely unpopular among certain groups. Social media was flooded with vicious verbal attacks and cruel comments, and the Secret Service had already responded to three assassination threats. None had turned out to be more than bluster. One woman had called for Ebbett to be drawn and quartered, apparently thinking that the phrase referred to a voodoo curse in which the governor's likeness would be sketched on a sheet of paper, which was then cut into four pieces, not to an actual form of execution, and a very unpleasant one at that. Still, Tomson and his team had to take these threats, and the ones that he knew would be forthcoming, seriously. Adding to their burden was intel from the CIA that, more than any other primary candidate in history, Ebbett might be a target of foreign operatives, due to his firm stance against military buildups by countries in Europe and Asia.

Another visual sweep of the convention center, outside of which both protesters and supporters were already queuing. Attendance would be huge; Ebbett's campaign committee had booked large venues for his events months ago, optimistically—and correctly—thinking that he would draw increasingly large crowds.

He glanced across the broad street, the lanes closed to handle the foot traffic. He noted his second in command, Don Ivers, close to the rope, surveying those present. Most of the men and women and a few youngsters had posters supporting the candidate, though there were plenty of protesters as well. Ivers and a half-dozen local cops, trained in event security, would not be looking the protesters over very closely, though. The true threats came from the quiet ones, without placards or banners or hats decorated with the candidate's name or slogans. These folks would have all passed through metal detectors, but given the long lead time for the event, it would have been possible for somebody to hide a weapon inside the security perimeter—under a planter or even within a wall—and to access it now.

Tomson much preferred rallies to be announced at the last minute, but of course that meant lower attendance. And for most candidates—and especially fiery Ebbett—that was not an option.

"Agent Tomson."

He turned to see a woman in her thirties wearing the dark blue uniform of the Pittstown Convention Center security staff. Kim Morton was slim but athletic. Her blond hair was pulled back in a tight bun, like that favored by policewomen and ballet dancers. Her face was pretty but severe. She wore no makeup or jewelry.

Tomson was unique among his fellow Secret Service agents; he believed in "partnering up" with a local officer or security guard at the venue where those under his protection would be appearing. No matter how much research the Secret Service detail did, it was best to have somebody on board who knew the territory personally. When he'd briefed the local team about how the rally would go, he'd asked if there were any issues about the convention center they should know about. Most of the guards and municipal police hemmed and hawed. But Morton had raised her hand and, when he called on her, pointed out there were three doors with locks that might easily be breached—adding that she'd been after management for weeks to fix them.

When he described the emergency escape route they would take in the event of an assassination attempt, she'd said to make sure that there hadn't been a delivery of cleaning supplies, because the workers tended to leave the cartons blocking that corridor rather than put them away immediately.

Then she'd furrowed her brow and said, "Come to think of it, those cartons—they're pretty big. There might be a way somebody, you know, an assassin, could hide in one. Kinda far-fetched, but you asked."

"I did," he'd said. "Anything else?"

"Yes, sir. If you have to get out fast, be careful on the curve on the back exit ramp that leads to the highway if it's raining. Was an oil spill two years ago and nobody's been able to clean it up proper."

Tomson had known then that he had his local partner, as curious as the pairing seemed.

Morton now approached and said, "Everything's secure at the west entrance. Your two men in place and three state police."

Tomson had known this, but the key word in personal protection is *redundancy*.

He told her that the entourage would soon arrive. Her blue eyes scanned the crowd. Her hand absently dropped to her pepper spray, as if to make sure she knew where it was. That and walkie-talkies were the guards' only equipment. No guns. That was an immutable rule for private security.

Then, flashing lights, blue and red and white, and the black Suburban SUVs sped up to the front entrance.

He and Morton, flanked by two city police officers, walked toward the vehicles, from which six Secret Service agents were disembarking, along with the candidate. Paul Ebbett was six feet tall but seemed larger, thanks to his broad shoulders. (He'd played football at Indiana.) His hair was an impressive mane of salt-and-pepper. His suit was typical of what he invariably wore: dark gray. His shirt was light blue, and in a nod to his individuality, it was open at the neck. He never wore a tie and swore he wouldn't even don one at his inauguration.

Emerging from the last car was a tall, distinguished-looking African American, Tyler Quonn, Ebbett's chief of staff. Tomson knew he'd been the director of a powerful think tank in D.C. and was absolutely brilliant.

The candidate turned to the crowd and waved, as Tomson and the other agents, cops, and security guards scanned the crowd, windows, and rooftops. Tomson would have preferred that he walk directly into the convention hall, but he knew that wasn't the man's way; he was a self-proclaimed "man of the American people," and he plunged into crowds whenever he could, shaking hands, kissing cheeks, and tousling babies' hair.

Tomson was looking east when he felt Morton's firm hand on his elbow. He spun around. She said, "Man in front of the Subway. Tan raincoat. He was patting his pocket and just reached into it. Something about his eyes. He's anticipating."

In an instant he transmitted the description to Don Ivers, who was working that side of the street. The tall, bulky agent, a former Marine and state patrol officer, hurried up to the man and, taking his arms, led him quietly to the back of the crowd.

Tomson and Morton walked up to the candidate and the agent whispered, "May have an incident, sir. Could you go inside now?"

Ebbett hesitated, then he gave a final wave to the crowd and —infuriatingly slowly—headed into the convention center lobby.

A moment later Tomson heard in his headset: "Level four."

A nonlethal threat.

Ivers explained, "Two ripe tomatoes. He claimed he'd been shopping, but they were loose in his pocket—no bag. And a couple of people next to him said he'd been ranting against Searcher all morning. He's clean. No record. We're escorting him out of the area."

As they walked toward the elevator that would take them to the suites, Ebbett asked, "What was it?"

Tomson told him what had happened.

"You've got sharp eyes, Ms. Morton," he said, reading her name badge.

"Just thought something seemed funny about him."

He looked her over with a narrowed gaze. "Whatta you think, Artie? Should I appoint her head of the Justice Department after I'm elected?"

Morton blinked and Ebbett held a straight face for a moment, then broke into laughter.

It had taken Tomson a while to get used to the candidate's humor.

"Let's go to the suite," Ebbett said. He glanced at Tomson. "My tea upstairs?"

"It is, sir."

"Good."

The entourage headed for the elevator, Tomson and Morton checking out every shadow, every door, every window.

Ten miles from Pittstown, in a small suburb called Prescott, the skinny boy behind the counter of Anderson's Hardware was lost in a fantasy about Jennie Mathers, a cheerleader for the Daniel Webster High Tigers.

Jennie was thoughtfully wearing her tight-fitting uniform, orange and black, and was—

"PVC. Where is it?" The gruff voice brought the daydream to a halt.

The kid's narrow face, from which some tufts of silky hair grew in curious places, turned to the customer. He hadn't heard the man come in.

He blinked, looking at the shaved head, weird mustache, eyes like black lasers—if lasers could be black, which maybe they couldn't, but that was the thought that jumped into his head and wouldn't leave.

"PVC *pipe?*" the kid asked.

The man just stared.

Of course he meant PVC pipe. What else would he mean?

"Um, we don't have such a great, you know, selection. Home Depot's up the street." He nodded out the window.

The man continued staring, and the clerk took this to mean *If I'd wanted to go to Home Depot, I would've gone to Home Depot.*

The clerk pointed. "Over there."

The man turned and walked away. He strolled through the shelves for a while and then returned to the counter with a half-dozen six-foot-long pieces of three-quarter-inch pipe. He laid them on the counter.

The clerk said, "You want fittings too? And cement?"

He'd need those to join the pipes together or mount them to existing ones.

But the man didn't answer. He squinted behind the clerk. "That too." Pointing at a toolbox.

The kid handed it to him.

"That's a good one. It's got two little tray thingies you can put screws and bolts in. Washers too. Look inside."

The man didn't look inside. He dug into his pocket and pulled out a debit card.

Hitting the keys on the register, the boy said, "That'll be thirty-two eighty." He didn't add, as he was supposed to, "Do you want to contribute a dollar to the Have a Heart children's fund?"

He had a feeling that'd be a waste of time.

The hallway of the suite tower's penthouse floor was pretty nice.

During his advance work—to check out the security here—Art Tomson had learned that in an effort to draw the best entertainers and corporate CEOs for events here, the owners of the convention center had added a tower of upscale suites, where the performers, celebrities, and top corporate players would be treated like royalty. Why go to Madison or Milwaukee and sit in a stodgy greenroom when you could go to Pittstown and kick back in serious luxury?

Paul Ebbett was presently in the best of these, Suite A. ("When I'm back after November," he'd exclaimed with a sparkle in his eyes, "let's make sure they rename it the Presidential Suite.") It was 1,300 square feet, with four bedrooms, three baths, a living room, a dining room, a fair-to-middling kitchen, and a separate room and bathroom actually labeled MAID'S QUARTERS. The view of the city was panoramic, but that was taken on faith; the shutters and curtains were all closed, as they were in the entire row of suites, so snipers couldn't deduce which room Ebbett was in.

In lieu of the view, however, one could indulge in channel surfing on four massive TVs, ultra-high-def. Tomson was especially partial to TVs because when he got home — every two weeks or so — he and the wife and kids would pile onto a sofa and binge on the latest Disney movies and eat popcorn and corn dogs until they could eat no more.

Special Agent Art Tomson was a very different man at home.

Only the candidate was inside at the moment. Chief of Staff Quonn was on the convention center floor, testing microphones and soundboards and teleprompters, and Tomson and Morton now sat in the hallway outside the double doors to Suite A. Tomson looked up and down the corridor, whose walls were beige and whose carpet was rich gray. He noted that the agents at each of the stairway doors and the elevator looked attentive. They didn't appear armed, but each had an FN P90 submachine gun under his or her jacket, in addition to a sidearm and plenty of magazines. Although armed assaults were extremely rare, in the personal protection business you always planned for a gunfight at the O.K. Corral.

Kim Morton said, "Wanted to mention: acoustic tile's hung six inches below the concrete. Nobody can crawl through."

Tomson knew. He'd checked. He thanked her anyway and cocked his head once more as transmissions about security status at various locations came in.

All was clear.

He told this to Morton.

She said, "Guess we can relax for a bit." Eyeing him closely. "Except you don't, do you?"

"No."

"Never."

"No."

Silence eased in like an expected snow.

Morton broke it by asking, "You want some gum?"

Tomson didn't believe he'd chewed gum since he was in college.

She added, "Doublemint."

"No. Thank you."

"I stopped smoking four years and three months ago. I needed a habit. I'm like, 'Gum or meth? Gum or meth?'"

Tomson said nothing.

She opened the gum, unwrapped a piece, and slipped it into her mouth. "You ever wonder what the double mints were? Are there really two? They might use just one and tell us it's two. Who'd know?"

"Hm."

"You don't joke much in your line of work, do you?"

"I suppose we don't."

"Maybe I'll get you to smile."

"I smile. I just don't joke."

Morton said, "Haven't seen you smile yet."

"Haven't seen anything to smile about."

"The two-mint thing? That didn't cut it?"

"It was funny."

"You don't really think so."

Tomson paused. "No. It wasn't that funny."

"Almost got you to smile there."

Morton's phone hummed with a call. She grimaced.

Tomson was immediately attentive. Maybe one of the other security guards had seen something concerning.

She said into the phone, "If Maria tells you to go to bed, you go to bed. She's Mommy when Mommy's not there. She's a substitute mommy. Like the time Ms. Wilson got arrested for protesting, remember? When they pulled down the Robert E. Lee statue? And you had that substitute teacher? Well, that's Maria. Are we clear on that . . . ? Good, and I do *not* want to find the lizard out when I get home . . . No, it was not an accident. Lizards do not climb into purses of their own accord. Okay? Love you, Pumpkie. Put Sam on . . ."

Morton had a brief conversation with another son, presumably younger—her voice grew more singsongy.

She disconnected and noticed Tomson's eyes on her. "Iguana. Small one. In the babysitter's purse. I stopped them before they uploaded the video to YouTube. Maria's scream was impressive, man, oh, man. The boys would've had ten thousand hits easy. But you've got to draw the line somewhere. You have children, Agent Tomson?"

He hesitated. "Maybe we can go with first names at this point."

"Art. And I'm Kim. By the way, it meant a lot when I met you. You didn't hit the ground running with my first name. Lotta people do."

"The world's changing."

"Like molasses," she said. "So, Art. I'm looking at that ring on your finger. You have children? Unless that is a terrible, terrible question to ask, because they all wasted away with bad diseases."

Finally a smile.

"No diseases. Two. Boy and girl."

"They learned about lizard pranks yet?"

"They're a little young for that. And the only nonhuman in the household is a turtle."

"Don't let your guard down. Turtles can raise hell too. Just takes 'em a bit longer to do it."

More silence in the hall. But now the sort of silence that's a comfort.

Inside the suite he could hear Ebbett had turned on the news —every set, it seemed. The candidate was obsessed with the media and watched everything, right and left and in between. He took voluminous notes, often without looking down from the screen at his pad of paper.

Morton nodded to the door and said, "He's quite a story, isn't he?"

"Story?"

"His road to the White House. Reinventing himself. He went through that bad patch, the drinking and the women. His wife leaving him. But then he turned it around."

Ebbett had indeed. He'd done rehab, gotten back together with his wife. He'd been frank and apologetic about his transgressions and he'd had successful campaigns for state representative and then governor. He'd burst onto the presidential scene last year.

Morton said, "I heard he came up with that campaign slogan himself: 'America. Making a Great Country Greater.' I like that, don't you? I know his positions're a little different and he's got kind of a mouth on him. Blunt, you know what I'm saying? But I'll tell you, I'm voting for him."

Tomson said nothing.

"Hm, did I just cross a line?"

"The thing is, in protection detail we don't express any opinion about the people we look after. Good, bad, politics, personal lives. Democrats or Republicans, it's irrelevant."

She was nodding. "I get it. Keeps you focused. Nothing ex— what's the word? Extraneous?"

"That's right."

"Extraneous . . . I help the boys with their homework some. I'm the go-to girl for math, but for English and vocabulary? Forget it."

He asked, "You always been in security?"

"No," she answered. A smile blossomed, softening her face. She was really quite pretty, high cheekbones, upturned nose, clear complexion. "I always wanted to be a cop. Can't tell you why. Maybe from a TV show I saw when I was a kid. *Walker, Texas Ranger. Law & Order. NYPD Blue.* But that didn't work out. This's the next best thing."

She sounded wistful.

"You could still join up, go to the state police or city academy. You're young."

Her eyes rolled. "And I thought you agents had to be sooooo observant."

Another smile appeared.

"Anyway, can't afford to take the time off. Single-mom thing."

Tomson saw Don Ivers approaching quickly. Tomson and the younger agent had worked together for about five years; he knew instantly there was a problem. Noting the man's expression, Kim Morton tensed too.

"What?" Tomson asked.

"We've got word from CAD. Possible threat triad."

Tomson explained to Morton, "Our Central Analytics Division. You know, data miners. Supercomputers analyze public and law enforcement information and algorithms to spot potential risks."

She nodded. "Computer game stuff."

"Pretty much, that's right."

Ivers continued, "About an hour ago there was an anonymous call about a white male in a red Toyota sedan. Plate was covered with mud. The driver was standing outside the car and making a cell-phone call. The citizen who called 911 heard this guy mention *Ebbett* and *rally*. That's all he could hear. But he saw there was a long gun in the backseat. It was outside a strip mall in Avery."

"About five miles south of here," Morton said.

Ivers continued, "That put all red Toyota sedans on a watch list."

"The caller say anything more about the driver?"

"He was in combat or camo, medium build, bald with an old-timey mustache. Droopy, like gunslingers wore. The computers started to scan every CCTV—public, and the private ones that make their data available to law enforcement. There were two hits on the target vehicles. At nine this morning one was spotted in a parking lot near a gun shop in Haleyville."

Tomson turned to Morton, his eyebrow raised.

She said, "*Twenty* miles south."

"He parked in front of a closed-up drugstore in a strip mall," Ivers said. "The closest active store was the gun shop. We got their security video. The first customer of the day was a bald white male, thirties to forties, with a drooping mustache." Ivers sighed. "He bought forty .338 Lapua rounds. Prepaid debit card he paid cash for. Owner said he was a scary guy."

"Brother," Tomson said, sighing. He added to Morton, "Lapuas are high-powered sniper rounds."

"And he didn't park in front of the shop," she said, "to avoid the camera in the gun shop."

"Probably."

Ivers added, "Then another hit. Two hours ago the Toyota was videoed parked near—but not in front of, again—a hardware store in Prescott, twelve miles away. He bought a toolbox and six three-quarter-inch PVC pipes. No CCTV inside, but the clerk's description was the same as the others. Same debit card as before."

"Where'd he buy the card?" Tomson asked.

"A Target in Omaha a month ago."

"Been planning this for a while."

Morton grimaced. "Those towns? That's a straight line to where we are now: Haleyville, Prescott, Avery."

Tomson asked, "Status of vehicle?"

"Nothing since then. He's taking his time, sticking to back roads."

"What would he want the pipes for?" Morton asked. "To make bombs?"

Tomson said, "Probably not. That's pretty thin. You couldn't get much explosive in them."

"A tripod for his gun?" she suggested.

An interesting idea. But when he considered it, that didn't seem likely. "Doubt it. Anybody with a gun that fires Lapua rounds would have professional accessories to go along with it. And in an urban shooting situation like here, he could just use a windowsill or box to support the weapon for a distance shot."

Tomson said, "Put out the info on the wire. Let's advise Searcher."

He knocked on the suite door. "Sir. It's Art."

A voice commanded, "Come on in."

The candidate was jotting notes on a yellow pad. Presumably for his speech that night. He'd do this until the last moment. A transcriptionist was on staff, and she would pound the keys of the computer attached to the teleprompter until just before the candidate took the stage. Open on the table was Barbara Tuchman's brilliant—and disturbing—book about the First World War, *The Guns of August*. One of the first items on Ebbett's agenda as president would be to revitalize the U.S. military—"make a great army even greater!"—and stand up to foreign aggression.

Tomson said, "Sir, we've received some information about a possible threat." He explained what they'd discovered.

The candidate took the details without any show of emotion. "Credible?"

"It's not hunting season, but he could be a competitive marksman, buying those rounds for the range. The camo? A lot of men wear it as everyday clothing. But the license plate was obscured. And he's headed this way. I'm inclined to take it seriously."

The candidate leaned back and sipped his iced tea. After he'd reinvented himself, this was the strongest thing he imbibed.

"Well, well, well . . . hm. And what do you say, Ms. Morton?"

"Me? Oh, I'm just a girl who spots tomato-throwers. These men know all the fancy stuff."

"But what's your gut tell you?"

She cocked her head. "My gut tells me that with any other candidate this'd probably be a bunch of coincidences. But you're not any other candidate. You speak your mind and tell the truth and some people don't like that—or what you have planned when you take office. I'd say take it seriously."

"She's good, Artie." A smile crinkled his face. "And I like that she said *when* I take office. Okay. We'll assume it's a credible threat. What do we do?"

"Move the press conference inside," Tomson said. "The location's been in the news and a shooter would know that's where you'll be."

The conference, planned for a half hour before the candidate's speech at the rally, was to be held in an open-air plaza connected to the convention center. The candidate had wanted to hold it there because clearly visible from the podium was a factory that had gone

out of business after losing jobs overseas. Ebbett was going to point
to the dilapidated building and talk about his criticism of the present administration's economic policies.

Tomson had never been in favor of the plaza; it was a real security challenge, being so open. The choice had been Tyler Quonn's,
but Ebbett had liked it immediately. Now, though, he reluctantly
acquiesced to moving the conference inside. "But I'm not changing one thing about the rally tonight."

"No need, sir; the center itself is completely secure."

"The press'll probably like it better anyway," Ebbett conceded.
"Not the best weather to be sitting outside, listening to me spout off
—as brilliant as my bon mots are."

Tomson noticed that while Kim Morton got the gist of what he
was saying, she didn't know the French expression, and this seemed
to bother her.

English and vocabulary? Forget it. . . .

He felt bad that his partner was troubled.

Tomson called Tyler Quonn and explained about moving the
press conference. The chief of staff apparently wasn't crazy about
the idea but agreed to follow Tomson's direction. Then Ivers
opened his tablet and they studied the area, setting the iPad on
the coffee table. Tomson explained to Morton and Ebbett, "Assuming he was going to try a shot at the press conference, we'll locate
where a good vantage point would be. Get undercover agents and
police there to spot him."

Then Ivers added, "I keep coming back to the pipes. The PVC.
And the toolbox."

"He could slip into a construction site, fronting as a worker. You
know, bundle the gun up with the pipes." Tomson shrugged. "But
there's no job site with a view of the plaza."

"There's construction going on there," Morton said, her unpol-
ished nail hovering over the screen. She was indicating a city block
about a mile from the convention center.

"What is it?" Ivers asked her.

"A high-rise of some kind, about half completed. All I know is
the trucks screw up traffic making deliveries. We avoid that road
commuting here."

Tomson picked up the tablet and went to 3-D view. He moved
his fingers over the screen, zooming and sweeping from one view
to another. He grimaced. "Bingo."

"Whatcha got, Artie?" Ebbett asked.

"You'll be inside the convention center for the rally. But the only way to get into the hall itself is along the corridor behind this wall." He zoomed in on a fifty-foot wall, with small windows at about head height. The windows faced the job site.

Ebbett chuckled. "Artie, come on. It's nearly a mile away. At dusk. Who the hell could make that shot?"

"A pro. And shooting a Lapua round? It's so powerful, what'd just be a wound with another gun would be fatal with a slug like that. Sir, this is a level-two threat. I'm going to ask you to cancel."

Ebbett was shaking his head. "Artie, just let me say this: my enemies, and the enemies of this country, want to make us afraid, want to make us run and hide. I can't do that. I won't do that. I know it makes your job tougher. But I'm going to say no. The rally goes on as planned. Move the press conference inside, okay. That's as far as I'll go. Final word."

Without hesitation the agent said, "Yes, sir." Then, given his orders, he turned immediately to the task at hand. "Don, you get a team together. I want eyes on every CCTV from here to that job site, looking for that Toyota. And I want two dozen tactical officers inside and outside the job site. And I need to come up with a different route to get Governor Ebbett into the hall, one that doesn't involve any outside exposure. Not even a square foot."

Ivers said, "I'm on it. I'll call in when I'm in position." He hurried down the corridor.

Tomson said, "I'll find a covered route to get you to the hall, sir."

As he and Morton turned to leave, Tomson glanced down once more at the coffee table, where *The Guns of August* sat. It hadn't occurred to him earlier, but now he remembered something; the cause of the First World War, in which nearly twenty million people died, could be traced to one simple act—a political assassination.

In conclusion, my fellow Americans:

This country was founded on the principles of freedom and fairness. And I would add to those another principle: that of fostering. You may remember someone in your youth who fostered you. Oh, I don't mean officially, like a foster parent. I mean a teacher, a neighbor, a priest or minister, who took you under his wing and saw within you your inner talent, your inner good, your inner spirit.

And nurtured your gifts.

Freedom, fairness, fostering . . .

Together, you and I will invoke those three principles to make our nation shine even brighter.

To make our strong nation stronger.

To make our great nation greater!

God bless you all, God bless our future, and God bless the United States of America.

Governor Paul Ebbett looked over his notes and rose from the couch. He practiced this passage a few more times, then revised other parts of the speech. Little by little he was closing in on the final version. He still had a couple of hours until showtime.

He smiled to himself.

Little by little.

Which was exactly the way he was creeping up on the presidential nomination. So many people had said he couldn't do it. That he was too brash, too blunt. Too honest—as if there was such a thing.

A knock on the door. "Sir?" It was Artie Tomson.

"Yes?"

"Your dinner's here."

He entered, along with the woman who had saved him from tomato target practice. He liked her and was sorry she was only a security guard and not on his full-time staff. They were accompanied by a white-jacketed server, a slim Latino, who was wheeling in the dinner cart. Under the silver cover would be his favorite meal: hamburger on brioche bread, lettuce, tomato, and, since the first-lady-to-be was not present, red onion—the sandwich accessorized with Thousand Island dressing and a side of fries.

And his beloved sweet tea.

The man opened the wings of the table and set out the food.

"Enjoy your meal, sir." He turned to leave.

"Wait," the candidate commanded.

The convention center employee turned. "Sir?" His eyes grew wide as Ebbett pulled his wallet from his hip pocket, extracted a twenty, and handed it to him.

"I . . . oh, thank you, sir!"

Ebbett thought about asking, as a joke, if the man was going to vote for him. But he didn't seem the sort who would get humor and he worried the server might actually think it was a bribe.

The slight man scurried off, clutching the money, which Ebbett bet he was going to frame rather than spend.

Artie Tomson was giving him an update about the potential assassin, which really was no update at all. They hadn't learned anything from the state police about local threats, or from the NRO, NSA, or CIA about foreign operatives. There was a full complement of tactical officers—some undercover in construction worker outfits—in and around the job site. But there was no sign of the bald, mustachioed suspect or the red Toyota.

As they spoke, Ebbett glanced across the living room and noted Kim Morton on her phone, head down, lost in a serious conversation.

Tomson received a call and excused himself to take it.

Ebbett strolled casually to the table and plucked a fry from the basket. Nice and hot. He dunked it in ketchup and, salivating already, lifted the morsel to his lips as he turned to the TV to check the weather and see if the predicted storm would possibly keep people away. No, it looked like—

Then a crash of china and glass, and with a sharp pain in his back, Ebbett tumbled forward onto the carpet. He realized just before he hit the floor that he'd been facing away from the curtained window, and he wondered, with eerie calm, how the assassin, who was apparently across the street, nowhere near the job site, had known exactly where he would be standing.

Art Tomson was in the hall, surrounded by a half-dozen other Secret Service agents and local police, all facing him as he gave them calm, clear instructions on how to proceed.

One by one, or two by two, the agents and cops turned toward the elevator and headed off for their respective tasks.

Ivers walked up to him and Kim Morton, who stood silently beside the senior agent. Ivers's face was even paler than normal as he displayed his phone. "Here's the answer."

Tomson was staring at the words on the screen. Then he nodded to the door of Suite A. "Let's go."

They walked into the hotel room, Kim Morton behind them.

Searcher, Governor Ebbett, was sitting on the couch, a heating pad on his back.

That was the only medical attention he'd needed after being

tackled while about to take a bite of French fry, dipped in what they suspected might be poisoned ketchup.

Tomson said, "Sir, we're awaiting the analysis of the food. But the substance in question is zinc phosphide."

"The hell's that?"

"Highly toxic rodenticide, used to kill rats mostly. Ingest some and it mixes with stomach acid and a poisonous gas is released."

"What's going on, Artie?"

He nodded to Kim Morton and said, "I'll let my partner here explain. She's the one who thought of it."

With her eyes on Ebbett's, she said, "Well, sir. I was thinking that this guy . . . perp, you say perp?"

"We say perp," Tomson said.

"I was thinking if this perp really was some brilliant assassin, well, he didn't seem to be acting so smart. Conspicuous, you know. Parking suspiciously. Talking about the rally in public while he had a rifle in the back of his car, and he wasn't too concerned if anybody heard him. Wearing camouflage. Buying the PVC pipes and toolbox so we'd think he'd be in a job site . . . I mean, it just seemed *too* obvious that he was planning to shoot you. And I looked at those windows in the hallway again. I mean, even if he was a pro, that'd be a hell of a shot.

"So what might other possibilities be? I thought I'd call the places we know he'd been: the gun shop and the hardware store. We know what he bought, but what if he'd *shoplifted* something that could be used as a weapon—a tool or a knife or a can of propane to make into a bomb? Nothing was missing at the gun shop, but at the hardware store—where there weren't any video cameras—I asked the clerk if anything was missing. They did an inventory. Two cans of rat poison had been stolen.

"When I saw you go for that fry, sir, I just panicked," Morton said. "I thought whatever I said, you might still take a bite, so I just reacted. I'm sorry."

He chuckled. "No worries. It's not every day a beautiful woman launches herself into me . . . and saves my life at the same time."

Tomson said, "We've closed down the kitchen and concession stands and analyzed the HVAC system. No sign of poison yet. But all of your food and beverages will come in from outside, vetted sources."

"Don't have much of an appetite at this point." He grimaced. "Had to be the fucking Russians. They love their poisons. Look at Litvinenko." The Russian expat murdered in London by Moscow agents, who slipped polonium into his tea. "And the Skripal poisoning in Salisbury—that Novichok toxin . . . Jesus."

"There was no chatter about it in the intel community," Ivers pointed out. "Washington's been monitoring."

"Of course there's no chatter," Ebbett muttered. "They're not talking about it overseas—the communications would be picked up. No, they hired some locals to handle the operation—where the CIA can't legally monitor phones and computers without a FISA warrant. Tell the attorney general I want the bureau and the CIA to check out the known Russian cells and anyone with a connection to them. I want them to use a proctoscope."

"Yes, sir. They've been alerted."

"And the car? That Toyota?"

Ivers said, "Never got close to the job site. Like Officer Morton was saying, it was a diversion, we think. A CCTV in Bronson, about thirty miles east, spotted it, headed out of the state. We're still looking, but after that sighting, it's disappeared. I've got one team going through the hardware store, looking for trace evidence and prints. Other teams are going over the convention center service entrance, kitchen, the suppliers, and onsite staff. We're looking at the tea in particular."

"Bastard messing with my sweet tea?" Ebbett grumbled in mock rage. Then his eyes slid to Kim Morton. "A local security guard took on a pro assassin . . . and kicked his ass."

"I just had some thoughts. It was Agent Tomson and Agent Ivers who did everything."

"Don't play down your role." He looked her over for a moment. "Artie was telling me a few things about you. How you always wanted to be a police officer."

"Oh," she said, looking down. "I guess. That didn't work out. But I'm happy with my life now."

"That's good. Sure . . . But you know my campaign slogan."

She said, "Making a great country greater."

"So what if I could make your happy life *happier*?"

"I'm not sure what you mean, sir."

"What I mean is, you did something for me; now I'd like to do something for you. Artie, leave us alone for a few minutes. There's something I'd like to discuss with Ms. . . . I mean, with *Officer* Morton."

"I'll be outside, sir."

At exactly 10:20 that night Governor Paul Ebbett's speech concluded with "And God bless the United States of America." The last word vanished in the tide of screams, whistles, and thunderous applause. Thirty thousand people were on their feet, waving banners and tossing aloft fake straw hats.

Art Tomson, who'd been onstage for the full event, now walked down the steps and joined Kim Morton, who was standing guard at the doorway that led to the underground passage through which Governor Ebbett would exit in a moment.

The evening had gone off without a hitch. In a few minutes Searcher would be in the SUV and speeding to the airport.

"Good speech," she said.

Tomson, who'd heard it or variations of it scores of times, simply nodded noncommittally.

Then she lowered her voice and said, "Thank you."

"For what?"

"Did the governor tell you what he's going to do for me?"

"No."

Morton explained what the candidate had said in their private meeting. "He's going to get me into the state police academy here. He's a friend of our governor, who owes him for something or another." Her face broke into a smile. "And he arranged for a stipend —almost as much as I'm making here. He said one favor deserves another. He did that all because you told him I wanted to be a cop."

"He was asking about you. He thought you were sharper than some of the people working for him." Tomson added with gravity in his voice, "And the fact is, none of us came up with that idea about the poison."

"Just a theory is all."

"Still, in this line of work, better safe than sorry."

Thomson tapped his earpiece and heard: "Searcher's on the move."

Into his sleeve mike he said, "Roger. Exit is clear."

Tomson shook Morton's hand. She gave him a fast embrace.

Never in his years of being an agent had he hugged a fellow personal protection officer. He was startled. Then he hugged her back and peeled away to join the candidate and his escort hurrying to the waiting SUV.

III

May 24

The main room at Earl's wasn't smoky, hadn't been for years. Even vaping was prohibited.

But the aroma of tobacco persisted, as the owners of the place had made no effort to clean the smell away. Because men, alcohol, and semiclad women somehow demanded the scent of cigarette smoke—if not the fumes themselves.

Bil Sheering was at the bar, nursing a Jack and Coke, looking at the scruffy audience sitting by the low stage and at unsteady round bistro tables. While he knew they all could figure out "Exotic Dance," he was wondering how many had a clue what an "Emporium" was. He wondered too why Earl—if there was, or had been, an Earl—had decided to affix the name to his strip joint.

Then his attention turned back to Starlight, the woman on center stage at the moment. Some of the dancers who performed here were bored gyrators. Some offered crude poses and outsized flirtatious glances. And some were uneasy and modest. But Starlight was into dancing with both elegance and sensuality.

He was enjoying her performance when his attention slipped to the TV, where an announcement was interrupting the game. On the screen was a red graphic: BREAKING NEWS.

Somebody beside him chuckled drunkenly. "Don'tcha love it? 'Breaking news' used to be a world war or plane crash. Now it's a thunderstorm, vandals at a 7-Eleven. Media's full of shit."

Bil said nothing but kept his attention on the grimy TV. A blond anchorwoman appeared. She seemed to have been caught unprepared by what was coming next. "We now bring you breaking news from Washington, D.C. We're live at the campaign headquarters of Governor Paul Ebbett for what he has said is an important announcement."

Bil watched the man stride to the front of the room. Cameras fired away, the thirty-shots-per-second mode, sounding like silenced machine guns in a movie.

At Ebbett's side was his wife, a tall, handsome woman on whose severe face was propped a stony smile.

"My fellow Americans, I am here tonight to announce that I am withdrawing from the campaign for president of the United States." Gasps from the crowd. "In my months on the campaign trail, I have come to realize that the most important work in governing this country is on the grassroots level rather than inside the Beltway. And it's in those local offices that I feel I can be of most benefit to my party and to the American people. Accordingly, I will be ceasing my efforts to run for president and returning to my great home state, where I'll be running"—he swallowed hard—"for supervisor of Calloway County." A long pause. "I'm also urging all of my electoral delegates and other supporters to back a man I feel exhibits the best qualities of leadership for America, Senator Mark Todd."

Another collective gasp, more buzzing of the cameras.

Ebbett took his wife's hand. Bil noted she didn't squeeze it but let him grip the digits the way you might pick up a gutted fish in a tray of shaved ice to examine it for freshness.

"Senator Todd is just the man to lead our party to victory and"—Ebbett's voice caught—"make a great nation greater. Thank you, my fellow citizens. God bless you. And God bless the United States of America."

No applause. Just a torrent of questions from the floor. Ebbett ignored them and walked from the room, his wife beside him, their hands no longer entwined.

The scene switched back to the brightly lit newsroom and the anchorwoman saying, "That was Governor Paul Ebbett, who just yesterday seemed unstoppable on his route to his party's candidacy. But there you heard it: his shocking news that he is dropping out of the race. And his equally stunning endorsement of Senator Mark Todd. Todd, considered a far more moderate and bipartisan politician than Ebbett, has been the governor's main rival on the primary campaign trail. Although Todd avoided personal attacks, Ebbett rarely missed the chance to belittle and mock the senator."

Reading from what had to be hastily scribbled notes on the teleprompter, the blond anchor said, "A lot of people were surprised by the success Ebbett enjoyed in the primary campaign, which played to the darker side of American society. His positions were controversial. Many in both parties thought his nationalist-charged rhetoric was divisive. He openly admitted that his campaign phrase, 'Make a Great Country Greater,' meant greater for people like him, white and Christian. He promised to slash social spending on education and the poor.

"He alarmed those both in this country and abroad by stating that one of his first acts in office would be to mass American troops along Russia's borders. Some pundits have said that Ebbett might have targeted Russia not for any political or ideological reason, but because he believed a common enemy would solidify support around him.

"We now have in the studio and via Skype hookup our national presidential campaign panel for an analysis of this unexpected announcement—"

"Hey, Bil," came the woman's voice behind him.

Bil turned to see the dancer who'd just been up onstage sidling up to him, pulling a shawl over her ample breasts. Bil wasn't completely happy she'd donned the garment.

He knew she went by Starlight at Earl's, but he couldn't help but think of her by her real name: Kim Morton.

She smiled to the bartender, who brought her a scotch on the rocks. The headline dancer began to pull bills out of her G-string. As tawdry as Earl's was, it looked like she had been tipped close to two hundred dollars—for twenty minutes at the pole. She sipped her drink and nodded at the screen. "You did it."

"*Me?*" Bil asked, smiling. "*We* did it."

She cocked her head. "Guess I can't really argue with that one."

We did it . . .

They sure as hell had.

Six months ago the National Party Committee had become alarmed, then panicked, that Paul Ebbett was picking up a significant number of delegates in the primary contests, beating out their preferred candidate, Senator Mark Todd. They were astonished that Governor Ebbett's bigoted and militant rhetoric was stirring up a groundswell of support.

The committee knew Ebbett was lose-lose. If elected, he would destroy not only the party but probably the economy and perhaps even the nation itself—if he managed to start World War III, which seemed more than a little possible.

Committee chairman Victor Brown wanted Ebbett out. But backroom attempts to negotiate with him to drop out were futile. In fact, the effort incensed him and fueled his resolve to win . . . and purge the ranks of those who had questioned his ability to lead the country.

So extreme measures were required.

Last March Victor had called in Bil Sheering, who ran a ruthless political consulting company in Washington, D.C. Bil had hurried back from his hunting lodge in West Virginia to his M Street office and got to work.

For the plan Bil came up with, he needed a pro—by which he meant a call girl based in the region of the midwestern state where Governor Ebbett would be holding a big rally in May. After some research he'd settled on Kim Morton, aka Starlight, a dancer at Earl's with an escort business on the side. He'd found her to be smart, well-spoken, and without a criminal history. She also had a particular contempt for Ebbett, since her husband had been killed in Afghanistan, which she considered an unnecessary war, just like the one Ebbett seemed to be planning.

Victor had given Bil a generous budget; he offered Morton a quarter million dollars to take a hiatus from dancing for two months and get a job as a security guard at the Pittstown Convention Center. She used her charm and intelligence to talk her way onto the security team working with the Secret Service at the rally, earning the trust of the senior agent, Art Tomson.

The day of the rally, Bil, who'd grown an impressive mustache and shaved his head, dressed in combat gear and smeared mud on the license plate of an old hulk of a Toyota he'd bought at a junkyard. He'd made his way toward the convention center from Haleyville to Prescott to Avery, making intentionally suspicious purchases: sniper bullets and PVC pipes and hardware. He'd also made the anonymous call about a man having a phone conversation about Ebbett and the rally with a rifle in the backseat of his car.

Meanwhile, Kim Morton continued to ingratiate herself into the Secret Service operation . . . and get the attention of Ebbett himself. She'd spotted the suspicious man in the crowd, armed with two rotten tomatoes (the kid was an intern from National Party headquarters given a bonus to play the role). Finally she'd offered her insights about the sniper attack being a diversion—poison-

ing might be the real form of assassination. (There never was any
toxin; at the hardware store Bil had not stolen the rodenticide but
had merely hidden the cans in another aisle; when they were later
discovered, the Secret Service would conclude the attack was a
product of the security guard's overactive imagination.)

The script called for Morton to tackle Ebbett to "save his life."
Following that intimate and icebreaking moment, Kim Morton had
fired enough flirtatious glances his way to ignite latent flames of
infidelity. After he'd asked her to stay and Art Tomson had left the
suite, Ebbett slipped his arm around her and whispered, "I know
you want a slot at the police academy. An hour in bed with me and
I'll make it happen."

She'd looked shocked at first, as the role called for, but soon
"gave in."

The ensuing liaison was energetic and slightly kinky, as Morton
told him she was a bit of a voyeur and wanted the lights on. Ebbett
was all for it. This proved helpful, since the tiny high-def video camera hidden in her uniform jacket, hanging strategically on the bedroom doorknob, required good illumination.

She'd delivered the video to Bil, who uploaded the encrypted
file to Victor Brown. The head of the national committee had
called Ebbett last week and given him an ultimatum: withdraw or
the tape would go to every media outlet in the world.

After a bit of debate, in which Ebbett had apparently confessed
to his wife what had happened (the fish-hand thing suggested this),
the man had reluctantly agreed.

Eyes now on the screen, Morton said to Bil, "He's actually running for county supervisor?"

"That's the only bone they'd throw him. He's up against a twen-
ty-two-year-old manager at Farmer's Trust and Savings. The polls
aren't in Ebbett's favor." Bil leaned close and whispered, "I have
the rest of your fee."

"I've got one more show. I'll get it after."

Bil had an amusing image of himself sitting in the front row
and, as Starlight danced close to him, tucking $150,000 into her
G-string.

"This worked out well. You interested in any more work?" he
asked.

"You've got my number."

Bil nodded. Then he lifted his drink. "Here's to us—unlikely partners."

She smiled and tapped her glass to his. Then she shrugged the silky wrap off her shoulders into his lap and walked back to the stage.

JOHN M. FLOYD

Rhonda and Clyde

FROM *Black Cat Mystery Magazine*

THE STRANGEST TWO days of Helen Wilson's life began with a skiing trip to Appaloosa Resort one winter Sunday. The trip itself wasn't unusual: Appaloosa was a popular location, and only forty miles from her home in the town of Lodgepole, Wyoming. What was unusual was that Helen had gone there in the company of friends. Helen Wilson didn't have many friends.

Even as a child she'd been a loner, and her school years had given her little reason to change. She also had no desire, after graduating with an accounting degree from UW, to leave her hometown to pursue a career. Instead she hired on as a bank teller, a safe and unpretentious job on a safe and unpretentious street near the house her late parents had left her. Ten years later Helen was still there, a sensible woman of reasonable means but no ambition, one of those rare people who doesn't require much in order to be happy. Even so, she was pleasantly surprised when two total strangers engaged her in conversation one day at a neighborhood coffee shop, and even more surprised to find that she enjoyed their company.

Rhonda Felson and her husband, Clyde, were new to the area, Helen discovered—writers who had rented a cabin in the mountains nearby and who spent most of their time hiking and sightseeing and creating what Helen suspected would one day be masterpieces of literature. During the days after that first meeting, the three of them had gotten together twice for dinner in local restaurants, and the following weekend Rhonda had invited Helen to accompany them to Appaloosa. The trip ended badly. Helen, who had never before been near a pair of skis, suffered the fate of many first-timers: six hours later she found herself medicated and hobbling on crutches through the exit doors of the local ER. More painful to her than her injuries was the knowledge that she'd been so much trouble to her new friends—they'd driven her to the hospital and then home afterward—and she found herself apologizing nonstop for spoiling their outing.

"Nonsense," Rhonda said for the tenth time. She used Helen's key to open the apartment door and stood aside as Clyde helped Helen maneuver down the hallway to her bedroom. "These things happen. I'm just sorry it happened to *you*."

Helen sagged backward onto the bed, propped her bad leg up on pillows, and sighed. "Thanks, guys," she said. "I'll be okay now."

Rhonda was frowning. "Maybe I better stay. Clyde can come fetch me in the morning—"

"I'll be fine," Helen said again. "Oh, I just remembered—where'd we put my purse?"

"It's in the other room."

"Could you get it for me? My cell phone's inside it, and I need to call my boss."

"Now?" Clyde asked. "It's past ten."

"He stays up late. He knows a lot of the folks at the resort, and if he hears about my mishap I want him to know I'll still be coming in to the bank tomorrow."

Both Felsons blinked at the same time. "You're going in to work?" Rhonda said.

"This isn't exactly life-threatening. I just want to forewarn him. I don't want everybody mooning over me when I limp in with my cast and my new wooden legs." Helen closed her eyes for a second and added, "Whoa—I can't believe I'm so tired."

"Tell you what. I'll make the call for you. You need to rest. What's your boss's number?"

Helen gave it to Rhonda and watched sleepily as the two of them left the room. It occurred to her that from now on she would stick to tennis . . .

Sheriff Marcie Ingalls had never fully adjusted to cold weather. Her parents had moved the family here from Alabama when she was nine, and she was sometimes convinced that she'd lived in balmy climes just long enough to thin her blood. But she'd married a local guy and her mother was still here, so Marcie made the best of it. She dressed in three or four layers, never complained, and even on subzero mornings usually got to the office before anyone else.

Today, though, she arrived to find the door unlocked and coffee brewing. Jerry Pearson, her only deputy, was at his desk in the back corner, feet propped up and a copy of *Guns & Ammo* in his hands.

"You're early," Marcie said. What a detective she would've made.

"And full of news," Pearson replied in a bored voice. "I put a ticket on a car parked in the alley off Fourth Street, a twenty-foot limb fell from an oak in front of the courthouse, and the bakery has jelly doughnuts on special today."

Sheriff Ingalls shrugged out of her heavy coat and took a seat at her desk. "Was it blocking traffic?" she asked.

"What, the limb?"

"The car."

"No, just blocking the alley." Pearson tossed the magazine onto his desktop. "Illegally parked. You saying I shouldn't have ticketed it?"

"I'm just saying it's not even seven a.m., and nobody ever drives through there anyhow."

He snorted. "Where I come from, they'd tow it away."

"You're not where you came from, Jerry. We do things a little different here."

"You can say that again." He nodded toward the window. "Hear that sound?"

Marcie frowned, listening. Sure enough, something was pounding on something, in the distance—*bam . . . bam . . . bam,* sharp and clear in the brittle morning air. She was about to reply, then stopped as Wanda Stalworth, the dispatcher, pushed through the door in a bright red parka. They exchanged greetings, Wanda headed for her desk in the other room, and Marcie looked again at Jerry Pearson.

"I hear it," she said. "What is it? Hammering?"

"Yeah. Roscoe Three Bears. He's fixing Maude Jessup's front steps."

"Good. She's almost ninety, and that's a high porch—it'd be too bad if she fell."

"What I can't figure is why he does it. Splits her firewood for her too. Roscoe's banned from the rez and dirt poor, and I hear she never pays him. Probably never even thanks him."

Marcie took a pair of reading glasses from her pocket and started riffling through her in-basket. "He does it because Maude's old and there's no one else to help her, Jerry."

He shook his head. "Maybe one of these days I'll understand that kind of thinking."

"I doubt it," she said.

From the dispatch desk Wanda called, "Are you two arguing again?"

"Not me," Pearson said. He rose to his feet and picked up his coat. "I'm going to do something to make me feel good for a change."

"You quitting?" Marcie asked.

"Not that good."

"Where you going, then?"

"To buy some jelly doughnuts."

Two hours later and two blocks away, in the bank on the corner of Western and Fourth, branch manager Spencer E. Spencer looked up from the papers on his desk to see loan officer Ernest Polk standing in his office doorway. Both men were wearing thick winter jackets, and Polk even had on a fur hat with earflaps. He looked like a movie poster for *Fargo*.

"Any word on the heating situation?" Spencer asked him.

"They're sending a repair crew from Casper," Polk said. "It'll take a couple hours. Until then I guess we'll just have to stay bundled up."

Spencer sighed. He had come in this morning to find the bank lobby as cold as Siberia, although the lights and the computers all seemed to be working. When he'd phoned the bank's home office, they had instructed him to call the heating-system people and to —above all else—remain open for business. He glanced through the glass wall of his office at two of his tellers, who were huddled at their stations like ice fishermen. Both were wearing mittens and had the hoods of their coats pulled up over their heads. He found himself dreaming of Florida.

Spencer E. Spencer was still staring at the lobby when his third teller clomped through the door on a pair of crutches. Helen Wilson was encased in a brown parka from the top of her head to her knees, and what little of her could be seen wasn't good: one eye was squeezed shut, her nose was bandaged, and a long comma of black hair hung in her face. Looking at no one and saying not a word, she solemnly made her way to her teller cage and wrestled herself onto her stool. The other two women muttered sympathetic words to her, their breath making little white clouds in the air, but otherwise the room was dead silent.

The two men in the office couldn't help staring. "She's in worse shape than I expected," Ernest Polk whispered.

Spencer, who had already alerted the staff, said, "That friend of hers—the one who called me last night to tell me Helen was coming in?—said she skied into a tree."

"She must've knocked it down."

"Tough lady," Spencer said. He reached for his phone and punched a number. When he saw Helen Wilson pick up her receiver, he said, "Sure you feel all right, Helen?"

"I'b vine," her voice said. "Doesn'd hurd doo bad."

"Looks like it would, from here. And what's wrong with your voice?"

"My doze is all stobbed up, dad's all. Like I god a gold."

"Okay," he said. "You let me know if you need anything." He hung up and said to Polk, "Maybe she'll have an easy morning—we shouldn't get many customers anyhow, with no heat."

But as soon as he uttered those words, the front door opened again and a short redheaded man entered carrying two duffel bags. On the nearest bag were the printed words PARADISE VALLEY CASINO. He walked to Helen Wilson's station, set the bags on the counter, and grinned at her. The tired smile she gave him in return looked more like a grimace to Spencer, but the man didn't seem to mind. He also didn't seem bothered by the frigid temperature.

"Thank God for the casino," Spencer said. "They deposit more money in a week than most of our customers deposit in a year."

"I believe it," Polk said as he turned to leave. "I'll keep a watch out for the repair folks."

Spencer nodded and went back to his paperwork, wishing he could do it with his gloves on. He also wished he didn't know the Paradise Valley Casino quite as well as he did. Sadly, some of those funds being deposited had probably once been his.

It took him twenty minutes to sign off on the earnings reports and finish a long phone call with the bank's IT crew about an upgrade to his ATM software. Finally Spencer leaned back in his swivel chair, burrowed lower into his coat, looked over at the tellers—and frowned. No one was sitting at Helen Wilson's station. Earlier, around the time the casino courier was here, Spencer had noticed Helen leaving her stool to make several trips to the vault. That made sense: the casino's deposits were always large, and her crutches would prevent her from carrying too big a load at once. But now she was gone. He picked up the phone to call the head teller, but before he could hit the intercom button, Ernest Polk stuck his head into the office.

"Know what we should do, Spence?"

"What."

"We should have a promotion and give away those big duffel bags like the casino does."

"What?" Spencer said again. His mind was on injured employees, not bank giveaways.

"You know—those bags like the ones the guy was carrying earlier, with the name printed on the side. That's great advertising, and—"

"Wait a minute," he said, still holding the receiver. "Are you saying the casino lets anybody have those, for free?"

"Well, not free," Polk said. "You have to spend at least fifty bucks at the slot machines. But that doesn't take long."

Spencer frowned. A vague uneasiness had crept into his bones. Shaking it off, he said, "Thanks, Ernie. I'll consider it." Then, without waiting for a response, he pressed the button for the head teller and, when she answered, said, "Libby? Is Helen taking her break?"

"She left for home ten minutes ago, Spence. Said she wasn't feeling well after all. I'm not surprised—she shouldn't have tried to come in."

"Thanks, Lib. I'll give her a call." Which he did, after allowing her five more minutes to get home. That should be plenty—Helen's house was barely a mile from the bank.

But her cell phone didn't answer. It rang four times, then went to voicemail. Rather than leave a message, he found her home number and tried her landline. After three rings, she picked up.

"Helen?" he said. "It's Spencer, at the bank. Just wanted to make sure you're all right."

Helen Wilson said, a little groggily, "I'm fine—thanks for checking on me."

"Well, you sound better, anyway. More like yourself."

"Excuse me?"

"Your clogged nose," Spencer said. "It must've cleared up, right?"

Hesitation. Then: "It's my leg, Spence, not my nose. I broke my ankle."

"But—when you were here earlier . . ."

"There? I wasn't there. I've been here at home all morning."

Spencer felt a cold ripple move through his stomach. "What?"

"My friend Rhonda phoned you last night, right? At first she was going to call and tell you I'd be coming in anyway, but she later said she'd taken the liberty of telling you I'd be staying home sick today. She was right, I guess—I needed the rest. So I stayed home."

Silence. Spencer tried to respond, but his throat seemed to have closed up.

"Didn't she call you?" Helen asked him. "What's going on?"

He swallowed. "I don't know. I mean—the person who called said you'd be coming in, like always. She didn't say anything about taking a sick day."

"Oh my. She must've misunderstood. Or maybe I misunderstood *her* . . ."

"Listen, Helen—this is important. Who's Rhonda?"

"I told you, a friend. I met her last week, she's the one who invited me to go skiing with her and her husband yesterday. The one who fell on my leg."

"Fell on it?"

"Well, it was an accident, but yeah, she fell and landed on my leg."

Spencer was sweating now, his heart thudding in his chest. "Hold on a second, okay?"

He rose and walked stiffly into the lobby and around to the teller area. Underneath the counter, in front of Helen's chair, he found it—a huge stack of bills. But they weren't bills at all—they were cash-sized bundles of blank paper. Helen's trips to the vault, he realized now, weren't to transport cash to it. They were to transport cash *from* it. If he'd been paying attention, he'd have noticed that the duffel bags the casino man had taken out of the bank were probably stuffed as full as they had been when he came in—but with real bills this time.

Quick as a flash, he pressed the alarm button under the counter, to alert the sheriff's department, then sprinted back to the phone in his office. "Helen?" he said. "What did they look like, your two friends?" But he was afraid he already knew.

"Look like? Well . . . the guy's short, reddish hair, glasses. His wife is—I don't know, about my height and weight, I guess. In fact it's a little spooky how much she does look like me, with the black hair and—"

"Names," Spencer blurted. "Do you have names?"

She gave them to him: Clyde and Rhonda Felson. He scribbled them onto a pad, looked up at the window, and saw Sheriff Ingalls's patrol car screech to a stop at the curb. As he leaped from his desk and hurried to meet the cops, Spencer realized he was trembling.

But not from the cold.

"I can't believe it," Helen murmured. She was still propped up in her bed, her leg cast resting on a pillow. Her face was noticeably free of bruises and bandages. "Rhonda told me she told you I wasn't coming in . . . when in fact she told you I *was*. She was setting the stage for"—Helen swallowed hard—"for impersonating me."

Gathered around her were Sheriff Marcie Ingalls, Deputy Jerry Pearson, and branch manager Spence Spencer.

"That seems to be what happened," Marcie agreed.

Spencer, who seemed to have aged ten years, said, "You didn't hear her make the call?"

Helen shook her head. "No, she used my cell phone, from the other room. I was a little woozy anyhow, from the painkillers. But I remember her coming back in and waking me up and telling me you'd said that taking a day off was fine, and to get well soon."

"She must've been crazy, to stroll into the bank like that," Marcie said. "But it worked."

"Without that damn parka it wouldn't have worked," Spencer said. "Between it and the fake bandages, we couldn't see much of her face. Also, she disguised her voice."

"And her partner, husband, whatever—he walked out with . . . how much?"

Spencer shrugged. "We don't know yet. A lot." He ran a hand over his face. "With bags the casino gave him for free, for playing the slots. Insult to injury."

"You'll get me the security video, right?"

"Ernie Polk's holding it for you. And our main office has already offered a reward."

The sheriff nodded and looked at Helen. "Clyde Felson, you said? And Rhonda?"

"Yes." Helen repeated the descriptions she'd given to Spencer on the phone. "She really does look like me. She's prettier than I am, though." She sighed. "He called her Ronnie."

"Ronnie and Clyde?"

"Why not?" Deputy Pearson said.

Everyone turned to look at him.

Pearson shrugged. "They rob banks."

Marcie and Pearson continued questioning Helen for another half hour, trying to come up with some kind of lead. The only thing helpful at all was the fact that the robbers and fake friends (Helen had to admit that's what they were) drove a black Toyota Tundra. At least that's the vehicle they'd taken Helen to the resort in. As for today, nobody remembered seeing what the imposter had driven to the bank.

Sheriff Ingalls said it had probably been Helen's Ford Focus, because of the possibility that someone *might* see it—and the fact that its keys were missing from her purse. In any case, the Ford was now parked in its rightful place behind Helen's house. The sheriff said they would check it over for prints but that it would probably yield no clues; Rhonda Felson would almost certainly have kept her gloves on during the drive to and from the bank.

"Wait a second," Helen said. "I think they might've had *two* cars. One that I never saw."

"Why would you think that?" Marcie asked.

"We went to the resort in the Toyota, but Rhonda drove. Once, on Sunday, I saw Clyde take a set of keys from his pocket. It was only for a moment—he was looking for his ticket for the ski lift—but the biggest key on the chain wasn't for their Tundra."

"What kind of key was it?"

"A Honda."

"Are you sure?"

"Yes. It had that funny curved *H* that's bigger on top than on the bottom."

The sheriff and her deputy exchanged a look. Both were thinking the same thing: since the robbers knew Helen had seen the Toyota, they would probably ditch that vehicle someplace and use another for a getaway. They could always steal one, but if they already had a second car waiting in the wings . . .

"Okay, that helps. They're probably driving a Honda," Marcie said. "Anything else?"

"Not that I can think of." Helen heaved a sigh. "They even stole my crutches."

A silence passed. Marcie used it to look carefully around the room. When she noticed the old-fashioned telephone sitting on the floor between Helen's bed and the potty chair, she blinked.

"Helen, is that the phone you used earlier, to talk to the bank?"

"Yeah, Spence called me on it. I had to dig it out from under the bedside table. It's still connected, obviously, but I haven't used it much since I got my cell phone."

"Where's your cell phone now?"

"Same place as my crutches, probably. Rhonda used my cell to call Spence last night, and must've kept it." Helen looked up and added, "I bet they figured they were taking my only phone, so I wouldn't be able to call anyone at the bank today—or get a call *from* anyone—and screw up their plans. They wouldn't have seen my landline."

The room fell silent again. Then Marcie had a thought.

"If your cell phone's still turned on," she said to Helen, "we can track it."

"It's still on," Spencer E. Spencer said. "Or at least it *was*, after the robbery."

Everyone turned to face him. Marcie had actually forgotten he was still there, and then realized he was probably reluctant to go back to an unheated bank and a heated interrogation by his bosses. As he'd mentioned, he hadn't even determined yet how much money was taken.

"How do you know her cell phone's on?" she asked him.

"Because I tried to call her on it first, and it rang. No one picked up, but it rang several times and went to voicemail—it didn't give me a not-in-service message or anything."

"Okay," Marcie said, deep in thought. "That's good. We'll see if we can get the cell towers to triangulate the signal, try to pin down the whereabouts of the phone."

All of a sudden Helen's eyes widened. "You won't have to," she said.

"What?"

For the first time today, Helen Wilson smiled. "It has a GPS chip."

"Excuse me?" Marcie asked.

"A GPS locator. My aunt bought me the phone a few months ago and said if I ever lost it, this feature'll find it. There's an app that'll point us straight to it."

"How exactly does that work?" Pearson said.

"We just need Aunt Lettie's phone. It's tied to mine—you click the app on her phone and it shows where my cell phone is, on a map. And where the Felsons are, if they still have it."

"Where does she live, your aunt?"

"Over past Battle Creek, near the edge of the reservation. About twenty miles—"

"I know her house," Marcie said. She pointed to the landline. "Will you call her?"

Within minutes Sheriff Ingalls and her deputy were in her cruiser and headed for Lettie Wilson's home. As usual, Jerry Pearson sat silent and brooding in the passenger seat. Marcie glanced at him from the corner of her eye. She liked him, but could never quite figure him out. He'd been a Seattle cop for years before moving here to be near his wife's folks, and had always seemed either unable or unwilling to adapt to local ways. Marcie sighed. Here she was, in a high-stress/low-pay job, freezing her butt off every year between September and May, with a deputy who was always in a bad mood. She couldn't imagine two better examples of ducks out of water.

She forced her mind back to the matter at hand. "Something's worrying me here, Jerry," she said. "Remember what the banker said about the heat being off in the building?"

"I remember. What about it?"

"He said if it hadn't been off, if the imposter hadn't stayed bundled up in winter gear, he and the staff would've probably recognized that she wasn't Helen."

"And?"

"Seems pretty convenient," she said, "that heating-system failure."

Pearson lapsed again into silence. Then: "Are you thinking they—"

"I don't know." Marcie chewed her lip a moment. "But the people coming to fix it should be there by now. Why don't you call Wanda, have her connect you to the bank. Ask to speak to the head fred on the crew." She turned, and they locked eyes. "Humor me," she said.

Two minutes later they had the repairman on speakerphone.

"You fellas see anything strange?" Pearson asked him.

"Dern right we did," the guy said. "The wires were cut to the heating system."

Pearson blinked. "Did you say *cut?*"

"Yep. As in severed. Somebody took a crowbar to the panel door and cut the wires. The *correct* wires—nothing else was affected. Whoever did it knew his way around a power board."

"Where is this panel? Somewhere in the bank?"

"Above the bank. On the roof."

Pearson thanked the man, disconnected, and turned to the sheriff. "Whoa," he said.

"Sounds like they decided to improve their odds a bit."

"Sure does," Pearson said. "They get two bags with the casino's logo, find a bank employee with the right looks, befriend her, cause her to have a disabling accident, create a situation that makes a disguise even easier . . . They know what they're doing, these two."

"So do we, now. We know one of them has teller experience and one's an electrician."

"Does that make us any closer to catching them?"

Marcie shrugged, her eyes on the road. "The more we know, the better off we are."

"We also know they're smart," he said.

"Let's hope they're not smart enough to turn off Helen's phone."

Helen's aunt Lettie took a while to find her cell phone, but when she did, she loaned it to them with her blessing. Marcie and Pearson arrived back at Helen's apartment within an hour.

And found that they had company.

Two men in dark suits were standing in the bedroom. One of them, who looked like he'd just taken a bite out of a lemon, said, without a handshake, "Detective Murphy. State police." He pointed to his partner and added, "This is Detective Ellington. We'll take it from here."

Marcie glanced at Spencer, gave him a *Did you do this?* look. He shrugged and appeared clueless. She figured the big boys at the main bank had called the big boys in Cheyenne.

"I doubt you have the vast resources required for something like this," Murphy said.

Grinding her back teeth, Marcie said, "The crime happened in my county, Detective."

"But I suspect the criminals are no longer *in* your county, Sheriff." He looked down at the cell phone in Marcie's hand. "And it sounds like this will tell us for sure. Ms. Wilson, would you do the honors?"

Helen, still in bed, took her aunt's phone from Marcie, tapped some buttons, studied it a moment, and handed it back. Everyone crowded in to see.

On the screen was a map with a red dot in the middle. The location wasn't approximate; it was exact. According to the GPS, Helen's missing cell phone was now at an address on the northeast corner of Hill Street and Lancaster, in the small town of Florence. Sixty miles south.

They watched the screen for several minutes. The red dot didn't move.

Detective Ellington took out his own phone and Googled the address shown on the GPS map. After a moment he looked up at his partner. "Two-twenty Lancaster Street," he said, "is a place called the Traildrive Motel."

Murphy nodded, his eyes on the screen. The red dot stayed put.

"We got 'em," he said.

Rhonda Felson, although that wasn't her real name, kicked off her shoes, stretched out on the too-small bed, and blew out a sigh. Her husband, Clyde, although that wasn't his real name, hefted both duffel bags onto the rickety table in one corner of the room and stared at them lovingly. "So far, so good," he said.

"I'm glad you're pleased," she murmured, her eyes closed. "I'll be pleased when we're in Florence, Italy, and not Florence, Wyoming."

"All in good time, Ronnie my dear."

Outside, the traffic on Lancaster Street, which consisted mostly of pickup trucks, was sparse. That was to be expected, probably: it was 11 a.m. on a weekday. But Clyde had a feeling traffic here was always sparse.

"So this is part of your plan?" she said. "Check into a motel only an hour away from the scene of the crime, in broad daylight?"

"This is one of the final phases of my plan," he said. "We're almost done here."

"We'll be done, all right, if they find us."

He smiled, still looking at the bags. "They won't find us."

Sheriff Marcie Ingalls pushed through the door of her office, tossed her hat onto the desk, and sagged into her chair. Deputy Pearson followed.

Seconds later Wanda Stalworth stuck her head in, from dispatch. "What are you guys doing back?" she said. "Did you catch 'em?"

"We're here because we were told to be," Marcie said. "It's not our case anymore."

"Then why are you frowning?"

Marcie rubbed her eyes. "Because something's bothering me." She looked all around, studying her surroundings as if seeing them for the first time. "Something small, something I think we talked about, right here in this office. I just can't put my finger on it."

"You think the state cops are wrong about heading down to Florence?" Pearson asked.

"I'm just saying we're missing something. As for Florence, those two detectives are in no hurry. I heard Murphy say he'll be taking several state troopers along with them and making this a big deal. He wants all the glory, I promise you that."

Pearson snorted. "While we stay here and write parking tickets. Right?"

Marcie blinked, then scowled. Slowly she turned and focused on her deputy.

"What's the matter?" he asked.

"That's it. That's what I was trying to remember. That car you said you ticketed this morning, in the alley."

"What about it?"

"That alley runs beside the bank, Jerry. Right beside it."

"So?"

"And I bet there's a ladder on the side of the building, to the roof."

They stared at each other for a long moment.
"The car," she said. "Was it a Honda?"

Seventy-eight minutes later, Clyde Felson was relaxing in the room's
only chair, reading a travel brochure he'd found in the drawer of
the nightstand, while Rhonda counted the money in the two bags.
She'd been counting for half an hour now.

In spite of Rhonda's doubts, the motel was everything Clyde had
wanted: small, cheap, quiet, and perfectly located. He didn't plan
to be here long.

He turned to Rhonda, idly watching the glow of the lamplight
on her jet-black hair. He had just opened his mouth to speak to
her when he heard the screech of tires somewhere outside their
window. A lot of tires. Then the slamming of car doors.

Clyde was on his feet in an instant, dashing to the window and
easing the curtains aside to peek out.

The Law had arrived.

Detective Michael Murphy was pleased with what he saw. As soon
as he had assembled his team of patrolmen, they had hit the road
and headed south. Now they were spread out evenly along the inside of the U-shaped row of twenty-four motel rooms. Ellington
had already fetched the Hispanic owner—a man named Roberto
Gonzales—from the motel office, and had learned from the register that only one couple was checked in at the moment: a Mr. and
Mrs. Curtis Allen, from Laramie, in Room 12. Murphy was now
standing outside that door, his weapon drawn and his mouth dry.
As planned, he caught Ellington's eye and nodded once.

Ellington took Aunt Lettie Wilson's cell phone from his pocket
and punched in Helen's number . . . and everyone went dead
quiet. Helen had told them her ringtone was loud and distinctive:
the "Throne Room" theme from *Star Wars*. Every cop on the scene
held his breath, waiting and listening. Five seconds passed.

And then Murphy heard it. It was ringing. The phone was here.

But not behind the door of Room 12. The ringtone was coming from somewhere off to Murphy's left. He turned, alert and
searching, and saw others turn as well. Moments later they found
the source of the music: a small blue mailbox on the outside wall
of the motel office.

Frantically Murphy signaled one of the troopers, who fetched a tire iron from the trunk of a cruiser and pried open the lid of the mail drop. Inside were half a dozen stamped envelopes and a model 5 iPhone, which had finally stopped playing John Williams's music and was now calmly instructing the caller, in Helen Wilson's recorded voice, to please leave a message.

But that wasn't all. Rubberbanded around the phone was a scrap of paper with the printed words:

PLEASE RETURN THIS TO HELEN. THANKS, AND ADIOS.

Murphy stared at it silently for a minute or more, ignoring the looks of his fellow cops and a confused-looking elderly couple standing in the now open doorway of Room 12.

Detective Ellington and Mr. Gonzales were both peering over Murphy's shoulder to study the message. Ellington looked at Murphy and asked, "Adios?"

"Sí," Gonzales said.

A hundred yards away, on the other side of Lancaster Street, the Felsons stood at the back window of Room 7 at the tiny Hamilton Inn, watching the festivities across the road. The room's curtains had been pulled back and the lights switched off so no one could see in from outside. Rhonda had brought Clyde the binoculars he'd placed on the bedside table an hour ago, and he was smiling as he watched the policemen in the Traildrive Motel's parking lot mill around, disperse, and leave the scene. When all activity had died down he closed the curtains, switched the lights back on, and returned the field glasses to Rhonda's travel bag.

She stood there staring at him. "That was stupid. You know that, don't you? Stupid and risky. We should be miles away from here by now."

He gave her a smug look. "It was necessary. I wanted to know how safe we are."

"What do you mean?"

"I mean they sent the big guns after us. State troopers, suits, everybody at once. That tells me that pinpointing her phone with that app you saw on her screen — that was all they had. They know nothing else about us."

Rhonda didn't respond, but she did seem to relax a little.

"They'll never catch us now," he added. "We're home free."

"It was still stupid," Rhonda murmured.

He sat on the bed, put his shoes on, and laced them up. "Come on, let's get out of here."

"Thank God. I was afraid you'd want to stay the night."

"I've seen what I needed to see." He looked up at her. "We'll double back and be in Canada by tomorrow. Then, the world."

"Why'd you write *adios* on the note?"

"Misdirection never hurts," he said. "Whether they're after us or not."

Within two minutes they'd gathered their belongings. Rhonda handed Clyde her travel bag, then turned to leave the room key on the dresser. He looped the straps of the two casino bags over his shoulders, took his car keys from his pocket, and pulled open the door.

The gray Honda Accord was parked nose out in the space directly in front of the room. Clyde pushed the button to pop the trunk even as he stepped out onto the sidewalk, his wife right behind him in the doorway. Head down and intent on his task, he loaded the two bags into the trunk, tucked Rhonda's bag in beside them, and closed the trunk lid.

And saw, for the first time, that he wasn't alone.

Two uniformed policemen, a man and a woman, were standing against the motel wall, ten feet from the door. The lady cop had a sheriff's badge, and her gun was drawn and pointed.

"Guess I don't have to ask if this is your car," she said.

For a long moment the two suspects stood there, staring. Their expressions weren't scared, or angry, or even disappointed. Mostly they looked stunned.

Marcie Ingalls said, in a level voice, "Turn around, both of you. Slowly. Hands behind your backs." She kept her automatic aimed and ready while Pearson cuffed them.

When they turned again to face her, the man—Clyde Felson, Marcie assumed—said, "How'd you know?"

She shook her head. "We didn't at first. My deputy and I arrived at the other motel long before the cavalry did, and when we found that you weren't there we looked around to see where else you might be. In case you decided to hide and watch from a distance."

"Watch? What made you think we might do that?"

"Nothing. But it happens sometimes, and it was worth a try."

Without turning, she asked Deputy Pearson—who had already taken the car keys from Clyde—to check the bags. He opened the trunk and unzipped the two duffels.

"The money's here," he said.

"Main thing is," Marcie continued, "we knew you weren't at the other motel because your car wasn't in the lot. All we did then was check possible vantage points until we found it." She nodded toward the still-open doorway to Room 7. "The lady in the office confirmed that this was the room that went with the car."

"But—you had no way to know about our car."

Marcie smiled, took the parking ticket from her pocket, and held it up. "Yes, we did—not only the make and model, but the license plate number. Thanks to my deputy here, who wrote a citation for your Honda earlier today, in an alley beside the bank building. An alley with the only outside access to the roof." She smiled, watching their faces. "That was smart, disabling the heating system. Everything you did was smart, except for parking in the wrong place this morning and hanging around here too long now. Which, by the way, was downright foolish."

"I told you," the woman growled.

Clyde's jaw tightened. "Shut up, Ronnie."

Marcie took out her cell and called dispatch while Pearson finished checking the cab of the getaway vehicle. "Wanda? It's me," she said into the phone. "Do me a favor. Track down Detective Murphy and tell him he might want to turn himself and his vast resources around and head back here to Florence. We have the two suspects in custody, along with the stolen cash. Yep, that's right. Tell him we're across the street from the red dot. He'll know what I mean."

She disconnected and turned to Pearson. "Find anything interesting?"

"A couple things." To the Felsons he said, "What kind of people steal a woman's crutches?"

Rhonda snorted. "Good old Helen. Guess she was in the wrong place at the wrong time."

"I agree," Pearson said. "And she was wrong about something else too."

"What's that?"

"She told us you were prettier than she is."

Rhonda glared at him.

"Okay," Marcie said. "Let's go." Pearson gripped Clyde's elbow and steered him and his wife toward the cruiser.

"Ronnie and Clyde," Marcie added, walking behind them. "What are your real names?"

The man turned and gave her an even darker look. "Thelma and Louise."

Marcie smiled.

"They didn't end well either," she said.

Two days later things were back to normal. Around 9 a.m. Sheriff Ingalls was sitting at her desk, sending an email to the mayor regarding his highly publicized but understaffed Pothole Prevention Program. For some reason, complaints about the poor condition of town streets were finding their way to the county sheriff instead of the city Public Works Department, and Marcie considered it her duty to place that particular monkey on the correct back.

Aside from the usual administrative headaches, though, all was going well. The quick arrest of the bank-heist suspects and the recovery of the stolen loot had put smiles on the faces of everyone except the two robbers and egg on the face of one Detective Michael Murphy. An additional but unexpected result of the incident was that the injured but wiser Helen Wilson now had an upcoming dinner date with Detective Scott Ellington. Proof positive, in Marcie's view, that clouds do have silver linings.

She had sent the mayor's email and was scrolling through the others when Wanda Stalworth ambled in from the other room. Marcie looked up, then turned back to her computer and said, "For what reason has the Wanda Woman abandoned her post?"

"Business is slow. Where's Pearson?"

"Out front, trying to fix our flagpole," Marcie said, eyes on her screen. A windstorm last night had snapped it off, along with three trees and the steeple of a nearby church.

Wanda, never one to be distracted from the important things in life, said, "Is that a box of doughnuts on his desk?"

"Half chocolate, half cream-filled. Help yourself."

"You want one too?"

Marcie shook her head. "One of my rules: I only eat sugar when I hear good news."

"Why's that?"

"You got any good news?"

"I guess not."

Marcie nodded. "Well, there you go. It helps me stay skinny."

Wanda picked out a doughnut and took a bite. Chewing, she said, "I do have some gossip. I heard you told the bank folks that Jerry Pearson caught the robbers the other day."

"That's not gossip. It's a fact."

Wanda stared at her. "But he didn't, Sheriff. *You* solved the case —I was standing right here when you linked the criminals to the car that was parked beside the bank that morning."

"I didn't say Pearson *solved* it," Marcie corrected. "I said his actions led directly to their capture. If he hadn't ticketed that parked Honda, there would've been no record of the license plate, and we couldn't have found them." She leaned back in her chair, holding Wanda's gaze. "If law officers were eligible for such things, I'd have made sure Pearson got that reward the bank offered. And I'll tell you something else: if it'd been me, I wouldn't even have written that ticket. Pearson did what he felt was right, and it turned out to be the only thing that pointed us to the guilty party."

Wanda finished her doughnut and wiped her mouth with a napkin. When her hand came away, Marcie saw that she was smiling.

"What's so funny?"

"I seem to remember you hinting that morning that Pearson should change his way of thinking."

"Well, I take it back," Marcie said. "I'm not sure I *want* him to change."

Wanda seemed to consider that, then said, "You might be a little late."

"Why?"

"Because of the reward." Wanda tossed the wadded-up napkin into a trashcan and sat down on the edge of Pearson's desk. "Do you recall telling us yesterday that the bank had withdrawn the reward offer because no one had come forward with information leading to the arrest and capture, blah blah blah?"

"Yes," Marcie said. "What about it?"

"Libby Anders, the head teller at the bank, called me this morning. She said Deputy Pearson told the bank manager last night that the reward would have to be paid. Said that he—Jerry Pearson —was informed by two alert citizens early Monday morning that a strange car was parked in the alley beside the bank. Said he wouldn't have noticed it otherwise. Since information from that ticket, as you said, later led to the apprehension of the two suspects, Pearson insisted that those two people should be given the full reward. Ten grand, divided between them."

"Who were these two observant citizens?"

"Roscoe Three Bears and Maude Jessup."

Marcie blinked. "You're kidding."

"Nope. Pearson said they mentioned the illegally parked car to him on his way to the office that day. Then he walked over and wrote the ticket."

"But . . ." Marcie stared into the distance, thinking. "Roscoe was working on Maude's house at the time. Repairing her porch steps. To even talk to them on his route to work, Pearson would've had to climb three fences and cross two yards."

Wanda narrowed her eyes. "Are you wondering if that's what really happened?"

"Well . . . I'm wondering what Roscoe and Maude would say if asked about it."

"Pearson said they shouldn't have to be contacted."

"What?"

"He said Roscoe doesn't speak much English and Ms. Jessup forgets things sometimes."

Marcie thought that over, and felt a smile spread across her face. Slowly she rose from her chair and crossed the room to the front window. On the snow-covered lawn between the office and the street, a man in a furry brown coat stood surrounded by tools, his fists on his hips and his eyes on a new brace that had been bolted to the pole supporting the Stars and Stripes.

Marcie stared out the window at her deputy for a long moment. *Flagpoles aren't the only things you can fix, are they, Jerry?* She was surprised at the sudden warmth she felt in her heart.

"That sounds reasonable to me," she murmured.

"What?" Wanda said.

Before Marcie could reply, she caught a glimpse of Helen Wilson's maroon Ford. She saw it putter its way up the snow-cleared street and pull into a parking spot, saw Helen climb out and limp on her recovered crutches to the front door of the bank. Spence Spencer appeared then, as if he'd been waiting for her to arrive. Marcie watched as he held the door open for Helen, bowed theatrically, and followed her inside. First, though, Spencer turned and stared directly down the street at the sheriff's office. Directly at *her.*

Marcie knew he probably couldn't see her from that distance, but he raised a hand anyway, and so did she. She thought she saw a grin on his face.

"What was it you just said?" Wanda asked again.

Marcie blinked and turned from the window. "I said I think I'll have a doughnut after all."

"Chocolate or cream-filled?"

Once more Marcie felt herself smile. "One of each."

On Little Terry Road

FROM *From Sea to Stormy Sea*

BAD DAYS BEGIN with phone calls, so when his cell rang at 4 a.m., Dibbs rolled over with dread. He felt in the sheets for the phone. He didn't remember getting into bed but knew it had to have been after two, when the bars closed. He also didn't remember driving home. The phone rang again, and he found it. "Yeah?"

"Lolo?"

Jesus. "Ferriday?"

"I'm in trouble," she said.

He swung his feet off the bed. "Where are you?"

"That Indian motel."

"Are you alone? Are you hurt?"

"Yeah. Alone but not hurt."

He stood, glad he'd slept in his clothes. The curtains were bright with moonlight and the room so cold he could see the captions of his breath. She was apologizing, saying she didn't know how late it was.

"It's okay," he said. "I'll be there in fifteen minutes. Don't move or call anybody."

He hung up. He lived alone in this old hunting cabin in the woods, the fireplace in the den the only heat, and not too long ago it had occurred to him that not one other person had been here since he'd moved in three years before. His job—he was a deputy sheriff—kept him in plenty of contact with lowlifes, which went a long way in lowering his estimation of his fellow human beings, and besides the other deputies and police officers he worked with, there really wasn't anybody else.

Except Ferriday.

He killed his lights as he pulled around the back of the motel. As usual, the parking lot was nearly empty, a couple of junky cars, probably migrant workers. He hoped Fouad, the owner, was asleep and wouldn't see his lights. Dibbs eased past a green El Camino and parked in front of Room 12. He got out of the pickup and wiped his palms on his jeans and went to the door.

She opened it before he knocked, wearing a Star Wars T-shirt and panties. She had mascara smudged below her eyes and a thumbnail bruise on her cheek, and her long, wet red hair was a rat's nest.

She said, "Hey."

He came in, and she closed the door. The room smelled like cigarettes. When he turned, she was hugging him, saying his name over and over. His own hands he kept in the air, unsure what to do with them, aware of her breasts against his stomach, gradually letting his arms fall to her back.

"What happened?" His voice was thick in her hair, which smelled of motel strawberry shampoo.

"I was out at Little Terry's—"

"Jesus, Fer. What were you doing there?" Though he knew. It was the kind of place you went looking for trouble. Residence of a fuckhead dealer named Terry Little that everybody called Little Terry. Usually with him was his cousin Spike, who Dibbs had arrested more than once. Last time, couple of months back, Spike was "spiked up," as he liked to say, and clocked Dibbs in the jaw, resisting arrest. Dibbs had tuned him up a bit after that while his partner turned away. Took it a little too far, couple of broken ribs. The sheriff didn't say it in words, but Dibbs knew he had to pull back.

"Where you been staying?" he asked. "When'd you get back?"

"I don't know. Couple of weeks?"

So long. Last he'd heard she was living in Santa Fe. She was into photography. This a year ago. And now she was back? How had he not felt her in his bones?

"Tell me what happened," he said.

"I kept meaning to call you, but I needed to get myself sober first. I just wanted to go out there and get a little weed, you know?"

"What happened?"

She began to cry and pushed away from him and sat on the bed. He went and sat next to her and covered her long legs with a sheet and put his arm around her and began to untangle her hair. "Tell me."

She did, between bouts of crying. She wanted pot, but they told her they had some exceptionally clean crank and they wouldn't take no for an answer. They drank pink wine, smoked some pot. Then somehow she found herself in their dirty little kitchen, and they were snorting this yellow shit with rolled-up dollar bills. Then they were leading her into the bedroom and taking off her clothes. "I tried to stop them," she said, crying again.

"What happened?"

She took a breath. "They threw me on the bed, and then they started to argue about who went first."

"Spike and Terry?"

"Yeah." She said Spike pushed Little Terry, who was saying since it was his house, he got to go first, but Spike pushed him again and said *Bullshit*. Ferriday had looked on the nightstand and seen a pistol and began to scooch toward it while Spike had Terry in a headlock and Terry was pounding Spike's back with his fist.

"I got the gun and checked was it loaded and it was—"

It had been Dibbs himself who had taught her to shoot, when she was seventeen.

"—and I got off the bed. They didn't even see me till I was nearly out the door. I had to get my clothes. Then they both let each other go and came for me. I raised the gun and shot Spike and then Terry started screaming and I shot him too."

She began to cry, silent, the bed shaking.

He said, "Shhhhh." It was Tuesday, he thought. That was good. It was after 2 a.m. Also good. The place would probably be deserted until midmorning, when the early crankheads started to stir. He leaned forward and took her shoulders in his hands and turned her.

"Are they dead, Ferriday?"

She shrugged and shook her head. "I just ran, Lo. I knew I had to call you, that you'd help me like you always do. Even though I'm not your responsibility."

If she wasn't his responsibility, then what was she? A question he'd been trying to answer for ten years. She was the daughter of the woman he used to live with. Dibbs had been dating Barbara for more than a year, and they'd been talking about getting married. Then one night Ferriday showed up. It was the first time he knew she existed. Barbara had had Ferriday when she was sixteen, and the girl had been raised by her father and her father's wife and rarely saw her mother. But she'd fought with her father and step-mother, and there she was, with two suitcases. And as gorgeous a girl as Dibbs had ever seen, ever prettier than Barbara, with her same legs and smooth skin and red hair. Of course they took her in, though Dibbs felt uncomfortable with a sixteen-year-old girl living in the same house, a girl not his daughter or stepdaughter, a girl he didn't know. He and Barbara got along fine, always had, but it began to trouble him that she'd never once mentioned having a daughter.

"Are they dead?" he asked again.

Ferriday pushed away from him and lay on the bed and covered her head with the pillow. "I don't know. I threw down the gun and ran."

"It was their gun."

The pillow nodded.

"You're sure."

Another nod.

He rose and went and turned off the light and looked out the window.

"They were asking about you," she said, her voice muffled.

"Me? How?"

"Saying wasn't we related. Seemed to know all about you. Asking did we ever fool around, stuff like that."

They hadn't. After Barbara's death, there had been all kinds of tension between him and Ferriday. Sexual was just one of them.

A car passed on the highway, and he watched until it was gone. He felt his body temperature rising; his face felt red and hot. "What else?"

"Asking was there any dirt on you. Anything they could use."

"Use how? What'd you tell 'em?"

"Nothing, there ain't nothing to tell, far as I know. What you got going on with them two?"

"We had a little go-round a while back. I'm sorry it caught you up." And glad too, in some twisted way, because here she was. The thing about Ferriday, though, was that every way was twisted. It seemed all kinds of wrong, for example, how he felt about her. He was forty-four and she twenty-seven, for one thing. Not to mention that he'd once lived with her mother. "Nobody else was there?"

"No."

"Did you leave anything?"

"No, I got my purse."

"What about the gun?"

"I threw it down, I think."

He came back to the bed and sat down and looked squarely in her face. Her eyes were glazed; she was still high. She gave him a little trembly smile. In a way, this was them at their best, her needing him and him being needed.

"Stay here," he said. "Don't make any phone calls or text or let anybody in. I'll be back soon as I can."

She stood, and the sheet fell onto the floor. "Where you going?"

He picked up her car keys. "Your El Camino?"

"Belongs to a friend." When he gave her a look, she said, "I borrowed it, okay?"

He put the keys in his pocket. "It's something I want to ask you. When I get back."

She started toward him, but he slipped out the door before she could hug him again (during their last long goodbye, she'd picked his pocket). He got in his truck and started the engine and sat thinking about what he was going to do. What he was willing to do. He'd have to quit his job, for one thing, but that was okay with him. God knew this place could grind you up under its heel. They'd have to leave town too, maybe the state. When he thought about it, Arkansas was the place he thought about going, the Ozarks. Maybe she'd stay with him if there were mountains.

By the time he turned off the four-lane, the heater had kicked in. He slowed and veered onto a two-lane and then, soon after, a smaller two-lane and then a dirt road known as Little Terry Road, where there had once been a barn in which the owner hanged himself. Dibbs turned off his lights and stopped a hundred yards from the house. He got his personal, unregistered Glock out of the glove compartment and worked its smooth action. His service weapon, a Glock identical to the one he held now, was under the seat. He stuck a pair of rubber gloves in his pocket and checked his ankle holster, the tiny .22 in its place. He left his jacket on the seat despite the temperature and stuck his Maglite in his back pocket and, pistol in hand, trotted down the road, his breath trailing in the cold. The house came into view lit up like Christmas, the whole night world lit further by a high white spotlight of a moon. You wanted darkness, a no-show moon, on nights like this.

There were three vehicles in front of the house, a new SUV with its windows lowered and a car and a truck. These last two looked abandoned, tires flat, weeds growing along the doors. He crept past, his shadow morphing beneath him in this weird moonstruck night. He noted an old shed ahead. He'd have to check it next.

The door to the house was ajar. He nudged the door, and a messy room swung into view. A naked man lay on his belly half in, half out of the room, not moving. Facedown. It was Spike. Ferriday said she'd shot them in the bedroom, so he must've been trying to crawl out. He didn't seem to be breathing, and there was a huge puddle of blood beneath him.

"Shit," Dibbs said, glancing behind him.

Here. Now. Here and now was his last chance to call for backup. Every step from this moment on would be the step of a criminal.

He took it, went forward and peered beyond Spike into the bedroom, where the floor was smeared in yet more blood, a yellow rug now turning brown. Careful not to bloody his boots, Dibbs stepped over Spike and into the room. Following the Glock, he moved into the corner; nothing behind the bed.

He went back into the front room. He scanned the floor, looked beneath the old sofa, the chairs, nothing. Beyond Spike's body, Dibbs noticed a bloody footprint—a man's sneaker, looked like —in the dark hall. He eased forward and saw another print in the kitchen in the back of the house and saw that the door was open and the screen door ajar. He pushed it open the rest of the way and eased down the steps into the night, darker back there because of the trees.

"Help!" a voice called.

Dibbs clicked on his Mag and followed its light into the woods. He was on a path, careful not to snag a thread of his clothing on a briar, careful where he stepped so he wouldn't leave a print. Going this slowly, this carefully, it took him a full two minutes to find where Little Terry lay.

He was passed out, lying flat on his back in the middle of the path that some part of Dibbs's brain understood would eventually lead to the river.

Dibbs's light showed that Little Terry's long johns shirt was heavy with blood, his jeans too. Like his dead cousin Spike, Terry had bled a few gallons. Dibbs shone the light around the man, trying to see if he'd grabbed a pistol or a phone, but he didn't see anything. He came forward, the Glock ready, knelt, and, with the back of his hand, tapped Little Terry's pockets, feeling for the familiar weight of a handgun.

Nothing.

He stood and looked back toward the house, lights blinking through the dark trees. Where was the pistol? Ferriday said she'd dropped it. He made his way back and checked the shed. He came out and walked around, shone his light in the tall grass, into the interiors of the SUV and the junk cars next, a 1967 Thunderbird and an old Dodge Ram. Nothing, nobody.

Count yourself lucky, he thought. So far in a situation where a thousand elements could have gone wrong, none had. Yet. If only Little Terry would be dead when Dibbs went back . . .

He wasn't.

His eyes were open, squinting against Dibbs's light. He tried to lift a hand to shield his face but couldn't. He was young, early twenties, Caucasian, pimples on his cheeks and kind of a goatee thing around his mouth.

"Who's that?" he asked, in a voice stronger than Dibbs would've expected.

For a moment Dibbs considered not answering.

But he had questions of his own.

He lowered the light and came forward, the Glock loose in his right hand. "Hey, Terry."

In the darkness it took a moment for recognition to change Little Terry's face. People looked at you entirely differently when you wore the blue. Dibbs in his flannel shirt and jeans could be anybody.

"Thank God!" Terry said. "I never been so glad to see a fucking cop in my life."

"I heard y'all was looking for me."

"Not me, but Spike was."

"Well, here I am."

"You call 911?"

Dibbs took out his phone and looked at its bright face. No new calls.

"Thank God," Terry said. "That fucking bitch shot me."

Dibbs put the phone away. "What bitch?"

"Is the ambulance coming?"

"You didn't say who. You didn't say why."

"Why call the ambulance?"

"Why she shot you. Who she was."

"Does it matter? We can discuss it in the fucking hospital. Are they coming?"

"Let's talk now."

Little Terry gaped. He was clutching his stomach with both hands, his shirt soaked. "She came looking for crank. She's been coming the last few days, and we all been having fun. I was about passed out on the sofa when they woke me up yelling in the bedroom. Screaming at each other, him saying she was robbing him. Then she shot him, and then she came out and fucking shot me!"

"Ferriday"—Dibbs said the name out loud in the night like a hex spoken—"said y'all was fixing to rape her."

"Oh Jesus, Dibbs, that's a fucking lie! She's the one wanted to buy off us and didn't have any fucking money. She said she'd blow us both if we set her up."

"Did she?"

"Blow us? Hell yeah, she did. Like a pro."

Sad part was that Terry's version of the story was likely as true as Ferriday's. Now, though, it was becoming Dibbs's story. Or he was making it his. He knew Terry's past. Everybody did. Terry had a bad dad, sure, but so had Dibbs. Terry's file at the police station was full of things he'd done to people, starting in his early teens. The couple on Second Avenue. That lady's dog that time. How he threw that kid off the railroad trestle at Chance. Lately he'd been helping his cuz Spike distribute low-grade crystal meth.

Dibbs knew all of this and knew that Ferriday had had an even worse time. Who could blame a girl for acting the way she did when she'd been raised by a father who (it turned out) sexually abused her? Barbara had had no idea but tried to make it up to the poor girl, and Dibbs had tried too, taking them to dinner, floundering, watching movies "as a family." That weekend of redfishing at Gulf

Shores. Crossing into Mississippi for the Neoshoba County Fair.
The Lyle Lovett concert where Barbara and Ferriday danced and
even Lyle noticed.

Barbara's aneurysm killed her as quickly as a bullet to the brain,
the doctor said. Dibbs began to drink. Ferriday stayed in her room.
For two months the two of them were a pair of ghosts haunting
different rooms of the same house. He kept volunteering for
nights, and she was a senior in high school. When she came into
his room one night, about three months after Barbara's funeral,
he was drunk. She slid into his bed and was kissing him and his
hands filled with the weight of her, but it wasn't Barbara's weight. It
wasn't her smell. When he opened his eyes it was Ferriday, stoned
out of her mind. He pushed her off and stumbled out of bed. She
ran from the room and outside and was gone. The next day she'd
called from an uncle's house, her father's older brother (a lie), and
said she would be living there.

Terry's eyes had been closed for several minutes, his breathing shallow, and Dibbs hoped this might be it. For a while he'd been shiv-
ering; now he stopped. His eyes opened. "This wasn't my fault," he
said. "I swear. Most of the times it is, you know. Most of the times
I'm the one fucking up." He began to shiver again. "It's so cold.
Can you at least get me a blanket?" He started to cry and repeat
that he was cold. He promised he would do anything Dibbs wanted,
he'd say whatever Dibbs wanted him to, he'd say that Spike tried
to rape Ferriday if Dibbs would call 911, please, he was so fucking
cold.

Then he said, softly, "I know why you murdering me. It's 'cause
of Ferriday. You think you're gone save her, don't you?"

Maybe. Dibbs turned and went down the path toward the house,
Little Terry calling after him. He walked to the edge of the woods
and watched the house and considered turning off its lights and
reconsidered. The less he touched, the better. He walked to the
pickup truck, which was missing its tailgate, and sat on the edge.
He lit a cigarette and adjusted his ankle holster. Terry still calling.
The moon had moved, and he felt a little better concealed in this
darkness, perhaps the way he would feel for the rest of his life. He'd
crossed one line; now here he was looking at a whole other line.
The question was, when would the lines stop?

He checked his watch. Five a.m. It had been quiet for a while, down there. Dibbs's cigarette had burned to the filter and he crushed it out on his boot toe, put it in his pocket, and went down the path to make sure Little Terry was dead.

He got back to the motel at dawn and knew before he turned the corner that the El Camino would be gone. He'd taken her keys, but she still had the knowledge he'd once taught her, hot-wiring a car.

The room was empty too, of course, except for the smell of strawberry shampoo and cigarettes. He stood staring at the rumpled bed and then went in the bathroom. He rolled toilet paper around his fingers and knelt at the edge of the tub and cleaned the long red hairs she'd left, flushed them. He emptied the ashtray and took her little bag of garbage and went around the room rubbing away her fingerprints and trying not to think about how he had snapped on his rubber gloves and put his hand over Little Terry's mouth and nose, expecting a fight but all the fight gone, Little Terry's lips moving in silent words. It happened barely an hour ago, but Dibbs felt centuries removed and regarded the man he'd just been—hopeful at seeing Ferriday again—as the fool he was.

He sat on the bed. Sometime later this morning, somebody would go to Little Terry's house for a fix and find Spike dead. They'd steal shit first, cell phones, the television, maybe the gun Dibbs couldn't find, then eventually somebody would call 911. The crime scene would be contaminated as hell and there'd be a crowd at the door by the time Dibbs and his partner, Chaney, got there.

Dibbs rose from the bed and went to the window and looked out. A few big trucks trundling over the road, the sun beginning to redden the pavement. He needed to get to the station. He'd let Chaney drive the cruiser this morning. He was younger and liked it behind the wheel. Dibbs would suggest they get an early bite at Keller's on Highway 3. He wouldn't mention how close the place was to Little Terry Road, which, as everybody knew, was where you went if you wanted trouble.

RICHARD HELMS

See Humble and Die

FROM *The Eyes of Texas*

A SUMMONS. A dumb subpoena. All I had to do was slap it into the guy's hand, tell him he'd been served, and pocket the forty-seven-fifty for the job. Should have been simple as a wet dream, especially for a former Texas Ranger looking for something to stave off boredom after punching out with thirty-two years of service.

Sick and tired of sitting around, watching TV, and waiting for something critical to break and put me on the dark side of the grass, I registered a DBA with the Houston clerk of court and hung out a private investigator shingle. It was something to do. I put a listing in the Yellow Pages, my granddaughter made a web page, and business trickled in from time to time. Maybe every two or three weeks some drab, nervous housewife would sidle through the door, her makeup smeared with tears, and demand that I catch her husband banging his secretary. I usually gave them a one-week turnaround. Sometimes, if the philandering husband was a real horndog, I wrapped the case before the end of the evening news.

I met an insurance guy in a bar in Sugar Land, just west of Houston, about a year back. We struck up a conversation. When he found out I had been a Ranger, he started asking me a lot of questions. Then he found out I was a private cop. He almost peed himself.

"No shit?" he said. "You're like a real private eye? Don't get me wrong. I don't mean nothing by it, but aren't you a little . . . well . . . *old* to be a private eye?"

"Want to arm wrestle?" I said. "My usual opponent is still in a cast. I stay in shape. And I know things."

"Like what?"

"Wear a badge for three decades and you learn tricks. It's not all about knuckles. There's a lot of know-how to the game. Besides, it ain't like you see on the TV. My days of tracking felons and punks are in the past. Most of what I do these days is sit around and wait for someone to do something stupid."

"I think I can get you some work," he said.

"Yeah? What kind?"

"Insurance fraud," he said. "Let's order another round and talk about it."

So every month or so I get a call from Dallas to check on a claim. I once accidentally rear-ended a guy in San Angelo. It was nothing. A couple of crinkled bumpers at a stoplight. I couldn't have been going more than three miles per hour. I hopped out of the car and checked on the other driver, who said he was perfectly fine. No problem. By the time the uniform cop arrived to take a report for the insurance companies, the other driver was holding his neck and declaring that he had shooting pains going all down his arm. I shrugged and handed my information over to the cop.

Two days later I caught the guy on my dashcam, doing backflips on a trampoline in his backyard. Needless to say, his personal injury claim died on the spot.

That was the kind of work I got from Dallas. Lots of folks trying to put one over on the insurance company. Some of them were legit. Most were bullshit. I saved the insurance company in Dallas a lot of money.

Then there was the process serving. An old friend at the courthouse called me one day. Said he'd heard I'd opened an office. Wondered whether I'd like to pick up a hundred or so a week to serve warrants and subpoenas. Probably wouldn't take more than a couple of hours.

I bit. The pay is pocket change, but like I said, I'm not in this for the money. Not entirely.

I drop by his office each Monday morning, and he has three or four orders to be served waiting for me. It's usually local stuff. I served a guy just down the street from me a couple of months ago. Walked over after dinner, found him in his front yard mowing his dirt. Slapped him with a subpoena and was back in my house, all in ten minutes. They're not all that easy. In most cases, though, it's a piece of cake.

People don't walk around expecting legal papers to drop out of the sky. It's a cinch to get close to them. The easiest are the ones you catch at home. Ring the bell, ask for Mr. About-to-Be-Served, tell him you're a courier, and hand him the envelope. Bingo bango, dinner for two at Golden Corral in your back pocket, with a few bucks left over for ice cream.

I'm partial to ice cream.

Sometimes you catch a guy who's been given a heads-up. This is especially true in divorce cases, where the wife has already screamed something like "I will steal your fucking dreams, you cheating son of a bitch!" Those guys are on the lookout. Getting to them sometimes takes a little finesse.

I know a woman in town who's in the process-serving game. Her name's Amy. She's middle-aged, but time has been kind to her, and she still gets lots of looks from guys half her age. She snags a lot of divorce paper services. Her game is to catch the subject in a bar, start up a conversation. Somewhere along the line, she gives him a fake name, and he—naturally—gives his real one. She repeats the name, as if she's heard it before. The guy says, "Yep, that's me!" and she lays it on him. He goes home with a subpoena in one hand and his dick in the other. Works every time. Nobody expects a hot southern lady to come bearing a summons. She has perfect camouflage.

Won't work in my case, unless I'm serving divorce papers to little old ladies in rest homes. I work the codger angle. There's always a guy out there willing to talk about the good old days. Sometimes they buy me a beer before I serve them. It's not really ethical, but I hate to be antisocial.

The boss at the courthouse knows what kind of guys are likely to respond to Amy and which will respond to me. He's kind of psychic that way. He gives Amy the young guys, and I get the old-timers.

I received the call on a Wednesday morning.

"Got a job for you, Huck," my guy said.

I'm Huck. Huck Spence. It's short for Huckleberry, my middle name.

"What's the job?" I asked.

"Guy named Ralph Oakley. Should be a milk run, no big deal. He skipped out on jury duty. Chose exactly the week the district judge's diverticulitis was flaring up. Judge was in the mood to knock broomsticks up some asses. He issued orders to bring in every scoff-

law who failed to show for the jury pool, so they could account for
their lack of civic engagement, but mostly so he could rake them
over the coals and vent his spleen. There's a fine for dumping out
on the call, also."

"I'm familiar with it," I told him. "Word in the halls is the money
goes into a fund that's split evenly among the judges at the end of
the year."

"Beats me," he said. "I have no idea whether it's true, but I've
heard the same rumor."

Ralph Oakley lived in Humble, about fifteen miles north of the
center of Houston. Humble is the ghost of an oil boomtown, which
lent its name to an oil brand at some time in the murky past. A hundred years ago it was the richest-producing field in the entire state.
The oil dried up, and the petro circus pulled up stakes and moved
on, leaving Humble very humble indeed. At its height, Humble
burst at the seams with roughnecks and wildcatters and mud log-
gers and doodlebuggers making small fortunes by pulling dead
stuff out of the ground. These days population tops out around
twelve thousand, mostly truck farmers and day laborers and field
workers and timbermen, the kind of people who sweat out their
paychecks and try to raise families on the precipice of poverty. It's
your typical small suburban Texas town, a simple satellite of the
metropolis to the south. It's a hundred square miles of desperation
and hope and churches and resignation, with a few bars thrown in
to keep the sidewalks flat on Saturday night. The best thing Humble has going for it is a high school football stadium that would
make most college fields weep with envy. They take high school
football extra serious in Humble.

It also has twice the average crime rate for towns its size. It's that
kind of place.

I had an address for Ralph Oakley. It was close to the city limits with an unincorporated community called Borderville, close
enough to the freeway to hear the cars zooming by. To get there
I had to drive through the center of Old Humble, a section that
might have inspired Anarene in *The Last Picture Show*.

I pulled up in front of the house where Oakley lived. A woman
wearing a flowered house robe answered the door. She looked like
someone had wrapped a refrigerator. Her voice sounded like someone grooming a cat with a belt sander.

"Yeah?"

"I'm looking for Ralph Oakley," I said.

"Ralph? Ralph ain't lived here for a year and a half. Can't say I'm sad about it, either. Guy was a fuckin' cheapskate, pardon my French. Practically had to beat the rent out of him every month. Why you want him? What's he done?"

"Just wanted to catch up. Do you know where he moved?"

"You're a friend of his, you should know."

"I haven't seen him in years. I'm just passing through. This was the last address I had for him."

"Well, you might catch him at work, if he ain't been fired yet. Check out Borum's Butcher Shop. Five blocks thataway. Cain't miss it. Got a big plywood bull hanging out over the sidewalk. Last I saw him, he was working in the back."

She was right. There was no missing Borum's Butcher Shop. I walked through the front door. Texans pride themselves on their beef, and Borum was no exception. The floor was spotless. The cases were polished to a sheen, the glass crystal-clear. Cuts of rib eye, thick as a man's wrist, were stacked inside. I walked down the case, building an appetite. Porterhouses, New York strips, fillets. I started thinking about grilling that night.

"Help you?" a man said as he walked in from the back room. He was shorter than me, but massively built, in the way you get cutting up two-hundred-pound steer carcasses for a couple of decades. His face was open and smiling, that fake sort of grin people slap on their faces when they want to sell something.

"Ralph Oakley?" I said.

"Bob Borum. You a cop?"

"Nope. Are you?"

He grinned for real this time. "Was, once. Long time ago. Thought I smelled it on you."

"Left over from my days in the Rangers, but that was a long time ago too. Ralph wouldn't be around, would he?"

"Off today. Mind if I ask your business with him?"

"Some legal stuff. Nothing big."

"None of my business anyway, right? It's cool. Way Ralph's been moping around and skipping out on work lately, he probably won't be working here much longer. What happens to him is on him, right?"

"Couldn't agree more. I dropped by the address I had for him, but they said he moved away."

"He's in a motel, three streets over. Been living there for quite a while now. Not a bad deal, I suppose. Fresh towels every day, fresh sheets every week, and you don't have to lift a finger. Not a lot of square footage, but how much room does a man need, anyway?"

"I reckon we all wind up with more or less the same space," I said.

"Ain't it the truth?"

"Let me take care of this business with Ralph, and I'll drop back by. That rib eye there looks like it's got designs on my stomach. Think you can wrap it and have it ready for me? I don't want to leave it in the car."

"You got it."

The place was what we used to call a "drive-up motel." It wasn't a chain place. It had likely been around for half a century. The entire motel was on a single level, all the room doors opening directly onto the parking lot. The outside walls were painted cinder block. An ice machine with a wheezing, rattling compressor stood against the outer wall alongside a Pepsi machine. All the "sold out" lights on the machine were lit.

Bob Borum had given me Oakley's room number, so I didn't have to shine on the desk clerk. I backed my car into a space across the lot, facing his door.

A couple of years back, a process jockey in Houston was beaten to death with a baseball bat when he tried to serve divorce papers on a guy who'd stoked back too many PBRs. Since then I carry a GoPro camera on my dashboard. It's motion-activated and connected to a drive that can record up to a week of images at a time. If I ever catch the off-world shuttle on the job, I figure someone might find evidence on the camera to catch the guy who did it. It also protects me from claims that I dump paper in the trash and still claim the pay for serving it. It's happened.

The whole deal took less than a minute. I slipped an oil change receipt from my glove compartment onto a clipboard, added the subpoena, turned on the dashcam, and crossed the lot to his door. A Latina cleaning woman stepped out of the room two doors up just as I rapped on Oakley's door and said, "Maintenance!" The cleaning woman looked at me strangely. Guess she never saw a maintenance guy in a corduroy jacket and a Stetson before. I held a finger to my mouth and pointed at the door. She nodded and retreated into the room she had been cleaning. That door closed, and I heard the lock trip. Guess it was that sort of neighborhood.

Oakley opened the door. He was about an inch shorter than me, maybe six feet in his socks. He was blond, his hair shaggy and maybe a little stringy, and otherwise an attractive sort, as best as men can determine that about other men. He looked sweaty and nervous. His eyes were red, and I caught a whiff of weed from the room. None of my business.

"Got a call about your AC," I said.

"I didn't call nobody," he said.

I checked the oil change receipt on my clipboard, which looked official enough if you didn't examine it too closely.

"Ralph Oakley?" I asked.

"Yeah, that's me."

I took the envelope with the subpoena and held it out. "This is for you."

He took it, reflexively. My job was done.

"The original notice of jury duty was sent to your old address. They didn't know where to forward it. Tell the judge that story, and you might talk your way out of a fine."

"What?" he asked, but by then I'd turned and walked away. His rose-colored eyes told me he wouldn't remember the advice anyway.

He closed the door. I sat in the front seat of my car and filled out the service log detailing when I'd completed the job. As I did, a Honda Accord pulled into the parking slot in front of Ralphie's room. A woman stepped out. From behind, she had a decent figure. Nice legs. She wore a scarf over her hair, which I thought strange, but then she knocked on Ralph's door. He opened it and she looked over the parking lot furtively, but she was in shadow and I couldn't make out her face. I thought she stared at me for a long time, then stepped inside, and it all made sense. I'd spent time sitting outside motels spying on philanderers for longer than was healthy. I recognized a clandestine rendezvous when I saw one.

I drove back to Borum's, where Bob had my steak wrapped and rung up.

"How'd it go?" he asked as he made change.

"Smooth. No biggie. A misunderstanding. He seems a nervous sort."

"Ralph? Never noticed."

"Maybe it's because his girlfriend was on the way over."

"Didn't know he had one. Hey, you enjoy that steak, y'hear?"

Sunday morning I was lounging on the screened porch at the back of my house, reading the newspaper. I'd dispensed with the sports and the funnies and was perusing the local section. I keep an eye on the obituaries these days, mostly because it's become sort of a game for me to outlive people. I had just taken a sip of coffee, and I nearly sprayed it all over the newsprint when I saw the notice.

Ralph Mark Oakley. Age forty-three. Butcher. Died on Friday, May sixteenth. A smattering of survivors. Services to be held, so forth and so on. Two paragraphs. Forty-three years of breathing, and his entire life had been digested into two paragraphs. Short paragraphs at that. No cause of death listed. The picture looked like the guy I'd served at the motel, except the hair was shorter.

I had Saturday's newspaper still in the rack in the den. I'd been working Saturday and had only glanced at it. I yanked out the local section and searched it. Found the story on page three. A cleaning woman—probably the one I'd scared—found Ralph's body in his hotel room late on Friday afternoon, after seeing the door slightly open. The reporter tried to pretty things up, but it was easy to read between the lines. It had been gory. Ralph had been bludgeoned and stabbed multiple times. He had to be identified by his prints. Police were investigating, but there were no suspects.

I sat on the porch, scratching my aging cat Boudreaux's lumpy head as she basked in the sunlight, and I thought. Bob Borum had told me he didn't know Oakley had a girlfriend. I wondered if anyone else knew. I had seen the woman visit him surreptitiously in his motel room. People who sneak around have things to hide. What if the woman thought she had been discovered? She had looked right at me. Maybe she thought I was spying on her, and she decided to eliminate her cheating problem. It didn't gel completely in my head, but it was something to work on.

And, I had a way to find her.

I retrieved the dash camera from my car. It took a couple of minutes to hook it up to my laptop computer.

I was in luck. Since I'd parked directly across the lot from Oakley's door, I had a full-on view of his visitor's car when she parked in front of me. I jotted down the license number and saved the file on my computer.

Here's the thing about being a retired Texas Ranger. It's like being in the mob. You might cash out, but you never really leave. Looking back, I probably should have gone directly to the Humble Police Department. I'm a cop, though—or at least I used to be —and the tendency to do it yourself is kind of strong in cops. I called my old office. It was Sunday, but there was always someone on duty. I was lucky. I got Wade Stanfield. We used to call him Wade the Blade because in his day he was definitely the sharpest knife in the drawer. That was a long time ago. We've all dropped a half step toward second since then, which was probably why they had him working the slowest day of the week.

"Blade, need you to run a license for me."

"What's up?" he asked.

"Don't know. Could be something. Might be nothing."

"Like always. Gimme the number."

What we were doing was technically illegal. Like I said, though, once a Ranger, always a Ranger. You never completely punch out. It would have been a lot worse if Wade had checked a license for some guy on the street who had never worn a badge or body armor. I read the number off the paper and heard him muttering a little.

"No can do, podjo," he said. "System's down for maintenance. Ain't that the way? They always do these things on Sundays. Should be up tomorrow morning. Maybe later tonight. Tell you what. I'll run it as soon as I can, and I'll call you. Gonna cost you two beers and a burger."

"Cheap at half the price," I said. "You're on."

Sunday turned into Monday, and no word from Wade the Blade. I wasn't surprised. Like most government agencies, the Rangers were stuck with a computer system that should have been junked years ago. Sometimes shutting it down made it lazy about booting up again.

I had nothing to do, and the Rangers didn't have the only computer system in the state, so I drove over to Humble and introduced myself to the detective who'd caught Oakley's murder.

His name was Ken Sheeran. My bona fides as an ex-Ranger got me into his office pronto. He was in his middle forties, a lifer. He was thick around the middle. His shirt gapped between the buttons when he sat down, probably because he saw extra-large shirts as an assault on his vanity. He had thick pewter hair and a gaze that could cut glass. The first time I saw him, I had a feeling he was a good cop. You get a sense for these things.

"How can I help you?" he asked.

"Maybe I can help you. I served papers on Ralph Oakley last week, a couple of days before he died."

"Did you now?" Sheeran asked. "So you're the one. Yeah. I see it now. You match the description."

"Description."

"Tall, lean guy like you, in his late sixties, with silver hair and a thick salt-and-pepper mustache. Voice like a cement mixer. Wearing a cream Stetson just like the one in your lap there. Sure. Several folks came forward and said you were poking around town last week asking about Ralph Oakley. Serving papers, you say?"

I showed him my PI license and a copy of my process service log. "He ditched out on jury duty. Judge wanted to have a word with him."

"Guess that ship has sailed. I do recall some legal papers we retrieved from the trashcan in his room. You scared the piss out of that cleaning woman at the motel. I mean, like, literally. She peed her pants when you came knocking on Oakley's door. She thought you were there to kill him. Don't suppose you were. That would make my day."

"Here's the thing," I said. "I was sitting in my car at the motel where he was shacked, and a woman came to visit him. It looked like she didn't want to be seen entering his room. Has anyone said anything about him having a girlfriend?"

"Not as I recall. Can you describe this woman?"

"Five-five, nice figure. Good legs. I only saw her clearly from behind. I got her license number, though. Caught it on my dashcam."

I handed him the slip of paper with the number and a thumb drive with the video segment from the cam.

"We'll run this right away. I'd like to thank you for coming in." He extended his hand. "This could be a big help."

I started to shake hands, but my telephone beeped. It was Wade Stanfield. I held up a finger to Sheeran and answered.

"Sorry it took so long to run that number, buddy," he said. "Computers just came back up this morning, and I had a backlog."

"Did you get a hit?"

"Sure did."

He told me the car owner's name. I glanced at Sheeran.

"You need to do a safety check," I said.

He tried to make me wait at the station, but we both knew that was unlikely. I followed him across town in my car. We parked in front of a wood frame house with a deep covered gallery. I followed him up the steps to the front door.

A woman answered when he knocked. I had never seen her face before, but the figure was familiar.

"Mrs. Borum?" Sheeran asked, flashing his shield. "Mrs. Margery Borum?"

"Oh, my God!" she said, her hand rising to her mouth. "What's happened?"

"I think you know," I said. Sheeran shot me a warning look.

"You," she said to me. "I recognize you. You were the man sitting outside—" She stopped, cutting off the very end of the last word.

"Mrs. Borum," Sheeran said. "We need to talk."

She led us inside. She was flustered and sweaty, and she nearly forgot her manners. Finally she asked us to sit and even offered iced tea. We declined.

"Tell us about Ralph Oakley," Sheeran said.

"He worked for my husband," she said.

"He wasn't working last Wednesday," I said. "I know, because I served him a subpoena at his motel room. I saw you there minutes later. Were you in the habit of visiting him when your husband was at work?"

She started to cry. I sat back and let her. I did hand her a box of tissues from the table next to the couch. Her entire world was crumbling. I'd seen it a thousand times. It never got easy, but sometimes you just had to wait it out.

After a few minutes she calmed a little.

"We . . . Ralph and I . . . started seeing each other a few months back. It got out of hand, but I couldn't stop. He couldn't stop. We were talking about running off together. It seems silly, now that he's dead. It never would have worked."

"Why?" Sheeran asked.

"No money. Cash just burns holes in Ralph's pockets. He can't hold on to it. I don't know what I was thinking."

"Where were you on Friday?" I asked.

"In Houston, visiting a friend. We went shopping and had some drinks at a restaurant there. I know what you're thinking. I was no-where near Ralph on Friday. By the time I returned, around eight on Friday evening, the news was spreading around town. I've been a nervous wreck ever since."

"Where's your husband?" I asked.

"He's at work, of course. He'll be there until six."

Sheeran told her not to call her husband. I followed him several streets over to the Borum Butcher Shop. When we walked through the door, the sales floor was empty. I pointed toward the door to the back.

"I'm calling for backup," Sheeran said as he pulled a walkie from his pocket. I moved toward the door to check the parking lot. Sheeran started to follow me. I heard the blow that dropped him. It sounded like beating a watermelon with a wiffle bat. I turned. Sheeran was sprawled out on the floor, a pool of blood spreading from the back of his head, his eyes oddly unfocused. He twitched and jerked on the linoleum. Bob Borum stood over him, holding a honing steel, which dripped blood. In his other hand was a cleaver.

"You!" he shouted when he saw my face. "This is all your fault!"

"What did you do?" I knelt next to Sheeran and checked his wounds.

"Why in hell did you have to say anything about Ralph's girl-friend?" Borum pleaded. There were tears in his eyes. "Twenty-three years. We been married twenty-three great years. Then you come in and tell me Ralph's knocking off a little, so I decide I'll swing by and see who he's shagging. Thought it'd give me some-thing to rib him about. I get to the motel, and there's my own car sitting out front of his room. I followed her the next night, when she told me she was going out to a Grange meeting with her friend Sally. Sure enough, she went straight to that bastard Ralph."

I backed toward the door. The confines of the butcher shop were too close for comfort. I pined for the open air, where I could dodge any swipes he might want to make with the cleaver. I had palmed Sheeran's walkie. As I backed up, I quickly raised it and made an "officer down" call, adding the butcher shop address. I suddenly wished I'd also palmed his gun. I don't carry one.

I hit the door, but it didn't budge. I recalled that it opened inward from the street.

"You ruined my life, you son of a bitch!" Borum cried as he strode toward me, real tears streaming from his eyes. "Ain't nothin' left for me here. I either go on the road or on the gurney. Cain't kill me twice, can they? I done took out Ralph, and now I done a cop. Ain't nothin' to keep me from doing you too."

"When did you kill him?" I asked, trying to buy time.

"The next morning, on the way to work. I called his phone. Told him I'd drop by, give him a lift. I gave him a lift, all right. Lifted his cheatin' ass all the way to fucking heaven!"

He dropped the bloody honing steel and raised his hand to wipe at the tears running down his face. I took the opportunity and charged him, the way a tackle sacks a quarterback. My shoulder rammed into his midsection, just below the ribs, crushing against his solar plexus. The air rushed out of him in an explosive gasp. In the back of my mind, I heard the sirens in the distance. I felt a sharp, searing pain along my left shoulder blade. He had swung at me with the cleaver and had connected. The cleaver hit the floor and skittered across it into the corner under a baseboard heater. My stomach lurched, and I tasted metal in the back of my throat. My heart raced as I grappled with the burly butcher, him trying to suck air into his lungs and me trying to hold him down. We rolled and scrabbled about in Sheeran's blood. I got in two good punches just as the cruisers pulled into the parking lot, and I saw his eyes roll up in their sockets as he went slack beneath me.

It was touch-and-go for Ken Sheeran. They had to remove part of his skull because his brain was swelling. He was unconscious for almost a week, but slowly came around. He took a disability retirement. I had a call from him a few weeks back. He was thinking about the PI game. Wanted to know how to get a foothold. My long silence spoke volumes.

Bob Borum's lawyer managed to make a deal for aggravated manslaughter mitigated by passion, but he'll still spend the better part of the rest of his life in prison.

His wife divorced him while he was in jail waiting for trial. She moved away, I think to San Antonio. She showed up to testify, but otherwise nobody in Humble saw her again.

It took seventeen stitches to close the gash in my shoulder. Borum also fractured my scapula, so I was in a sling for a couple of months. You heal slower as you get old. It put a crimp in my PI activities, but that was okay. I needed a while to process things.

Bob Borum wasn't a bad guy. Neither was Ralph Oakley. They weren't criminals. They weren't evil. They were two men in love with the same woman, and I walked into their lives, a stranger come to town, who innocently catalyzed their self-destruction. There were no bad guys in this, just people set on the path of disparate fates.

Borum blamed me for his life turning to shit. In a way, he was right. If I'd kept my mouth shut about seeing the woman go into Ralph Oakley's motel room, probably none of this would have happened. At least it wouldn't have happened because of me. Humble's a small town. Sooner or later, one way or the other, the word would have gotten back to him. Killing Oakley was on him. I triggered it, though. That's a lot of responsibility to carry around.

I would have to learn to live with that.

RYAN DAVID JAHN

All This Distant Beauty

FROM *Mystery Tribune*

NOAH BECKETT WAS standing in front of a small airplane hangar, watching the bruise-purple sky turn dark. He lit a cigarette while he waited for George Beverly, his pilot, to pull a small Cessna out onto the faded tarmac. Beverly was a skinny old man with the sad, wet eyes of a basset hound, and he dressed like you might see him stamping paper on bingo night. Noah had never worked with him before, but he used to run drugs for the Medellín cartel before retiring to a stucco bungalow in Valle de Bravo, and a man who'd lived through the life of a drug runner was a man who could handle himself.

Once the plane was out on the tarmac, Beverly pushed the tug back into the hangar and closed the roll-up door. Then he hesitated, looking at Noah with his sad, wet eyes.

"What is it?"

"You seem like a nice guy," Beverly said. "This job you took, there's a reason the cops are leaving it alone. You follow through, you'll probably get yourself killed."

"Don't worry," Noah said. "I'm not a nice guy."

"It's your skin, kid."

"I'm forty-three."

Beverly shrugged. "My man should be here in about twenty minutes. I have a parachute ready to go, but if you wanna repack it yourself I wouldn't be offended."

"I'll trust you."

"How much experience you have jumping?"

"Had airborne training in the army."

"Static lines rather than ripcords?"

Noah nodded, took a drag, flicked his butt away.

"My advice? Pull as late as possible. A parachute's a big fucking target and they probably have armed guards all around that island. We're doing our flyover at night, but that don't make you invisible. Wait till you're at four hundred feet—two hundred if you're feeling a little suicidal, and I'm guessing you are."

"This has nothing to do with my mental state. It's just a job."

"Bagging groceries is a job."

Noah first read about the kidnapping four days earlier in *El Reformador*, the Mexico City newspaper at which the victim, journalist Sofia Trujillo, worked. According to the paper, she'd been investigating an international human trafficking ring when she vanished from her apartment, the only evidence of trouble a broken door frame. A day after the piece ran, the newspaper's owner came knocking.

Noah was sitting at the kitchen table, drinking coffee in his underwear, when he heard three staccato raps. He cursed to no one, got to his feet, and padded across the cool tile floor. When he pulled open his front door, he found himself looking at a brick of a man. He wore a well-tailored suit, his hair and nails immaculate, but his nose had been broken at least once, the bridge doglegging left midway down, and his eyes were moist. A thick manila folder was gripped in his fist.

"How can I help you?"

"Mr. Beckett?"

"He's not in. Can I tell him who stopped by?"

"My name is Santino Garcia." The voice was thinner than you'd expect from a man of his build, as if the sound of a flute came squeaking out of a tuba. "I own a newspaper and something has happened to one of my journalists. I believe Mr. Beckett might be able to help."

"Is this about the kidnapping?"

"You heard about it."

"I read about it. Why don't you come in? We can talk in my office."

"You're Mr. Beckett." It wasn't a question.

Noah nodded, then stepped left to let Santino inside. He led the man to his kitchen, gestured toward his table.

"This is your office?"

"Wait here. You can have a seat if you'd like."

When Noah returned—now wearing a pair of threadbare cut-off shorts, flip-flops, and a T-shirt—Santino was pouring coffee into a chipped mug, the manila envelope left resting on the counter. "I hope you don't mind."

"Help yourself."

Santino sipped his coffee.

"Who told you I might be able to help?"

"Dante Lopez."

Noah nodded. He didn't advertise his services, as they tended to be illegal, and only accepted clients if they could name someone he'd worked with before. "What do you think I can do for you?"

"I want you to find Sofia."

"Do you think they kidnapped her for ransom?"

"I don't believe so, no."

"Then there's nothing to be done. She got too close to something and they wanted her dead."

"That is my fear, of course."

"So why are you here?"

"Because I might be wrong," Santino said. "She's my stepdaughter, Mr. Beckett. If she's still alive, I want her home safely."

"Any idea where they might be holding her?"

"I have the notes from her investigation." He picked up the envelope and held it out to Noah, who took it from him. "My hope is you'll read something in there that will help you find her."

Noah flipped through the paperwork. "It's almost all in Spanish."

"You don't speak Spanish?"

"I speak it okay—I've been in Mexico a long time—but I read at a third-grade level."

"I can provide a translator."

"I guess I'll make do. I don't like coworkers. But first we need to talk about terms."

"I can pay you fifty thousand dollars up front and another fifty if you make her mother stop crying. That is every penny of liquid cash I have. I cannot negotiate. Your expenses will have to come from the money you're paid."

"Okay," Noah said.

Noah didn't know that he believed the man, but fifty thousand dollars in cash would allow him to engage in nothing but fuckery

for the next year if he wanted to, even after expenses. The second
payment didn't enter into his calculations at all. Sofia Trujillo was
almost certainly dead, which meant the money would never come,
but he'd still do what he could to find her.

He spent the rest of the day going through the dead woman's investigative notes and found himself impressed by her work. He
was no investigator himself—at best, he was a mercenary given to
sloth—but he wasn't so stupid he couldn't tell when someone had
managed to find worms under a rock. She'd uncovered dozens of
money transfers to and from prominent men; the names of half a
dozen orphanages from which girls aged five to sixteen frequently
went missing, and the orphanages' financial ties to several of those
prominent men; she had uncovered what looked to be a reasonable approximation of the trafficking ring's hierarchy, with a few
names missing; and, finally, she'd uncovered a base of operations,
which appeared to be Isla de Zapatos, a private island off the coast
of southern Mexico whose rubber trees were once harvested for a
shoe company, now defunct.

   If she'd already been murdered, she was probably buried out in
the desert somewhere or stuffed into a wall. But if her abductors
had for some reason kept her alive—maybe they wanted her to tell
them who'd betrayed them by talking to her and giving her docu-
ments—he might find her on Isla de Zapatos.

   Based on Sofia Trujillo's research, the trafficking ring held girls
on the island until buyers came to get them, which meant it had already been set up as some sort of prison camp, the perfect place to
hold a kidnapped journalist from whom you wanted information.

   It was a long shot, of course, but everything was.

Noah was lighting another cigarette when Beverly's guy showed up
in an old powder-blue Ford pickup that was dotted with rust holes
behind the wheel wells. The guy parked in front of the hangar
door, killed the engine, and stepped out into the night. He looked
at Noah, stepped over to Noah, and held out his hand.

   "How you doing? Name's Gael."

   Noah shook his hand and told him his name.

   "Cool, man, cool. Are we ready to go?" He was young and had
more enthusiasm for life than Noah liked, but that came with
youth. All the things he dreamed of doing hadn't yet become the

things he'd never done. Give him another fifteen years, let regret calcify his soul, and Noah predicted he'd turn into the type of man you could sit next to in a bar and not hate.

"I'm ready."

"Where's Bev at?"

"On board."

Gael stepped up onto the plane and Noah went back to smoking. He looked up at the sky. The bone-colored moon was a thin hooked blade, which was good; the lack of moonlight would increase his odds of getting onto the island unseen.

Satellite images he'd looked up of Isla de Zapatos revealed an utter lack of construction on the south end of the island, nothing but white beach leading into a mangrove forest. If he dropped in there, he might be okay. It'd mean a daylong hike to the north end of the island—maybe two days if the terrain was treacherous—but he'd just have to live with that. It was preferable to getting riddled with bullets while falling from twelve thousand feet.

The satellite images he'd seen had also revealed the compound, a plane on a dirt runway, and a dock with a boat tied to it on the north end of the island. Noah couldn't fly a plane, but he could drive a boat, so this was his one and only plan for escape.

Gael poked his head out of the plane. "We're ready when you are, man. Let's do it!"

Noah nodded, stoic, took a last drag from his cigarette, and flicked it away. He grabbed his rucksack from the tarmac. It held two changes of clothes, an extra pair of shoes, a small tarp, a blanket, enough food for two days, a hundred feet of twine (you never knew when you might need it), and a flint. A fanny pack already strapped to his waist held a pack of cigarettes and a lighter, a fold-out knife, a compass, his flip phone, a Glock 20, and fifteen 180-grain 10mm rounds. The fanny pack was supposed to be waterproof, but everything in it was bagged anyway, in case of a water landing. He also had a full canteen clipped to his belt.

He walked up into the plane and Gael shut and locked the hatch behind him.

The wind whipped through Noah's graying hair. The ground below, free of any artificial light, was covered in shadows. The seawater was black ink. He felt sick to his stomach. They were at twelve thousand feet and nearing the jump point. He lowered goggles over his eyes.

Gael tapped him on the shoulder. He nodded, turned on a strobe light attached to his rucksack, and threw it out into the night. For a moment he watched it drop, seeing only the rhythmic flashing of the light, then he jumped out into the darkness after it.

He arched his back and put himself in a neutral position, the wind whipping against his body, louder than the plane engine had been.

It was impossible to orient himself in the night. He could make out the silhouettes of trees and occasionally see the moonlight reflecting against the seawater, but had no way to gauge distance.

He looked at his altimeter. Nine thousand feet.

He was gonna pull his chute as late as possible, which would mean a hard landing.

Six thousand feet.

He looked to the north and saw lights in scattered buildings; saw tall lamps surrounding the compound.

Four thousand feet.

He looked down and saw the blinking light on his rucksack. It was still falling—then it wasn't. It landed and the light went out.

Two thousand feet.

He angled down, cutting through the wind.

One thousand feet.

He could now see the world below him more clearly. He was heading for a water landing—but not too far from shore.

Eight hundred feet.

He hoped the water had depth where he hit or he might break his legs.

Six hundred feet.

He started to feel genuine panic. Up to this point he'd been flying, but with the ground rushing up at him he knew for sure he was falling. If he'd jumped off the Empire State Building, he'd be about halfway to becoming a smudge.

Two hundred feet—you could buy a length of rope that long.

One hundred and—

He pulled the ripcord.

The chute burst open, caught air—one second, two seconds—and he splashed into the water, going under completely, feeling the sting of the landing even through the soles of his shoes. For a brief panicked moment he felt disoriented, it was dark underwater and he didn't know which way was up, but then he surfaced and saw the beach. He began gathering his parachute, stuffing it back into the pack. He'd either have to carry it with him or hide it, but it couldn't be discovered.

He scanned the water but couldn't see his rucksack, so he swam toward shore. If it came down to it he still had a knife, a gun, and some water. But when he reached the shore he saw it lying on the beach. The light, still flashing, was half buried in the sand. He lay on the beach beside it and looked up at the sky, heart pounding.

No one had shot at him, which meant he probably hadn't been seen. Either that or a group of men with guns was cutting its way through the woods to find him.

He reached into his fanny pack, pulled out a sandwich bag holding his cigarettes and lighter, and lit himself a smoke. When he got near the compound he'd probably have to lay off — he wouldn't want to give himself away — but for now he thought he was okay.

Once he'd finished his cigarette, he snuffed it out in the sand and put the butt into his pocket. He got to his feet and trudged across the beach, past a group of box thorns with fat green paddles and red bulbs, and into the mangrove forest. He walked some distance, listening to the night animals, looking for a flat surface to lie on. When he found a place, he pulled his tarp and his blanket from his rucksack and laid them out, putting the tarp down first. He undressed and hung his wet clothes from tree branches. He loaded his Glock's magazine with the fifteen rounds, lay down, wrapping himself up like a human burrito, and with the pistol gripped in his fist, closed his eyes.

Noah woke early the next morning to the sound of distant birds and the sensation that he was being watched. Before he did anything else, he reached for the grip of his pistol, which he'd let go in the night, and then, lying as still as possible, shifted his eyes left, then right, seeing what he could without moving his head.

About ten feet away, sitting among the mangrove trees, was a black jaguar. Its face and head were the color of midnight, but the darkness faded enough that you could see the shadow hints of spots on its flank. Its tail was curled around its body and it was looking at him with its yellow eyes. It was a large cat, at least a hundred and fifty pounds, but it was relaxed, giving Noah no sense that it was prepared to attack. Still, if it changed its mind, he had no doubt that it'd be able to kill him — unless he managed to shoot it first.

But hc had no intention of doing that unless the thing made an attempt on his life. He wouldn't murder an innocent creature—he had more love for animals than people—but also he didn't want the sound of a gunshot echoing across the island.

He slowly pushed the tarp and blanket off himself and sat up, still holding the pistol. He got to his feet. The jaguar continued to watch him, but it didn't move, so he pulled his clothes off the mangrove branches and put them back on. He snapped his fanny pack in place but tucked the pistol into his waistband for easy access. He buried his parachute, stuffed his tarp and blanket into his rucksack, and strapped it onto his back. He looked at the jaguar.

It didn't move.

He didn't think he could read the jaguar's mind—wild animals were mysterious to him—but it did seem that it was waiting for him to do something. He pulled his compass from the fanny pack, oriented himself, and began walking, glancing over his shoulder at the jaguar every once in a while, not fully trusting it wouldn't attack.

After about ten paces, it began to follow.

He continued to look over his shoulder as he walked, and it continued behind him, never coming closer or falling back.

Every once in a while he would hear the calls of frigate birds or cormorants and glance up to see them flying overhead, far beyond the canopy of trees. The sky was pale blue, like a bolt of faded denim, but he could see dark clouds to the east blowing toward him.

As he continued walking, as he began up the rocky slope of the hill that separated the south end of the island from the north, as he got farther from the shore, he saw them less frequently.

The black jaguar continued to follow.

It got very hot out. Sweat beaded on his forehead and ran down his sun-pinked skin, and the runnels caught on his eyebrows. He wiped them with his arm when they began to tickle and continued on. Sweat ran down his torso. His socks grew damp.

The mangroves were thinning as the terrain grew rockier and the water beneath it less brackish, but new types of foliage appeared, tall grasses mostly, cacti, an occasional cypress, and flowering plants he didn't recognize.

About noon he discovered a cave in the hillside. It was surrounded by red bursts of panic grass, so he nearly missed it. But didn't. He entered the cool, earthen-smelling interior of the cave. Somewhere deeper inside he could hear the steady drip of rainwater filtered by the rocks splashing into a standing pool. He shrugged out of his rucksack and sat down. He looked to his left and saw the black jaguar sitting on a boulder about ten feet from the mouth of the cave, looking at him, waiting. He opened his rucksack and pulled out a large bag of beef jerky he'd made a week earlier. He didn't have a food dehydrator, so he clipped the marinated steak to a box fan he put in his kitchen window and let the sun-heated air do the job. He took a piece out and tossed it to the jaguar, who sniffed it, then ate it. He bit into his own piece, washed it down with a swallow of water from his canteen.

After lunch he strapped the rucksack back on and continued his trek, the jaguar following.

About four o'clock he reached the top of the hill and stood there beneath the sun, looking out on the terrain to the north, the island stretching out before him. It looked to be a completely different habitat. He could see jacarandas on the downslope, and then, as the terrain grew less rocky, black sapotes, big-leaf mahoganies, and panama rubber trees, a forest of them, with the blue sky and the ocean beyond—seabirds circling the waters, looking for fish; clouds like pulled cotton Scotch-taped to the firmament. He just stood there a moment, looking out at all this distant beauty, and for a moment he felt completely at peace.

But though he wouldn't go so far as to call the beauty a lie, it was a half-truth. Once you got close enough you saw the danger: predators lurked in the shadows of the forest, and the sea was haunted by death. Always had been.

It started to rain as he began navigating the rocky slope down. It would have been a relief, except it made the ground beneath him slick and treacherous, slowing his journey. Fortunately, despite falling twice, he avoided any injury worse than a scraped elbow.

It was nearly dark before he reached the base of the hill, and he decided he was finished for the day. It was still raining, he was tired, and he didn't want to walk through unknown terrain in darkness.

He strung a length of twine between two trees, about three feet off the ground, and put the tarp over it, forming a makeshift tent, then put rocks on the corners of the tarp to keep it from flapping about in the wind. He sat in the mud, listening to the

rain thwack against the tarp, and smoked his first and last cigarette of the day.

The jaguar sat beneath a black sapote and waited.

The next morning he and the jaguar reached the rubber tree forest. The trees had great gouges carved into them for the exudate
to run down once they'd been tapped, and there were old white-
coated buckets scattered among leaves and fallen branches, most
of them half buried.

Soon after that they came across an old camp, housing for the
laborers who worked the rubber plantation probably. The camp
consisted of two dozen wooden huts with corrugated steel roofs,
now rusted and falling in.

"Should we go inside one of them, Chloe?"

The jaguar didn't respond. Noah wasn't sure she liked her new
name.

"I'm gonna check it out," Noah said. "You can wait here if you
want."

He pushed open a wooden door, the bottom rotted away, and
stepped into a small hut. Beams of light stabbed their way in
through the rusted roof, dust motes swimming around in them like
minnows. The hut held two cots and a table, and on the table an
old oil lantern. It was otherwise empty. He thought about the men
who must have worked and lived on this plantation and felt brief—
but overwhelming—sadness. This island was beautiful, but there
was something rotten about it, something bad seeping up through
the soil. The men who had harvested rubber, even if they'd been
paid a pittance, had almost certainly lived lives of desperation—
their hopes and dreams stolen from them by a shoe company so
it could make high-tops for kids in Indianapolis—and now the island was being used to hold young girls who were being bought
and sold into slavery of a different sort. It made him feel sick in his
stomach to think about it.

A wolf spider crawled across the table.

Noah looked at it for a moment, then turned and left the hut.

Chloe was sitting just outside the camp. She looked at him as he
approached, her face expressionless.

"Let's get going."

Noah continued to walk, heading north, and the jaguar followed.

*

He heard the men talking before he saw them, and, as soon as he did, stopped all movement. He hadn't looked at his watch for some time, but the sun was low and the sky was streaked with orange and pink, so—despite the heat and sweat dripping from his body— evening had arrived. He pulled the Glock from his waistband and listened to the conversation, which turned out to be an argument.

"Estoy cansado. Es tu turno."

"Todavia tengo ampollas de la ultima vez."

"¿Cómo es mi maldito problema?"

"Porque estoy haciendo tu problema, imbécil."

Noah took one careful step forward—then a second, a third, and a fourth.

He could now see the men between the trunks of the trees. They were standing in a clearing next to a hole they were digging, a hole they had been digging, anyway, before they decided to fight about whose turn it was to work. The larger of the two, olive-skinned and dark-haired, was holding the shovel like a baseball bat, threatening to hit the smaller one, a pale redheaded man, with the spade end, but the small one didn't appear to be all that concerned.

"¿Cómo se supone que debo cavar si me estás amenazando con la pala?"

This was a solid point and seemed to convince the large one that his threat was pointless. He lowered the shovel, hesitated a moment, and then handed it over. The small one swung it around hard and it whacked against the large man's skull with a hollow *thwack* that rang out briefly like a broken bell. The large man collapsed to the ground and the small man hit him in the head again, and again—with quick, brutal blows—then threw down the shovel and spat.

"Fucking stupid dumbfuck," the small man said with a Texas accent Noah hadn't heard in his Spanish. But just listening to those three words in English, Noah knew this was a man who'd wersh his clothes rather than wash them.

He raised his pistol and stepped out into the clearing.

The Texan had his back to Noah, still looking down at the guy he'd hit in the head. The skull was cracked and seeping blood into the soil. The blood looked black and thick as crude oil in the evening light.

Noah walked up behind the Texan as quietly as possible, knowing that with each step he might reveal himself—with a snapped twig or the sound of his breathing — and once he was close enough, he yanked the revolver from the guy's waistband.

The Texan jumped, startled, and turned to look at him.

"Who the fuck are you?"

Noah tucked his Glock away but kept the revolver aimed. "I'm pointing a gun at you and you're unarmed — except the ankle piece, and if you go for it, I'll do you. That means I'm the one who gets to ask the questions. A woman was brought to this island. Where is she?"

The Texan shook his head, as if confused. "I don't know what you're talking about, man."

"Bullshit. Tell me where she is."

"I don't know no woman."

It might have been true. She might as easily have been dead in a ditch on the mainland.

Then Noah saw why the men had been digging — something large was on the ground behind the pile of dirt they'd excavated. It was wrapped in a bloodstained sheet.

"What's the grave for?"

The Texan nodded toward the sheet. "Go look."

"I think you need to tell me."

"You can't shoot me. If you do, a dozen men'll be here in less than five minutes."

"I won't be here in five minutes, but you'll still be dead, dumbass. What's in the sheet?"

The Texan shook his head.

Noah stepped forward and used the revolver to whack the man's temple. The Texan stumbled back dazed, slipped, and fell into the grave, but didn't seem to like it there much, because he immediately tried to scramble out. Noah decided not to let him. He kicked the guy back into the hole, aimed the revolver at him.

"Tell me where the woman is or get comfortable where you're lying."

Chloe slunk out of the shadows as silent as a ghost, her body moving fluidly, and sat down beside Noah, looking at the man in the grave. The man looked back, scared.

"She's been with the girls most of the time." He pointed toward the compound — clearly more afraid of Chloe than he was of a man with a gun. Noah didn't blame him. Wild animals hadn't learned the niceties of civilized life and didn't care about laws or justice.

They were instinctual, and instinct without thought was not only dangerous but unpredictable.

"Is she alive?"

"I don't know—she was."

"When?"

"What?"

"When was she alive?"

"I saw her about two hours ago."

During the course of his conversation with the Texan, it had occurred to Noah that he might have to kill him. If he didn't, the man would talk, everyone else in the compound would know he was here, and that would make it difficult to get off the island alive. He told himself the guy was part of a human trafficking ring and if he killed him he'd be doing the world a favor. It was probably even true. The man had caved in another man's skull over whose turn it was to dig a hole. He clearly placed no value on human life. But Noah found it was difficult to put himself in the right frame of mind. He'd killed people when he was in the army, had even shot someone once as a cop for the LAPD—before he was kicked off the force for stealing cash from the evidence locker—but in those situations his life had been threatened. He'd been reacting to danger. Killing a man in cold blood was another thing altogether.

"Where in the compound are they?"

"In the green building. It's a converted shipping container. You'll see it. But if you try anything you'll only get yourself killed."

"How many men are in the compound?"

The Texan did a mental count. "Sixteen." Then he looked at the man on the ground with blood seeping from his skull. "Fifteen."

"Counting you?"

The Texan shook his head.

Fifteen men, probably heavily armed, and some of them were certain to have had military training. Not great odds, but better than the lottery, and he still bought a *Melate* ticket every once in a while.

Noah rubbed the revolver's hammer spur, feeling it rough against the pad of his thumb, and thought about what he was going to do. The Texan looked back at him with wide frightened eyes. Noah thought about his mother back home in Dallas or Houston, wondering what had happened to him. He thought of his sister crying at the funeral after the body had been discovered in a shallow grave.

"Stand up."

The Texan stood up.

"Turn around."

The Texan turned around.

Noah hit him at the base of the skull with the revolver, and he collapsed to the ground unconscious. Noah then stepped into the grave and pulled the man's shirt off. He tore off a sleeve and shoved it into the mouth. Then tied the rest of the shirt around the head to keep the sleeve in place. Finally he hogtied the man with twine and left him where he lay — let God pass judgment.

Noah didn't need him dead, just silent.

He stepped out of the grave and walked to whatever was wrapped in the bloody sheet. After pausing a moment, not sure he wanted to see, he pulled the sheet away and found himself looking at the blank face of a teenage girl, maybe sixteen years old. Her left eye had been bruised shut, her nose had been broken, her lower lip was split. Her neck was bent at an unnatural angle. Her right eye stared at him, blank as a broken television screen.

Something inside him shifted and he went cold all over.

He stepped into the grave and stabbed the Texan in the back of his neck, twisted the blade, yanked the knife back out, and watched blood ooze out of the wound.

Maybe God was busy. Maybe sometimes judgment couldn't wait.

Noah stood beside Chloe, smoked a cigarette, and waited for dark. He told himself this would be the last cigarette he ever smoked if things went bad. Well, everybody died sometime. He might as well do it while trying to accomplish something good, especially after all the bad he'd done. Two ex-wives he hadn't treated as well as he should have; a daughter who refused to speak to him; money and girlfriends stolen; friends betrayed. He hadn't been lying when he told Beverly he wasn't a nice man. But he hadn't been telling the whole truth either. He wasn't a nice man — but he tried not to be a bad one. He tried to find some kind of balance, to do enough right that it offset the wrong.

The sky went dark.

"Are you ready?"

Chloe looked back at him, but her expression was—as always —unreadable.

"I'm going," Noah said.

He walked toward the compound, telling himself not to look back. But he couldn't help himself. He glanced over his shoulder, expecting the jaguar to be close behind, but she wasn't. She had walked to the dead girl's body and lain down beside it, resting her chin on the girl's breast. She watched him with her yellow eyes, expressionless, but that was it.

It seemed as though their brief friendship was over.

Noah told himself not to be stupid. The jaguar was a wild animal. There was no telling why she'd decided to walk with him for as long as she had, maybe just curiosity, but they hadn't been friends and he never should have named her.

Yet he'd taken some kind of comfort in the knowledge that they'd be going into the compound together, and now he was going in alone.

Noah stood in the shadows and looked at the compound. It was made up entirely of shipping containers that had been converted to buildings. They sat on concrete blocks, had windows and electricity and plumbing, had slant roofs for the frequent rains to run off of. He could see the green building at the other end of the compound. A girl, maybe thirteen, was looking out the barred window.

Noah was certain there were others inside.

Several armed guards—Noah counted six of them, and there were probably others he couldn't see—were standing around the perimeter. They were dressed in army BDUs and holding M16A2 rifles. At the opposite end of the compound was a dirt runway with a small single-prop airplane parked at the end of it. Beyond that, at the shoreline, the dock feeding into the water and the boat he'd seen on satellite images. And surrounding the entire place, the dock excepted, were high-pressure sodium-vapor lamps, set up about every twenty feet, so that there was almost no space for shadow between them. Noah had no idea how he was going to breach the perimeter without being killed almost immediately. So he stood there for a long time, looking in on the place.

He glanced from one building to the next, looking into the windows to see if he could learn anything else. Behind the third window, he saw Sofia Trujillo standing across from a man Noah recognized as a legislator and prominent member of one of Mexico's national political parties. This was the man Sofia thought was running the entire human trafficking ring, and now she was standing across from him having an apparently relaxed conversation. The legislator said something and patted her arm. She laughed.

It was possible Sofia had managed to put herself in the legislator's favor in order to get herself out of a bad situation. But she didn't appear to be the victim of a kidnapping. She didn't appear to be the victim of anything.

She hugged the legislator, kissed him on the mouth — lips parted — and picked a purse up from a table. She made her way outside, carrying the purse, and walked to the green shipping container in which the girls were kept. She pulled a key from her pocket and snapped open a padlock. She slipped it out of the staple, flipped open the hasp, and pulled open the door. She stepped inside.

This might be Noah's only chance — if it was a chance.

He walked through the shadows along the perimeter of the compound, looking for a way to get into the building without being seen. But even as he moved, he thought about what might happen if he was seen. He wondered to himself whether the steel of a shipping container might stop a bullet. The walls were made from fourteen-gauge high-strength low-alloy steel — he'd once had a friend who wanted to convert one into a bomb shelter, and the motherfucker wouldn't shut up about it — so he thought they'd at least slow down most bullets to the point of nonlethality. They weren't dealing with aluminum foil here. But there was only one way to find out for sure, and he hoped he didn't have to.

He was now positioned directly across from the unlocked door, but there were about a hundred feet of well-lighted ground between him and it — and no protection. There was also an armed guard positioned so that he'd see Noah the second he stepped out of the darkness.

Noah shrugged out of his rucksack and set it down gently beside the trunk of a tree. He exhaled in a sigh and removed his knife. He gripped it tight, but it felt slick with sweat. He reached up, grabbed a tree branch, and yanked it down. It snapped loudly. He hid himself behind the trunk of a tree and watched.

The armed guard looked toward the sound — seemed to be looking right at Noah, though that was impossible — but for a moment he didn't move. Finally he decided to check it out, so he walked toward the woods. Noah held his breath, hoping the guard suspected a capybara or something rather than a human, and watched as the man took step after step through the light before entering the woods and covering himself with shadows.

The guard was now only ten feet away from him—now he was eight.

If he turned his head to the right, he'd see Noah, but he didn't turn his head. He was looking toward the ground, looking to see a creature on the forest floor.

Now he was only five feet away and Noah knew he needed to move—if the guard kept walking, he'd only put distance between them.

He jumped out of his hiding spot and wrapped an arm around the guard's head, covering his mouth with the palm of his hand. The man struggled and elbowed Noah in the ribs. He tried to turn the M16 around so he could fire at him. But Noah ducked left and jammed his knife into the throat just below the jawline. Blood throbbed out of the wound around the blade, each gush timed to the guard's heartbeat. But soon enough the bleeding stopped with the heart and the guard went limp as a wet towel.

Noah let him drop to the ground, let him sag down, then leaned over, picked up the M16, and strapped it over his shoulder. His right arm was covered in the man's blood, and more was soaking into his shirt. It smelled strongly of metal. Noah ignored it and walked to the edge of the woods. He looked out at the compound. It was quiet, still. No one had yet noticed the guard was missing.

Noah paused a beat, inhale, exhale, and ran for the building —shot out of the darkness and into the light. His heart thumped in his chest. His eyes darted as he looked for danger, but he saw no one, and he believed no one saw him.

He reached the door and pulled it open.

He stepped inside, shut the door behind him, and stood there with his back to it. Seven faces floated in front of him like moons —six girls, aged five to sixteen or so, and Sofia Trujillo. From the looks of it, Sofia had been putting makeup onto the youngest girl. She already had eye shadow on, and Sofia was holding a dark red lipstick in her hand. But nobody was doing anything now. Every face was turned toward him, staring, silent.

Noah looked at Sofia. "Santino García sent me here to rescue you—if you were still alive—but I'm not sure you need rescuing."

"You shouldn't have come here. You're gonna get yourself killed."

"That may be, but before I do, I'd like you to tell me what's happening here."

"I don't owe you an explanation."

"That's where we disagree. You're the reason I'm here, so I think you owe me something."

"I'm here to help these girls."

"By putting makeup on them while they're being held captive? I read your research. I know what this place is. How you can participate in it is—"

"You need to talk to Jose Luis."

"Ramos?" She didn't answer, but her eyes said yes: Jose Luis Ramos, the legislator. "Why is it you think I need to talk to him?"

"Because you don't understand what's happening here. I didn't either, not at first. But they're getting these girls out of a life of poverty and into new homes in the United States. Into new homes with families who will love them."

"By keeping them locked in a storage container?"

"For their own safety—ask them yourself."

"I don't need to. They'll repeat the lies they've been told."

"You're wrong."

"Then why is one of the girls lying beside a shallow grave a quarter mile from here with her fucking neck snapped?"

"Ana?" Sofia looked confused.

"I didn't get a chance to ask her her name. She was about sixteen. Black hair, cut at the jawline, like a short bob. Big brown eyes."

"That's Ana. She went to her new home yesterday afternoon."

"If her new home is a grave, she's right next to it."

"I don't believe you."

"What do you think happened to her? How do you think I know what she looked like?"

"I saw her step on a plane with her new father."

"But what you probably didn't see is what he tried to do to her on that plane. How she fought back. How he killed her for it. And you didn't see Ramos's men unload the body after dark and drag it out into the woods."

"That can't be true. Jose Luis is a kind man. He screens the adoptive parents. What he's doing—it might be illegal, but he's doing it to help these girls."

Noah glanced over to the girls. They were clean and well fed and staring at him wide-eyed and fearful. As if he were the bad guy. For just a moment he almost allowed himself to believe Sofia's story. It would make this much easier. He could walk out of here and not look back. Only he didn't believe her story. He believed that *she* believed it, but that was all.

"How much money do you think he's making off them?"

"A person can't make money and do a good thing?"

"Let me ask you this, Sofia: why is he only 'rescuing' girls?"

"His sister died in an orphanage, and the normal adoption process takes so long and—"

"You're sleeping with him."

"I don't—"

"I've read your research. You're too smart to believe any of this bullshit. You dug your way to the truth and now you're denying facts that *you* uncovered. The only explanation is, you're falling for him. Love makes everybody stupid."

Sofia looked toward the corner for a long time. When she looked back at him there were tears in her eyes. "You're right. I let myself fall in love with him. I didn't mean for it to happen—I met with him to confront him with what I knew—but it did." She looked down at her hands, at the lipstick and cap she was holding. She twisted down the lipstick, put the cap on it, and tucked it into her purse. "So what do I do now?"

The question was answered by a gunshot. The bullet thwacked through the glass and dinged against the far wall of the building, denting it. It flew by close enough that Noah felt the air move in its wake. Someone outside had seen him and decided to shoot rather than investigate.

The girls screamed and huddled into a corner of the room. Noah shoved Sofia out of the line of fire and ducked down.

People outside were yelling in Spanish, and he could hear the heavy thudding sound of boots pounding earth.

Noah's plan—if it could be called a plan—had been to find Sofia, sneak her out of the compound, and get to the boat. But the time for sneaking around had ended with a gunshot. Now he had to react.

In Spanish he told the girls to lie on the floor, facedown. Then he looked at Sofia. "You got a compact in that purse?"

She nodded.

From outside: "Come out of the building with your hands up."

Noah didn't respond to the request. He reached over to the purse and grabbed it, dropping it at his feet. He dug through it till he found a Mac foundation compact. He opened it and let the applicator pad fall to the floor.

"We have you surrounded; come out of the fucking building with your hands in the air."

Noah looked at Sofia. "Real good people here, shooting into a building with six innocent girls inside — and you."

She looked back at him but said nothing.

With his back to the wall, sitting on his haunches just below the window, he held up the compact to get a view of the situation outside. He saw three of the guards standing about thirty feet away, aiming their rifles at the building. Then one of them saw the mirror's reflection and fired. Noah saw a brief muzzle flash and the compact exploded in his hand.

"Fuck."

He glanced at the door.

It remained closed — for now.

He listened for the sound of footsteps outside but heard nothing.

"You have one more chance — come out with your hands in the air."

He was in the soup now, and didn't know how to get out of it. After a beat, he decided there wasn't an elegant solution to this inelegant situation. He'd have to be blunt.

He crawled to the cots on which the girls slept and pulled a mattress down from one of them. It was about six inches thick and filled only with foam; no chance it would stop a bullet, but it would at least block the guards' view of what was happening inside. He yanked it toward the window and pushed it up, blocking the bullet-punctuated glass. Then pushed it enough to the side that he'd have an inch or so of room to see — and to fire.

He flipped the M16 to three-shot bursts, knowing he wouldn't have time for precision shooting—he wasn't the world's best shot anyway—and got to his feet with his back to the wall. He closed his eyes, inhaled, exhaled, and opened his eyes.

He looked through the strip of glass and pulled back.

A bullet thwacked against the wall, denting it, but didn't penetrate.

The three guards were standing in the same positions. The other guards—and who knew how many there really were; there might be up to ten of them—could have been anywhere, but his guess was that they were planning to burst through the door, so he'd have to keep an eye on it.

He waited a moment—and then another moment. He looked at the girls and, in Spanish, told them to cover their ears. Then he looked at Sofia. "You too."

He turned around, fired three three-shot bursts through the window, moving from left to right, taking no time to line up his targets, then put his back against the wall again. The sound of the gunfire in the building, in this small metal room, was deafening. His ears rang with tinnitus.

He glanced quickly through the window.

One of the guards was on the ground. Another had been shot in the shoulder but wasn't incapacitated. The third he'd missed altogether.

And he had twenty-one rounds left in the M16—if the thirty-round clip jammed into it had been full, of which there was no guarantee.

The door flew open with a bang and a guard in a bulletproof vest barged in, aimed at Noah, and—

Noah angled the gun toward the head and fired a three-round burst.

The head split open as if it'd been cleaved with an ax and the body dropped, leaving a mist of blood hanging in the air, behind which another man stood.

Noah fired again—but not before he took a round to the gut.

The two men—Noah and the second guard—went down simultaneously. Noah felt hot blood pouring into his lap before he felt the pain, but he knew there could be more men in the doorway, so he aimed toward it and fired blind, pulled the trigger again and again and again and again, until the gun only clicked. The room was now full of smoke and the stink of cordite.

He pulled the Glock from his waistband—he must've dropped the revolver while running—and aimed at the doorway, but the doorway was now empty.

He listened to the silence while pain radiated out through his body in waves from the gunshot wound in his stomach.

He crawled to the doorway and rolled the first guard out into the dirt. He looked at the four other men lying outside beneath the light of the sodium-vapor lamps. One of them lifted his head to look at Noah—he'd only been hit in the bulletproof vest: had the wind knocked out of him, maybe broke a rib or two—and raised his rifle.

Noah shot him in the face and shut the door.

He sat on the floor and bled. None of the men in the doorway had been the same as those outside his window, which meant there were at least two more guards—but as many as seven—and he felt sick and sweaty and weak, and the pain was nearly unbearable.

He was forty-three years old. His hair was turning gray. He had a beer belly that flopped over his belt. He smoked a pack of cigarettes a day when he wasn't on a job, two if he went out drinking. His back hurt every morning when he got out of bed. Nobody out of high school would mistake him for an old man—but he was too fucking old and too fucking tired to do shit like this anymore. Unfortunately, he had no job, no skills besides these ones—which amounted to half-forgotten military training combined with amoral misanthropy—and until the morning Santino had written him a check, he'd had about two thousand dollars to his name. What else was he gonna do with his life?

The silence stretched on.

He looked from the girls to Sofia—they were all okay.

"You still thinking Jose Luis Ramos is a swell guy?"

Sofia didn't respond. She was pale and sick-looking, which was to be expected. Nobody liked violence up close, even those whose job it was to engage in it.

"Are you still alive in there?" Noah recognized the voice. He'd heard it on television and the radio. It was Ramos speaking to him this time.

"No—you killed me," Noah said. "You can leave now."

"Send the girls out. We don't want them to get hurt."

"Then stop shooting at them."

"You have to know there's no way out of this for you. You'll never get off this island alive."

"I've killed seven of your men. That means there's eight more men on this island, including you. Even if they're all trained, I don't think my odds are too bad."

"If you don't let the girls walk out of that building, their deaths are on you."

"Listen, Ramos?"

"Yes?"

"I don't wanna be rude, but you're kind of an asshole."

"Finish it." This time softer, not speaking to Noah.

Gunfire exploded outside the building. Dozens of shots all at once.

Bullets pounded against the steel wall. Dents hammered themselves into the metal, the paint flaking off in star-shaped bursts. Every fifth or sixth round managed to punch through. Noah was hit by fragments as he lay on the floor. They shot into his back and neck and his hands, which he was using to cover his head. They weren't even trying to keep the girls alive at this point. They probably weren't trying to kill them either—they were valuable merchandise as far as Ramos was concerned—but Ramos was willing to lose them if it meant Noah died too. And willing to lose Sofia, despite whatever love he may have professed.

The shooting stopped.

Noah waited where he lay prone, half expecting another burst of gunfire, but he heard only silence—and the sound of the younger girls crying. He looked over at them. The older ones had lain on top of the younger during the gunfire. One of the older girls was bleeding in her neck, another in her arm, but the injuries didn't appear to be lethal.

He looked at Sofia—she was dead.

A bullet had punched through the metal and struck her in the temple. Her eyes stared at him with nothing behind them.

"Goddamnit," he whispered to himself.

He had to end this. One way or another it was going to end soon anyway. He'd been bleeding for some time, and every minute that passed he grew weaker.

"Fuck it."

He crawled toward the door and pulled it open as quietly as possible. He almost hoped that a gunman would be there to finish him off—he was so tired he didn't really want to go on—but no one was there. He picked up an M16 from one of the corpses and stumbled to the far side of the building, feeling dizzy, black dots floating in front of his eyes.

He stood in the shadow of the building for a moment doing nothing, then looked around the corner. He saw Ramos standing there, a pistol hanging from his fist. He was flanked by the men who remained on the island. All of them. He suddenly wished he'd thought to bring an explosive device. If he had, he could finish this now.

Well, he supposed, it was about to be finished anyway.

He estimated he had thirty rounds in the M16 and another fifteen in the Glock—but he seriously doubted he'd live long enough to fire off forty-five rounds.

He stepped out of the shadows and began to shoot in bursts, sweeping back and forth across the line of men, walking forward even as they began to fire back at him, even as he felt sharp pain in his left ear and hot blood began pouring down his face, even as something else kicked his right shoulder back and caused more pain to radiate through his body, and when something tore at his right leg he limped forward, and when the M16 was empty and there were three men left standing, he pulled the Glock from his waistband and continued to shoot, watching the men drop, blood hanging in the air beneath the sodium-vapor lamplight, and then it was only him and Ramos standing there, maybe ten feet apart, and each of them was aiming his pistol at the other.

Noah pulled his trigger—*click.*

Ramos smiled a sick smile, a malevolent smile, his face spattered with the blood of his men, and pulled his own trigger—*click.*

Noah watched him reach to the ground for a weapon even as the black jaguar leaped out of the shadows, silent as a ghost, sinewy muscle rippling beneath her shiny black coat, and in two bounds she was upon Ramos, her teeth tearing at his throat as a grumbling roar as loud as a truck engine left her mouth, and she shook her head back and forth, ripping at the flesh, and hot blood poured out into the soil, and then—like that—it was finished.

Noah looked at her.

She turned her head to look back with her unreadable yellow eyes and licked the blood from her muzzle.

"I'm sorry I didn't get here in time to save you, Ana," he said, knowing he was being superstitious. But he believed his superstition nonetheless. "I'm very sorry."

She walked over to him silently, licked his fingertips once, her tongue as coarse as sandpaper, but that was it. She turned and walked back into the woods. She didn't look back, but he continued to watch until the shadows enveloped her.

He loaded the girls onto the boat and began the drive back to the mainland. The youngest, a five-year-old who told him her name was Luna, stayed beside him while he manned the wheel and talked to him about how her parents had died in a car accident. She was holding a stuffed rabbit named Nicolas, stroking his left ear, which was dirtier and more threadbare than the other—her small comfort. Luna was a pretty child with long hair that had been pulled back into a braid, and she wore leggings, a Pikachu T-shirt, and a pair of sneakers. Her eyelids were green with the eye shadow Sofia had put on them, and the eyes themselves—despite what they'd seen tonight—sparkled with innocence.

During a long silence, the shoreline now coming into view in the early morning light, Luna tapped his arm, and when he looked at her, she said, "*¿Por qué estás tan triste?*"

"I'm not sad," Noah said in Spanish. "I'm tired. And I'm in pain."

"You are sad. You're very sad—here."

She held out Nicolas the rabbit. Noah tried to refuse, but she shoved it at him again, so he took it and held it while he drove. Luna remained beside him the rest of the trip.

George Beverly and Gael were waiting in the powder-blue Ford pickup when Noah and the girls reached the shore. Beverly helped Noah into the back of the truck, where he could lie down, and the girls piled in after him. By the time the truck engine had begun to rumble, before it had even been put into gear, Noah had passed out.

He woke up on a veterinarian's metal table as a woman in a white lab coat was digging a bullet out of him—but he was only conscious for seconds, and didn't feel anything. He saw the stainless steel surgical tools on a tray, he saw the vet herself, and he saw Nicolas the rabbit sitting on a counter in the corner. Then his head dropped down again and he was gone.

*

He recovered over a period of months. News about what had happened on the island got out. It filled front pages during the first week, worked its way toward the back, then vanished altogether. No one identified him by name and the police never came knocking. He would forever be a "mysterious man," which, in his line of work, was fine. He didn't want to be on anybody's radar. He got jobs by whispered reference only. And as far as the police were concerned he was a burnout American who'd fled trouble in the States, a not entirely inaccurate assessment.

Late spring the following year he decided to take a trip to the beach for a week. He could lie out in the sun and drink ice-chest beer and forget about everything. He made reservations for a beach house rental—his only major indulgence since he'd been paid fifty thousand dollars by Santino Garcia—and loaded the trunk of his car. Then he and his companion were on the road.

Luna, who'd turned six since the events on the island, looked out the window, excited as the world streaked past. She held Nicolas the rabbit, stroking his left ear. He'd given the rabbit back to her on the day she moved in with him, but she'd assured him that Nicolas was both of theirs, to share.

He told himself he'd invited Luna into his life only because she was an orphan and he had a spare bedroom. But somewhere inside he knew it was also because he wanted to try to be a dad again, and maybe this time he wouldn't fuck it up.

When the beach came into view, he pulled to the side of the road and just sat there, looking at the sea stretching its way to the horizon—all this distant beauty.

"Are we gonna go?" Luna asked. "I wanna swim."

He looked at her with what might have been love, and he smiled.

Then put the car into gear, pulled out onto the road, and drove toward the sea.

SHEILA KOHLER

Miss Martin

FROM *Cutting Edge*

I

WHEN DIANE COMES back from boarding school this summer, she finds her father waiting in the still afternoon air. Diane usually walks to their quiet town house on a shady side lane in East Hampton, but today her father lounges in his tight blue jeans and his Panama hat in the shade of a tree at the bottom of the station's steps.

"Oh, there you are, Kitten," he says, his narrow face brightening, as she descends from the platform, dragging her fancy suitcase behind her. Diane's father calls her *Kitten* or sometimes *Pussy Cat* because of her soft dark eyes, he says. He keeps, she knows, a photo of her as a little girl with blond curls and a bow in her hair on his desk in his office in an oval silver frame.

Diane is aware her father is considered a distinguished-looking man, with his fine profile, the delicate pointed nose, though he has lost much of his hair. He wears the Panama hat all through the summer to protect and hide his bald pate. Tall and slender, he moves quickly to take her suitcase from her and to kiss her hard on both her cheeks. "I'm so glad you are home," he says, looking into her eyes.

She says politely, "Thanks for coming to get me," as he swings her suitcase into the trunk of his old gray Mercedes, though she worries immediately that he is here in order to reprimand her in the privacy of his car. She is afraid her headmistress, Miss Nieven, might have phoned him from the school as she had threatened to do. What if they have decided to expel her?

Her father, a lawyer, has very strict ideas of what is right and wrong and often holds forth at length about the evils in the world: dishonest politicians, corruption in the government, and unfaithful wives, always sounding shocked and angry.

But when she gets into the familiar car and her father starts the engine, he says nothing about school. Instead he turns to her and confides apologetically that the work which was supposed to be done on their house has not been completed.

"They told me they would have it finished weeks ago, but of course they are still working on it," her father warns, speaking of the new sleeping loft he has installed on one side of the house. "They haven't put in the stairs yet," he adds, and glances at her anxiously with his close-set, intensely blue eyes.

"Does she like it?" Diane asks, referring to her father's second wife. It is the first time Diane has been in the house without her mother and with Miss Martin — Diane always thinks of her as Miss Martin — who was her father's secretary and is now his wife.

He glances at her with something close to impatience and purses his thin lips as though her question is extraneous. "No, she calls it the slave quarters," he says with sarcasm and scowls, driving skillfully down Town Lane, threading in and out of the cars, pale clouds vanishing across the sky.

Diane just looks at him and wonders why he has bothered to go to the expense of altering the house now that her mother has gone. She thinks of her maternal Kentucky grandmother saying, "Closing the barn door when the horse has bolted."

Could it be simply out of spite?

Diane's father is from an old New England family where thrift is prized and ostentatious wealth frowned upon. She knows her father does not like unnecessary expense. Though he is more than generous with her at times, he is basically a thrifty man who despite his excellent salary in the law firm and his inheritance never takes a taxi and says disparagingly that first class on an airplane is "for people with fat behinds." Diane's father does not have a fat behind, she knows. He keeps himself trim by running for an hour at six every morning and eating little.

The sleeping loft was something her mother wanted to have

built. She always found the two-bedroom house too small, too cramped, claustrophobic. "It's like a boat!" she would say in exasperation — Diane can hear the way her mother says *boat* with such disgust, as if she were naming something much more damning and using some other, unmentionable word.

When her father shuts the car's engine off in the driveway of the white clapboard house, he glances at the small red Renault parked there and whispers, "Things are rather disorganized at home, I warn you. We will have to be patient, Kitten."

She sits beside him uncomfortably in the shade of the magnolia tree, looking up at the house with some apprehension.

She stares at the creeper-covered dormer window of her small bedroom and thinks of her large, sunny dormitory at school, which she shares with two other girls and where she makes her narrow bed so neatly, with hospital corners, pulling the bright plaid blanket tightly across the top. She keeps her one small bookcase close by her bedside with her favorite books, which she has organized since she was quite small in alphabetical order. She thinks of her history teacher, who has given her an A+ for her paper on regicide — she wrote about Charles I, Louis XVI, and Nicholas II of Russia. Mrs. Kelly had read the paper to the class as an example of excellent work. "Listen to the scope of this paper!" she had said, while Diane sat feeling her face turn crimson. What will Mrs. Kelly say now if she hears about what Diane has done? What if she can never return to her history class?

Diane stares at the creeper-covered house, with its small dormer windows, where she has lived all her life, as though she has never seen it before, hesitating to enter until her father says, "Come along, Kitten. Got to face the music," and they enter the living room together, her father carrying her suitcase.

II

The first thing Diane does in the house is climb up the long ladder which is propped against the wall of the dining room, going into the high loft that runs all the way above the kitchen and dining room.

"Wow!" she says when she gets to the top, standing in the part of the loft where the sloping roof is highest. "You could sleep seven up here." She peers at the expanse of the long, low room and then down from the open door to her father, who stands watching her from below.

She thinks of her mother, who always said the space above the kitchen and the dining room was wasted. She had said, in what Diane understood was an effort to persuade her father, that this way Diane could have lots of friends over if she wanted to in the summers, when everyone liked to come to a house near the sea. It would be good for her. Diane, despite her house near the sea, has never had lots of friends who want to come over. She is too quiet, too shy, too bookish, to have made many friends. She is not one of the popular pupils at school. She likes spending her holidays alone in the small, shaded back garden with its white roses that her mother grew in shiny blue pots, just reading or swimming in the sea.

Sometimes Diane thought her mother wanted to put *her* in the sleeping loft on the other side of the house, so that her mother could have a room of her own where she could work on her books, or even just sleep on her own if she was so inclined. Diane had often found her father on the leather sofa in the living room when she came down in the morning for her breakfast. He would watch her coming down the stairs and sigh sadly, shrugging his shoulders as if to say, *You see how your mother treats me.*

"Come down now and say hallo," her father calls up to Diane. "Be careful, Kitten, come down backward," her father says, holding the long ladder as Diane descends fast into the small dining room, which opens onto the living room.

She expects Miss Martin to come forth from the kitchen in her narrow dark skirt with the small slit up the back, with a cup of delicious frothy coffee in her hands, as she would as her father's secretary.

But to Diane's surprise Miss Martin is not in the kitchen whipping up a soufflé and must be upstairs in one of the bedrooms. She soon comes wafting down the stairs and into the cramped living room with its overflow of Victorian furniture, the pink chintz-covered chairs, the leather sofa, and the large fireplace. She looks too tall for the low-ceilinged room, and she is smiling in a silly way.

Miss Martin, Diane will later learn when she goes to study abroad in France, is what the French call a pretty/ugly woman. She has a strong profile, a large nose, plump lips, and high cheekbones.

Her glossy dark hair, which in the office was expertly coiled at the back of her head, is now springing rebelliously around her face despite the strange sort of *Alice in Wonderland* ribbon which circles her head, as though she were a child. Her makeup, Diane notices, has changed. Though Diane does not yet wear any, as her father prefers she does not, she has been studying the question. In the office Diane noted that Miss Martin's makeup was impeccable: the lipstick discreetly pink, the mascara a faint blue echoing the color of her pale eyes, the foundation cream perfectly smooth and light. Now it has become suddenly violent: she has glossy red lips and dark mascara and dark foundation cream.

She is not in her skirt but instead a long loose dress with lots of bright red flowers, which Diane feels does not suit her at all. She seems to be wearing strong perfume.

She does not shake Diane's hand firmly as she would do in the office, but lurches forward and seems almost to fall on Diane. She enfolds her in a huge hug, hanging on to her as though she cannot stand on her own. She gives her a damp kiss, which Diane is tempted to wipe from her cheek. Why is she kissing her! Diane hates physical contact with strangers. Miss Martin gushes, "Goodness, how you have grown up! A young lady! I love your hair like that!" Diane has cropped her fair hair short like a boy's. She just looks at Miss Martin, aghast.

There is a moment of awkward silence. Then Miss Martin laughs in a girlish way and says they are both just to relax; she will bring in lunch in a jiffy. Diane is hungry, not having had time for breakfast before she took the early train, and she imagines that Miss Martin, despite her strange attire, will make something splendid for this first luncheon together.

III

Diane first heard about Miss Martin before she met her. Miss Martin was, Diane's father said, smiling in a satisfied way, "the perfect secretary, remembers everything but is utterly discreet, always there when you need her, never there when you don't."

Miss Martin moved around her father's office in her perfectly pressed long-sleeved blouse, the smooth sheer stockings on her long legs whispering seductively as she walked. The first time Diane saw her she wanted to touch the stockings and perhaps even the slim legs which seemed to go on forever.

Diane was immediately fascinated by Miss Martin's obvious efficiency, the neatness of her desk, and her very high-heeled patent-leather shoes, which rapped out commandingly on the parquet floor. She was fascinated by the way she moved so fast around Diane's father, the way she answered the telephone so swiftly, as though plucking up a weed from the garden, and the clipped way she pronounced the names of her father's law firm. Diane presumed Miss Martin was English until her father said she came from South Africa. "Albee, Melbourne, and Morton," she said commandingly, as though announcing the regiments in an army. Diane's father is the Morton part.

"Why did they put your name last?" Diane once asked her father.

"Alphabetical order," her father replied quickly. Diane wonders if that was true.

IV

Diane and her father sit opposite one another in the pink armchairs in the dark living room beside the empty fireplace in the steamy summer air. There is no air-conditioning in the house— "waste of energy," her father says. Faintly in the distance they can hear the sound of waves. The house is not far from the shore. Diane's father loves the sea and still likes to take his daughter there sometimes at twilight in his car.

"How's school? Did you miss me?" he asks.

There is not much Diane can say under the circumstances, and her father hardly seems to be listening anyway. "Fine. I got all A's." She glances around the room. She has never had problems at her school before this. She loves her classes, most of her teachers, and has always had the best marks in the class.

There is a moment of silence, and Diane notices that the photo of her and her mother that always stood on the top of the old English dresser is gone. "The photo!" she says to her father, who shrugs and looks a little embarrassed.

"We put it upstairs in your room, Kitten."

Diane is about to say something rude but decides it would be better not to, considering her situation.

It was her mother who with considerable difficulty had persuaded her father to send Diane to a select girls' boarding school in Connecticut, which costs, as her father says, "a fortune."

"It would actually save you money, as she would not be around for you to spoil rotten," her mother had said, staring severely at him. Despite his thrifty upbringing, her father would from time to time buy Diane expensive gifts from the fancy shops in East Hampton: soft cashmere sweaters in pastel colors, gold bracelets, once a charm bracelet with a heart.

Her father had protested, sulked, asked her if she no longer loved him, insisted the school catered only to snobs, the rich and the privileged, and he had finally driven her there in silence the entire way when she went off for the first time at thirteen. He had lingered on in the long driveway when all the other parents had left. She had watched him from the dormitory window sitting there in his car, the sun sinking between the old oaks at the end of the driveway, his shoulders shaking. She hoped no one else had seen her father weep.

She is expected to contribute to her exorbitant school fees in any way she can. ("At least you could make an effort to help me," her father had said.) When she turned sixteen this year, she was allowed to work in the mailroom, sorting the mail at the school for a small hourly wage. "It's not much money," Diane told her father apologetically. He just smiled and said he was proud of her and kissed her hard. He said it was not the money but the willingness to work that was important in life. Diane's father admires people who work hard, whatever they do, or so he says. He says that the less one is paid, the more meaningful the work often is, though he is very well paid himself as a lawyer, though she knows he does do pro bono work occasionally.

Diane imagines he admired Miss Martin because she was so good at her work as a secretary, taking down his every word so exactly, and dealing with the complexities of the computer so efficiently, something he has never learned to do, all for a small salary. He must have thought she would make a good, hardworking wife.

They sit opposite one another in silence, listening at the same time to certain ominous noises coming from the kitchen.

"So, nothing to report?" Diane's father asks.

She shrugs and shakes her head.

Her father seems not to have heard about the missing letters and packages in the mailroom (sometimes there was cash in the envelopes, sometimes delicious cookies in the packets). The headmistress, Miss Nieven, has apparently not called, as she had threatened, to discuss the matter. "I will have to decide with your parents what to do about this, Diane," Miss Nieven had said ominously in the seclusion of her dark, book-lined study. "Quite frankly, I don't really understand your behavior. You come from an affluent family, after all, your father a lawyer, your mother a full professor, a house in East Hampton. You are always beautifully dressed. I know you have had difficult changes in your life to cope with recently, but you have everything you need, surely?" Miss Nieven had said, staring at her. "You realize this is a serious matter. How would you like it if your father had sent you a package and you never received it?"

"My father has never sent me a package or even a letter," Diane had replied. Her father only gives her presents in person. She looked at Miss Nieven and thought that now perhaps, as her mother was in France, where she had gone off with her lover, a French professor she met at the university in Southhampton where she teaches philosophy, she might send her packages. She hopes her mother will send her some French books. She is learning to speak French at school. She would like to speak a language that is not her mother tongue.

At this point they are distracted by a great clatter of dishes and pots and pans and the strong odor of something burning.

"Perhaps you better go and see if you can help, Kitten," her father suggests.

Miss Martin is standing in the middle of the big, hot kitchen with its glass-fronted cabinets and old wooden table with several pots bubbling furiously on the stove, a frying pan smoking, and a serving platter—Diane sees it is the good blue-and-white Wedgwood one, which her father inherited from his Connecticut grandmother—that has broken at her feet. She is, to Diane's consternation, weeping.

"Can I help?" Diane says as her father comes striding into the kitchen. He turns off the gas under the smoking pan and the bubbling pots and takes out a broom from the closet. He vigorously sweeps up the broken crockery from the floor into a dustpan and throws the pieces into the rubbish bin. Diane and Miss Martin stand and watch. He says severely, "I will get some sandwiches," and Miss Martin weeps even louder as he walks out of the house, slamming the door behind him.

V

At night in her bedroom Diane lies awake reading. It rained earlier that evening, and with her window open she can hear the sound of the waves in the distance and smell the fresh odors of the garden mixed with something dead. In the faint light of the bedside lamp, she looks at the photo of herself and her mother on the dresser and the small silver pitcher of white roses that someone has arranged beside it. Could it have been Miss Martin? From the bedroom next door Diane hears her father's loud voice and Miss Martin's cries. She hears her wail, "What do you want me to do?"

In the morning at breakfast, when Diane goes down into the kitchen, her father has bought a coffee cake and makes the coffee and even squeezes the oranges for juice himself (he likes his orange juice freshly squeezed). Miss Martin sits red-eyed at the kitchen table in her dressing gown, her hair in disarray, staring blankly before her, her big hands folded in her lap, as though she were an unhappy guest.

Then Diane's father says he has work to do but will be back and would like his lunch promptly at one, if that is not too much to ask. He leaves them sitting side by side in silence at the wooden table where Diane's mother would chop vegetables and make her delicious soup.

When the door shuts on her father, Miss Martin starts weeping again, and Diane wants to give her a shake. What is wrong with the woman? She does not seem able even to clear the kitchen table of the breakfast dishes or the orange peels, which Diane does, stacking the dishes in the dishwasher with a clatter. Obviously Miss Martin is not used to kitchens but offices.

Miss Martin looks up at Diane and says, "A mistake. A terrible mistake! I thought it would be so different! He seemed such a good man, such a devoted father!"

Diane thinks about this and is not sure what to say in response, though she would like to agree. Then she says, "What can I do?"

Miss Martin looks at her, apparently thinking about the matter.

"I just wish I could escape—marriage is so different from work, where you get to escape, at least in the evenings and on the weekends, to gather your wits. This just goes on and on!"

Diane laughs and says that is true. "I know just what you mean about wanting to escape."

"You do?" Miss Martin says.

Diane thinks of how often she had wished to escape before she finally managed to persuade her mother to send her to boarding school when she turned thirteen.

Once she had tried to tell her mother about her father and what he would do in the car at the beach in the gloaming. She must have been nine or ten, but her mother had interrupted her in the midst. When she said something about her father's hand and where it went, her mother had looked uncomfortable and sighed. She said, "Pet, all little girls make up stories in their minds about their fathers. It's difficult to sort out what is real from fantasy in life. I remember doing that myself as a child. One day you will read Freud and understand why."

Diane could think of nothing to say to that at the time. Now she tells Miss Martin, "Yes, I wanted so badly to leave home. Sometimes I thought of running away."

"To get away from your father?" Miss Martin says, and looks at Diane and seems to understand.

She nods and says, "I tried to tell my mother, but she didn't understand."

What Diane wanted to tell her mother was that she would never make up a story like this: this was real, her father driving her to the beach at twilight, leaving the car motor running and staring as if mesmerized at the sea, murmuring to her on and on like the waves beating against the shore about things she would have preferred not to hear. He would sigh and breathe in an odd loud way, his hand straying so strangely and surprisingly. Each time, though she feared it was coming, it was a shock, the long fingers slithering from his knee across to hers and finding their way like a snake between her legs, stroking her like a kitten, almost as if the hand had nothing to do with her father.

Yet he would eventually say, "You like that, don't you?" and she, weeping, would shake her head.

"Please don't," she would beg him.

"Oh, you do like it, I know you do, that's why I have to do it," he would repeat, the awful hand going on stroking and probing in her.

And the terrible thing was that the hand did excite her, making her damp until she came — she didn't even know what was happening, but she felt the great sickening release, when she would gasp, and he would say, "And now you must help me, please, Pussy Cat. You know your mother won't," pulling her head down into his lap. Afterward he would give her expensive presents, designer suitcases, fancy pens, bright beautiful scarves, and her mother would complain. Her only escape was school.

"Your mother didn't want perhaps to understand," Miss Martin says now.

"She did finally get Father to send me to boarding school," Diane says.

Miss Martin pushes her dark curls back from her face, and exclaims, "Oh, yes, boarding school! I'm sorry, with all this going on I forgot to tell you. I spoke to your headmistress. She sounded quite cross!"

"You did?" Diane says, abandoning the dishes and sitting down opposite Miss Martin, looking at her face with its red blotches and the dark curls which fall lankly about her cheeks, the dressing gown which is half open on her bony chest. "What did she say? What did *you* say?"

"I said that sometimes stealing can be a way of asking for help, that your mother had left so suddenly and unexpectedly and your father had up and married his secretary right away, that you are, after all, such an excellent student — one of her best and an asset to the school, obviously Ivy League material. That mollified her a bit. But she really changed her tune when I said your father and I were considering a gift to your excellent school — I sent quite a substantial check, actually."

"You did? What did Daddy say?" Diane asks, putting her hand to her lips.

"Oh — I didn't think it necessary to mention the conversation to him. I just said I thought it wise to be generous with your school. After all, your college applications are coming up soon, and you will need good references. That did the trick. He actually complimented me on my quick thinking and thanked me for watching out for you."

"Gosh!" Diane says, opening her eyes wide with admiration. Miss

Martin, despite her red eyes and her greasy hair, despite the dishes, looks fascinating to Diane again. How did she manage to think of such a thing? she wonders.

Suddenly Diane feels glad to be sitting in the sunny kitchen at the old wooden table where her mother would cut up vegetables and where Diane would fill in the pictures in her coloring book. She feels hopeful, as she did sometimes as a little girl, looking out the window at the branches of the tall magnolia tree stirring in the breeze against the blue sky, thinking she has all the summer before her to enjoy the beach and the sea and that she will be able to go back to her school in the fall.

"Luckily, your father opened a joint account for us before we married, though I'm afraid now that . . ." and she begins to weep again.

Diane says, "I think I know how we could manage at least an afternoon off."

VI

Of course they do not expect him to try to jump. It is so easy to remove the ladder when he is up in the sleeping loft alone one afternoon, and then to grab their swimsuits and take off in Miss Martin's red Renault. Despite the woman's incompetence in the kitchen, she is a fast and excellent driver. They just drive down to the sea and go for a long swim — Miss Martin, it turns out, is a good swimmer. They swim out together, leaving the shore behind, ducking under the big waves and then riding them back onto the shore.

Then they drive all the way to Montauk to Diane's favorite restaurant, which looks over the sea, where they order clam chowder, lobster, and cheesecake, which they pay for with Diane's father's credit card while he is pacing up and down in the attic, increasingly incensed.

When they arrive back, Diane's father has tried to jump down from the loft, which might have been possible without injury but he has fallen on the ladder, which Diane left on the floor below. He is lying there making the sort of noises Diane remembers from the car. He has difficulty breathing. The doctors will later discover he has punctured a lung.

Miss Martin takes control of the situation as if she were his secretary again. She calls 911; then she speaks to Diane's father, leaning down to talk in his ear with her South African accent as he lies gasping on the floor. She says nothing about the ladder but tells him that in her opinion it might be wise not to antagonize his daughter in any way in the future, as she is a remarkably enterprising young woman (and indeed Diane's father does not bother her again and watches her warily at all times until she leaves for college).

Then Miss Martin shakes Diane's hand firmly, wishes her all the best, and takes off immediately in her car to go—Diane discovers later—to empty the joint account. Diane never sees her again, but she still thinks about her at times and considers that her father's initial estimation of her skills was correct: "Remembers everything, is utterly discreet, always there when you need her, never there when you don't."

JAKE LITHUA

The Most Powerful Weapon

FROM *The Odds Are Against Us*

ARIYA WOKE AT DAWN, carefully easing her way out of bed so
as not to wake her so-called husband, Imran. He would wake soon
himself; and if his breakfast of flatbread, bean paste, and fried egg
was not ready by the time he was dressed, he would hit her. *Perhaps I
will kill him today,* she thought. She always began her mornings with
the thought of killing her husband, her master, her jailer. It made
the rest of the day more bearable.

She stifled a grunt as she dressed in the long shapeless abaya
dress demanded by Islamic State mujahideen of their women, the
fresh bruises on her arms and back making her wince. In public
she would also wear a double-layered veil, which would at least hide
her ice-blue eyes and dirty-blond hair—rare features that marked
her as Yazidi. Ariya had been only twelve when she was taken, with
no time to cry over her murdered family. Yazidis could expect no
mercy from the Islamic State. And seeing the brutality meted out
to the other captives, she realized she had to make a choice. And
so she did.

My goal is escape, she thought in her native Kurmanji, repeating
the daily litany that she had created three years ago. *To do that, I
must survive. So I play along with Imran for now, so that I can be free in
time.*

How much time? came a mocking whisper from the back of her
mind, but Ariya ignored it. Soon the smells of breakfast filled their
tiny house, made of mud brick and scrap metal. It had once belonged to an Iraqi tailor and had been given to Imran by the Islamic State, part of his benefits as a mujahid. Once there had been

money too, and Ariya could eat fairly well. But then the airstrikes began and the money tapered off, and so Ariya often went hungry so that Imran could be full. It had been worse when he had had two wives, but then Imran had strangled Zahra and it was just the two of them again.

Zahra had been foolish, Ariya thought with a pang. *She got him angry.*

"Morning of goodness, my wife." Imran was up. He was short and had a pale, pinched face; his dark hair was close-cropped, but his beard was long and stringy. When he was given the girl Ariya as a wife, Imran had been eighteen.

Ariya flinched minutely. "Morning of light, *ba'ali,*" she replied in her now familiar Arabic, using the word that meant both "my husband" and "my master." Imran insisted on it, no doubt to flaunt his power over her. (Most native Arabic-speakers would have used *zawji* instead, but Imran had grown up in a place he called Biljika, in Europe, and learned Arabic late.) "Breakfast is ready."

They ate silently, cross-legged on the bare floor. Imran did not believe in luxuries. On the rare occasions that Ariya could talk to the other wives in the village, they sometimes gossiped about Islamic State fighters who engaged in *fusuq* by drinking alcohol or listening to Western music; but Imran was a true ascetic. When he was not on duty, he was usually kneeling on the floor, reciting haltingly from the Qur'an or the Hadith. Ariya was glad, because it meant that she only had to worry about his moods during meals —and at night.

When he was finished, Imran rose, went to the closet, and slung his battered AK-47 over his shoulder. "My company is going out today," he announced. "We will not return until Thursday, maybe later."

That meant a combat operation. "May you find victory over the enemies of Allah," Ariya replied mechanically as she rose to her feet. *I hope you die,* she thought to herself without changing expression.

"Clean the house while I am gone," Imran said. "Study the Surah of the Cave and be ready to recite it for me by heart when I return."

"Nothing would please me more, *ba'ali.*" She despised reading the Qur'an. Ariya had been an indifferent Yazidi at best in her youth, but the book of her tormenters was like ashes in her mouth.

"Do not leave the house except to go to the market."

He would check on her with the neighbors, of course. She would have no freedom at all, even while out of his sight! Her stomach churned at the thought. "*Ba'ali*," Ariya said, "I will need to gather herbs in the hills." She hesitated, bracing herself, then continued. "Money is scarce and we have little food left—"

He struck her across the face with his fist, as she knew he would. "Do not speak to me about money!" he snarled. Ariya fell back against the wall and made a show of whimpering in pain, which was not difficult; satisfied with this display of his power, Imran said, "Gather in the hills, then. But be back before dusk."

Good. Now I can get some fresh air. Ariya had become skilled at exploiting Imran's temper, by necessity. A few more hurts done to her battered body were a small price to pay sometimes.

Ariya waited an hour after Imran left, scrubbing the pots and sweeping the floors, checking that the door was locked and the window shuttered and tensely counting the seconds. Then, when she was sure he was truly gone, she stripped off her stifling sack of a dress and flung it into the corner of the room with a curse. *Melek Tawuse,* she prayed, not knowing or caring if anyone was listening; *Give me strength to be free!*

In her underclothes, Ariya bent down and heaved herself into a handstand, holding the position for almost two minutes until her corded arms were trembling violently and sweat dripped down her face onto the bare floor. Then she did squats; then a plank, moving from one exercise to another with savage focus. When she had first been captured, Ariya knew she was too weak to resist; since then, every chance she got she would do strength training. It made her thin as a rail but tightly wound with muscle. Perhaps one day she would be strong enough to kill Imran and escape.

(She had heard that overexercising made it harder to conceive. Good; the thought of carrying that monster's child was abhorrent, and Ariya did everything she could to prevent it—exercise, herbs, disguising her cycles. If Imran ever succeeded in impregnating her, Ariya might just kill herself.)

When she was too worn out to continue, Ariya ate from her secret stash of parched grain, throwing a handful to the chickens in back when she was full. The rest of the day she spent practicing baking cigar-nut pastries, which she had heard were Imran's favorite. In the evening she read from the Surah of the Cave, laboriously committing the hated words to memory.

The next day was the same, Ariya not yet willing to risk leaving the house. But on Monday the food ran out; she had to get more or go hungry. She swaddled herself in the abaya, took her canvas satchel, and headed for the hillside overlooking the village to the east. She took one of Imran's robes with her; *I'll need a way to wipe off if I get muddy,* she thought spitefully.

The day was cool, and a biting wind pierced all her layers of clothing. The scents of early spring rose from the moist earth around her. As she picked herbs, gratefully munching on sweet grasses as she went, Ariya could almost imagine that Imran didn't exist, that the Islamic State didn't exist, and that she was still a child of twelve gathering flowers for her mother. *Can't think like that. Can't lose control. I am fifteen and a grown woman, and I have only myself to rely on.*

The sudden *crack-crack* of gunfire. Ariya flinched and threw herself to the earth, squeezing her eyes shut. Then she swore; the gunfire was back in town. *You stupid coward. Now your clothes are dirty.* The shooting continued, the dull chattering bark of AK-47s along with the higher crackle of pistol fire. Faint shouts reached her ears, Arabic intermixed with something else, and Ariya's eyes widened. *Kurmanji? Are those Kurds?* For a second a wild hope that she had never allowed herself to feel rose up in her chest. She ran heedlessly down the hill slope.

Most of the mujahideen had gone with Imran, but there were still some left in the village. Three of them were making their way around houses on the edge of the village, calling to one another and firing their rifles as they advanced. One mujahid staggered and fell; Ariya nearly let out a whoop before catching herself. Yet the others continued forward; the firing went on, but by the time Ariya reached the bottom of the hill, it had petered to a halt. Then came the cries of *"Allahu akbar!"* and Ariya's stomach knotted. Sudden tears burst from her blue eyes. *The Peshmerga couldn't have killed all of them so quickly. Those are Islamic State cries, not Kurds.*

Her rescuers were dead. No one would save her. No one even knew she was alive, probably. She was trapped here forever. Ariya squeezed her fists shut. *Stop it, stop it, stop it!* She would never escape Imran. She was being childish when she thought she could. *Stop it!*

When she finally worked up the courage to walk back into the village, Ariya passed seven bodies that had been covered with bloodied sheets and laid out in a row, just outside the marketplace. Four looked like Islamic State fighters, judging from their thin tan hiking shoes, which stuck out from under the sheets. Three, wearing thicker boots with stiff rubber soles, were not. *God, give these poor men their rest,* Ariya thought, and averted her eyes.

As dusk was approaching, Ariya was finally returning to the house through deserted dusty roads, carefully balancing a sack of barley on one shoulder and beans on the other, still carrying her satchel of herbs. She had just come in sight of her door when something out of the corner of her eye made her halt. The alley on her left was strewn with splintered boards and old furniture and discarded rusty metal, as always, but today it looked different than usual — almost as if someone had gathered some of the junk into a pile near the alley mouth.

Her breath caught. Fresh blood glistened wetly on one remaining leg of a ruined stool, almost invisible in the gathering dark. For a moment Ariya shrank back. Then her mind flashed back to the hillside. *Are you going to grovel again, you coward? Was everything you ever told yourself for the last three years a lie, you weak fool?* Gritting her teeth beneath the abaya, Ariya set down her sacks in the road and crept forward carefully.

One moment she could see nothing, but then her eyes focused and a man suddenly appeared behind the refuse, as if by magic. Ariya gasped. He was curled up in a ball, dressed in a faded tan military uniform without insignia, which was torn in several places and soaked with blood. He had dark hair and eyes but did not look Arab; his skin was pale, almost cream-colored beneath the dust and blood. His jaw was clenched in agony, but his eyes were clear and fixed on hers. So was a small black pistol, held in one trembling hand.

"Quiet," he whispered in thickly accented Arabic.

Ariya frowned; the accent was strange. "Peshmerga?" she breathed. "Do you speak Kurmanji?"

He relaxed a fraction and lowered the pistol. His face was wider than Imran's, though drawn in pain. His long, straight nose looked like it had been broken once or twice. "A little," he said in hesitant Kurmanji. "Yes, I fight with the Peshmerga."

Her eyes widened. *He's a foreigner! Maybe American?* She glanced around her, suddenly afraid, but no one was nearby.

"Help, please," he breathed. "I need a house. Healing."

Ariya's blood froze. If Imran caught her helping the enemy, she would be dead for sure! And not just Imran, but anyone else in the village. There would be no way to hide him for long.

A new thought came to her. *True. But it might be just long enough.* "If I help you," she whispered slowly, "would you kill my husband?" The man frowned, and Ariya added, "He's a mujahid."

At that the man nodded. "I will kill him. If I can."

Ariya licked her lips, amazed at her daring. "Can you walk?"

The man clenched his teeth on a piece of torn cloth and heaved himself to his feet, hissing and going even paler. Ariya saw that he had been shot in the right thigh and arm; blood oozed through the makeshift bandages he had tied around the wounds. He swayed but stayed upright. "A little. Slow."

"Wait." She pulled out Imran's robe. Soon, wearing the robe over his bloodied uniform, the man was hobbling painfully toward the house. Miraculously, no patrol came by; perhaps the remaining few mujahideen were busy mourning their dead.

By the time Ariya had locked the door behind them and cast aside her veil with a snarl, the American's wounds were bleeding again. His face ashen, he slumped down onto the cushions she provided. "Water, hot water," he gasped in Kurmanji. "With salt. And cloth, for the—for the blood."

Ariya understood. She lit the stove and put on a small pot of water to boil. As she waited, she gave the man water to drink and a small piece of flatbread. Then she laid out Imran's best keffiyehs to clean the wounds with. *Either he's going to die soon or I will, so why not?* She grinned a little at the thought.

The American had sunk back on the floor. He looked very weak, his eyes half closed. Ariya surveyed his bloody uniform. It would have to come off; there was no way around it. "Can you take off your clothes, or should I?" He hesitated, going pink. She snorted. "Imran has been my accursed *husband* for three years; I know what a man looks like."

His dark eyes widened in shock; for an instant his face filled with fury, and Ariya reflexively shrank backward. But the fury passed and he gave a tiny shrug, then gritted his teeth and fumbled one-handed. By the time the water was boiling, he was dressed in only a thin white shirt that clung to his chest and short cloth pants that ended midthigh. The two gunshot wounds were exposed to the air, dribbling blood onto the cushions. Ariya felt sick in the back of her throat and had to close her eyes for a moment, remembering with awful clarity what her older brother had looked like—how the blood had poured from the gaping wounds in his chest that day.

Shaking her head sharply, Ariya brought the boiling pot down to the floor and poured a handful of salt into the water. Then she dipped a cloth and swabbed the blood away from the American's arm. "More, make it clean," he managed, breathing heavily; she winced but swabbed the wound thoroughly. She did the same to the other side of his arm, where the bullet had come out, then tied a thick bandage around the arm. Then she treated his thigh wound; before she was finished, the American mercifully fell unconscious.

She sat back on her heels and gazed at the man, this man who would rid her of Imran. *In theory.* Right now he looked weak unto death. He was bigger than Imran, more muscular too. But it would do him no good if he could not stand and fight. She bit her lip. *What have I done?*

Still, he was tough. That he had not cried out when she dressed his wounds was testament enough to that. Perhaps he could kill Imran after all. *I will just have to nurse him back to health—and quickly.* She covered him with a wool blanket and waited.

"What's your name?" she asked later, as she knelt by his side and fed him warm gruel and milk.

"Tristan," he replied, then coughed.

"*Te-rees-tan,*" she said slowly, hesitating on the unfamiliar syllables. "Why are you here? Are you Ameriki?"

He nodded. "I fought in the war, before Daesh." Ariya flinched at the word *Daesh;* the Islamic State hated the nickname, which was considered a slur. Tristan hesitated, looking for the right words, then said something that sounded like *green berei.* "It means I teach soldiers. Kurds, Iraqis. Teach them to fight for home." His eyes hardened. "Then Amerikis go. My students are alone, to die. Daesh kill them. So I stay."

Ariya frowned. "Why not go back to Amrika? You almost died today. Why not go home?"

Tristan smiled briefly. "Too stupid. I want to stay with my friends. Rajan, Serhat, Alexander." For a moment his eyes took on a faraway look; then he shook his head and said, "And you? What is your name?"

"Ariya."

"Where did you come from?"

"Kurdistan," she said shortly. She spooned out more gruel and thrust it into his mouth, suddenly wary of more questions.

He chewed, his dark eyes never leaving hers. Ariya tensed, but he finished eating silently. When the gruel was finished, he smiled and said, "Thank you for your hospitality. And for the bandages."

She nodded graciously. "Rest now."

Tristan was soon asleep. Still, Ariya felt too self-conscious to do her strength exercises, not with a strange man in the house. And she realized with a rush of elation that she would never need to read the Qur'an again. *Because you will be dead soon,* a nasty voice said in the back of her mind. She ignored it. Part of her wished that Tristan were still awake; she had so many questions about what life in Kurdistan was like now. Most important of all—she licked her lips—what would *happen* to girls like her? Would she be taken in by someone, the government perhaps? Or would she be cast aside, despised as the enemy's whore? The thought made her stomach clench.

She heated more water for when Tristan would need his bandages changed, and prepared bean paste for them both. Once she was done, there was little left to do but wait.

His small black pistol lay in the bundle of his cast-off uniform. Ariya licked her lips. Tristan would surely hit her or even kill her if he saw her touch it; but he was still deep asleep. Quietly she knelt and picked it up. Her father had showed her how to use his old rifle when she was six; carefully she opened the action just to be safe, and nearly dropped the pistol in shock.

The chamber was empty. The magazine was empty too. Tristan had pointed an unloaded weapon at her, before. Ariya felt the blood drain from her face. *How can he shoot Imran without bullets?*

"Your gun is empty." She said it accusingly, unable to stop herself.

Tristan shrugged. He had slept through the night, waking at dawn and hobbling to the latrine with muttered curses. Now he was lying back on the cushions, eating slowly. "I used my bullets in the fight. I did not have many. We did not want to be seen, so no rifles, no more magazines."

Ariya slammed down her metal plate, her ice-blue eyes flashing.

"But what about Imran? *You* said you would kill him! And now he's going to kill you and me both!"

She felt her eyes sting. Grimacing, she wiped her eyes, then stared openmouthed at the tears dampening her fingers. It was the first time she had cried since Zahra had been strangled, more than a year ago. Suddenly she was sobbing, her thin body shuddering; ashamed, she tried to stifle her cries, but they only became louder. She rose to flee to the bedroom.

"Ariya."

He said it firmly, as a command, in a hard voice that compelled obedience. She froze. He reached up, wincing in pain, and shockingly took her hand and pulled her back to a seated position. His hand was rough and callused, and she could feel its strength. He stared at her until satisfied that she would stay, then let go. She pulled her hand back toward her chest, sniffling.

"What is the most powerful weapon, Ariya?" he said, still in that hard voice. "Not a gun. What?" She hiccupped and shook her head. He pointed at his temple. "It is *this*. And *this*," and he pointed at her head. "A gun is just one tool. If I want to, I can fight with many tools. But I have to *want* to, to know it in my head. In *your* head too."

She shook her head again, suddenly terrified, and he leaned forward. "Yes, Ariya. You too. My wounds hurt; what if I'm—" He paused, then said in English something like *enfektid.* "What if I'm sick? What if your husband kills me? What are you going to do? Lie down and die?"

Why am I so scared? Shame slithered deep into her belly. *Isn't this what I've been hoping for? Haven't I spent three years hoping for a way to kill Imran? Or was that all just an act?* She firmed her jaw. *No. I am not a coward!*

Tristan saw the change in her face and nodded. "Okay. Now see, there are many weapons in this house. Knives. Wooden poles. Even your pots and pans. It is not easy; if your husband has a gun, you will have to hit him from behind. But you finish the mission, Ariya. You *always* finish the mission, always. There is always something more to do, some other way to fight. Because you have no choice, Ariya. We win or we die."

Ariya breathed heavily. After an eternity, she rose and retrieved the carving knife from the cramped kitchen. Her hand trembled on the hilt. *Could I really have killed him myself, all this time?* In a small voice she said, "Teach me how to use this."

It was Wednesday evening. Tristan was getting stronger, but his wounds had acquired an angry red color around the edges and were hot to the touch. Ariya cleaned them again and again, until the pile of bloody cloths was nearly a foot high, but it seemed not to help. The American did not complain, but she could see in his eyes that he was worried. Sipping cool water carefully, still lying on the floor, he said in his rough Kurmanji, "We have to take an auto and go, while I can still drive."

"How?" Ariya turned up her hands. "You can't walk very far, and we have no good way to steal someone else's car without being caught. It has to be Imran's Jeep."

Tristan grimaced. "Then your husband needs to come soon."

"Stop calling him my husband!" Ariya flared up suddenly. "He's a murdering kidnapping pimp! He may have taken me into his bed, but he is not my *husband!*"

"You called him that first," Tristan said, and raised an eyebrow.

She flushed and looked down. "Well, I shouldn't have." The words echoed in her mind and she repeated more softly, "I shouldn't have."

The American gazed at her, then smiled approvingly. "Good."

That afternoon when he tried standing up, his injured leg buckled beneath him and he pitched forward onto his face. Ariya cried out; Tristan grunted and forced himself to his knees but could not stand again. His face was sweaty and red. Ariya brought over his cushions and a blanket and gave him food and water, a queasy knot forming in her stomach. *He's very sick. There's no way he can beat Imran like this. He might lose consciousness before Imran even gets back.* A sudden thought chilled her. *What if Imran doesn't come back? What if he's been killed or wounded in combat? That means no Jeep. Maybe I can find another way to escape, but it won't be soon enough to save Tristan. He needs to get back to the Peshmerga soon, or he'll die. Melek Tawuse, help us now!*

Melek Tawuse apparently had a dark sense of humor. The low, heavy growl of Imran's Jeep suddenly reached her ears, along with the crunch of tires on gravel in front of the house. Ariya's pulse hammered in her ears. *He's early!* She looked around the house wildly, seeing the pile of bandages against the wall, the discarded plates scattered over the floor, the pot of saltwater boiling on the stove—and most of all the groaning American stretched out in the middle of the floor.

Her wits frenzied, she grabbed a large white bloodstained sheet and threw it over Tristan, covering his whole body. "Lie still," she hissed. "Quiet." The sheet sank to the floor, contouring itself to his body. It was still obviously a person under the sheet, but maybe it was a dead person and hence not a threat. Not something Imran would expect, anyway.

Footsteps came up to the door, and the lock rattled. "Wife!" Imran called. "I'm back!" He sounded surly; perhaps the battle had gone against Daesh. Ariya's chest seemed to freeze. Panting, she snatched up the carving knife with one hand and a heavy ceramic jar with the other and ran soundlessly behind the bedroom doorway.

The front door swung open. "Wife!" Imran called again, striding into the house, his shoulders slumped with weariness, his camouflaged robe stained with sweat and mud. Then his eyes registered the sheet-covered body, and he stopped dead. "Wha—" He stiffened and lifted his AK-47. Without looking away from Tristan's body, he called again, "Wife!" Ariya said nothing, vomit rising in the back of her throat, her hands sweaty. Her heart was beating so fast, it felt as though it would burst.

Imran took a careful step closer to Tristan, his rifle trained on the center of the American's body. *God, let him stay still!* Ariya thought. Imran took another step. Then Ariya leapt around the door frame and hurled the jar with all of her strength, right at Imran's head.

He never saw it coming. The jar smashed against his skull and he staggered like a drunk, the rifle dropping to the floor. Letting out a shriek as if the spirits of her murdered parents had returned for vengeance, Ariya charged across the room with the knife clenched in her hand.

The best way is to stab hard, Tristan had told her. *Like you're punching him with all of your strength. Not just once, but do it again and again and again until he dies.* He had made her drill with a wooden spoon, stabbing the wall for twenty minutes straight until her arm ached and her fingers chafed. Only then was he satisfied. *Your instinct is not to hurt,* he said. *Good people have to learn to hurt, or bad people will win.*

She slammed the knife into Imran's side, below the ribs. It went in at a shallow angle but still sank deep into his flesh. She yanked it out and stabbed him again, this time more solidly in the belly as Imran turned to face her. His expression was rapidly turning from shock to fury. "*Putain de merde*," he growled. She tried to stab him again, and he slammed his fist into her jaw. Her eyes went blurry, her knees buckled; the knife went spinning aside in a spatter of blood.

Seemingly not even noticing the wounds in his stomach, Imran wrapped both hands around Ariya's throat and smashed her slim body back against the hot stove. She couldn't breathe; her throat was being crushed. Pain throbbed through her jaw; the fire's heat beat against her back. Wildly she scrabbled at Imran's snarling face, at his inexorable hands around her neck, but it made no difference. Black flecks filled her vision. The world went dim.

Stop. Calm down. You only have enough air to do one more thing, so make it count. And then, in Tristan's steady voice, came another thought: *Finish the mission.*

She allowed herself to relax and let her hands drop away from Imran's. A feral grin spread across his face. He leaned forward, resting his full weight against her body.

And then he screamed. Ariya had grabbed the pot of boiling saltwater from the stove and flung the water into his face and eyes. Moaning, Imran reflexively let go and stumbled backward. Ariya took in a shallow breath and coughed horribly, but her vision was already sharpening and she did not hesitate. She swung the pot like an ax, bashing it against his head with all of her strength. Then she did it again. And again.

She didn't stop until Imran's body had stopped twitching and the pot was dented and bent, its bottom spattered with blood.

She stood there for a long moment, her chest heaving, gulping sweet air down her burning throat. Then she knelt next to the bloody corpse of her former captor. Ignoring the blood and the unsettling feel of his too-still flesh, Ariya rifled through his pockets until she found his key ring.

She loaded the car with food and tools and Imran's weapons. Tristan was lucid enough to drive, barely, and they left the village under cover of darkness with the headlights off. Once they were ten minutes away, Tristan brought the Jeep to a stop. He was too weak to continue; instead, he coached Ariya through her first hour of ever driving a car and told her to keep driving until she saw

Peshmerga, before passing out. She drove gingerly, her head barely making it over the dashboard, keeping the speedometer below 30 kilometers per hour and being careful to stay on the road.

I don't know what my life will be like tomorrow, she thought. *It could even be worse than before. But I don't care anymore. I'm done letting things happen to me. My life is my own.*

But not just *her* life. In the passenger seat, Tristan was breathing shallowly; he desperately needed the medical care he could only get in Kurdish territory. His life depended on her now. The thought actually made Ariya smile. She was no longer helpless; she mattered. *Perhaps I will save more people tomorrow.*

The Jeep drove on through the darkness. Dawn would come soon.

RICK McMAHAN

Baddest Outlaws

FROM *After Midnight*

THE CREECHES OF Clement County were the baddest outlaws
I've ever known. That's a pretty big accomplishment when you
look at that statement in the larger scheme of things. Many Kentucky counties are known for being rough, with some having whole
communities damn near lawless. Even folks outside the state have
heard of Harlan County. The region's reputation started way back
during the blood spilled during the feuds between the Hatfields
and McCoys, but it was the Depression-era coal wars that cemented
Bloody Harlan's violent name.

People in the know, the crooks and cops who truly know the un-
derbelly of the commonwealth, might say the Cornbread Mafia had
the roughest criminals. They would have a point. After all, Johnny
Boone's crew all came from Marion County, and that county has a
long outlaw history. Back during Prohibition, it's said, Al Capone
himself traveled to Marion County to make deals for alcohol to
feed his Chicago-based speakeasies. Moonshine and running outside the law, some would say, runs deep in the DNA of Marion
County. Decades later, Johnny Boone turned that outlaw way from
moonshining to growing and selling marijuana on a large scale.
The Cornbread Mafia had a reputation for protecting their own,
demanding fierce loyalty. It was said that those who went against
the Cornbread Mafia or talked to the law were met with swift, violent retribution. To this day the Cornbread Mafia is the boogeyman
to would-be informants. You snitch and the Cornbread Mafia will
kill you. They'll nail your house shut with you inside before they
torch the place. They'll grab you and put you in a dark hole. Even

though the feds arrested most of the Cornbread Mafia members, not a one turned state's evidence and testified. Not one. So there must be something to the loyalty and fearsomeness of the Cornbread Mafia.

Still, my money is on the Creeches. And I think if you listen to what I'm about to tell you, you too will agree that the Creeches of Clement County are the baddest outlaws in the whole Commonwealth of Kentucky.

I was sent to Clement County fresh out of the Kentucky State Police academy. This was the time before cell phones and social media and instant communication. CDs were the rage, but many folks still had cassette players in their cars or on their home stereos, and DVDs were slowly winning the battle with VHS tapes. As a rookie trooper, I was destined for the midnight shift. Clement County is one of the commonwealth's biggest counties in terms of land, but not so much of people. We rode shotgun with old dog road troopers, learning the hollers and back roads of the county. At the same time those troopers eyed us to see if we were going to measure up to the standards of the thin gray line. They wanted to see if we had the mettle to be the only law in the county at 3 a.m. when we stopped a car alone.

First time I had a Creech sighting I'd been wearing my badge all of two weeks. I was on day shift partnered with Shawn Morman, a grizzled bear of a trooper whose presence took up most of the front seat of a Ford Crown Victoria. He was a large, imposing man who smoked cheap cigars and could wither you with just a look. He had been a Kentucky state trooper longer than I had been alive. We were driving along when he stabbed his two fingers holding his cigar at the windshield and declared, "That's the most dangerous man in Clement County."

I looked where he was pointing. There was a single car parked in front of the gas pumps at the Texaco, but no gas was getting pumped. The only person in sight was a guy leaning against the front fender of a long Caddy in a tough-guy pose. Arms crossed. Hard stare.

"Londell Creech," Shawn said. "King outlaw of the Creeches." Shawn eased his foot onto the brake of the Crown Vic, and we eased in front of the gas station. Morman rolled his window down.

"Lonnie," he called out.

The man leaning against the fender never broke eye contact with Morman as he pulled a pack of Camels from inside his leather jacket and shook one out. Firing up his smoke, he gave a curt nod of his head. Creech wore a fancy dress shirt underneath his jacket, a large collar folded over the lapels. He had on khakis and brown ankle boots that zipped up one side. I saw the boot only because his foot was wedged against the shiny front hubcap. His shoulders barely cleared the side-view mirror.

"Mister Graybelly," Londell Creech said as introduction. He took a long drag on his cigarette. He and Morman blew out tendrils of smoke almost in unison.

"How's that Brahma bull of yours doing?"

"Blue's dead," Londell said nonchalantly.

"Blue?" Morman asked, perplexed.

"Yeah, Blue," Londell explained. "Like Paul Bunyan's bull."

"Ah, I see," Morman said. "How'd he die?"

"Too damn stupid to live," Londell said. "One time he got to chasing me in the field next to the house. He was serious, so I had to show him I was more serious. Hit him in the head with a hammer to get him to stop." He shook his head. "Was never right after that." He let out a fog of smoke. "We made the best of a bad situation. Barbecued old Blue for the family reunion."

After a polite pause to mourn Blue's passing, Morman said, "I heard Hobart came home."

"Yeah," Creech said, drawing the words out. "Them big cities weren't for him. Mountain's in his blood."

Morman nodded, then patted his hand on the side of the cruiser. "My partner and I have to move along. Gotta keep the county safe, so you stay out of trouble now, Lonnie."

"Wouldn't think of it, Mister Graybelly," Creech said as we pulled away.

As Shawn rolled up his window, he mumbled, "Paul Bunyan, my ass. I don't think Lonnie can read." The Crown Vic picked up speed as we pulled away. Morman gave me a sly smile as he said, "He hates being called Lonnie."

I was thinking I was being played. I already suspected that Master Trooper Shawn Morman was the one who had sent me on a run up a lonesome mountain road to locate Mr. Squatch, whose car was broke down. When I called back for a first name, I was told Sas.

"That guy is the king of the roughest outlaws in Clement County?" My disbelief was obvious in my tone.

Shawn threw me a sideways withering glance that cut me off. He clamped his cigar in his mouth, chewed on it a minute. Finally he said, "I'm hungry. Let's get lunch."

Slinging the wheel with his hand, he spun the cruiser around and headed back into town.

There weren't too many fine-dining options in Clement County, so when Shawn turned the car around I knew where we were going. Poppa's place. There was a sign out front that simply said POPPA'S. A few years later, when the rock band Papa Roach made it big, since the old man's last name was the same, though spelled differently, Poppa put up a new sign. POPPA ROCHE'S PLACE. I heard the band made a special trip to visit the store when they came through Kentucky.

Poppa's was more of an everything store, with various additions sprouting this way and that on the building, sprawling uncontrolled on the lot. What started out as a general store had morphed into more. One area rented VHS movies, another had foodstuff and kitchenware. Another had generally everything you'd need and a lot you didn't, usually things Poppa bought on the cheap out of derailed rail-car sales. One week he might have a sale on those Chia Pets and the next he might have a whole pallet of parrot food cheap. You never knew what he'd have. But us troopers were interested in the small side room with mismatched tables and chairs where he served breakfast and lunch. Poppa's place was probably the most protected establishment in all of Clement County.

Trooper Shawn Morman waited until we had finished with the lunch plate special of chicken-fried steak and sweet tea before educating me further about the hierarchy of criminals in Clement County. Pushing back in his chair, Shawn started unwrapping a fresh cigar as he explained, "Trooper Stokes, don't underestimate the Creeches. They are dangerous. Every one of them."

I nodded and was smart enough to keep my mouth shut.

"Most dangerous group you'll find in this here county," Shawn declared. "I know what you saw—a midget. Whatever's the right way to call 'em—midgets, small people, little folk. Dwarfs. I don't know what the correct phrase would be, but I can tell you this, they're dangerous. They're the baddest outlaws in all of Clement County."

"Are they all . . ." I began, and trailed off.

"That small?" Shawn asked as he put the cigar cellophane wrapper on his discarded plate. "Not all of the women, but every man carrying the Creech name is small. In fact, old Londell is a bit on the tall side for a Creech."

"And they're Clement County's worst criminals?" This time I wasn't able to keep the disbelief out of my voice.

He pointed his unlit cigar at me from across the table. "That most definitely is part of their DNA, as sure as their short stature. Each and every one is a born crook. The Creeches do anything crooked to make a buck." He paused to light the cigar before continuing. "Hell, I think they do some stuff just to do when they're bored. Or out of meanness. But most anything illegal, the Creeches have a hand in — dope, stealing, chopping cars. You name it, they do it. And Londell runs all of it."

"So he's the king of the outlaws?" I asked. He could still see the doubt on my face.

"He is that," Shawn said in an even voice. "Londell runs the whole show." He paused to fire up his cigar and take a long pull. "Boy, I know at the academy they taught you that with that campaign hat, that badge and gun, you boys are ten feet tall and bulletproof."

Damn straight, I thought. I felt myself sit up straighter.

"Well, don't let your notion of things blind you to facts," Morman said. "Watch yourself when you run across a Creech. Don't let their size fool you. They're dangerous."

Being a trooper is a great job for a young twentysomething full of piss and vinegar. You get paid to drive fast and fuss and fight. And in a big old rough place like Clement County you did all three on a regular basis. You learned fast. I kept my eyes and ears open and tried to pick up from the experiences of older troopers. I quickly learned that listening and talking to folks could calm down most situations, but I also learned when the time for talking was done. Sometimes you just had to fight. You hit fast. You hit hard. And you damn sure hit first.

Still not completely sure that Trooper Morman was shooting me straight about the Creeches, I made a point to learn a bit about the clan. At first there was nothing. I just would spot a Creech around town. Mostly it would be Londell driving his long Caddy, his head tilted back so he could look through the windshield. Usually he had heavy metal music blaring so loud you could hear him coming a mile away. He favored AC/DC and Def Leppard. Sometimes he would have passengers, usually a full-sized blonde or brunette hanging all over him like he was a movie star. The car was spotless, and I wondered how he kept it so clean and ding-free on our rutted roads and with all the trucks flinging coal from their open beds.

Then I'd listen to old-timers talk. Every so often the Creech name would come up in conversations around town. Citizens and crooks alike just said the same thing. *You don't mess with them. They're bad news.* Other cops who talked about the Creeches echoed what Trooper Morman had claimed—the Creeches did anything dishonest to make a dollar. They were great con artists. The biggest con had been pulled off by the Creeches' late mother. There are plenty of charities that come and help the poor in the hills of Appalachia. Well, apparently Mother Creech convinced one such group that her kids needed a special house, and the group built a large rambling brick house at the head of the holler on Whitehouse Road. All of the Creeches resided up and down that road, but Londell and his brothers lived in their mother's house halfway up the mountain. Though none had scammed as well as Mother Creech, the rest who could would get on the draw for food stamps or disability. Other Creeches' criminality was less finesse and more pure blunt action. Some Creeches stole. Others fenced said stolen stuff. And they were big into marijuana. Rumor was most marijuana fields were owned, if not tended, by a Creech. Still, the first Creech I arrested did nothing to cement my belief that they were a hardcore group of bandits.

I was on my own working the midnight shift, which is a misnomer, since we actually went eleven to seven, an hour before the witching hour. I was working on my second cup of coffee, sitting on a logging road turnabout just outside of town. From my spot I could stay hidden, but I could also see the ragged two-lane highway down below, and I could pick out likely speeders for good felony stops if I wanted to get into something. I had just settled in with not much traffic on the road when my radio crackled to life.

"Unit 322?" dispatch called out. I keyed the mic, letting them know I was awake and listening. "We have a call of a child riding down Main Street on a bicycle. In the middle of the street."

There was a pause and I was about to key up a 10-4 when the dispatcher continued a little slower. "Three twenty-two, be advised, caller says the child is riding a black Huffy."

"Ten-four," I said as I fired up my Crown Vic, which really sounded like a death rattle; as rookies we got the oldest, most raggedy cars the Kentucky State Police could find.

"Further," dispatch continued.

I was beginning to think dispatch was enjoying this.

"The operator of said Huffy is wearing a black bowler."

I looked at the radio. Even though my mind told my mouth not to, I keyed up the mic anyway and said, "Dispatch, please repeat."

"Three twenty-two, caller advised the operator of the Huffy is wearing a bowler hat." Pause. "Nothing else."

That time I did hear laughter in the background. I was betting the night sergeant and other dispatchers sitting at post two counties away were yucking it up at my expense. I noted that the time was well after midnight, and I was wondering who in their right mind would let a kid out on a school night. And I didn't even think about the clothes. I kicked the car into high and headed toward town. Did I mention before that we young road troopers loved to go fast every chance we got?

The town's main drag wasn't much, and the stoplights went to flashing yellows after ten. The storefronts were closed, though some light leaked out onto the sidewalks. We didn't have much of a downtown, but we did have sidewalks on what we had. It didn't take me long to find the bike in question. Indeed it was a Huffy and indeed the rider was naked except for a small black bowler. I turned on my lights and hit the siren just one chirp. Without looking back, the bicycle's operator raised his arm, making the signal for a right turn, and pulled to the curb, where he promptly fell over.

It wasn't a pretty sight awash in my headlights. All limbs and naked torso matted with dark hair. And the bowler had fallen off to reveal a bad case of male-pattern baldness.

Sliding out of my cruiser door, I yelled out, "Sir, are you okay?"

The nudist got himself free of the bike without catching any needed parts in the spokes or chain and stood wobbly at attention, hands stiffly at his sides. My eyes caught a glimpse of something glowing just under the bike's spinning front tire.

"Trooper," the nudist said. All deep bass voice as steady as his legs weren't. The pungent odor of marijuana rolled off him.

Making a leap of logic, I asked, "Mr. Creech, where are you headed?"

He didn't answer. He just stood there at attention, rocking slightly back and forth. As I got closer, his eyes blinked, trying to focus on me. He had a heavy five o'clock shadow.

Squatting, I reached underneath the still-spinning front wheel and picked up the dying doobie. The joint was as big and fat as a good Havana cigar. Cheech and Chong would have been proud.

"This yours, Mr. Creech?"

"I don't mind sharing," he answered, breaking out into laughter.

As I stood there looking at this naked stoned midget, I couldn't take Shawn's words seriously. I couldn't believe this guy was a member of a hardcore criminal clan. He never gave me a bit of trouble. Just climbed in the back of my cruiser and fell asleep. I tossed the bike and bowler into the trunk of my cruiser. The doobie went into an evidence envelope.

When I booked him into the jail, I learned I had arrested Hobart Creech, Londell's younger brother. Hobart had spent the last few years in New York City, presumably working (or being a criminal) before moving back home. While I was filling out the citation, the jail staff tried to find a jumpsuit that would fit Hobart, but none were small enough. In the end one of the jailers went to her car and gave him a pair of her kid's pants and a Power Rangers T-shirt to wear.

That small arrest turned into something big in my learning about how the Creeches handled things. While I was finishing up my shift, Hobart Creech and another inmate named Eddie Tremayne got sideways with each other in the drunk tank. It seems that while Hobart was mellow while stoned, Eddie was a mean drunk. He sucker-punched Hobart and proceeded to stomp the downed Creech into unconsciousness. The next morning the jail staff asked what had happened, and Hobart Creech refused to say a word. A few days after that, both Tremayne's house and his truck burned to the ground while he was in jail, trying to make bail. By then he knew he had made a major mistake. In fact, he refused to make bail when he could, thinking jail would protect him. Eventually, though, Tremayne had to leave. Now, we know Ed Tremayne walked out of the county jail. From there no one knows where he went. Rumors were that he wound up at the bottom of some well or coal mine, but for all we knew, he hopped a Greyhound bus out of Clement County.

But that still didn't convince me that the Creeches were the baddest outlaws in Clement County. The next time I encountered the Creeches I became a true believer.

Talk all around town and most all of Clement County was the burglary of Poppa's place. Someone had cut the electricity to the building before knocking down the side door. After that they just backed a truck up to it and waltzed out with everything they wanted. Every cop on every shift wanted the hides of those thieves. Now, the reason the cops were fired up was because whoever broke in took Poppa Roche's big stove and griddle, and Poppa wasn't sure if and when he could replace them. No stove, no lunch plate specials. Which meant there were a lot of hungry, angry cops.

Though it seemed like the burglary was the work of a professional crook, the randomness of what they stole had us all scratching our heads. The thieves took the time to tote out the restaurant-sized stove and grill, but they didn't touch any of the guns in sporting goods. The same thing for the rings and earrings in jewelry display cases. Yet they did take twenty rolls of plastic that farmers and landscapers use to protect plants. They then waltzed down aisles picking this and that, with a particular interest in chips and Twinkies.

Besides the kitchen appliances, the biggest and most bizarre item stolen was one of the most controversial products ever featured for sale at Poppa's. Like I said, Poppa would bid on shipments from damaged or derailed box cars, sometimes sight unseen. Before the burglary Poppa's was already the talk of Clement County for cases of products stacked knee-high all over the store. More conservative church groups were offended that every other aisle at Poppa's displayed bottles of something called The Love Doctor's Personal Lubricant.

I am not a prude, but I did think Poppa was never going to sell all of the Love Doctor's product, even if every person in Clement County bought two of the economy-sized bottles. The Love Doctor lube wasn't flying off the shelves until the burglars came along and loaded up as many cases as they could carry off. Did I mention that each one was the economy-sized half-gallon plastic pump bottle?

Nope. I'm not joking. I didn't think they packaged that stuff in such large containers.

Some of the people around town thought the break-in was the result of some bored teenagers' prank that got out of hand. Another theory was that some overzealous members of the Holiness Congregation had taken it upon themselves to rid Clement County of the horribleness that Poppa was peddling. But everyone was betting that if the cops caught the thieves, there would be plenty of mountain justice handed out before the thieves made it to jail. Not so much for the burglary, but for disrupting the public servants' favorite eating routine. You don't mess with cops and their meals.

About a week after the burglary at Poppa's, well past midnight, I was once again perched upon my favorite hiding point above the state two-lane. Like a hunter in a duck blind, I was watching the highway, waiting for a speeder, able to see a long ways in either direction. Calls and disturbances on midnight shift rolled in ebbs and flows in Clement County. Weekends you were going call to call from drunk and disorderly to domestic disputes to just general stupidness. Wednesday nights were usually pretty calm. You might get a call now and then, but mostly after 1 a.m. it was quiet, so you either worked at staying awake or tried to stir something up. Even though there was only myself and Jack O'Bannon, another rookie trooper, working the whole county, I wanted to get into something, so I was hawk-eyeing the highway. I was in the middle of eating the peanut butter and jelly sandwiches my wife made for my dinner when Jack O'Bannon radioed dispatch that he was pulling a car over for speeding.

I started my cruiser, thinking if the car rabbited on Jack we might get in a good chase. Young cops love chasing people. I was no different; whether it was a car chase or running someone down on foot, I ate that stuff up. Instead Jack almost immediately radioed dispatch that the driver had pulled to a stop. Jack called in the car tag. Listening, I thought it was odd that the car was from a county almost all the way across the state from us. Jack called back and said he had made contact with the driver and all was fine. Settling back in, I was about to open my little cup of applesauce when Jack keyed up the radio.

"Unit 322, you in service?" Jack asked. Looking down, I noticed that Jack had called me on our car-to-car radio channel, which didn't reach outside the county. We used that when we didn't want our talk overheard back at post. Rattling off a mile marker on a road outside of town, he asked, "Can you meet me at my location?"

Shoving the applesauce in my lunch pail, I answered, "Ten-four."

Though it wasn't chasing someone, I did get to drive really fast to get to Jack's location. I found Jack's cruiser sitting on the side of the road. In front of his car was a Ford Mustang. What surprised me was a man was sitting on the grass at the rear of Jack O'Bannon's Crown Victoria. Getting out of the car, I walked up, and as I got closer, the bigger this guy got. Jack's easily six-foot-six in his stocking feet, and I would bet this guy was just as big. But his arms were pumped up like Popeye's, and his arms barely made it behind his back to meet the cuffs. I saw the full-sleeve tats and the pale pallor of a man not used to sunlight.

"What's going on, Jack?" I asked as he intercepted me outside earshot. A small breeze was blowing, and I got a distinctly weird smell wafting off of Jack's prisoner. Something chemical. And something else I couldn't quite put my nose on.

Leaning in conspiratorially, he said, "I stopped this guy doing almost a hundred. I mean, he was screaming, but once I lit him up he just pulled over like a kitten."

I nodded. I got it. An easy stop.

"When I asked him where he was going in a hurry, he said, 'I want to get out of this crazy county.'"

I shrugged. Jack was excited, but I didn't see why. "Okay."

"Just listen to what he has to say."

I made a noncommittal grunt, already regretting that I had left my applesauce for this.

"Trust me, Bo. This is great. You'll see." Leading me over to the guy on the ground, Jack nudged him with his foot. The man looked up with hangdog eyes. "Tell my partner what you told me."

The guy shook his head, droplets of water flinging off the ends. "Man, if you're going to take me to jail and violate me, just do it. I don't want to be made fun of." I tipped my flashlight and shined it on the man. He was completely wet. Hair. Clothes. Shoes. Not just wet. He was soaked through, and here we were in a drought.

"Ronnie," Jack said before I could ask about how Ronnie got wet. "Tell the story. We might can help you."

I shot Jack a look. He just smiled.

Ronnie cleared his throat. "Okay." Long sigh and another head shake. "I'm out of the joint just two weeks. I owe a guy a favor from when we were locked up together." He glanced at me and Jack. "Don't ask, I'm not going to tell you the guy's name. No way. I'm not going to snitch that way."

As I stood there, the chemical smell was getting stronger, and the other smell was too. It was a weird one. Like someone had tried to replicate a natural odor and didn't get it right.

"Ronnie, get to the story," Jack said, directing the guy back on point.

"Okay, okay," Ronnie said, hair falling into his eyes. "So my friend gives me a piece of paper. Directions. He says just drive over to Clement County and pick up five pounds of weed. No money. It's all on the front. All I have to do is go see the little dude."

Jack smiled at me, really broad.

Ronnie kept on rolling with his tale. "Only my guy told me, 'Don't call him little, dude, or midget, he don't like that.' I said, 'Cool, man. I just go pick up five pounds of homegrown from a dude and drive it back.'"

"And you got five pounds?" I asked, my excitement growing.

Ronnie sighed, tilting his head back. "No, man, you can check. I don't have any weed. No cash. Nothing."

Now I was getting into this. I knew he had to be talking about Londell Creech.

"Tell him," Jack prompted.

The smell was distracting me. I couldn't place it, though it kind of smelled familiar. Almost like suntan lotion.

Ronnie gave us a ticked-off look like he thought we were making fun of him. Another sigh. "So I drive out in the middle of nowhere on this road. Whitehouse Road. I remember because it made me think of D.C. and the president. And I went way back, and just like my guy said, there's this big old brick house on cleared land. It's lit up like the Vegas strip. Music going. Every light on, like a party. I pull up in the yard, thinking there will be a ton of folks there, but no one was around. I rang the front door. I yelled."

"And?" I asked.

"No one answered. I walked around the back, where this big old steep hill was. There's one dude and a chick. All stoned. And they're slip-sliding."

"Slip-sliding?"

"Yeah," the guy said. "You know, those things kids have that are slick plastic. Lay it down and hook a hose up and they slip-slide on it."

"Got it," I said.

"This little dude is running around smoking a big old doobie and is only wearing a leopard-print man-thong. And the chick is naked. They are slip-sliding. Except this is the longest, biggest slip-slide I think ever was made." He paused. "So I said hello and asked about the weed. He said his brothers were gone and I had to see one of them. He said I could wait. So we smoked some weed, and they slid down the hill."

"Tell him about the water," Jack prompted.

Ronnie gave a disgusted snort. "It wasn't water on the slip-slide."

Coconut! The funky not-right smell I was smelling: it was coconut.

Ronnie kept talking. "They had tons of these industrial-sized jugs of the stuff. Poured on the plastic and rubbed it on themselves." He made a disgusted noise.

"Love Doctor's Lubricant?" I asked.

"Yeah," Ronnie said. "It was everywhere. Empty jugs thrown around. And more stacks of full bottles waiting to be used. So the chick and the dude were sliding around. I sat and smoked a little. Somewhere along the way the dude grabbed one of those funny hats like foreigners wear."

"A bowler," I said. Hobart Creech.

"Whatever," Ronnie said. "The slide had to be close to a football field long and ran straight down this big-ass hill. They'd pump some of that stuff on their hands, rub it all over, and dive onto that plastic. Slicker than snot, they'd shoot down the hill. Laugh all the way down. Walk up the hill. Smoke dope. Slide down again." He looked at me. "I got bored. I had just drove halfway across Kentucky, so I was already tired. A few tokes on a joint and I was out like a light. It was awesome weed. I woke up just as they rolled me onto the plastic, and that little dude gave me a shove, and I started downhill headfirst."

He glanced back and forth between Jack and me. "Man, once you hit that stuff there was no stopping. And the worst part was that little dude jumped on my back like I was a sled or something. I'm a big dude."

"And gravity," I commented.

"Yeah, gravity. Just like in school," Ronnie said. "Gravity sucked us down faster and faster. We were zipping down this hill, between trees. Rocks. Whatever. And then it ended. And we skidded another twenty feet, damn near slamming right into a boulder. The little dude laughed all the way down the hill. That ride scared me."

Falling back into the grass, Ronnie looked up at the sky. "Man, I've been in some fights in prison. Shanks and knives. But I was more afraid zipping down that hill inches away from a big old oak or a rock splitting my head open. I said, forget this. My guy told me the main dude I was to deal with was crazy. And he wasn't the one nearly banging my head off the land riding down that slip-and-slide. That dude in the leopard-print thong was crazy enough for me. I didn't want to meet his brother. I got the hell out of there intending not to slow down until I got out of this county."

Jack pulled me away a few steps. "What do you think?"

Raising my voice, I said, "Ronnie, I think we can let you off with a warning this time."

After we had Ronnie give us all the info he had about the house, Jack and I raced back to the office, where we came up with this great idea. Others would call it harebrained. But to us two rookies, it was a great plan. We used Ronnie's statement about where he went (the Creeches') and who he met (Hobart Creech) as well as the description of the slip-and-slide (matching the type of material stolen from Poppa Roche's) and the brand and enormous quantity of Love Doctor lube (ditto for Poppa Roche's burglary), and we thought we could get ourselves a search warrant for the Creech residence. Even better, with only a stoned and half-naked Hobart there, the two rookies could easily be the heroes and solve Poppa's burglary. One stoned Hobart against two of the finest of the thin gray line. No problem. It was a foolproof plan.

When we knocked on the county attorney's door with our freshly typed affidavit in hand, he was more than a little mad. However, after he read our work and saw what we were doing, he was all in. Did I mention that the prosecutor and judge also liked eating at Poppa's place? From there we went to the judge's house, where Jack swore out the search warrant.

When we finally got the warrant, it was after 3 a.m., so we figured even the ne'er-do-well relatives on Whitehouse Road would be asleep or passed out drunk or stoned and not be able to rouse old Hobart. Our plan was to ease up Whitehouse Road. Not going too fast. Not going too slow. With a little luck we would get to the Creeches' big brick house while Londell and the others were out doing Lord knows what. We would snatch up Hobart, and once we located the missing stove and griddle, along with all of the plastic and Love Doctor's product, it would be time for first-shift troopers to come in to work. All of those senior troopers could come help us heroes tote out all of the stolen property.

Sounded like a great plan.

Jack and I slid into his car and headed toward our destination. We waited until we were already headed down the road before I keyed the radio to dispatch. "Dispatch, be advised Units 322 and 575 are en route to 1072 Whitehouse Road."

A long pause as the night dispatcher probably rubbed the sleep out of her eyes. "Unit 322, I don't have a call for that address."

"Dispatch, we will be serving a search warrant for stolen property there," I said. Then I keyed the microphone and made static noises and half words. "Dispatch we . . . when . . . contact post when we're ten-seven."

Jack suggested we switch off the radio. I didn't do that, but I did turn the volume all the way down, so we could honestly say we couldn't hear dispatch call for us.

To get an idea of Whitehouse Road, you have to picture a small, barely two-lane road that snakes this way and that. More curves than straightaways. Hillside on one side and wooded drop-offs on the other. Every little bit, a house or trailer would be in a flat spot or just visible through the trees. Most with only a porch light on, or a lone bulb glowing in through a window. The rest was darkness and shadows of trees, the road only illuminated as far as the light from the headlights.

As we drove deeper into the holler, the thicker the trees got and the farther apart the houses were. And the darker it seemed to get.

We rounded one long curve and there was a great big house and driveway. And it was lit up like it was on the Vegas strip. We didn't have to worry about anyone hearing us roll up. AC/DC's "Back in Black" was pumping out of a huge stereo someone had dragged out into the driveway with an extension cord running back into the house.

Jack pulled the Crown Vic to a stop at the bottom of the driveway, and we quietly got out, each taking one side of the driveway. Heading up the gravel drive, we kept our eyes open and one hand on our holstered pistols. As we passed the stereo, Jack reached down and gave the cord a yank, killing the music. The silence was deafening.

Together, Jack and I eased around to the back of the house, since that was where Ronnie said Hobart had been when he left. Moving through the carport, we took a flagstone path toward the rear of the house, where I could see at least an acre or more of cleared land sloping down to the bottom of the hill. As I rounded a corner, my foot kicked into something that skittered away, bouncing into the night. Looking down, I saw there were empty plastic bottles scattered along the pathway and into the yard. Love Doctor's Lubricant. Sure enough, there was a long tongue of black plastic rolled all the way down the backyard out of the range of the light into the darkness. The slide started fifteen feet from a nice concrete patio with lounge chairs and a grill. Two of the lounge chairs were occupied. Curled up on one was a woman as naked as the day she was born. Flopped in the second chair with his legs and arms spread out in a wide *X* was Hobart Creech. Still wearing the leopard-print thong and bowler. Snoring away. Tucked in at the corner of the patio were neatly stacked cartons. You guessed it. More Love Doctor product standing by, ready to slather up and slide down.

Jack kicked the side of Hobart's chair with his shoe. "Mr. Creech. MR. CREECH!" Raising his voice had gotten a slight stir out of him. "MR. CREECH. STATE POLICE!" Jack had a booming voice that could rattle your teeth.

Hobart stirred and opened an eye. Lazily a hand rose, pointing. "I know you."

I nodded. "Trooper Stokes and Trooper O'Bannon, Mr. Creech. We have a warrant to search your house for stolen property."

Now, you would think a man stoned and slow to stir would not be so quick, but my words must have been like a starter pistol going off for a track star. Hobart sat up bolt straight and yelled, "I'm not going to jail."

"Now, Mr. Creech," Jack said, reaching a hand to grab the man's wrist. Hobart yanked. His hand slipped right out of Jack's grasp.

Jumping up, Hobart cried, "I'm not going to jail." He leapt between Jack and me to make a dash toward the front. Running between us should have been a mistake, because we both instinctively grabbed for him, but our hands just slid off his skin. Hobart was lacquered up in Love Doctor slippery action formula in layers like wax on a surfboard. And for a small fellow, Hobart sure could run fast. About every time his foot came down, he yelled, "I'm not going to jail. I'm not going to jail."

Jack and I gave chase. Now, Hobart's advantage was he had a good start and he knew the lay of the land. Jack and me weren't stoned and we had greater strides on Hobart. Still, he rounded the corner into the carport and made it into the house in time for the screen door to slam closed. Pausing, Jack ripped the door outward and off its hinges in one yank, and in we went.

"Hobart, calm down and stop," I said. The carport door led us into the kitchen. Hobart was already across the linoleum floor into the living room, two angry state troopers on his heels. There was a large couch in the middle of the room, and Hobart paused on the back side of it to catch his breath, keeping the couch between us.

"Troopers, I'm not going to jail," he said in between ragged breaths. Jack edged toward the left side of the couch. I moved to the right. I had to move quick, because I thought Hobart might try to make it to the front door on my side and run into the night. Hobart feinted toward me but spun on his heels and tried to squirt past Jack on the inside of the couch. He almost would have made it, but Jack dove onto Hobart and both of them rolled onto the carpet in a mess of limbs.

"I'm not going to jail!" Hobart wailed, thrashing.

Jack had a hold of one of Hobart's arms and was trying to fish a pair of handcuffs out of his belt pouch with his free hand. I grabbed Hobart's other arm, figuring that between the two of us, we should be able to hang on to one arm until we could get him cuffed.

Now, if this was the worst of our plan falling apart, we could have handled a little slicked-up thief trying to get away. But no. What we didn't know until later was that the other Creech brothers had been gone all evening trying to pull Londell's Caddy out of a ditch. They tried to use their second car to pull Londell out, but all they succeeded in doing was getting both cars stuck and having to hitch a ride home. We knew none of this as Jack and I tussled with Hobart on the living room floor. Hobart had quit screaming. It was taking all of his concentration to keep us from cuffing a hand. It was all we could do to hang on to him. I felt like I was in an oil wrestling contest. And I was losing. We were all grunting and squirming. Rolling this way and that.

Then I had this feeling that someone was watching me. I looked over my left shoulder at Londell Creech, the king of the Creeches, standing in the doorway. Behind him was a line of Creeches. Without a word, Londell took off at a dead run toward us, the other Creeches following right behind, like a charge of warriors from a medieval battle.

Rolling away from Hobart, I tried to get to my feet but only made it to my knees when the first body slammed into me, followed by a second piling on top. A rain of kicks and punches started hammering me. Luckily the body armor under my shirt absorbed a lot of that energy, but my head took a few shots. For several minutes it was a mass of bodies rolling around and around, trying to gain leverage and the upper hand. I think we wrestled from one end of the living room floor to the other. Londell Creech was trying to choke or hit me, and one of his brothers was trying to wrap up my legs. At one point Londell scrambled onto my back, slipping his arm around my throat. Choking me. My lungs screamed for oxygen, but none was coming. Desperately, I flailed my arms, trying to get him off me. I was hoping to hit any body part. Then I started trying to pull his hair. When my fingers found a nostril, I dug in deep. Yanked. Hard. The arms choking me dropped away as my attacker howled.

Pausing to suck in lungfuls of air, I looked over and saw that Jack had managed to stagger to his feet with a Creech latched onto each arm. Windmilling his body back and forth, he threw one Creech into a wall behind him. When he pivoted the other way, he let that one sail across and land in a cupboard. Standing straight up was Jack's downfall.

Hobart had gotten up but had not run away. Instead of shooting out the front door, he scrambled onto the back of the couch, standing at full height, sort of reminding me of Nature Boy Ric Flair on the top rope of a wrestling ring. Once Jack was upright, Hobart let out a banshee scream and jumped off the couch, his fist hitting Jack right in the face. Blood spurted from Jack's broken nose as he toppled back to the ground.

At that point I had my own hands full. Both of my attackers had clambered up on me and ridden me to the ground. One smacked my head into the floor, sending bright shards of pain through my brain. I felt a pair of hands clawing at my holster. Now, I don't know if they would have killed me if they got my gun, but I locked my hand down on my pistol, feeling panic rise in me. Here we were just wanting to be heroes with an easy bust, solve a crime and show the old guys we knew what we were doing. I really didn't want to shoot someone over a stolen kitchen appliance, some plastic sheeting, and all the Love Doctor lube in the world. I knew if this kept up, either I would lose my gun or, if we couldn't get them to stop, I'd have to shoot. The hand pawing at my holster was relentless. And the other one was pummeling my sides and back.

I felt the holster give and the heavy Smith slide. Instead of pushing the gun back in, I frantically grabbed the grip, swinging the heavy hunk of steel this way and that in a wide arc. On one swing I felt the blade of the front sight hit something fleshy. Shifting around, I rolled until my gun grabber and I were almost face-to-face, but I had rolled on top. Rearing up, I smacked the gun down, splitting his head open.

Struggling to my feet, I put my back against a wall, wildly pointing the gun this way and that, sweeping the barrel over every person standing in the room. I thumbed back the hammer on that big-old-hogleg .357 Magnum.

With one hand I reached down and helped Jack stand up. He was wobbly on his feet, blood pouring from his nose, staining all the way down his torn shirt. My badge was halfway torn off of mine.

My desperation must have been plain on my face. Motioning with the muzzle, I told the Creeches, "The first one that even moves wrong, I'm going to shoot." They saw I was serious and raised their hands. Londell was bleeding from his own ruptured nose. A Creech I didn't know had his hand held to his scalp where I'd laid him open. Another one was nursing a broken arm.

Marching them out into the front yard, I had them sit on the ground, arms still up, while Jack staggered back to the cruiser to radio for help. I was beyond caring about the immense trouble Jack and I were going to be in. I just kept hearing Morman's voice in my head telling me to take plenty of backup when dealing with the Creeches.

Over the years I've dealt with criminals who have wanted to fight. But I have never had a knock-down drag-out fight like that night. Those Creech boys were small but they were determined. It dawned on me right then that they might be disadvantaged as criminals. It's easy being a bad hombre when you're as big as my friend Jack O'Bannon. It's another to be a bad outlaw when your genes have shortened your stature. The Creeches hadn't shied away from their outlaw ways. They relished it. Yet they had to be twice as tough and twice as mean to make it as criminals.

In my book, pound for pound, inch for inch, no criminal is as flat-out bad as the Clement County Creeches.

I'm here to tell you, them Creeches are the baddest outlaws alive.

LISA MORTON

What Ever Happened to Lorna Winters?

FROM *Odd Partners*

FOR SOME IT'S the handshake at the end of the meeting. The smile at the restaurant table that tells you the answer is yes before you even ask. The email that makes you laugh. The sure knowledge — the kind that's *so* sure you feel it in every fiber — that the person next to you will do something great, but only when they work with *you.*

For me it was that moment when I realized the blonde getting murdered in the old 16mm film was Lorna Winters. I knew then that those three minutes of black-and-white footage were going to become an important scene in the story of *my* life.

The battered old steel reel holding the nearly sixty-year-old footage arrived at my workstation the way most movies arrived there: in a box with other films and the accompanying paperwork.

I'd worked for BobsConversionMagic.com for two years and an odd number of days. When I'd taken the job, I'd been stupid enough to think it was a temporary fix for my unemployment problem. Since graduating with a film degree, I'd somehow failed to set Hollywood on fire. I'd tried all the usual approaches to getting a foot in the film industry door: I'd made two short films that I'd entered into festivals (the second one, *Raw Material,* had won a runner-up prize somewhere in Michigan), I'd written three feature screenplays that I kept in the trunk of my car at all times, I'd joined a writers' group that gathered once a week for breakfast at a Westside eatery, but everyone I'd met had been other writers as desperate as I was. I wrote a blog on the history of film noir that had a few dozen followers but had yet to lead to anything else.

And I was flat broke. I was a terrible waiter, an even worse burger-flipper, and my car was so badly in need of a paint job that signing up for some driving app just seemed useless.

So the day my old college buddy Elliott called and said he could get me a film job, I jumped at the chance.

It turned out the "film job" was actually working for a place that converted old home movies into DVDs. And the company was in San Bernardino. I wasn't thrilled with the idea of leaving Hollywood behind for the Inland Empire, but I was even less thrilled at the thought of living on ramen and friends' futons forever. The pay was decent, I figured apartments in that area would be cheaper than L.A., and maybe six months of transferring Uncle Harold's old Christmas movies to digital would be enough to finance one more short film that I thought had a great script.

And two years later I was still pulling battered reels out of boxes and threading them through Bob's old telecine.

Bob Zale, who owned the company, had turned out to be a damned decent boss to work for. He was a guy in his forties who, like me, had walked away from a Hollywood crash-and-burn, and, also like me, he loved old movies. My college bud Elliott may have left the company not long after setting me up there (he moved back home to South Dakota, where his parents' basement beckoned to him with its siren song), but Bob and I bonded over many late-night beers and Robert Mitchum, Gloria Grahame, and Humphrey Bogart. We knew every bit player, the location of every rain-soaked street, the title of every forgotten gem.

Here's how my days usually went: I'd arrive at work around 9 a.m. (Bob didn't freak out if I was late, so long as I got through the day's work). There'd be a few boxes of movies waiting for me; they'd already been received and checked in by Joanne, who ran both receiving and reception at Bob's (we didn't get much walk-in; most of the business came via the website). I'd pull out a reel, load it onto spindles on a flatbed, add a take-up reel, and crank through it by hand just to inspect the film. I could do basic fixes—repair splices, simple cleaning. Then, once I'd made notes about problem areas and solved what I could, the reel was loaded onto the telecine machine. Bob had two of them, both old Marconis that were probably far from the high-tech devices most customers imagine, especially if they'd watched Blu-ray supplements about digital remastering. We weren't sitting in front of a bank of computer screens carefully watching a transfer to color-correct and paint out imperfections; instead I perched on a wobbly wooden stool peering into a screen the size of a paperback novel, just making sure the digitization was really happening.

That day's first two transfers were typical stuff: faded footage of a backyard barbecue, and a family of wife and two girls horsing around on a deserted beach (Dad was presumably the cinematographer). In my two years working for Bob, I'd seen this stuff hundreds of times.

The next movie I threaded onto the machine from the same box was black-and-white. It seemed to be shot at night, on the back of a yacht. It opened on an empty deck surrounded by a low metal railing. In the background, light glimmered on moving water.

After a few seconds a woman entered the frame. Her back was to the camera, but she carried herself with such natural poise that I guessed she was beautiful before she turned. She walked to the edge, leaned on the railing, bent down to look into the water. Her long blond hair blew in the breeze caused by the boat's cruising. She wore an elegant sleeveless black dress; it must have been a warm night, because her exposed shoulders didn't huddle against any cold.

She turned to face the camera at last. It was a full shot, but even on the small telecine screen I could see I'd guessed right: she *was* beautiful.

I squinted and leaned in, trying to get a better look. Just then a man walked into the shot. The woman reacted with surprise—not the *good* kind—at seeing him. In fact, she backed toward the railing, her eyes narrowing.

It was that expression—the calculating coolness hiding the alarm—that confirmed who she was. It was one of her trademarks, a look that had made her one of film noir's greatest icons.

She was Lorna Winters.

I nearly stopped the transfer in disbelief. *Lorna Winters!* I watched a few more seconds to be sure, but there was no doubt. Her tall, lean figure, the long blond hair with a few streaks of light brown, and that face . . . Lorna Winters, who had slapped Richard Conte in

Rat Trap. Lorna Winters, who had raised male temperatures across the country when she'd flirted with Sterling Hayden in *Bullet's Kiss.*

Lorna Winters, who'd made seven low-budget film noir gems, one last expensive studio production (*Midnight Gun*), and vanished without a trace in 1960.

I watched, breathless, as she argued with the man who'd entered the scene. He was a big man, wearing a suit with no tie. Lorna tried to walk around him, but he turned to block her, facing the camera. He had a classic thug's face, heavy features, slicked-back dark hair, white scar over one eye.

I'd seen him before. There'd been one shot of Dad in the backyard barbecue movie. He'd grinned, lifted his long fork, waved it in a jaunty way when a little girl ran up to him.

Now I was watching this same man pull a gun out of his jacket and level it at Lorna Winters.

Her chilled façade nearly cracked, but she forced a smile and a nod toward the gun. I didn't need sound to know she was saying, "You're not really going to use that."

His jaw clenched; he pulled the trigger. The gun went off. Lorna staggered back, grasping her chest, her mouth open in shock.

She came up against the railing, and he fired again. Her feet went out from under her on the slick deck, causing her to flip right back off the end of the boat into the sea. He calmly walked forward, leaned over the railing to search the night waves, then holstered the gun.

The film ended.

I was so stunned that I dropped the reel getting it out of the telecine. I got it wound up nice and neat again, checked the digital file, burned it to a DVD, and rushed off to my workstation. I had to see it on a decent-sized monitor. I had to be sure.

The DVD started playing. I held my breath as the woman walked into the shot, finally turning.

No question—it was Lorna Winters.

What was I watching?

It seemed logical to assume it was a scene from a movie . . . but if it was, it was a Lorna Winters movie no one had ever seen, because I'd seen her eight films enough times to know every shot, and this was definitely not in any of them. An unfinished film, maybe? It couldn't be a deleted scene, because her character hadn't died by being shot on a boat in any of her existing movies. And the man who shot her . . . he wasn't an actor in any of the movies. In fact, if he was an actor at all, I'd never seen him in anything.

And what studio would've let Lorna Winters flip off the back of a moving boat like that? They would've saved that for a stuntwoman, adroitly substituted for Lorna after a cut.

The knot in my gut told me what I'd just seen was real. The answer to one of Hollywood's greatest real mysteries: *What ever happened to Lorna Winters?*

I stopped the playback, yanked the disk out of my computer, and went to Bob's office. He was there, seated behind a desk piled high with papers and movies, the walls around him lined with crowded shelves and boxes.

He was on the phone, saying something about how "the transfers looked great" and he'd make sure we "sent a tracking number." He saw me, waved a hand indicating that I should wait, and finished the conversation. When he finally ended the call ("No problem, Mrs. Simmons, always nice to hear from you"), he shook his balding head. "That is one bored old woman. Jesus, she does this with every order—"

Bob must've seen something in my expression, because he broke off, concerned. "Hey, what's up?"

I handed him the DVD. *"This."*

"What is it?"

"An order I just completed. You need to see it."

"Why?"

"Just watch it."

He eyed me uncertainly for a second before sliding the DVD into his own computer. I didn't even bend over to watch it with him; instead I watched his expression. When his mouth fell open, I knew he'd gotten it. "Is that . . . ?"

"Lorna Winters. Keep watching."

He did. The film finished. Bob continued to stare at the screen. "Jesus H. Christ. Is that *real*?"

"You tell me."

He considered for a few seconds, staring at the frozen last frame on his monitor. "It's gotta be a scene from a movie—"

"The man is no actor. He's Mr. Family Guy in the other movies included with this lot."

Bob leaned forward to bring something up on his computer. I waited as he read through some text. "I'm looking at her Wikipedia entry, says she disappeared in 1960, just after finishing *Midnight Gun*. She'd been dating some mobster named Frank Linzetti, but they could never tie him to anything." He stopped reading and looked up at me. "You think that guy in the movie is Linzetti?"

I shook my head. "Google Linzetti—he was a good-looking guy. But maybe this dude worked for him."

After a long exhale, Bob pulled the DVD out of his computer. "Christ. We've got to hand this over to the police. And we'll need to talk to the customer. Who is it?"

I'd brought the order with me. "Name's Victoria Maddrey. She has an Encino address, so she probably has money." I saw Bob squirming at the thought of all this, so I added, "Let me do it."

He looked at me, surprised. "Really? Dealing with the cops?"

"I don't mind. I *want* to do it. I mean, think about it, Bob: we could be the ones to figure out what happened to Lorna Winters."

Bob smirked. "I love you, Jimmy, but you know that doesn't belong to us. We can't make a bundle selling it, at least not legally."

"I don't want to sell it. I want to work with it. I want to *know*."

Bob tossed the disk to me. "Knock yourself out, amigo."

The next day I headed west on the 10 freeway. I had an 11 a.m. appointment with the Cold Case Homicide Special Section of LAPD's Robbery-Homicide Division, and a 3 p.m. with Victoria Maddrey at her home.

Despite traffic (how does it keep getting worse?), I made it to downtown L.A. in time, paid a ridiculous amount to park, and was waiting for Detective Dorothy Johnson at 10:55 a.m.

The detective assigned to talk to me turned out to be a tired-looking middle-aged African American. I told her who I worked for, handed her the disk, gave her the CliffsNotes version of The Lorna Winters Story, and let her take a look.

If you base your notion of cops on movies and television, you probably think they all dress in tailored suits, work closely with forensics teams in glistening blue-lit labs, and are obsessed with every case they get. But as I waited for Detective Johnson to finish watching the movie, I realized nothing could be further from that. The truth was that her desk was a cluttered little island in a sea of

other cluttered little islands, that her pantsuit was old enough to
be seriously out of style, and that she was underwhelmed by what
I'd brought her.

She finished watching and turned to me. "So first off, Mr. Guerrero," she said, in a tone that told me this wasn't going to go well,
"we're actually talking a missing persons case, right?"

"Before yesterday I would've agreed. But then I saw this."

"And what makes you think this is real?"

I squirmed, suddenly—irrationally—feeling as if that movie
were a friend who'd just been insulted. "I know Lorna Winters's
work inside and out, and that's definitely not a scene from any of
her movies. And no studio would've let a star take a dive off a moving powerboat like that."

Johnson looked at me a few more seconds. In her eyes I saw
a lifetime of disappointment—with people, with what they were
capable of, and with what she'd never unravel. "You say this Lorna
Winters disappeared in . . . what, 1960?"

I knew where this was headed. I just wanted to be out of there.
"Right."

She pulled the disk from her machine. "This is a copy we can
keep?"

"Yes."

She spoke as she slid the disk back into its little glassine envelope. "You have to understand that there's not much here. See
these?" She tapped a stack of folders on her desk. "These are all the
cases I've got actual evidence on, mostly DNA. With this case . . ."

"But you get a good look at the guy who shot her."

"And maybe he really shot her, or maybe that's just practice for a
movie, or somebody's gag reel. Otherwise . . . look, if I get a break
from the other cases, I'll see what I can do."

Detective Johnson would never get a break, because people had
been killing one another in this city from Day One, and around
nine thousand of those murders had never been solved. I got to
my feet, trying to sound sympathetic. "I understand. Thank you for
your time."

"We'll be in touch if we need anything."

I knew I'd never hear from her.

Fortunately, my second appointment of the day was far more productive.

Victoria Maddrey was a slim, attractive woman in her late fifties. Her house was in the foothills at the southwest end of the San Fernando Valley; even though the house was older, it was immaculate, and I could only imagine what the property taxes must've been. It was surrounded by a lush garden of hibiscus and bougainvillea, with a tall old magnolia tree dominating the front yard. Victoria was simply but tastefully dressed, with the air of a proud woman who'd put a lot of work into her life.

She took the box of films and disks that I handed her, set it aside, and invited me into a comfortable living room. I wasn't used to this kind of money, even as I realized this wasn't the high end of the wealth scale in L.A. She brought me a cup of coffee, and then we got down to business.

"Ms. Maddrey, I'd like to show you something that was on one of the films you sent us."

"Please, call me Vick."

I pulled out my iPad, which I'd already loaded with the film. I brought it up, hit Play, and passed it to her.

I have to say, she impressed me. Her face remained implacable as she watched, not a flicker of emotion. When it was done, she handed the iPad back to me without speaking.

"The woman," I said, "is an actress named Lorna Winters, who disappeared in 1960. Can you tell me anything about the man?"

She took a sip from her own cup and then said, "The man is my father. Vincent Gazzo."

I had to set my coffee down before I choked. "Your father?"

For the first time her elegant surface cracked, but it was a hairline crack—all she did was look down. "My father liked to call himself a 'security consultant,' but he really worked for the Mafia. Do you know the name Frank Linzetti?"

"Yes. He was dating Lorna Winters—the woman in that film."

Another hairline crack, but this time of curiosity. "Was he? How interesting. My father worked for him."

"And your father is . . . ?"

"Dead. He died in 1990, of a heart attack. Ironic, isn't it, that he spent a lifetime hurting others and making enemies but ended up dying because he'd eaten too many cannoli." She gestured around the perfect room. "He left me this house. I know I should've sold it at some point, but my husband and I are really quite fond of it."

"It's a beautiful house." Secretly I wondered how much the Mafia's equivalent of a grunt made. Even sixty years ago, this would've been an expensive house.

An uncomfortable silence passed. I knew she wanted me to go, that she just wanted this painful reminder of the father she was ashamed of to be gone. "There's something you should know: we had to report this to the police. I don't think they have any intention of following up on it, but . . ."

"Of course. I understand. I'm still amazed that Father never did time for anything worse than tax evasion."

I finished the coffee — possibly the best I'd ever had — and stood. "I won't trouble you anymore. I know this must be difficult."

She stood, offering me a hand and a small smile. "You'd think I'd be used to it by now. Thank you, Jimmy. You've been very kind."

I wondered then what her life had been like. I realized she must have been one of the little girls I'd seen romping on the beach in one of the other movies, or the one laughing as she bit into the hot dog her daddy had just grilled for her. I imagined her growing up, as she realized who her father had really been, how she'd built a wall to protect herself from either loving him or hating him too much. And I thought about the film I'd just shown her; if it had been human, it would've just told her that Pop was a killer while we both watched her, waiting to see how she'd take it.

She and the house both looked good, but I was glad to get back onto the crowded freeway and head home.

Back in San Bernardino, I filled Bob in on both meetings. He listened, then gave me the best news I'd had all day. "Dug this stuff out of some old boxes for you."

He tossed a stack of yellowing, brittle old magazines at me. I picked up the top one: it was a 1959 movie-star tabloid called *Confidential,* one of the real sleazebag rag sheets from the time. The cover had photos of celebrities looking drunk or bewildered, plastered against bright red and yellow backgrounds, while the nearby text shrieked something like *"Why Sinatra Is the Tarzan of the Boudoir"* or *"James Dean Knew He Had a Date with Death!"*

In one corner was a photo of Lorna Winters, holding the hand of a young man in a suit, both looking like they wished they were anywhere else but near that camera lens. *"Lorna Winters Steps Out with Director!"* bellowed the text.

"I bookmarked the article," said Bob.

I flipped to the piece of paper he'd stuck in. It was a one-page piece on Lorna Winters and David Stander, director of *Midnight Gun*. There were two photos: the same photo of Lorna and David Stander, holding hands, turning their heads away from the photographer, and a smaller inset of Lorna and a different man—dark, handsome, with a toothy grin, who looked like a shark about to chomp. They were seated in an extravagant restaurant booth; the caption read *"Lorna and Frank Linzetti, together in happier times."*

The accompanying text speculated that Lorna had fallen for her director on *Midnight Gun* and had two-timed Linzetti, who she'd been involved with for a year.

My gut performed an acrobatic flip. "Oh my God . . ."

"Yeah," Bob said, "so she dumps her mobster beau for this director, Linzetti flips out and sends his hired gun to take her out."

I thought for a second. "And the hired gun has to film it to prove to the boss that the job's been done."

Bob nodded.

I went home after that. Bob suggested we hit our favorite margarita joint, but I told him I was tired from the day of driving.

That was a small lie. All I really wanted to do was go home and watch the film (*my* film) again. And again.

I put it up on my television. The image quality wasn't great blown up that big—grainy, high-contrast, the result of a cheap transfer—but it made details clearer. Now I could see a life jacket hanging on the railing at the left of the frame. A white blob at the right I knew had to be the moon, probably covered by a light fog. There was Lorna . . .

I hit the DVD Pause when she came on so I could get up, come back with a bottle of tequila, then hit Play again. "What are you trying to tell me?" I muttered. "You're hiding something from me. C'mon, partners don't keep secrets from each other . . ."

Lorna . . . beautiful young Lorna. What could she have been if she hadn't had the bad luck to hook up with a bad-tempered gangster? She'd just made her first big studio picture, and she was good in it—*damn* good. She could've been the next Kim Novak or Lauren Bacall. Hell, she was young enough that she could've been the next Jane Fonda or Faye Dunaway. She died at twenty, just as the wildest decade in movie history was in preproduction.

I watched the film two, three, four times, getting progressively drunker. I watched over and over as she was shot—that look on her face, that instant of shock, that spasmodic clutch at the lethal wound, that tumble over the decking. With enough tequila in me, I kept talking to the film, urging it to spill its secrets, to stop teasing me with the promise of revelations. "You gotta tell. C'mon, baby, spill . . ."

I think I was on the fifth viewing when something pinged off the back of my sodden brain. Something *wrong*.

I wound the scene back a few seconds, to the moment when Vincent Gazzo pulled out the gun. I got off the couch, not even caring that I spilled the half-inch left in the tequila bottle, and walked up to stand closer to the television.

"Yeah, that's it . . . give it up . . ." I muttered as I hit Play again.

There was the shot. There was Lorna grabbing at her chest—

There was no blood.

I paused the image, trying to peer through the heavy digitized grain. Lorna's hand looked pale, spotless. She was wearing a black dress, so with the poor quality I shouldn't expect to see anything there, but . . . wouldn't her fingers have been at least a little splattered? Wouldn't blood have seeped through them?

There was something else, though, and it wasn't until I watched the movie again, from the start, at half speed, that I got it: in the beginning the boat left a clear wake, a *V* of white water.

When Lorna was shot, the water behind the boat was still.

The boat wasn't moving.

I fell back on my ass then, too drunk and too stunned to get to my feet. "You *fake*," I snarled at the frozen picture on my screen, stopped at the point where Lorna was halfway over the rail, her delicate high-heeled feet no longer on the deck. "God*damn*it! You were fake all along! And I went along with you!"

I stopped the player, slid the tray open, grabbed the disk, and hurled it across the room. It collided with a wall, bounced off, and hit the floor. I collapsed on the rug, wanting to howl over the betrayal. "Son of a *bitch!* How could you do this? I thought we were in this together."

I felt like the noir hero who gets set up and knocked down by a dirty partner. I almost called Bob to tell him, but instead I passed out.

I woke up in bed the next morning with no memory of having dragged myself there. My head throbbed with the agony of a thousand exploded blood vessels, although three glasses of water and two cups of coffee helped. A little.

I did call in then, to tell Bob I was running late. "It's a fake," I told him, "a goddamn fake. She's not really shot, and she flips into calm water. The boat's not even moving."

"Well," Bob said, "it's still a newly discovered piece of Lorna Winters film. I say we talk to the owner again, see if she'll consider selling it."

I got into the shower after that. As warm water sluiced over me, easing the pain in my head, I thought. I still wanted to know what the film represented—a promo reel for a new movie? A gag? Vincent Gazzo had died a while back, so we couldn't ask him, and his daughter knew nada. Frank Linzetti had also died, in 2009, in a federal prison where he'd been serving time for money laundering. Wherever Lorna Winters was—dead or alive—remained unanswered. That left one person who'd been involved with the whole thing back in 1960: the director David Stander.

I turned off the water, wrapped a towel around myself, and practically ran to get my phone. A few seconds later I had the facts about Stander: He'd made a few more movies for Columbia but had never really hit it big. He found more success in television and had directed every show from *Bonanza* to *MacGyver* before retiring in 2008. He'd married his secretary, Nora Chilton, in 1962, and they lived now in the Cheviot Hills area of Los Angeles.

Bob had a friend who worked in the office at the Directors Guild; one little white lie to his friend about wanting to film an interview with David Stander got us his phone number. I called it that afternoon.

When a man answered on the first ring, I asked, "Is this David Stander?"

"Yes, it is."

"Mr. Stander," I began, hoping I sounded convincing, "my name is Jimmy Guerrero. I'm working on a documentary about Lorna Winters, and I was wondering if it might be possible to meet for a brief interview?"

"I'm sorry, no."

No explanation, no excuse . . . but he also didn't hang up, so I pressed on. "Oh, that's too bad, because we've got some newly discovered footage of Miss Winters that we were hoping you could shed some light on."

"What kind of footage?"

"Something filmed privately. It shows Ms. Winters on a boat, and . . . well, it looks like she gets shot."

There was a pause. Then Stander said, "Where did you find this footage?"

"It belonged to a man named Vincent Gazzo."

Another long beat. When Stander finally spoke again, he said, "I can meet you at five p.m. today."

He gave me his address. I told him I'd be there and hung up.

I got dressed, went into work, and asked Bob for the rest of the day off. When I told him why, he closed the door to his office, sat down behind his desk again, and said, "Jimmy, what if Stander watches the film and then tells you he doesn't know anything about it?"

I started to say, "So what if he does?" but I realized it would be a lie. Bob was right; David Stander was the dead end. If he couldn't —or wouldn't—supply an answer, it would hurt. Bad. "I don't know," I answered.

"I think . . ." Bob trailed off, trying to find the words. "I think you might be counting on this too much."

It was true. The film was like a living thing for me, a partner who whispered promises, who offered the reward of giving me that shot in film history I hadn't earned otherwise. I could be the one who brought one of Hollywood's greatest secrets into the light. If my own talents—or lack thereof—as a filmmaker couldn't give me fame, maybe this could.

"Maybe," I said to Bob, a guy who was me with twenty years added. "But don't tell me you don't want to know too."

He shrugged. "'Course I do."

I left early, given traffic on the 10, and made Cheviot Hills by 4 p.m. I killed time just driving—past the massive 20th Century Fox lot, past what had once been the MGM lot, past the Westwood cemetery. I figured the last was the only one I might ever have a shot at getting into.

Finally 5 p.m. approached, and I headed to the address David Stander had provided. I negotiated my way past manicured lawns and houses that had once been middle-class but were now homes to millionaires. I pulled up and parked before a lovely two-story Tudor-style, with a rose garden leading up to the front door. It was

4:55 p.m. I took my iPad and a copy of the disk—in case he wanted to see the film on his own TV—and walked up to the door.

"Don't let me down," I whispered to the disk.

My knock was met a few seconds later by a man in his eighties who was still straight and trim, wearing casual slacks and a polo shirt. Even with thin gray hair and lines in his face, I recognized him from the tabloid photos, when he'd been holding Lorna Winters's hand.

"Mr. Stander," I said, extending a hand. "I'm Jimmy Guerrero."

He took the hand but released it too quickly—he wasn't comfortable with any of this. "Yes, Mr. Guerrero. Come in."

David Stander had kept himself in good shape; he still moved well, with only a slight slowness to his gait as he led us to an entertainment room. But he was tense—*too* tense for this to be a casual interview. He turned to me before a large television screen and said, "May I see the footage you mentioned?"

I handed him the DVD. He put it into a player, turned it on, and stayed standing to watch.

As the scene played out, his expression changed, or should I say *opened*—he moved from anxious and guarded to noticeably shaken. As Lorna Winters fell into the sea, he collapsed into a padded armchair.

I asked, "Are you all right, Mr. Stander?"

"Yes, I . . ." He broke off and looked up at me. "What is it you really want, Mr. Guerrero?"

"Please, call me Jimmy." I told him everything then: about Bobs ConversionMagic.com, about my sad attempt at a Hollywood career, about how much I loved Lorna Winters, about what those few minutes of film meant to me.

When I finished, he nodded and rose. "Jimmy, my instincts tell me I can trust you. Besides, this has gone on long enough."

"What has, Mr. Stander?"

He turned to leave. "Excuse me a moment."

Stander was gone only a few seconds. I heard soft conversation from another part of the house; after a minute he returned with a woman. "Jimmy, I'd like you to meet my wife, Nora."

I started to extend a hand—and froze, too shocked to move.

I was looking at Lorna Winters. Older, yes; aged, yes. But she was still beautiful, with those unmistakable high, broad cheekbones and chilled blue eyes. Her hair was silver, but she still wore it long.

She reached out and grasped my hand, and when she spoke it was with Lorna Winters's husky-around-the-edges voice. "Jimmy, I'm so pleased to meet you. David tells me you've brought us something quite special."

I was speechless as David started the DVD again. She watched it silently until the onscreen Lorna flipped over the railing, and then she laughed. "I still remember how cold that water was."

David said, "Probably my finest accomplishment as a filmmaker."

"*You* made this . . . ?"

Nodding, Stander said, "You see, Frank Linzetti had gotten his nasty hooks into Lorna. He was an evil, abusive son of a bitch — when she showed up for our first meeting on *Midnight Gun,* she had to wear oversized sunglasses because of a black eye."

Lorna sat down nearby. "That was because I'd just tried to leave him."

David sat on the arm of Lorna's chair and took her hand; the way she smiled at this simple motion was testament to not just their love but their *care* for each other. "We fell for each other," David said, "and Frank found out. He threatened me first, but I told him I didn't care. That was when he sent Vincent Gazzo. Fortunately, Gazzo liked Lorna, so we were able to buy him off."

I thought about that. "You bought him off . . ."

"Not with money — I didn't have enough of that. But I had my family's house. We got creative with some paperwork and made it look as if Vincent had inherited a house from an uncle, but really it was what I gave him to help us make that movie."

"His daughter still lives in that house. So you convinced Linzetti that Lorna was dead."

Stander nodded. "Then it was just a matter of getting her a new identity and keeping her out of the limelight."

"Which," Lorna said, "I was happy to do. I missed the acting, but not the rest of it." She looked at me and frowned slightly, then handed me a tissue from a box on a nearby table.

I hadn't even realized I was crying.

Because Linzetti was gone and it was safe at last, they let me reveal everything. Not long after the big news broke, the American Cinematheque held a tribute to Lorna, and she invited me as her special guest.

I know this will all fade soon, that Lorna will get her privacy back and I'll be just a guy making old movies into DVDs again. Still no Hollywood breakthrough for me, but that's okay, because I've got something better.

And I've got a three-minute movie to thank for that.

JOHN SANDFORD

Girl with an Ax

FROM *From Sea to Stormy Sea*

THE GIRL WITH the ax got off the bus at the corner of Santa
Monica Boulevard and Gower Street and started walking the superheated eleven blocks down Gower to Waring Avenue, where she
lived by herself in a four-hundred-square-foot bungalow with an air
conditioner designed and manufactured by cretins.

The girl was slender, with wheat-colored hair cut close over high
cheekbones and pale blue eyes, bony shoulders under an unfash-
ionable blue shift from JCPenney. She had a nice, shy smile that
could light her face when she let it out; she wore cross-training
shoes chosen for their durability, and golf socks.

The ax was heavy in its hard case and banged against her leg as
she carried it down the sidewalk. She'd spent all morning and half
the afternoon at the Bridge recording studio in Glendale, and her
amps were still there, along with two less valuable guitars.

Her name was Andi Holt.

The name, the pale eyes, the shy smile, and the wheat-colored
hair were all relics of her Okie ancestors, who'd come to California
out of the Dust Bowl. Andi knew that, but she didn't care about
it one way or another. They were all dead and long gone, buried
in cemeteries that bordered trailer parks, along with that whole
Grapes of Wrath gang.

Gower Street ran down the side of the Paramount Studios lot, but
like most native Angelenos, she didn't care about that either. To
care about Paramount would be like caring about Walmart.

Waring made a T-intersection with Gower, and she took the

right, tired with the day's work and the bus ride, which had required three changes. She'd be riding the route in reverse the next
morning, for the last session of this set. Her car's transmission had
gone out, and she was temporarily afoot in Los Angeles. She could
have called an Uber for the ride, but money was money and the
bus was cheap.

Andi lived a few houses down Waring, a neighborhood of tiny
bungalows worth, now, absurd amounts of money. She didn't own
hers but rented it, for what was becoming an absurd amount of
rent. Somebody once had told her that Waring Avenue was named
after the inventor of the Waring blender and she'd believed it—
why would anyone lie about something like that?—but when she'd
repeated the story, she'd been ridiculed: the street was actually
named after a long-dead band leader named Fred Waring, who
had nothing to do with blenders.

But the guy who told her *that* story had been massively stoned on
some primo Strawberry Cough, so she'd never repeated the Fred
Waring story.

Andi's house was gray.

The one just before it was a faded brick red and larger—six
hundred and twenty-five square feet, or a perfect twenty-five by
twenty-five. Andi's was twenty by twenty. She obsessed over the
numbers. Hers was like living in a closet; the red house, small by
any sane standards, felt expansive by comparison.

Just the way it was, in L.A.

As she passed the red house, she stopped to peer at it. The house
was partly owned by Helen McCall and partly by a rapacious reverse-mortgage company called Gray Aid, which hovered over Mc-
Call like a turkey vulture, waiting for her to die.

Andi was friends with the old woman. They'd share a joint or a
margarita or even two on a warm evening, and Helen would tell her
about Hollywood days, or, as she pronounced it—you could hear it
in the words—Hollywood Daze.

Helen had been an actress, once . . . or almost an actress. She
had the stories to prove it.

And it occurred to Andi that she hadn't seen Helen for, what,
three days? She thought three days. Helen was ninety-nine years
old.

With the ax banging against her leg, Andi continued to her house, but the thought of Helen stuck like a tick on her scalp. Inside, where the ambient temperature was possibly 120 degrees, she turned on the air conditioner and took the ax out of the case—a 2007 Les Paul custom—and stuck it in a cabinet that maintained a temperature of 72 degrees and a relative humidity of 40 percent. Five other guitars resided in the cabinet, not counting the two of them still at the Bridge, with her Fender and Mesa amps.

The instruments were all sturdy enough, but even with the ocean, L.A. got dry enough in the summer that Andi liked to keep her guitars somewhat humidified. She'd like to keep herself somewhat humidified as well, but in the tiny house, with the piece-of-shit air conditioner that she suspected had fallen off a truck, probably in Chechnya, that was difficult.

She was a dry-looking girl; parched.

And she hadn't seen Helen.

She got a beer from the refrigerator, popped the top, and since the house was too hot to stay in anyway, she walked next door and knocked. No answer. Knocked harder. Still no answer. She trudged back to her place, a little apprehensive now, a little scared, and found the key that Helen had given her.

She opened her neighbor's door and smelled the death.

Not stinky or especially repulsive, but death all the same. To be sure, she walked back to Helen's bedroom, where the old lady lay on her bed, in a nightgown with embroidered flowers across the chest, her head turned to one side. She looked desiccated, like a years-old yellowed cigarette found under a couch when you move.

"Helen?" Andi knew she was dead but called her name anyway. Then she called the cops.

Of all the stories Helen had told Andi, the most interesting was about a famous artist who'd painted her back in the late thirties, and that the painting itself had become famous, and now hung in a Kansas City museum. Helen had never been the star of a movie, or even the third banana, but she'd been the star of Thomas Hart Benton's *Hollywood*, standing straight, tall, and only skimpily clothed in the center of the work. She'd shown Andi a book about Benton's relationship to motion pictures, and to *Hollywood* in particular;

and a black-and-white photograph of herself with Benton, who was holding a paintbrush and whose head came barely to her shoulder.

Andi knew some famous people—singers—but they were work-aday people who'd happened to push all the right buttons and had gotten rich and famous, or one or the other. Just people. To be in a famous painting was something else: something that would carry you into the future, long after you were gone, and your music was gone, and your songs were gone. . . .

The cops came and were quick and professional. They looked at the undisturbed body, sat Andi down, interviewed her and took a few notes, especially emphasizing the time between her discovery of the body and her call to 911—Andi estimated it at thirty seconds. She was allowed to return to her house but was asked to stay around until a medical examiner's investigator could speak to her.

That happened an hour and a half later. The investigator, a weary-looking woman in shoes like Andi's, named Donna, told her that the cops had been interested in the timing of her call to be sure she hadn't looted Helen's house after she discovered the body.

"She didn't have anything to loot, except maybe her wedding ring," Andi said. "She was living on Social Security and payments on a reverse mortgage."

Donna asked if Andi knew about survivors.

"Her son died two years ago, from being too fat. That's what Helen said. She has a granddaughter and some great-grandchildren who live in San Diego, I think. She has one of those old Rolo things with their names written in them. Their name is Cooper. The daughter's name is Sandra Cooper. I met her once, a couple of years ago."

"A Rolodex, I saw that. I'll notify the Coopers . . ." Donna made a note and asked, "Do you think she might have taken her own life? There was no note, no pill bottle or anything."

"No, I don't think so. She was a lively old lady. Not in pain or depressed or anything, as far as I could tell. She was looking forward to turning a hundred next fall. She was ninety-nine."

They talked a while longer, and Andi cried a little, and Donna patted her on a knee, and when she was leaving told her, "I kind of think that most people wouldn't want somebody to say this after they die, but . . . her death looks to me like it was totally routine. She got old and died."

Andi nodded. "That's what I think. But she lived so long. She knew so much. Now that's all gone. Gone."

"You gonna be okay?"

"Sure. I'm okay. Sad."

"And you're a musician?"

"Yes. Play guitar, I do session work. I work a couple nights a week over at the Guitar Center on Sunset," Andi said.

"I think you're probably good folks." Donna nodded. "You take it easy, girl."

The girl with the ax got off the bus at the corner of Santa Monica Boulevard and Gower Street and started walking the superheated eleven blocks down Gower to Waring Avenue, where she still lived by herself in a four-hundred-square-foot bungalow with an air conditioner designed and manufactured by cretins.

She took the right on Waring, and the first thing she saw was a U-Haul truck and an SUV parked outside Helen's house. The truck's back doors were open, and she could see Helen's two-cushion couch and television inside it. She walked past, looking through the open door, and could see a man pushing a desk across the wooden floor. He looked out and saw her, and she lifted a hand and went into her own house, unlocked it and put the ax in the humidifier cabinet and got herself a beer.

It had been two weeks since Helen died, and a piece of cop tape had been stuck on the door ever since, to keep people out. Andi had gotten her guitars and amps back from the Bridge and had been working at a place called Grassroots in Pasadena, laying down tracks for a Bakersfield country band that was, she had to admit, really pretty good. The front man had spent some time chatting her up, and she'd liked it; and she'd noticed that the band's own lead guitarist had some kind of ego conflict going with the front man.

She was thinking about the singer, whose name was Tony, and thinking that if he lost his lead guitar and she went on the road with the band, how she'd wind up sleeping with him. That prospect was pleasant enough—the sex part, not the road part—but then she'd lose her place in the L.A. session world, which kept her in a house, and the job at Guitar Center, which kept her in fish sticks and fries.

The fact was, she was $1,450.88 from being broke, and the transmission was broker. Summer was slow; even with no crises along the way, she needed every dollar she could find to keep her head above water until the busy season started again, in October. She wasn't desperate, she'd been here before, financially, but from where she was, she could *see* desperate.

Halfway through the beer, the man she'd seen at Helen's house rang the doorbell. He was sort of piggish, she thought as she walked toward the door. Probably her age, in his later twenties, middle height, overweight, with a short, oily flattop over heavy pink cheeks. He was wearing a black T-shirt and tan cargo shorts. The T-shirt showed a slogan: THAT'S TOO MUCH BACON and in smaller letters, beneath, . . . SAID NO ONE, EVER. He apparently tried to live up to it.

"Can I help you?"

The man looked at a piece of paper in his hand. "Are you Andi Holt?"

"Yup."

"You found my great-grandma when she died?"

"Yes, I found Helen."

"Could you come over for a minute? My brother and sister and I are going through the place, checking out what she had."

"Sure."

On the way over, she asked, "What's your name?"

"Don Cooper. My brother's Bob, my sister's Cheryl. There's about a ton of paper shit in there; we're trying to figure out what to do with it."

The three Coopers were a matched set: dark hair, overweight, shorts and T-shirts with slogans. Cheryl's read, NOPE, STILL DON'T CARE. Bob's read, PETA and beneath that, PEOPLE EATING TASTY ANIMALS. All three shirts were sweat-soaked; Helen had had a window air conditioner, which was sitting in the middle of the living room.

Helen's house had only one bedroom, but it had another small room, which might have accommodated a twin bed and which Helen had used as a home office: a couple of filing cabinets, rarely used, a midcentury office chair, a tiny desk, pictures on the wall. No computer. An elaborate old steamer trunk, probably dating back to the 1930s, substituted for a coffee table. It had been full of scrapbooks and other memorabilia, which now lay on the floor with the contents of the filing cabinets. The filing cabinets and trunk were gone, apparently loaded into the U-Haul. All the pictures that had been on the wall had been stripped of their frames, which were gone, the pictures scattered on the floor.

"Here's the deal," Bob said. "If we don't leave for home in an hour, it'll take us three hours to get down the Five. We need to get all this crap outta here so we can sell the place. We were thinking we could throw you a few bucks and you could bag it and stick it in Helen's trashcan and your trashcan over the next couple of weeks, and that way we don't have to pay to haul it and you get a few bucks, which you look like you need anyway."

Andi ignored the implied insult. "What's a few bucks?"

"Fifty?"

Andi looked at the mess on the floor. "Fifty is a pizza for two and a couple of beers. For cleaning out this house?"

"Well . . . tell you what. You play the guitar, right? I saw all those guitars. Helen had a guitar in the closet. We'll give you the guitar."

"Let's see it."

Bob went out to the U-Haul and came back a minute later with the guitar. Solid body, weighed a ton. Two rusty strings still attached, four broken and curled around the neck, specks of rust on the bridge and the tuners.

"Electronics are probably shot," Andi said. She squinted down the fretboard. "But . . . neck looks straight, anyway." She grimaced and hefted the guitar. "Okay."

"Great," Don said. He waved at the paper, the photos, a round rag rug on the floor. "Just dump everything. The rug smells like a cat shit on it."

"Cat died a couple of years ago," Andi said. "It was seventeen."

"Good. Hate fuckin' cats," Bob said.

"I gotta ask," Cheryl said. "You didn't help yourself to anything when you found Helen, did you?"

"What? No! Jesus!"

Cheryl shrugged. "Had to ask. You'd think she would have built up a little more of an estate, you know. She was ninety-six or something. We got her rings, the diamond was like a half carat, about the size of Don's dick."

"And she'd know," Bob said.

"Fuck you," Cheryl said.

"We got that camera," Bob said. An old camera sat on a window-sill, an Argus C3. "That's gotta be worth something."

"She was ninety-nine," Andi said, still pissed about being asked if she'd taken anything.

"Whatever," Cheryl said. She had a cigarette in her hand, lit it with a yellow plastic Bic lighter, blew smoke. "Got the house, any-way. We looked at houses around here on Zillow; that's a nice piece of change. One down the block like this sold for eight-fifty. Mom said the three of us could split half and she keeps the other half."

"Hello, cherry-red Camaro," Don said.

"Piece of shit," said Bob. "I'm going ZR1!"

"What's that?" Andi asked, waving smoke away from her face.

Bob did a spit take. "Corvette. Play your cards right, I'll give you a ride, sweetpuss."

"Yeah, well, before you spend the money, you better talk to Gray Aid," Andi said.

"What's that?" Don asked.

"Reverse-mortgage company. Helen had a reverse mortgage," Andi said. "I'm not sure, but I don't think there was much left. Maybe some."

"What the fuck? The old twat spent the house?"

"Most of it. Not all of it yet," Andi said. "She told me that she wouldn't get paid anymore after she turned 102, so she planned to die before then." She gestured at the papers on the floor. "The con-tract's probably in there. I'll go through it, see if I can turn it up."

Cheryl slapped her forehead. "Ah, Christ! She spent it? What about us?"

"Let's see if we can find the contract," Bob said, and kicked a pile of the papers.

"That won't do it," Andi said. "It's only going to be a few sheets of paper, probably."

They spent fifteen minutes looking, then Cheryl said, "Let's get the air conditioner in the U-Haul. We gotta get moving. If there's a mortgage, the hired hand can find it."

"We called and had the water company turn off the water," Bob said. "The toilets don't work. You think anybody would see me if I took a dump in the backyard?"

Andi: "Hey, I gotta live here . . ."

"And I gotta go," Bob said. He walked down the hall to the bathroom, reappeared with a half roll of toilet paper, and went out the back door.

"He's a real classy guy," Cheryl said. She lit another cigarette. "He'd take a dump on the White House lawn if he had to go. One time at a rock concert—"

"So fuckin' hot in here," Don interrupted. "Shoulda left the air conditioner to last."

"You really don't want all the pictures and photo albums and stuff? You don't think your mother would?" Andi asked. "It's Helen's whole life in here."

"Shit-can it," Bob said. "We don't care about that shit."

"You know, Helen once told me that she posed for a painting for a really famous painter," Andi said. "Back like . . . eighty years ago."

"You see a painting in here?" Don asked.

"No, but . . ."

"Then fuck it," he said.

Bob came back, threw the remnants of the roll of toilet paper on the floor, and he and Don staggered out of the house with the air conditioner. Cheryl was stacking plates and glasses into cardboard boxes and said to Andi, "Don't just stand there; you want the fifty," so Andi helped out. The dishes were old and never had been expensive: "I'll unload them on the wetbacks down at the flea market," Cheryl said. "That's a hundred bucks right there."

Bob and Don came back and carried boxes out to the U-Haul. Helen had had a couple of hundred books, many of them old *Reader's Digest* versions of fifties novels, along with a complete set of *Encyclopedia Britannica,* which Andi knew from her own flea market experience were virtually worthless. It amused her to see the two men sweat them out to the trailer.

And it went on for an hour like that: "Fuck her, fuck this place, fuck you."

When the house was empty, except for the thousands of sheets of paper and folders of old memorabilia, the Coopers headed out for San Diego. Bob gave a final kick to the stuff that had been in the steamer trunk, the photo albums, sending it exploding across the floor, faces of forgotten men and women, forgotten times, black-and-white images of men in army and navy uniforms . . .

"Old bat," he said.

Andi: "How about my fifty dollars?"

*

The Coopers had gone.

Andi took a closer look at the guitar, decided to leave the broken strings on it, placed it in a clear corner of the living room, and went to work on the paper. There was a lot of it: she went through it carefully, into the evening, and halfway through one of the stacks that had apparently been dumped from the file cabinet she found the reverse-mortgage papers, and also the original mortgage on the house, which apparently had been paid off in the sixties.

Most of the paper on the floor really was trash and should have been thrown out years earlier: old bills, old warranties, old canceled checks. Some of it was interesting, though: fliers for movies in which Helen had appeared, a stack of love letters bound together in their original envelopes, with a rubber band, from her husband, Gary, who'd fought in World War II, then Korea, and finally Vietnam, where he'd been killed in a car accident in Saigon. The letters all began with the same five words: "Hey Babe, Miss you bad."

Bob Cooper had left his cell number with her, and when she called it and told him she'd found the papers from Gray Aid, he gave her an address and she said she'd mail them. "How long before you get the place cleaned?"

"I'll have the papers cleaned out tonight . . . and I'll sweep it tomorrow, as a freebee, 'cause I'm not working. All these pictures and stuff . . ."

"We told you to shit-can it."

"You mind if I take them? She was a friend of mine."

"We don't care, just get them the fuck out. We've got a Realtor coming around to look at the place on Monday, gotta be cleaned by then. Could you wash the windows?"

"Not for fifty bucks, no. The Realtor can take care of that."

She finished with the paper that night. One of the last things she looked at was a crumbling brown file pocket, the kind with a fold-over flap. When she opened it, she found a carefully folded sheath of semitransparent paper. She unfolded the sheets, each about three feet by two, like the paper used by architects for their plans.

Drawings.

Men with old-fashioned movie cameras and microphone booms, some wearing old-timey workmen's hats. A man in what must've been an expensive suit, turned away, with a thirties haircut. One of Helen herself, holding what looked like a long dowel rod that extended over her head. Andi recognized it immediately: the star of the *Hollywood* painting, Helen as a nineteen- or twenty-year-old, wearing nothing but a bra and underpants. Another drawing was perhaps a different view of Helen, she thought, the blond woman shown from an overhead view; she might have been nude.

She stared at it for a bit, then carefully folded all the papers and put them back in the file pocket and set it aside. The house was still hot, but she crawled around the floor, picking up photographs, glancing at them, setting them aside, until she finally found the one that Helen had shown her, of herself with Thomas Hart Benton. She put the photo in the brown file pocket with the drawings.

By midnight it was done. Andi had five garbage bags of paper but had been unable to throw away the photos and the movie memorabilia.

Helen had told her about her movie life.

"You'd look at me on a screen, and you'd hardly see me," Helen had said one night as they sat in her backyard, sharing a joint. "Some of the girls—Lauren Bacall—they'd light it up. You'd look at me, and you wouldn't even see me," she said.

"I'm sure that's not true," Andi said.

"It was true. You had to figure it out, and that took a while, but it was true. Still, I made a living. I even have a SAG card. Haven't seen it in years. I'd be a secretary who'd bring in some papers, and I'd say, 'Here are the papers, Mr. Shipley,' or whatever. I was in seventy movies like that, because they knew I was reliable. They'd call me in, I'd sit around for a couple of days, I'd get thirty seconds onscreen, and I'd go home. One time this Japanese guy—Japanese American—got in an auto accident on the Pasadena Freeway on the way to the studio, and they were shooting a war film and they needed a Jap to fire a machine gun from a bunker, and I was small and they put a lot of makeup on me and a helmet and had me in the bunker firing this machine gun, and then in another shot they had me charging with a gun and bayonet and screaming, 'Banzai! Banzai!' That was sort of the peak of my dramatic career."

And she laughed, and she blew a little pungent smoke out into the evening air, passed the joint back, and said, "You get the best shit, Andi. Musicians always have the best shit."

As Andi was locking up Helen's house, she noticed an unfamiliar and unhappy odor at the back door and stepped outside: Bob had indeed taken a dump in the backyard, in fact in Helen's flower bed.

She locked the door and went home.

Andi mailed the reverse-mortgage papers to the Coopers. She had a spotty series of gigs over the next couple of weeks and picked up three extra shifts at Guitar Center when a salesman quit unexpectedly. A FOR SALE sign went up in Helen's yard, and one day she saw Bob and Cheryl Cooper talking to an agent. When the agent left, she walked over, and Bob said, with a grim shake of his head, "Bad as we thought—we're gonna get a hundred thousand if we're lucky, and my mom is backing out of the deal. She's gonna throw us ten grand each and keep seventy, greedy bitch."

"Don't talk about Mom like that," Cheryl said. She was smoking, dug a second cigarette out of her purse, used the first one to light it, and flicked the used butt, still burning, into the street.

"You suck up to her 'cause you're trying to get more," Bob said.

"Fuck you. You're an asshole."

"You want a ride home?"

"Fuck you."

The house sold in August, but Andi never saw the Coopers again. The deal had probably been done electronically, and she never found out exactly how much they'd cleared. She had a very nice ten-day gig at Fox for a TV series that needed some blues guitar and got the transmission replaced on her Cube.

Then she waited, and waited, and waited.

On October 1, a warm Wednesday evening, the girl with the ax turned down Gower Street at the corner of Santa Monica Boulevard, down to Paramount Studios, and then right, to her four-hundred-square-foot bungalow with an air conditioner designed and manufactured by cretins.

She unloaded her Les Paul and an Asher version of a Strat, went inside, put them in the guitar cabinet, turned on the air conditioner, got Helen's old guitar out of a closet, and went back outside to the Cube.

The trip to the Valley, to Van Nuys, took forty minutes because of a fender-bender on the 101. Loren's Fine and Vintage Guitars was located in a neatly kept strip mall next to a hat store; Loren was an old pal. She carried Helen's guitar inside, and Dale Loren came out and looked at it, and said, "Holy shit. I think . . . a '58?"

"When I first saw it, I was hoping it was a '59," Andi said.

"It's not. The neck's too fat. Come on back, Andi, let's look it up."

They went into the back room, where a worktable was covered with a soft rubber sheet. Loren examined the neck from the end, and both sides, ran his finger down the ends of the frets. "Neck is good. Frets are original."

"I thought so. I put a ruler on it, and there's no waves or twist, as far as I can see."

"We'll have to do a little more than put a ruler on it . . . Let's check the serial number."

The serial number was stamped on the back of the headstock. Loren had a paper printout of Gibson Les Paul serial numbers. He ran a finger down the list and said, "Here it is: 1958. So, 1958 cherry-red sunburst, even still shows a little bit of the red. They're usually pretty faded; they go yellow."

"Cherry red, like a cherry-red Camaro, almost."

"The same . . . The bridge and tuners will clean right up, the rust, that's not a problem at all."

He turned it over. "Has some buckle-rash"—he rubbed the rough spots with a thumb—"but not bad. Where'd you get it?"

"An old lady left it to me. She said it belonged to her husband —he was killed in Vietnam. He was in World War II and Korea and then Vietnam, and it finally killed him."

"Have any more guitars?"

"Not as far as I know . . ."

"Tell you what," Loren said. "I'll give you a receipt, and I'll have Terry clean it up. It'll take a while . . . I'll call you in two weeks."

"What's your cut?" Andi asked.

Loren shrugged. "I've got to make a living too, honey, and I have the techs who can restore it. I even got a guy who I think will buy it, like *right now*. I'll take thirty percent, and I'll tell you what, Andi, you won't do any better anywhere else. If this had been used by some famous rocker, then it'd be more, but . . . you say you don't know about that."

"Take it," Andi said. "And Loren . . . let's keep this under our hats, okay?"

"Absolutely."

Ten days later she got a text: "I got a buyer for $130,000. Your end will be $85,800. Yes or no?"
Yes.

Okay, so the late-model Porsche Cayenne was a basic version and used, but not very—thirty thousand miles. The Porsche dude said it would be good for two hundred thousand if she took care of it. He was mildly perplexed when she told him about the trade-in, but he walked out to take a look at the Cube. "Tranny's real good," Andi said.

And on a cool, bright day in December she drove over to the Getty and parked the Cayenne in the underground ramp. A curator and her assistant carefully unfolded the drawings on a library table, and the assistant said, "Oh, my God. You got them at a flea market?"
"I did," Andi said.
"If these are real . . . we'll want to look at them for a while, but that looks like Benton's signature on this one and his initials on that," the curator said. "Thomas Hart Benton had a very distinctive way of . . . you know, this might be one of his finest . . . a flea market? Really?"
"Sure. And I want to do the right thing," Andi said. "You can look at them as long as you want. If you could give me a receipt?"
"Of course, and we'll take some photos," the curator said. "If you'd consider selling them, I'd hope that you'd let us bid."
"Yes. I'd like to keep them in Los Angeles," Andi said. "I read about the painting, so they must've been here for eighty years. Los Angeles is their real home. I'd hate to see them go to someplace like . . ."
"Back to Missouri?"
"I was thinking, not even San Diego," Andi said.

That night, out in the backyard, lying in a lounge chair, with the L.A. glow overhead, Andi sparked up a fatboy and looked to where the stars should be.
"Thank you, babe. Miss you bad."
And she cried a little, but not too much.

Pretzel Logic

FROM *Die Behind the Wheel*

THE GUYS WHO come back the first time, they always say the biggest difference outside is the silence at night. They can't sleep because it's too quiet.

The guys who come back a second time, they generally ain't too self-aware. They say the biggest difference outside is the sensations. The food, it tastes so much better. The girls, they so much juicier. The air, it don't smell like week-old socks all the time.

Only one guy came back a third time when he was inside. That guy just scored himself a third strike with whatever he could pull off quick and easy that was barely a felony. That guy said the biggest difference is that everyone thinks there's a big difference between being inside and being outside. But there ain't.

I ain't never going back.

The red-blue strobe in his rearview mirror pulled his insides down. Adrenaline roiled him, and he tasted it at the back of his mouth. In his throat, electric and sour. He hit the blinker, searched for a polite excuse for whatever he might be told was the reason for the stop. *DWB*, dressed up like a burned-out bulb. *Yes, sir. No, sir.* An expired tag. *Thank you, sir, may I have another.*

He put the Kia in park. Rolled down his window. Spun the volume on WJAZ to zero. Put his wallet and phone on the dashboard. Put his hands at 10 and 2 on the wheel, fingers flung wide. Waited.

"Driver." A woman's voice through the speaker. "Step out of the car and place your hands on the hood."

His head sagged. He took a deep, slow breath. He complied.

The cop was young. If not a rookie, close. She'd be scared.

"Spread your legs," the cop said as she approached. Her hand rested on her pistol. "And don't move."

"Yes, ma'am." He couldn't read her name tag.

The cop started a frisk. "Plates say this car is registered to a Randall Baxter. That's you?"

"People call me Bax." Her frisk wasn't very thorough. "Yes, ma'am. I'm Randall Baxter."

"You prove that?"

"Yes, ma'am." Bax nodded toward his wallet. "My license is there. On the dashboard."

The cop reached through the open window. "Don't move," she repeated. She pulled the license and held it up to compare the photo to Bax's face. Replaced the license in the wallet, the wallet on the dashboard. "You know why I pulled you over, Mr. Baxter?"

"No, ma'am."

"I'm going to search your pockets. You got anything sharp in there?"

"No, ma'am."

"Nothing that's going to stick me?" The cop groped his back pockets, then started to crowd him, almost embracing him as she reached into his front pockets.

"Ma'am—"

"Shut up." The cop got up close and personal. "You hear me, Mr. Baxter?" Raised her voice to a shout. "I said shut. The fuck. Up." Spun him, backed him up against the side of the little SUV. Reached inside his jacket to search his inside pockets, then dropped something small and hard in the chest pocket of his shirt.

"Ma'am, I—"

The cop silenced him by grabbing bunches of his jacket in her fists, pulling him close. "Your code is Brooklyn," she whispered into his face before she shouted, "I told you to shut up."

"But I din't do nothin'," he shouted back. Then he whispered, "Brooklyn."

Bax's day had started like most days: coffee, eggs with bacon, and strawberry jelly with sourdough toast at the counter of the diner on the dividing line between the suburbs and his city. Flirting over the newspaper with Venetta, the morning shift manager. Who'd let him take her out a couple of times. Who'd refused a dinner date at his pal Napoleon's locally famous supper club until he started going to Sunday services with her, her daughter Margaret, and her mom. Who'd squinted up half her face when he'd offered the vaguest possible interpretation of his work.

He recognized the flash off his kid brother's blinged-out shoes in the parking lot. Recognized his boss's Lexus SUV.

"Ima take that booth over there," he told Venetta. "Don't you come wait on me."

Venetta started to speak but stopped when he shook his head once.

Bax slid into the booth before his boss's enforcer, Owsley, opened the passenger door for Reamer Kline. Bax's balls unshriveled a tiny bit when Owsley, so big that the SUV listed toward the side he sat on, didn't follow Mr. Kline toward the diner door. Bax knew Owsley's kind from his bit. Knew Owsley enjoyed the beatdown he put on Russell to persuade Bax to fix for Mr. Kline.

Mr. Kline waited at the diner's door until Russell figured out it was his job to open the door.

Bax saw some sullen fear in his brother's eyes and wondered what it was about this time.

Mr. Kline motioned for Russell to slide into the booth first, opposite Bax, so Mr. Kline could contain Russell. "Your idiot brother said I'd find you here." Keep the kid from rabbiting.

Bax narrowed his eyes. Gave his brother a hard stare. "I'm sorry it couldn't wait until I got to the shop, Mr. Kline." Waited for the waitress to serve coffee. "What do I need to fix for him now?"

Russell snorted a protest.

"Shut up, Russell." Bax and Mr. Kline said it at the same time.

Russell stared at the wall. Slouched lower.

"Your idiot brother went and got all . . . entrepreneurial." Mr. Kline waved off menus. "Managed to sell some—property—that already had a buyer."

Bax remained silent. Raced through Mr. Kline's lines of business to assess what property Mr. Kline might be talking about. "Is it property we can get more of?"

"It is not."

That ruled out cars and parts, some drugs, and girls. It left knock-off Japanese whiskey and—

"All them FNs," Russell said.

Mr. Kline's backhand across Russell's face flashed so fast Bax might have missed it if not for the split that opened in the middle of his brother's lower lip.

"Russell," Bax said, "you keep your own counsel for the rest of this conversation." He pushed his napkin across the table. Motioned for Russell to use it to stop the bleeding. "Mr. Kline—"

"I know you thought you'd work off Russell's debt in the next two, three years."

"Is this fixable?" *Or just more debt?*

"I sold that property to the originally interested party."

"The gentlemen from San Leon."

"Exactly." Mr. Kline paused while the waitress refilled his coffee. "And your brother somehow managed to secure a commitment to buy from the—how did you say it? The gentlemen from Tyler."

Bax covered his face with his hands. Cursed silently into his palms. *Decades more debt.* "I'm sorry, Mr. Kline." *Lifetimes.* "I—well, I'm just very sorry."

"Now, Bax, you don't need to apologize." Mr. Kline moved his hands like he was giving a benediction. "I know young Russell here is just a half-brother. So I can assume he acquired his extraordinary stupidity from his father, not yours."

Bax kicked Russell under the table to prevent his protest. "Yes, sir, Mr. Kline."

"Is this fixable, you ask." Mr. Kline wrapped his hands around his coffee mug. "All the ways I can think to fix this involve throwing your brother to one or the other of the two motorcycle gangs currently waging war over which will control Texas."

Russell's face melted from sullen fear to absolute terror.

Bax kicked him again. "Let me think on it for a bit, Mr. Kline, if you will."

"You can understand why I'd like to find a more successful resolution." Mr. Kline twisted the big nugget-looking ring that had opened Russell's lip. "Can't you, Bax."

"Yes, sir."

"But our time is short. Thanks to young Russell's commitment, now both parties expect delivery within two days."

"Two days, Mr. Kline."

Bax's boss nodded with his whole body. He pulled a long wallet from inside his jacket, opened it, and fingered through the bills.

He tugged out a fifty. "That Miss Venetta is quite a catch, Bax." Folded it under his saucer. "You take good care of her."

Bax hustled his brother out of the diner as soon as Mr. Kline's Lexus turned at the end of the block.

"Russell, how you find this much trouble to get into?"

Russell threw a dismissive hand toward the sky. "Man, get off my shit. I just—"

"*Your* shit?" Bax dope-slapped Russell. "I'm carrying that Wells deal you oughta got dead for, and you talk at me about your shit? You tell Mr. Kline the woman I'm seein', and you talk at me about your shit? How many times I got to tell you 'bout impulse control?" Bax didn't flinch as Russell reared back to retaliate for the dope slap. "You need to think before you swing on a man."

Russell sprawled himself on the smoker's bench, his ridiculous shoes pointed at Bax. "The Cossacks—"

"Shut up." Bax swiveled his head. "You stupider than I gave you credit for, you start name-checking the guys gonna peel your skin off."

"They reached out to me." Russell admired the rings on his left hand. "*They*. Reached out. To *me*."

"Why you think they did that, Russell? 'Cause you the brains of this operation?"

Russell puffed out his chest.

"Or 'cause you the likeliest to fuck up the deal the Bandidos already done for what both of 'em want?"

Russell's face blanked. His head tilted.

"Jesus, Russell." Bax rubbed his palms across his face. "Go back to the shop. I got to think. You just—just—"

"Gimme your keys, then."

Bax shook his head. "Call you a Lyft. Or hoof it. Just sit in my office. Don't touch nothin'. Or do nothin'. Watch some *SportsCenter* or some shit like that."

"But—"

"Don't you do nothin' or say nothin' till I get there."

Venetta's one arched eyebrow told Bax about all he needed to know. He showed her his palms as he straddled his regular counter stool.

"You told me you was going straight after your bit."

"I am."

"Well, I know who that was you was talking to." Venetta raised her other brow. "And people going straight don't spend a lot of time with Mr. Reamer Kline."

"I'm—that was my kid brother. With us."

"The one you did the bit for."

Bax had told Venetta most of the truth about his stretch downstate. He hadn't done what he pleaded to, but he'd pleaded to it to keep his brother out of the system. "Russell fell in with a crew belonged to one of Mr. Kline's lieutenants while I was doing his time. And he—he ended up owing Mr. Kline some."

Venetta turned her back to him. She started wiping the little spring-loaded pitchers of syrup. "I'm still listening."

"Mr. Kline, he got to me the day I landed at the halfway house. Told me I could pay Russell's debt if I fix—if I fixed up one of his businesses."

"Why you work so hard for Russell?"

Bax hadn't told her any of the truth about that. Not really. Just that doing Russell's bit had been the right thing for both of them because he'd done some stuff he hadn't been caught for, that he should've gone away for. "Russell, you know, he came up without a dad. He ain't had nobody to show him how to be a man. And he's my only family now."

Venetta let him keep looking at her back.

"Since our mom passed."

"I don't want no Mr. Reamer Kline in my diner."

"I don't want that neither." Bax thought carefully about his next move. Moves. Thought that what he really needed was time to think about motorcycle gangs and what they wanted with the shipping container that filled a not-too-noticeable hole in the salvage yard he ran for Mr. Kline. "Can I finish my breakfast here?"

"I saved it for you." Venetta turned and slid his plate across the counter. "But it gone cold."

In the diner's parking lot, the cold half of his eggs riding heavy and low in his belly, Bax opened the Kia's tailgate and lifted the floor panel covering the spare tire. He pushed the sidewall of the tire until it gapped away from the wheel, reached inside the tire, and fished around until he grasped his most recent burner. Flipped it open and tapped at the tiny keypad: *Hudson. U got any friends in DC.*

Bax bundled the phone among his newspaper and other trash from his car and stuffed all of that in the stinking, oozing can at the bus stop.

The lady cop had pulled him over between the diner and the salvage yard. Berberian had never responded to a text so fast. The DC ask must have lit a fire under someone important. Bax thought about how he might leverage that as he triple-checked that he'd deactivated all the sounds and shakers on the burner the lady cop had dropped in his pocket.

He found Russell in his office BSing with the guy who knew how to take apart Audis. Bax told the Audi guy to get gone with a chin twitch, then kicked Russell's feet off his coffee table. "Thought I told you not to say nothin'."

"I weren't saying nothin'."

"Russell, you want to get out of this alive, you need to understand that don't say nothin' mean don't say *nothin'*. To *nobody.*"

Russell turned this over in his mind for a few moments. "Even you, that means."

Bax felt the growl in his throat. "You know what, Russell? That's the best idea you've had in a long time." He played out the strategy a few moves, imagined all the ways Russell could fuck it up. "Here's your rule: unless you're answering a question I ask you, you don't say nothin' to nobody."

"Even Reamer?"

Bax shook his head. "That man's always Mr. Kline to you. And if he say something to you, the only options you got to reply are yes, sir and no, sir."

"What if—"

"Yes, sir or no, sir. Or answering my questions." Bax paused at the door to the bathroom. "You keep your mouth shut, maybe I can keep you breathing."

In the bathroom, Bax checked his burner.
Brooklyn. 1415 the park.

The park was Berberian's code for the commercial laundry where Bax took the salvage yard's floor mats.

Brooklyn, he tapped back to Berberian. *OK.*

Bax ordered Russell to collect anything going to the laundry and load it in the salvage yard's F-150. He went out to get chop suey for his crew and get rid of his most recent burner.

After lunch Bax stuck Russell's phone and his desk phone in a metal locker behind a padlock, then locked Russell in his office and told the Audi guy to make sure no one went in or out.

"This is Parker," Berberian said. "FBI."

Parker was a tiny thing, wiry and coiled. She looked like a kid sitting at the Ikea table in the laundry's back room. She wore a wedding ring with a diamond that looked the size of a bottle-cap.

"I'm Bax." Her handshake told him she punched above her weight. "Randall Baxter."

"Berberian tells me that you're his meal ticket," she said.

Bax didn't tell her that he couldn't care less whether it was Berberian's ticket he punched or hers. He knew only that if ratting on someone guaranteed that he'd never go back inside, he'd rat on anyone with a pulse. "I try to take very good care of Detective Berberian," Bax said.

"And why is that?" Parker said.

Bax felt her grip again, but more like it was around his neck. He glanced at Berberian.

"Bax is a man with a—" Berberian said.

"My brother—his name's Russell, and Russell's my only family —my brother made some mistakes when I was in prison," Bax said. "He screwed up a fentanyl deal for one of Reamer Kline's lieutenants. Cost Mr. Kline a lot of money. When I got out, Mr. Kline told me I could make up that money for him or watch his man Owsley kill my brother."

"So you're out to get Reamer Kline," Parker said.

"No, ma'am. I got no particular interest in Mr. Kline. But he's got a very particular interest in me. And I got no interest in going back to prison for whatever he's up to. But a lot of interest in keeping my brother alive."

Parker checked Berberian. "What's Reamer Kline's interest in you, Mr. Baxter?"

"Bax did a—"

"I did a bit for my brother. I stood up. Kept my own counsel. Mr. Kline, he likes people who know how to stay loyal. And I ain't had much school, but I'm pretty good at making sure things run smooth."

"You're just a good citizen."

"No, ma'am." Bax forced the gentle smile he'd perfected to soothe the warden's mind when it was troubled by uppity Negroes. "But I didn't much enjoy my time in prison, and I planned to go straight after I got out. Mr. Kline, he gave me no chance to go straight. What I do for Detective Berberian, it's about the only thing I can do to bend the curve back."

"And you obviously know how this game is played."

"I'm always trying to learn." Bax maintained his smile. "Ma'am."

That seemed to chill her out a bit, and she was silent.

Berberian couldn't abide silence. He said to Bax, "Why'd you ask me to call in the feds?"

Bax locked eyes with Parker. "You're aware of a shipping container from FN Herstal that the police in Los Angeles didn't get?"

The silence flattened and got heavy. Parker rapped her knuckles on the table twice. "Excuse me." A third time. Then she left.

Berberian took her chair. "Bax, what the—I mean, chop shops and drugs, right, but—shit. How did Reamer Kline get hold of—I don't even know what FN Herstal is."

"It's Belgian. I can't pronounce it—it's French, like, Fabric National. They make guns for the army, but also for cops."

"LAPD?"

"Crazy full-auto shit. Looks like the goddamn Terminator. One a those half-sized containers packed high and tight—"

Parker returned. She leaned against the door she'd just closed, tapping her phone against her chin. "Can you describe the contents of this shipping container you claim to know something about?"

"That, and more." Bax had grown used to people taking his word since he started fixing for Mr. Kline, and he forced himself to swallow his frustration. "I can give you the numbers off the side of the container, plus who wants to buy it."

Parker's phone made a Charlie Brown teacher noise. She held the phone to her ear, then said, "Hang on." She tapped the screen and put the phone in the middle of the table. "Mr. Baxter, could you—"

"Bax, please, ma'am."

"Sure. Bax, could you tell us the numbers on the container?"

Bax recited the digits he'd memorized, and then described the shipping seal his Jaguar guy had cracked. "It's a twenty-foot container. I ain't taken everything out of it to know the complete inventory, and Mr. Kline, he ain't showed me the manifest. But the one crate I did take out had four rifles, and there's a hella lotta crates in that container."

"How did Reamer Kline come into possession of this container?"

"The driver traded it. To buy his daughter out of Mr. Kline's stable in Memphis."

A voice came out of the phone: "You know where it is?"

"And who's bidding on it."

Parker said, "Bidding?" at the same time her phone flashed a text message.

Bax pretended he hadn't seen the message—*MAKE THE DEAL*—and said, "But I need something."

Bax returned with the three dozen Krispy Kremes that Berberian brought to the meeting to cover for why he'd been gone so long. His crew tore through the doughnuts so fast that only one was left by the time he unlocked Russell from his office.

When Russell started to whine, Bax said, "I ain't ask you no question."

Russell stuffed the entire doughnut into his sneer.

Bax pushed him into his office. "I got to go back out again tonight."

"You ain't locking me up—"

"The hell I ain't. The only question is, you want it to be here, or you want me to put a man on you at your room."

"Man, what you got to—"

"To save your life, brother." Bax grabbed Russell's shoulder. "You and me, Russell, we all each other got since Mom passed."

"Since my dad got killed."

Bax chewed his lower lip. "He weren't no kind of man for you to follow."

Russell threw off Bax's hand and started building up to something furious.

"No." Bax pointed at the couch. "I'm full up to here listening to your bullshit about how great your daddy was. I'm sorry you only had our granny to show you how to be a man, because she didn't have it left in her to tan your hide the way she did mine." Bax continued pointing until Russell finally sat. "Once was all it took."

"And look where you ended up."

Bax enclosed his fury in the safe he'd learned to build in prison, the lockbox that earned him a little grudging respect from the guards and privileges in the library, the commissary. He slowly, quietly closed his office door and turned on his brother. "I did your bit so you could stay in school. I ended up finishing my diploma in prison. You couldn't even finish your diploma in my old school. And when you started running with Ducornet's crew instead, you fucked that up so bad that I ended up in a whole 'nother prison when I got outta the first one I went to for you."

"Hey, Bax, I—"

"You shut the fuck up, boy, and you listen to me. Where I ended up is putting my life on the line to make sure you ain't skinned alive by the most bloodthirsty savages since you pissed yourself when we watched that chainsaw movie."

Russell looked out the window.

"So if I tell you I got to go back out and you got to choose where Ima lock you up, the only thing you say to me is here, alone, or in your room, with a babysitter."

Russell dug at the carpet with his toe. "I got Xbox in my room."

"Yes, sir, Mr. Kline." *Another burner.* "Since Russell introduced competing interests, I think we should keep you as far away from this transaction as possible." *Another boss.* "Russell handed his party off to me, and if you'll hand your party off to me, I've got a solution that will satisfy both." *Another deal.* "But I'm moving the product to a third-party location to limit your exposure."

Bax's crew was used to overnight hours, and the chop suey followed by Krispy Kremes had left them feeling like they'd finished a Thanksgiving meal, maybe Friday leftovers, so the grumbling about breaking the container into two truckloads for staging across town was good-natured, and no one asked him why they had to rustle up the lumber to build as many empty crates as they had crates full of guns and then pack them with recycling scrap picked from the yard to match weight.

The warehouse wasn't exactly abandoned, but the ownership had transitioned into the nether regions of not quite Southland Beverage's and not quite Bank of America's. The liquor distributor had built its warehouse across the state line. A single building that could ship into either state and comply with each state's different regulations and taxes and laws about selling on Sundays. A single building with a concrete wall that sat atop the legal and geographic boundary between the big, mirrored loading bays facing northeast and southwest and overseen by a dispatch room that could look at both sides simultaneously even though neither side could see the other.

And later, at the pizza joint where he bought pitcher after pitcher of Captain Jack to cloud his crew's faculties and memories, when a thick-necked, tatted-up crewcut set a burner on the counter between the bathroom sinks in which they were washing and said, "Your code is Queens," Bax said, "Tell Parker I owe this to my brother."

Bax hadn't known how Reamer Kline would keep his finger on the deal's pulse.

He'd known Mr. Kline would take his advice to stay away from any potential dispute between the Bandidos and the Cossacks, because they were as likely to set one another on fire as they were to rape the other's women or blow up their clubhouses. He'd also known that Mr. Kline's distance came with conditions, with remote sensors, that could get complicated.

So it was a relief, and some luck, when Kline sent only Owsley. Owsley alone probably was the best he could've hoped for. Just one extra guy would make everything easier to manage, but Bax knew Owsley only as a type—powerful, mean, not too smart, but singularly focused and therefore clever about what he applied his singular focus to.

As he had when he put Russell out of commission for five weeks to persuade Bax to fix for Mr. Kline.

Since then, Bax made a point of having as little to do with Owsley as possible. Bax figured that probably ended up as a wash: as much as he didn't know Owsley, Owsley didn't know him.

"We gonna be up here," Bax told Owsley, pointing at the dispatch room on the diagram he'd drawn. "The glass ain't bulletproof, but we laid a bunch of sheet steel on the floor and against the walls, so if anyone starts shooting, just get down. There's a door to the outside, down a flight of stairs, and we already hid a car there. There'll be plenty of concrete between us and the warehouse, and I've got a couple of guys watching it tonight to make sure no one scouts us before the deal goes down."

"Clean getaway." Owsley nodded. "Your guys strapped?"

"My guys are labor, not muscle." Bax rotated the diagram. "I'll have one on each side to meet the buyers. The Bandidos come in from the northeast side, the Cossacks from the southwest. Once my guys get them in the warehouse, you and me, we'll take over from the dispatch office and my guys take off."

Owsley nodded. "You strapped?"

"I'll have a nine on my hip and a thirty-eight on my ankle. You?"

Owsley opened his jacket to show twin shoulder holsters. "I carry forty-fives here and a thirty-two in my crotch." He grunted. "They never frisk your package."

"Smart." Bax had learned there weren't many things a dumb guy liked more than to have someone tell him how smart he was.

"What about your idiot brother?"

"I don't let him carry."

"He just hurt himself."

Bax forced himself to laugh along with Owsley. "You have no idea."

Bax had braced Russell twice—once before Russell went to sleep, once after he woke up—to make it sink in.

"You got one job," Bax told him the night before. "You stand behind me and look mean. The less you talk, the meaner you look."

In the morning, over coffee in the kitchen, missing his eggs with bacon and jelly with toast and Venetta with him, Bax said, "What's your one job?"

"Stand behind you and look mean."

"Good. And how you look mean?"

"By not saying nothin'."

"Very good. Now Ima tell you your second job."

"All right." Russell beamed. "What you—"

"Shut up." Bax opened the cabinet above the refrigerator and lifted out a big round tin of Danish cookies that had gone stale and hard years before. He wiggled the lid off, lifted out the first layer of cookies, and removed a .38 pistol. "This a Ruger LCP." He pointed it at the wall, at a framed poster he'd bought at Big Lots, a black-and-white photo of a coastline he didn't know where. "When you squeeze the grip"—a red dot appeared on the poster—"it's got a laser pointer. Now you do it." Bax handed the gun to Russell. "And don't point it at me."

Russell squeezed and released the laser pointer a few times. "This my second job?"

"If anything goes down, you point this at Owsley and pull the trigger before he starts doing the same to you."

"Wait—Owsley?"

"You keep pulling the trigger till ain't nothin' coming out of that gun."

"Owsley gonna be there?"

"Don't matter. Nothing gonna go down."

Russell started to fit the gun into his pocket.

"Gimme that back." Bax extended his palm.

"I thought—"

"Gotta load it." Bax took a magazine from the tin, slapped it in, and racked the slide. "You think Ima let you wave around a loaded gun in here?"

Bax had set up Berberian's most recent burner to text *QUEENS GO* when he pushed just one button, but he had to wear a jacket loose enough to keep the flip phone both open and hidden. He felt like a damn fool in one of Russell's pimped-out hip-hop jackets.

When Owsley gave him a critical glare, Bax jerked his head at his brother. "It's his OG jacket." Rolled his eyes. "Told me he'd feel better if I wore it."

"That coat, all his shiny banger shoes—he must be joking."

"I don't even know where he gets those shoes. But I'm his only family."

Owsley nodded, then shook his head.

"I hear you." Bax extended his fist for a bump and was gratified when Owsley did the same.

"I got the boys from Tyler," the Audi guy said through the radio. "Two blue box trucks and a white Escalade."

"Tyler is in the house," Bax replied. "Any sign of San Leon?"

"I think they missed the turn and gotta come back around." The Jaguar guy, his only other labor outside, was on the northeast approach. "Two Ryder trucks just went by on the—yeah, here they are. Two yellow moving vans and a—ah, shit, they got like a minivan." Laughter on the open channel. "A black Chrysler."

"Good. Don't make fun of their minivan, right? Get them backed up to the docks. Tyler at four and five, San Leon at fourteen and fifteen."

In the dispatch office, Bax couldn't hear anything outside, but he felt the bumps as the trucks hit the loading docks. "Tyler good?" Bax said into his radio.

"One truck at four," Audi said, "and one truck at five."

"San Leon good?"

"Fourteen and fifteen," Jaguar said.

Bax pushed the buttons that opened those doors. The Bandidos' and Cossacks' rented trucks were lower and smaller than the big rigs the docks had been built for, and sunlight mixed with the overhead fluorescents. A breeze swirled crispy leaves through the Cossacks' bay.

Bax told Audi and Jaguar to let the dealmakers through the staff doors on each side. "Then you guys head back to the shop. Clock in Russell when you get there, and then make sure that container we emptied out is completely shredded."

Moments later the Bandidos' and Cossacks' leaders entered their respective loading bays. Audi and Jaguar pointed their buyers at Bax perched in the dispatch office. They could see him, but neither could see over or through the concrete wall on top of the state line.

Bax hit the speaker switch for the loading bays. "I'm Bax. We talked last night. Up here are my associates, Owsley and Russell."

Cossacks and Bandidos began drifting out of the box trucks. They carried shotguns and rifles. A couple waved wicked-looking machine pistols. Half established a perimeter, half trained their weapons on the dispatch office.

"This look like the deal we talked about?" Bax said through the speaker.

The Cossack flashed two thumbs up. The Bandido said, "You hear me?"

Bax thought about his response, how he could respond without betraying that he was talking to two people instead of just one. "I can hear you when you talk."

The Cossack said, "This looks like what you said," and the Bandido said, "Looks like what we agreed to."

"Like I told you when we talked, you can grab any crate to check the contents are what you expect." Which would work as long as neither gang moved more than three stacks of crates and found the scrap filler.

Two men on each side slung long guns over their shoulders and approached the stacked crates. The Cossacks grabbed the closest crate on top. The Bandidos moved one stack of crates, then another.

"When you've confirmed the contents," Bax said, "then you'll show me your side of the deal."

He waited to see if the Bandidos would dig deep enough to get to a filler crate. He grasped the hidden flip phone, positioning his finger on the Send button.

The Cossacks opened their crate before the Bandidos chose a crate from the third stack.

Bax waited until both crates were open. While the guys pulled out sleek, ray-gun-looking rifles, horsed around with them, put them back.

"I showed you mine," Bax said. "You show me yours."

The Cossack whistled. The Bandido spun his finger in the air. Cossacks hauling rainbow-striped rectangular nylon duffels emerged from their truck. Bandidos dragging black roll-aboard suitcases strolled in from theirs. Both opened their luggage to show bundled stacks of cash.

Bax pushed Send in the same motion as he raised binoculars to look at the Cossacks—

"What the fuck you looking at over there?" a Bandido shouted.

That's when the windows shattered, when Bax yelled "Get down," when his ears popped and his eyes dazzled from flash-bang grenades, when he heard men yelling over gunfire, "U.S. Marshals —drop your weapons," when men started shrieking, when Owsley started for his shoulder holsters, when Russell painted a red dot on Owsley's midsection, when Bax bellowed, "Russell, what did you do?" when bullets clanked and plinked on the sheet metal, when a spurt of blood stained Owsley's shirt and Owsley fell to one side and drew his other pistol.

"Russell," Bax shouted what he'd rehearsed, springing at his brother, pushing him through the door to outside, drawing his pistol, "you traitorous piece of shit!"

Bax fired three, four, five shots over Russell's head and kicked the door shut behind him.

Russell was half over the railing when Parker grabbed his belt and hauled him back onto the landing.

Bax grabbed his brother's head, shook it. "Russell, listen to me." Got his brother's eyes. "This is Parker. She's going to get you out of here." They flinched as bullets pierced the transom behind them. "You're getting a new life somewhere else."

Russell's eyes got big, then rolled a bit as he pissed himself.

"Are you kidding me?" Parker muttered.

"Go," Bax said. "I'll tell you this now because I got to go in for Owsley and I won't see you again. Ever." He planted a kiss on Russell's forehead. "I'm sorry, brother," he whispered. "For everything."

Bax crouched low outside the door. "Owsley," he shouted. "You hear me? Ima open the door."

No response.

Bax cracked the door. The crescendo of explosions and gunfire shocked him, knocked him back. The smell of gunpowder and smoke covered the smell of Russell's piss. The plinks on the sheet metal had stopped as Bandidos and Cossacks concentrated their fire on the feds. He peeked in, saw Owsley on his side, leaking blood, one pistol trained on Bax.

Bax ducked. "Owsley—can you move?" Owsley didn't fire. "I got the car. I can get us out of here."

Owsley rasped, "That idiot brother of yours shot me."

Bax didn't tell Owsley that he'd loaded only a single round in the Ruger he'd given to Russell, figuring close range and a laser pointer would get Russell in the general vicinity of Owsley's bulk without being fatal.

"He set up Mr. Kline," Bax told Owsley. "That must be what his whole thing with the other gang was about." Bax crawled through the door. Owsley's gun arm had dropped. "He set us up and I killed him for it, but now I gotta get you out of here."

"I don't—" Owsley yelped. "I can't make the stairs."

"I'll carry you."

Owsley spit up some blood when he laughed. "You're as big

an idiot as your brother if you think you can carry me." Then he passed out.

Bax turned down the volume on the TV news coverage of the gang-war gun battle when Mr. Kline came out of the bedroom and closed the door. Behind it, Owsley lay in a queen-sized bed that he made look like a twin, breathing raggedly after the horse-farm vet pulled out the .38 slug and sewed up a couple of holes in one of his lungs.

Bax had held Owsley's hand through the surgery. His joints ached from the crushing grip.

"Owsley says you saved his life," Mr. Kline said.

Bax moved the morning's newspaper off the couch so Mr. Kline could sit. "He's heavier than he looks."

Mr. Kline chuckled, then grew solemn. "He also told me that you made sure your brother won't be assisting the feds he sold us out to."

"I'm real sorry about him, Mr. Kline." Bax let the real emotion of never again seeing Russell show on his face. Leak from his eyes. "After all you done for him—"

Mr. Kline patted Bax's knee twice. "It's not lost on me that you did a lot for your brother too."

Bax wiped his eyes. It wasn't beyond the realm of possibility that Mr. Kline knew what he'd gotten away with, what he'd stood up and done Russell's time for. But he knew better than to acknowledge it, than to give Mr. Kline even more power over him.

"However, I must be absolutely confident we're covered on that flank. I can blame Russell to the Cossacks, but my assurances to the Bandidos have been met with some . . . skepticism."

"Yes, sir. When Russell shot Owsley, I put four in his chest and he went over the railing onto the ground. After I got Owsley out, I put another in his head and put his body in the trunk. I can show you a picture on my phone." Parker's people had made Russell look like a chainsaw victim in the movie that had scared the piss out of him.

"Not for me, Bax. But the Bandidos might ask."

Bax put back the phone he'd started pulling from his pocket. "I drove Owsley here, to your ranch to see the doc, and then drove the car with Russell's body out to that quarry in Jefferson County. Wrapped the body with canvas and chain, like we do, and sank it separate from the car."

"Like we do."

"Yes, sir."

"I'm out both the guns and money I expected to get for the guns."

"Yes, sir, I understand that I'm still in your debt." Bax waited for Mr. Kline to acknowledge showing his belly and got a small nod. "I did hold out one crate of those guns for you."

Mr. Kline's mouth twitched to the right.

"The feds are telling the news that it was between the Bandidos and the Cossacks."

"I believe we shall find that sinking that driver in the quarry will pay greater dividends than I originally anticipated."

Bax flinched inside. Maybe Berberian could find out whether the driver's daughter was off the streets in Memphis. "The feds say the Bandidos stole the guns, and the Cossacks ambushed them while they were breaking down the container for distribution."

"Certainly that's not the story your brother fed them."

"I figure that's their cover for flipping Russell, because they ain't know I killed him." Bax shrugged. "But the closest they can get to you from him is me. And I know how to keep my counsel."

Venetta didn't take much care when she tossed his plate of eggs with bacon and jelly with toast on the counter.

Bax folded the paper he'd brought with him from the horse farm. "I missed you yesterday," he said.

She leaned over the counter, one hand planted deliberately over the front-page photo of the still-smoking, bullet-riddled ware-house. "I 'spect you musta been pretty busy yesterday."

"I finally got it through my brother's head that he needs a fresh start somewhere else."

"Mm-hmm."

"Spent the day packing his things and then put him on a bus to Houston. He got a cousin there who can help him get established."

"You said you's his only family."

Bax chewed on a slice of bacon. "I think I said he's my only family."

Venetta looked like she might raise an eyebrow, but she didn't. "Now that he gone, you gonna tell me the rest of that story?"

"You gonna let me take you to the supper club on Saturday night?" Bax finished his eggs, appreciating that they were still hot.

"I have never met Napoleon, but that ain't our deal."

Bax nodded. "My mom—she was Russell's mom too, you know —when I came along, she was a working girl. After I arrived, she got on a different track. Started waiting tables in a diner."

"Really."

"This diner." Bax smeared strawberry jelly across his sourdough toast. "I bused tables here, for tips, after school, when I was eight, nine years old."

Venetta perched on a stool behind the counter and took her hand off the newspaper.

"But Russell's dad, when she took up with him, he wanted her earning more. After Russell come along, he hooked her on dope so he could turn her out."

"Gonna put his baby momma on the street."

Bax wiped his mouth. "So I killed him."

Venetta cleared his plate and ran a towel over the counter. "You did Russell's bit for what you done that you ain't got caught for."

Bax took a twenty from his wallet and laid it on the counter. "I don't need no change."

Venetta extended his paper. She didn't let go of it when he tried to take it.

Bax looked at Venetta's hand. Its firm grasp on the news.

"Not Saturday night," Venetta said. "But you can take my daughter and me out for lunch after Sunday services."

Nightbound

FROM *At Home in the Dark*

"LEAVE HIM," Crissa said. "He's dead."

Adler was facedown in the alley, not moving, Martinez kneeling beside him. She could see the entry wound in Adler's back, the blood soaking through his field jacket. From the location of the wound and the speed he was bleeding out, she knew he was gone already, or would be soon.

They had to keep moving. Back at the stash house, the Dominicans would be recovering from the flashbang she'd thrown on her way out the rear door. The three of them had been halfway down the alley when one of the Dominicans had stumbled out of the vacant brownstone, firing blindly. She'd snapped a shot at him with her Glock, chased him back inside. But Adler had caught a round, gone down hard.

Now Martinez looked up at her, panic in his eyes, all that was visible through the ski mask. She shifted the strap of the gear bag, heavy with money, to her left shoulder, grabbed him by the coat sleeve, pulled him up. "Move!"

Forty feet away was the mouth of the alley, the street beyond. To their left, more empty houses. To the right, a high chain-link fence that bordered a vacant lot. The only way out was ahead.

More shots behind them. She spun, saw two men run out into the alley, guns in their hands. She fired twice without aiming. One round ricocheted off blacktop, the other punched through a plywood-covered window. The men ducked back inside.

She fired another shot to keep them there, shoved Martinez forward. The street ahead was still empty. Where was Lopez? The

Dominicans would be going out the front door as well, would try to circle around, block the alley. If they beat Lopez there, she and Martinez would be trapped.

Broken glass and crack vials crunched beneath her feet. She could hear Martinez panting behind her.

A screech of brakes, and the Buick pulled up at the end of the alley, Lopez at the wheel, the rear driver's-side door already open.

She tossed the gear bag into the backseat, threw herself in after it. A shot sounded. Martinez grunted and fell against her.

"Get in!" Lopez said.

She gripped Martinez's field jacket, pulled him to her, and they fell back onto the bag. His legs were still hanging out of the car when Lopez hit the gas. As the Buick lurched forward, she heard rounds strike the left rear fender. She pulled Martinez all the way in just as the Buick made a hard right turn. The momentum swung the door shut.

Martinez moaned. She rolled him off her onto the floor, sat up. They were in a residential area, dark houses on both sides of the street. The transfer car was still a couple of miles away.

"What happened back there?" Lopez said.

She pulled off her ski mask, had to catch her breath before she could speak. "Too many of them. Seven, maybe. At least. More than we thought."

Through the rear window she saw headlights way back there, coming fast. No other cars around.

"They're on us," she said.

"Shit." Lopez gunned the engine. The Buick swung a left, then another right onto a main thoroughfare, sped by darkened storefronts.

She pushed the mask into a jacket pocket. If she had to do a runner from the car, she didn't want to leave it behind. There would be hair in the material, DNA. Evidence if the cops found it.

Martinez moaned again. She laid a gloved hand atop his. "Steady. You're going to be all right."

They'd scouted this area of East New York for weeks, timed the route, and she knew the chances of running into a squad car were slim. It was midnight shift change, the same reason the Dominicans chose that time for their weekly money pickup. Lopez was an ex-cop, knew the area, the players. Martinez was his brother-in-law. The two of them had found the stash house, gathered the intel, then reached out to her through a middleman. She was the one who'd brought in Adler.

Two blocks ahead was the business district, an intersection controlled at this hour by only a blinking yellow light. She looked back at the street behind. A pair of bright headlights swung out onto it, moving fast.

"They're coming," she said.

Martinez made a slow sign of the cross. His breath was ragged now, wheezing. Collapsed lung, she thought.

Lopez took the left at the yellow light, cut it too close, the driver's-side tires bumping hard over the curb. A red light began to blink on the dash, in time with a soft beep.

"Fuck," he said.

"What?"

"They must have hit the tank. We're losing gas."

Behind them a dark SUV made the turn, staying on their tail. High beams flashed on, lit the inside of the car. The Buick began to sputter and slow. The next turn was still a block ahead.

"Get down!" Lopez said.

The SUV swept into the left lane, came abreast of them. The front passenger-side window slid down, and a shotgun barrel came through.

Lopez slammed on the brakes. It threw her forward onto Martinez. She heard the roar of the gun, an explosion of glass. The Buick slewed to the right, hit the curb, rolled up on it, and came to a stop. The SUV braked just beyond it, then reversed.

She heard the shotgun being ratcheted. Another blast, and safety glass sprayed over her.

She jerked up on the latch of the passenger-side door, pushed it open, and rolled out onto the sidewalk, the Buick between her and the SUV.

How many men? Two at least, driver and shooter, but maybe others in back. Likely more on their way from the stash house in another vehicle. She couldn't stay where she was, couldn't run without presenting a target.

A third blast, this time into the rear driver's side. The car rocked with the impact. She heard a door in the SUV open. They were getting out to finish it. *Now,* she thought.

She raised up, aimed the Glock over the roof of the Buick. The man with the shotgun stood there, lit by the streetlight. Shaven head, facial tattoo. She'd seen him at the stash house. He swung the muzzle toward her, and she fired twice, saw his head snap to the side. He fell back against the SUV, dropped the shotgun, and slid to the pavement.

She aimed through the open door of the SUV, but the driver was gone. The rear windows were tinted. She couldn't see inside or through.

She steadied the Glock with both hands, waited. Would he come around the front or back? Were there more men inside, ready to open a side door, start firing?

The driver popped his head over the top of the SUV, pistol resting on the roof. She fired once to get him to duck, then lowered the muzzle and began shooting through the SUV's side windows. The smoked glass exploded and collapsed. She could see the driver on the other side, saw him take the impact of the bullets. She kept firing until he fell out of sight. The rear of the SUV was empty.

Shell casings clinked on the sidewalk behind her. Gun smoke hung in the air. There'd been fifteen rounds in the Glock—fourteen in the magazine, one in the chamber. How many left?

She went around the front of the Buick. The man with the shotgun lay on his side. A rivulet of blood ran out from below him, shiny on the blacktop, coursed toward the gutter. She kicked the shotgun away, circled the SUV. The driver lay on his back, motionless, eyes open. She put a foot on his pistol, swept it into a storm drain.

In the Buick, Lopez was slumped over onto the passenger seat. He was dead or close to it. There was blood on the dashboard, the steering wheel, and what was left of the windshield. The fuel light still blinked red.

The rear door was pocked with buckshot holes. She pulled it open. Martinez lay still and silent on the floor. His own gun had slid partly out of his jacket pocket, the same model Glock as her own. She took it.

Headlights back at the cross street. She leaned into the car, hauled out the gear bag, swung the strap onto her shoulder.

A block ahead was another intersection, another blinking yellow light. To her right was a wide, unlit alley that ran behind a row of commercial buildings. Their storefronts would face onto that main street. High above, a bright half moon shone through thin clouds.

Headlights lit her, the vehicle coming fast. She took a last look at the Buick, then ran into the darkness of the alley.

Breathe. Think.

Fire escapes here, but their street-level ladders were raised and unreachable. She ran on, the bag thumping against her back. A cat darted from behind a dumpster, crossed her path, and disappeared.

She heard a vehicle brake on the street behind her. If it turned into the alley, she'd be caught in its headlights. They'd send someone to the other end too, to cut her off, try to pin her between them.

Ahead on the left was a one-story brick building with a loading dock, a green dumpster and a pile of discarded tires beside it. The metal pull-down gate was covered with graffiti. On the dock was a single fifty-five-gallon metal drum. She stuck the Glock in her belt, tossed the bag onto the dock, and climbed up after it.

There was a heavy padlock at the bottom of the gate. She tugged at it, but there was no give. She looked around, considered the dumpster for a moment. Knew that would be one of the first places they'd look.

No way in, and she couldn't go back. She felt the first sharp edge of panic. She tilted the barrel toward her, heard its contents slosh, smelled motor oil. The drum was half full. She swung and wheeled it closer to the gate, then scrambled atop it. It rocked unsteadily beneath her feet.

The roof was gravel and tarpaper, bordered on all sides by three limp strands of barbed wire. Broken bottles glinted in the moonlight. There was a silent air-conditioning unit in one corner, its grille dark with rust. A few feet away was a closed wooden hatch.

She climbed back down, the barrel shaking. She could hear urgent voices in Spanish on the street back there. They'd be coming this way soon.

Hoisting the gear bag to her shoulder, she climbed carefully back onto the barrel, almost overbalanced. She heaved the bag onto the barbed-wire strands, weighing them down, then crawled onto and over it. Pulling the bag free, she rolled away from the edge, the roof creaking under her.

She backed away farther, out of eyesight from below. Seven men at the stash house. She'd killed two at the SUV. By now they might have called for more men. Likely why they hadn't come down the alley yet. They were waiting for reinforcements.

She crawled toward the air-conditioning unit, got her back to it, tried to slow her breathing. The Glock's magazine was empty, with a single round left in the chamber. She took the full clip from Martinez's gun, transferred it to her own, and slapped it home. She pulled the bag toward her, unzipped and opened it. His Glock, her mask, and the empty magazine went inside.

She pointed her gun toward the edge of the roof, the butt resting on a thigh. There was nothing she could do about the drum. If they saw it, figured out what she'd done, then it would be all over. But she'd take out as many of them as she could before they got her.

With her left hand she rifled through the money. Packs of bills, some bank-strapped, some bound with rubber bands. Street money, hundreds, fifties, and twenties. She did a rough count in the moonlight. Maybe a hundred thousand altogether. Less than they'd expected. Lopez had said there might be as much as three hundred thousand at the stash house.

It hadn't been worth it. Lopez, Martinez, and Adler all dead, and everything they'd planned gone to hell.

Headlights below. She looked over the edge of the roof, saw a dark SUV come to a stop just inside the alley. Its high beams lit dumpsters, fire escapes, and brick walls. A side door opened and two men got out, both carrying pistols. They'd search the alley on foot. The SUV stayed where it was, engine running.

She could hide here for now, wait them out. But soon they'd know she hadn't come out on any of the neighboring streets, was still somewhere on this block.

How far away was the transfer car? Would she even be able to find it? It was a banged-up Volvo wagon, inconspicuous enough not to draw attention, too old and ugly to invite theft. Lopez had stolen it the day before in Yonkers, cracked the steering column so the ignition could be easily hot-wired again. She'd shown Martinez and Adler how to do it. If something went wrong or they got separated, anyone who could make it to the transfer car would still have a chance of getting clear. But now there was only her.

She gripped the gun, rested the back of her head against the cool metal of the air-conditioning unit, looked up at the moon, and waited.

*

When she looked at her watch again, it was one thirty. A half hour had passed. The SUV was still there. They'd turned off the engine but left on the headlights.

She crawled toward the front of the roof. The street was lined with dark stores, most with riot gates. No traffic. To the left, past the blinking yellow signal at the intersection, a storefront threw light on the sidewalk. Neon signs in the window read BURGERS PIZZA FRIED CHICKEN 24 HRS. There was a cab parked outside, no one at the wheel.

Stay or go? With the alley blocked, the only way out would be through the front, with the hope she could make it to the cab without being spotted, find the driver. Get away from here.

The other option was to wait until daylight. There would be more cars then, people. The searchers might have given up. But she didn't want to stay here in the meantime, trapped like some animal, her fate being decided by someone or something else.

She took two banded packs of money from the gear bag, stuffed them in her jacket pockets. The bag would be a burden, would slow her down. She'd have to leave it here, come back another time, hope no one found it in the interim.

She zipped the bag back up, wedged it behind the air-conditioning unit, covered it with a loose piece of aluminum flashing. It would have to do. If they searched the roof and found it, it would just be her bad luck. There was nothing for it.

The hatch was locked from the inside, but it was old wood. She took out her buck knife, opened the three-inch blade, and went to work on the hinges, slicing away wood until the screws were loose. She pulled the hinges free, then pried up that side of the hatch high enough that she could reach in. Her fingers found a bolt. She opened it, then lifted the entire hatch free, set it gently on the roof.

An iron ladder led down into darkness. The familiar smells of motor oil and rubber drifted up. She closed the knife, put it away, took out her penlight. She shone the beam inside, saw an oil-stained concrete floor, a lift pit with no lift. More tires. She switched off the light, put it away.

Go on, she thought. *You can't stay here and wait for whatever's coming.*

She tucked the Glock in her waistband, sat on the edge of the opening, swung her legs in, felt for the rungs with her feet. She let herself down slowly. Five rungs. Six. Her feet touched concrete.

To the front was a bay door, a single window set high in its center letting in streetlight. On the other side of the lift pit, an open doorway led to an office.

She circled the pit, staying out of the light. Inside the office was a battered metal desk and a filing cabinet. The cabinet's drawers were open and empty. The desktop was filmed with dust. On the floor was an auto parts calendar from 2015.

She took out the Glock, held it at her side. A wide-gridded riot gate covered the front window, faint streetlight coming through. To the right of it was a glass door in a recessed doorway, with cardboard taped over a missing panel. From here she had a clear view of the street in both directions. There was only one pole light working on the block, maybe twenty feet to her left. Beyond that, across the intersection, was the bright storefront. The cab was still there.

Headlights from the right. She stepped away from the door, back into the shadows, watched a dark Navigator approach and slow.

She took steady breaths. *Don't panic,* she thought. *Watch. Wait.*

Another pair of lights came from the opposite direction. It was a low-slung two-door Acura. The vehicles stopped abreast of each other, window to window, the drivers talking. The car drove off.

The Navigator crossed the intersection, pulled up behind the taxi. Three men she hadn't seen before got out and went inside the restaurant. After a few minutes they emerged and got back in the Navigator. She watched it pull away.

They might be doing circles, grids, looking for her. The Acura too. One or more of them might be coming back this way before long. It was time to move.

With her left hand, she unlocked the door. It had swollen in its frame, wouldn't open. She pulled hard, shook it. It rattled and creaked as it came free. Cool night air flowed in. She put the Glock in her pocket, kept her hand on it.

Outside, she cut left up the sidewalk, walking fast but not running. She crossed the street, stayed close to the storefronts on the other side. Ahead the yellow light blinked, lit the blacktop.

On the other side of the intersection, she stopped short of the restaurant, looked through a side window. It was bright and stark inside. Plastic tables and chairs, a counter window with thick bulletproof glass. Behind it a young Black man in a white T-shirt and apron was texting on a phone, thumbs busy.

A single table was occupied. A thin, dark-skinned man with glasses and graying hair was reading a newspaper.

She tried the rear door of the cab, wanting to get in, out of sight. It was locked. She went up to the window near where the man sat, tapped a knuckle on the glass. The second time she did it, he looked up from his paper. The counterman had put down his phone, was watching her.

She pointed at the cab. The thin man nodded briskly, took off his glasses and stowed them in a jacket pocket. He got up, left the newspaper on the table.

She waited beside the taxi, looking in both directions. No headlights, no police cruisers, no sirens.

The thin man came outside. "Miss, may I help you?"

He had an accent she couldn't place, West Africa or somewhere in the Caribbean.

"I need a ride," she said. "To somewhere not far from here."

He looked around, then back at her. "Are you alone?"

"Yes." Her breathing grew faster. She wanted to get in the cab, off the street.

"Where are you coming from?" he said.

"Queens. My car broke down. Can we go?"

With her left hand, she worked loose a bill from the pack. Her other hand stayed on the gun.

She folded the bill, held it out. It was a hundred.

"Just a few blocks," she said. "But we need to leave now."

He looked in the direction the Navigator had gone, then at her, the hand still in her pocket.

"Now," she said. "Let's go. Please."

He took out keys, hit the remote button, unlocked the cab. The headlights blipped.

"Of course," he said. "Anywhere you want."

She watched the signs on the deserted streets they passed, giving him directions through the grid in the Plexiglas divider. When they came to a block that looked familiar, she said, "Slow down."

She recognized the neighborhood now. Warehouses, muffler shops, and garages. Ahead was the side street where they'd left the Volvo. A dark White Castle on the corner had been their landmark.

"Turn left up there," she said.

From a wide alley on the right, an SUV charged out, blocked the street. The Navigator. The taxi driver braked hard, sounded the horn, stopped when he saw the men spilling out of the Navigator into the cab's headlights.

She threw herself across the backseat, clawed at the passenger door handle just as the first shots came through the cab's windshield. She got the door open, tumbled out onto the ground. The cab was still rolling. It thumped solidly into the side of the Navigator.

She pulled out the Glock, brought it up. Three men were still shooting into the cab, glass and upholstery exploding. They hadn't seen her get out.

She stood, took one of them down with a center-mass chest shot, swung her muzzle toward the next one, fired, and missed. The round blew out a side window in the Navigator. The two men dropped down behind the cover of the cab.

Farther down the street behind her, another vehicle was coming fast. The Acura. She ran into the alley the Navigator had come out of, heard the pop of guns behind her. A bullet ricocheted off the pavement to her right. She cut across the alley into a vacant lot, ran through thigh-high weeds. More shots. Something tugged at the tail of her jacket.

The Acura turned down the alley after her. There were men on foot as well, coming through the weeds. But she was away from the streetlamps now, and they had no clear target. She hurdled an overturned shopping cart and then she was back on cracked sidewalk, another empty street, this one wider. There was an elevated roadway ahead, cars speeding along it, a dark underpass below. She heard the men behind her, didn't look back.

She crossed the street, ran for the shadows of the underpass, cars humming above. The Acura turned left, caught her in its headlights. She made the underpass, lungs burning, came out on the other side. There on the right was a lot full of tractor trailers, surrounded by a high fence topped with razor wire. Parked in front of the closed gate, facing away from her, was a police cruiser.

She stumbled onto the weedy shoulder at the fence's far corner, about thirty feet behind the cruiser. She couldn't breathe. To her right, a dirt access road ran parallel to the overpass.

The cruiser's interior light was on. A uniform cop sat behind the wheel, drinking from a Styrofoam cup.

The Acura emerged from the underpass, the front passenger window gliding down. The car slowed and came to a stop, head-lamps illuminating the cruiser. The uniform turned to look back at it. Traffic rumbled by above.

The Acura didn't move. After a minute the window slid closed again, and the car made a long, slow U-turn away from the cruiser. Giving up.

She raised the Glock above her head and squeezed the trigger three times. The sharp cracks split the night. The Acura's tires squealed as it pulled away fast. The cruiser's rollers flashed into life, and the cop swung it into a hard U-turn, headed after the car, siren rising and falling.

Across the street, the lot was empty.

She sat down in the dirt of the access road, couldn't seem to get enough air. Head between her knees, she resisted the urge to be sick. She put the Glock away, felt the right side of her jacket, the rent where a bullet had passed through the material without touching her. *Pure luck,* she thought. *The only reason you're alive.*

From the access road, an embankment led up to the overpass. She started up it, heard another siren. A second cruiser sped past below, lights rolling, following the first. Backup.

Once on the elevated roadway, there was a shoulder wide enough to walk on. A car flew past, so close she felt its slipstream. Another slowed, beeped its horn, came abreast of her. She put a hand on the Glock in her pocket. A man yelled something at her from the passenger-side window, then the car sped up and passed her.

She walked on. There was a major intersection ahead, where the highway dropped down to cross another main road. On one side of the road was a dark strip mall. On the other, a three-story building with a bright lobby and a sign above it that read PARKWAY MOTOR INN.

She let two cars pass, then sprinted across the road toward the motel. The parking lot was less than half full. She stopped to get her breath back, brushed grit and dirt from her clothes as best she could.

She gripped the big silver handle of the glass door, pulled. It wouldn't open. Inside the lobby, a turbaned clerk stood behind bulletproof glass at the front desk. He frowned at her.

Wearily she took out the hundred she'd offered the cabdriver, unfolded it, and pressed it against the glass. She held it there, waited. The door buzzed.

She opened it and went in. She was done running.

The clerk took the two hundreds she gave him without a word, offered no change, and asked for no ID. A key card attached to a diamond-shaped piece of green plastic came back in the pass-through slot. Room 110.

The lobby smelled of stale cigarette smoke and disinfectant. There was a skinny ATM near the front desk counter, a couple of worn chairs, and planters full of dusty plastic flowers.

She went down the orange-carpeted hallway. An ice machine rattled in an alcove at the end of the corridor. She heard grunting from behind a door she passed.

The room was as she'd expected. Mirror on the ceiling over the bed. Dresser and nightstand, a single chair, and no windows. White shag carpet and a TV bolted to a brace on the wall. The cigarette smell was strong in here as well.

A door led to an adjoining room. The connecting door was locked. She put an ear to it. No sound inside. She closed her door again, bolted it.

The bathroom was small, the sink mineral-stained. She realized then how thirsty she was, ran water, cupped some and drank, then spit it out. It tasted of metal.

The chair went against the hall door, the top rail wedged under the knob. It would give her warning at least, if the clerk or someone else with a key tried to come in. Then she took the Glock into the bathroom, set it on the toilet tank, undressed, and showered, let the spray wash the last bits of safety glass from her hair, the tension from her shoulders. She would be sore and aching tomorrow.

When she was done, she dried off with a towel that smelled like burned hair, dressed again. She checked the doors a final time, then sat on the edge of the bed. She thought about the cabdriver. He was dead, almost certainly, and for no other reason than he had tried to help her.

She stretched out atop the comforter, not trusting the sheets, looked at her watch. Three a.m. Only three hours since they'd gone in the back door of the stash house. *You're alive*, she thought, *and a lot of people aren't.*

She needed sleep. Tomorrow she'd get a cab to take her into Manhattan. From Penn Station she'd catch a train south to New Jersey and home. It wouldn't be safe to go back for the money tomorrow. They'd still be looking for her. She'd have to wait, return another time, hope it was still there when she did.

She moved the Glock to the bed, in easy reach. She was too tired to turn out the lights, too tired to do anything. She looked up at her reflection and closed her eyes.

She woke in silence, not sure why, raised her watch. Four thirty.

Muscles stiff, she slid off the bed, picked up the Glock, went to the hall door, and listened. Outside, the hum of the ice machine. Then, from the direction of the lobby, the quiet voices of men, too low for her to make out the words. After a moment she realized they were speaking Spanish. Her stomach tightened.

She slipped on the jacket and gloves, pocketed the Glock, got out her knife. She went to the adjoining door. Still no sound from the other side. She worked the blade into the jamb of the inner door, pried at the deadbolt. The wood there was soft. The door opened easily.

This room was the mirror image of hers. She went in, closed both connecting doors behind her. On the far side of the room was another door. She used the knife again. The next room had the same setup but this time no connecting door. It was the last room in the hall.

She closed the knife, went to the hall door, looked through the spyhole, got a distorted, fish-eye view of the hallway, the vending alcove with the ice machine. Next to it a stairwell door.

She took out the Glock, held her breath. The voices down the hall had quieted. Easing the door open, she looked back toward 110. Three Dominicans stood outside the door. One of them held a gun to the back of the turbaned clerk's head. The clerk slid a key card into the reader, and when the door unlocked, they tried to push him inside, met the resistance of the chair. One of them hit the door with his shoulder, knocked it open. She heard the chair fall. They shoved the clerk inside, crowded in behind him. The third man stayed in the hall.

"Hey," she said, and raised the Glock.

He turned toward her, gun coming up, and she fired, hit him in the shoulder. It spun him around and dropped him. She ran to the fire door, slammed her hip into the panic bar, found herself in a dim concrete stairwell. To the left, stairs ran up. Straight ahead, another fire door, this one leading outside, with a sign that read EMERGENCY EXIT ONLY! ALARM WILL SOUND!

Shots from down the hall. A round hit the door frame behind her. She kicked the bar with the sole of her foot, jolted it open. An alarm began to bleat loudly. Outside was the rear parking lot. The way they'd expect her to go.

She took the stairs two at a time. At the third landing was a shorter flight that led to the roof. The alarm kept on, echoed through the stairwell.

Another door, another panic bar. Then she was out on a black-top roof. She could see the lights of the highway, the overpass. Far to the west, the glow of Manhattan.

In the front lot three dark SUVs were idling near the entrance, headlights on. One of them was the Navigator. She could see the missing window, the collision damage. Another car pulled into the lot behind them. The Acura.

People were stumbling out of the lobby doors into the lot now, some half dressed, unsure what to do, where to go. There were sirens in the distance.

From the side of the roof a fire escape ran down, its last level a hinged ladder. Flashing lights came down the highway and across the overpass, a fire engine and a police cruiser. They pulled into the lot.

She put away the Glock, swung out onto the fire escape, went down quickly. On the bottom rungs, her weight carried the hinged section down. She dropped the last couple feet to the pavement, landed wrong. Her ankle twisted under her, and she fell hard. A surge of pain ran up her leg.

Now the night was filled with sirens, people shouting, and the steady blare of the fire alarm. She got to her feet, braced herself against the wall, tested the ankle. It hurt but would bear her weight. She limped to the front corner of the building. Two fire trucks in the lot now, another cruiser. Red and blue lights bathed the vehicles, the people milling around.

The Acura and two of the SUVs were blocked in by the trucks. The third one, a dark Chevy Tahoe, was about fifteen feet from her, parked away from the others, engine running. The passenger door was ajar, the seat there empty. She could see the man at the wheel.

Pain flashing in her foot, she limped across the distance. When she reached the Tahoe, she pulled the door wider, pointed the Glock inside. The driver turned, saw the gun. Before he could react, she swung up and into the seat, pulled the door shut behind her. "Drive."

It was one of the men from the stash house who'd fired at them as they ran in the alley. He was younger than the others, with long hair slicked back. When he didn't respond, she aimed the gun at his groin. "Your call."

The interior of the Tahoe was washed in emergency lights, red, blue, and red again.

"You gonna pull that trigger?" he said. "All these cops around? I don't think so."

"I'm betting in all this confusion no one notices. You want to find out?"

An automatic was wedged between the driver's seat and the console, a 9mm Steyr. She pulled it out, put it in her left coat pocket.

"You the one we been chasing, eh?" he said. "Didn't think it would be a woman."

"Go."

He looked at her, then reversed, swung the Tahoe around clear of the emergency vehicles, pointed it out of the lot. Through the motel doors she could see that the lobby was full of firefighters and cops. There were horns blowing as people were trying to leave, their cars blocked in.

The Tahoe bumped onto the highway, turned right. Another cruiser, lights and siren going, passed them from the opposite direction, turned into the lot.

"Where?" he said. Staying cool.

"Just drive."

She tried to calm herself, figure out her next move. They were headed east, deeper into Brooklyn, the streets empty, the sirens fading behind them. Ahead on the right was the empty lot of a darkened pancake house.

She pointed. "Pull over in there."

He slowed, glided into the lot.

"Kill the lights," she said. "And get out."

He turned off the headlights, looked at her. "You the one got the money?"

She didn't answer.

"If you didn't, you know where it is, right?"

"Why?"

"Maybe I make you a deal."

"Like what?"

"You take me to it. You give me half. Then I take you wherever you want to go."

"What about your bosses?"

"Fuck 'em."

She looked at him, weighing it. "Why should I trust you?"

"You got the guns. What do I have?"

"A lot of balls, rip off your own people that way."

"Money's money."

"Half is too much for just a ride."

"A ride and a lie. You held a gun on me, was nothing I could do. I let you out somewhere up the road, don't know where you went. Part of it's true, right?"

"You think they'll believe that?"

"They'll have to, won't they?"

"Or I could just shoot you and take your ride. Not give you anything."

"You could do that. But I don't think you will."

In the console compartment, a cell phone began to buzz.

"They're looking for me already," he said. "Soon they're gonna know what happened."

He was right. It would only be a matter of time before someone found them.

"Put it in park," she said.

He did, turned to her. "What do you say?"

"Get out."

"You're making a mistake."

"Out."

He opened the door, stepped down. With the Glock still on him, she climbed over the console and into the driver's seat.

"They'll never stop looking for you," he said. "And when they find you . . . You'll be begging them to kill you. But first you'll give up the money. And then you'll have nothing, *puta*. Not even your life."

She thought about Adler and Martinez and Lopez. The cabdriver. Everything she'd been through tonight.

"It'll be bad for you," he said. "And it'll go on for a long time."
"I believe you," she said, and shot him.

She left the Tahoe on a dark street in Bay Ridge, two blocks from the Verrazano, keys still in the ignition. She walked down to the bayfront, squeezed through a hole in a chain-link fence, reached the cracked seawall. She tossed the two guns out into the water. The sky to the east had lightened to a pale blue.

She walked until she found a subway station, took the R train into Manhattan. Three hours later she was home.

"Slow down up here," she said. "But don't stop."

She powered the Town Car's rear window halfway down. The tire shop was ahead on the right. More people around now, more traffic, but a lot of the storefronts were still dark, riot gates in place, businesses that were gone for good.

Luis, the driver, looked at her in the rearview. "This isn't a good area. Even in the daytime. I know. I used to live here."

"Go around the block again."

She looked at the shop's recessed entrance as they passed. No one inside she could see, the door still closed.

She'd waited two days to come back, taken the train up from home. At Penn Station in Manhattan, she'd called a car service from a burner cell, used a fake name.

They circled the block, came back around.

"Pull up here," she said.

He steered the Town Car to the curb. She looked at the shop door, the darkness beyond it, wondered what waited for her there.

Three possibilities. The money was still here, hadn't been found. Or the Dominicans had searched the building and roof, taken it. Or they were there in the tire shop now, or somewhere close by, watching, waiting for someone to come back.

The Town Car stuck out here. It would look wrong to have it standing outside the shop too long.

"Wait five minutes," she said. "Then come back to get me." She opened her door.

"Maybe you should tell me what this is all about."

"Five minutes," she said. "That's all it will take. One way or the other."

She shut the door behind her. Her gloved right hand went to

the .32 Beretta Tomcat in the pocket of her leather car coat. She limped into the doorway of the tire shop. Behind her the Town Car pulled back into traffic.

She tried the knob. It was still unlocked. Inside, she eased the door shut behind her, drew the Tomcat.

The office was as she'd left it. In the bay, a shaft of light came through the roof hatch, lit dust motes. She went to the ladder, listened. No voices, no footsteps.

Up the ladder to the roof. It was empty. To the west, an airliner traced a white line across the sky.

She made her way to the air-conditioning unit, pulled back the flashing, and there was the gear bag. She knelt, unzipped it. The money was inside, along with Martinez's gun and the empty magazine. Her mask. Everything there.

She zipped the bag back up, slung it over her shoulder, stuck the Tomcat in her belt, climbed down the ladder.

Back in the office, she stood just inside the door, watched the street, the cars going by, feeling exposed. She glanced at her watch. Five minutes since Luis had dropped her off.

A dark SUV with smoked windows pulled up outside. She backed farther into the office shadows, took out the Tomcat. The SUV stayed there. She waited for someone to get out, come inside. She raised the gun.

Horns blew. The SUV drove on. Two minutes later the Town Car slid to the curb.

Deep breath. She put the gun away, opened the door. The front passenger window came down. Luis leaned over. "Sorry. Traffic. Everything okay?"

She went out quickly, ignoring the pain in her ankle. There was no sign of the SUV. She opened the rear door of the Town Car, tossed in the gear bag, climbed in after it, and pulled the door shut.

She met his eyes in the rearview.

"Just something that belonged to me," she said. "Something I had to leave behind."

"And now?"

"Let's go back to Penn."

He waited for a break in traffic, then made a U-turn across both lanes, headed back the way they'd come. She looked out the rear window. No SUV, no one following them.

They passed the all-night restaurant, crowded now, a line at the counter. She'd ask Rathka, her lawyer, to find out the cabdriver's name, if he had family. If so, she'd figure out a way to get part of the money to them. It was all she could do, but it wasn't enough. No amount would ever be enough.

"Luis, do me a favor?"

"Sure. What?"

She took four hundreds from her pocket, leaned over the seat, and held them out. "Tell your dispatcher when you got the call to pick me up, there was no one there."

He looked at the bills.

"You never brought me out here. You never saw me at all," she said. "Can you deal with that?"

"That's a lot of money."

"Can you?"

He hesitated. "I think so."

"Then that's good for both of us. Take it."

He did.

She sat back, looked out the window at the streets passing by, kept one hand on the gear bag.

"Glad you didn't hang around too long back there," he said. "That's a rough neighborhood."

"I know," she said.

ROBIN YOCUM

The Last Hit

FROM *The Strand Magazine*

THE THING THIS younger bunch doesn't understand is this: it's just not as easy to clip someone as it used to be.

I'm not making excuses. It's a fact. Nowadays there are cameras on the freeways, inside of buildings, outside of buildings—everywhere. You're always on camera. And if you're carrying a cell phone, the cops can track you by the pings off cell towers. It's crazy. That's how they nailed Joey Labitto for the Carsoni hit.

In the old days I could walk down an alley, through a back door, and *boom*, the job was done. Thirty minutes later Carlo and I would be at Undo's, eating bucatini with clam sauce, a bottle of Chianti between us. Maybe a cannoli for dessert. Carlo loved cannoli. We would laugh and talk, never about business but about women, baseball, or politics. We would treat ourselves to a nice dinner because we knew the next day the old man would slap our backs, hand us each a wad of cash, and say, "Thanks for your service, gentlemen." He was a man of few words.

Carlo and I worked together for more than four decades. Every cop and FBI agent in the tri-state knew who we were and what we did, but they could never put a finger on us. That's how good we were. Half the time I don't think the cops even tried to solve the cases. If they were honest, they'd tell you they were secretly grateful, because we were not exactly taking out Sunday school teachers.

I was a respected member of the family back then. I got invited to baptisms, weddings, and Sunday dinners, and if I went down to one of the whorehouses the old man ran, I never paid. *Never.* Of course, I'd tip for exceptional service, but that was it. Do you want to know why I never had to pay? Because I was trusted and respected. Now the old man is gone and the young guns look at me like I'm a dinosaur. There's no respect for me or the old ways. But let me tell you this: I'm seventy-two, and I'm still taking in oxygen. Most guys in my line of work don't make it that long, including Carlo.

The kid, they call him Little Tommy, he doesn't want to listen to anything I have to say. He gets a burr to take someone out, and he wants it done yesterday. I try to tell him that these things take time, that you need to be careful, but like I said, he doesn't want to hear any of that. "Just get it done," he says.

Before he died, his dad, Tommaso "Big Tommy" Fortunato, asked me to look after his only son. I promised I would. It's been six years since the old man stroked out, and I'm an afterthought in the family these days. I don't get invited to dinner. No one asks how I'm doing. I thought I'd be a mentor to Little Tommy, but that's not how he wants it. When I think of it, the only reason he hasn't already shoved me out the door is I know all the family secrets. I know where the bodies are buried—literally.

Every morning I walk down to the diner to get breakfast and read the newspaper. Sometimes in the afternoon I'll go over to the nursing home and visit Jimmy Nicolosi, who used to run the gambling operation for Big Tommy. Nickels, we called him. We spend some time talking about the old days. I do a lot of the talking, because Nickels doesn't even know who I am most of the time. I take my dinner at Cardone's and spend my evenings in front of the television in an old third-floor walkup.

I was a loyal soldier. Now, after decades of undying loyalty to the family, Little Tommy treats me like a leper. He used to sit on my lap and call me Uncle Ange. Now he hardly ever calls to see how I am doing.

But he called tonight.

He said, "I need you to do something for me."

The kid only calls when he needs something. I wanted to tell him that I wasn't interested, but I remembered my promise to his old man. "Sure," I said. "When?"

"Tonight."

Of course, no time to prepare. "I'll be right over," I said.

I pulled a black suit out of the closet and took a brush to my shoes. Dress like you have some respect for yourself and your job

—Carlo taught me that. I always took pride in my work, and I've done a lot of different jobs for the family, but my specialty is elimination. I can't tell you how many people I've taken out in my five decades of service to the Fortunato family. In all candor, I've lost track. It's not the kind of thing you log in a journal. I sometimes feel like an old man trying to recall his many sexual conquests. The faces start to blur after a while. I was there, I remember the hit, but did I do the deed or did Carlo? Who knows? But I know my body count is easily north of eighty. It's all I have done my entire adult life. And I believe every son of a bitch I killed is rotting in hell. I may be headed there too, but I'll worry about eternity later. In the meantime, it's no secret that I am on the outside looking in, now that Little Tommy is head of the Fortunato family.

A month ago I stopped by the diner for a coffee and a doughnut. I was sitting at the counter when a guy smelling of Aqua Velva sat down next to me. He wore a nice suit, polished shoes, boring necktie. I didn't know who he was, but I knew *what* he was the minute he sat down. There were fifteen empty seats at the counter, but he sat right next to me. As he was reading the newspaper, sipping his coffee, he whispered, "Hasn't been the same around the ranch since the old man died, has it?"

I didn't say nothin'. After a minute he slid a business card under my coffee saucer and said, "We'd like to talk to you."

I put my fingertips on the card, pushed it back under his newspaper, and said, "Christ Almighty, are you trying to get me killed?"

He kept drinking his coffee. After a couple of minutes he dropped three dollars on the counter and pushed the card back under my saucer. "We'll make it worth your while, Angelo," he said, and left.

His name was Braddock, Special Agent Lawrence G. Braddock of the Pittsburgh field office of the Federal Bureau of Investigation. I put the card in my jacket pocket. I didn't call him, but a week later he called me at my apartment. I said, "My number's unlisted. How'd you get it?"

He snorted. "You're kidding, right? I'm with the FBI. I can get any number I want."

On the outskirts of Aliquippa there is an abandoned brick factory where my father worked himself into an early grave. Behind it, nearly smothered by the encroaching brush, is a cobblestone wharf that extends into the Ohio River. That's where I met him. We were at the water's edge, tiny waves lapping in the shoals, the smell of oil and mud heavy in the air.

"In the old days," I said, "when this factory was humming, they used to bring barge loads of clay to this wharf, and my dad and a few of the other grunts would start shoveling. They'd unload the whole damn barge by hand."

"Honest work," Braddock said.

"Fool's work," I said. "He'd come home so stoved up and tired he could barely walk. He couldn't even go out in the yard and toss around the baseball. He died at fifty-seven, his body completely shot."

"Is that why you got in with the Fortunatos, so you didn't have to unload barges?"

"What do you think, Sherlock?"

He looked out over the river, picked up a flat stone, and skipped it across the dark water. "We want to make you an offer, Angelo."

I said nothing.

"In exchange for your help in our investigation of Little Tommy Fortunato, we're prepared to give you complete immunity and put you in the witness protection program."

"Are you miked up?" I asked.

This time Braddock said nothing. Of course he was.

"Why would I want immunity?" I asked. "You're implying that I've done something wrong. I've never been arrested, not once."

"They're making a lot of advances in DNA research. Sooner or later someone is going to make a link to you and one of the corpses that you and Carlo left all over the tri-state. All it takes is a little blood, maybe some saliva or a hair follicle. You didn't cap all those guys without leaving some kind of evidence behind."

"I don't know what you're talking about. Besides, you'd have to have my DNA to compare it to."

Braddock smirked. "We're the FBI, Angelo, remember? Do you seriously think we don't have your DNA?"

I gotta admit, that made my ass pucker.

"We want to take down Little Tommy," Braddock said. "He's a bad guy, Angelo, a real bad guy. In the old days, when Big Tommy was in charge, you guys were just running the illegal gambling and the whorehouses. No one cared. But Little Tommy's bringing heroin, meth, and cocaine into the area in truckloads. We can't

have that. We want him off the street, and you're the key. We know
you're on your way out of the organization. It's a win-win."

"You get Little Tommy, but what do I get?"

"Along with revenge on the guy that ran you out?"

I nodded.

"You get a new identity, a nice little place in the sun. I heard your
lungs aren't so good. The dry air in Arizona or New Mexico would
be good for you. And we'll get you a very generous stipend. You'll
be able to buy yourself a new Buick."

I turned and started up the wharf. "I'll think about it," I said.
When Big Tommy was around, I would never have considered such
disloyalty.

"Don't think too long, Angelo. My bosses are impatient men.
You're not the only guy we're trying to flip, and the first guy to the
door gets the deal. In the meantime, we're still working on that
DNA. There's no statute of limitations on murder."

It's a thirty-minute drive from my apartment to the Fortunato compound on the far east side. The property is encased by a black iron
fence with a fleur-de-lis at the top of each post. Red brick pillars
stand sentry at the entrance to the driveway. A matching brick drive
snakes around to the rear of the house.

When I pulled up in my Buick LeSabre, Big Tommy's widow was
in the garden.

"Hi, Rosebella," I said. "Picking yourself some daisies, I see."

She stared blankly for a moment, struggling to caption the image in her mind's eye. It didn't come. "Yes, picking daisies," she
finally said. "I like daisies. Have you seen my Tommaso?"

Tommaso, of course, had been dead six years.

"I haven't seen him lately, Rosebella."

"I'm starting to worry. I can't imagine where he's gone."

"If I see him, I'll send him right over."

She smiled. "I'd like that very much."

She had the Alzheimer's something terrible. For forty years I ate
nearly every Sunday dinner at her home. Her husband and I were
like brothers. Now I am nothing but a nameless character passing
through the last chapter of her life—another sign that my best
days with the family are behind me.

There were three guys, young like Little Tommy, sitting on the veranda. They were talking in hushed tones, most likely about me. They sniggered, and I overheard one of them say, "The fossil has arrived." They were wearing Hawaiian shirts, hideous floral things that hid the snub-nosed .38s they had tucked in the waistbands of blue jeans, and penny loafers without socks. The blue jeans, by the way, had holes in them when they were bought. Explain that one to me, please. They looked like they were on vacation in Key West instead of working at the Fortunato compound. No respect.

Before I could get to the shade of the overhang, the tubby one, the one called Gummy, got up and walked inside. Gaetano and the Tipplehorn kid, the harelip who heads up the drug operation, continued to sit; they acknowledged my presence with the slightest of nods. Tipplehorn had a glassy look in his eyes. He was high on something. That's one more thing that would never have flown when Big Tommy was in charge.

The drug game is a cancer on our society. That probably sounds odd coming from a guy who helped run Big Tommy's whorehouses and who puts tunnels the size of shooting marbles through people's brains, but that's the way I feel. The gambling and prostitution game was just supply-and-demand economics. The mill rats all demanded a place to squander their paychecks or step out on the old lady. The drugs, they turn people's brains to mush. But whether I like it or not isn't important. It's now the family business, and Little Tommy makes more money in six months than the old man made in five years. None of that is my concern. Little Tommy gives me a job and I do it. End of story.

Little Tommy walked out the back door and made a slight move of the head, indicating that he wanted me to follow him away from the crowd. We walked past his mother, who showed not the first sign that she recognized her only son, and stopped at the edge of the paver bricks. "You're taking Gaetano with you tonight," he said.

I could feel the heat building under the collar of my dress shirt. I hated that little punk. His name wasn't even Gaetano. It was Harold or Harvey, or something like that. He began calling himself Gaetano to make himself sound more Italian. Give me a break. He was one of Little Tommy's favorites and the one designated to someday take my place. That hadn't been said, but I know what I know. He had gone with me on the last three jobs. The first two I made him wait in the car. The last one he got to watch. If it bothered him seeing a gangbanger named Lucius get his brains scrambled, he didn't show it.

I took a few calming breaths; Little Tommy knew having a shadow didn't sit well with me. I'd been a solo act ever since Carlo bought it. "You know I prefer to work alone," I said.

"It's not an option," Little Tommy said. "Look, I don't want this to come out the wrong way, but you're not going to live forever, Uncle Ange. I need to have someone waiting in the wings who knows the ropes. You're the best in the business, the absolute best, and I want him to learn from you. Besides, what's this 'I prefer to work alone' stuff? You worked with Carlo for years."

"That was different. We were a team. I trusted Carlo. This one, Gaetano, he's not ready for this. He's careless."

"I want him on this one."

"I see what's happening here, Tommy. You have me train the kid and when he's ready I'm never going to get another phone call."

"Uncle Ange, please, that's not so." He raised his right hand alongside his face. "My right hand to God, as long as you're around, you're my guy, my number one. I swear."

There was no sense in arguing. "Who's the mark?" I asked.

"Gaetano has all the information." He put a hand on my shoulder and squeezed once. "I want him getting involved. I need to know if he's got the stomach for this."

I nodded. "I'll take care of it."

The mark, I assumed, was another gangbanger. I had dropped four of them in the past two years for encroaching on the family's traditional turf. For the most part the other crime families respect boundaries. That's not the case with the gangbangers. Respect is just another word they can't spell. They come into town with their loud music and gold jewelry and think they're going to take over. There's no talking to them. The only thing they understand is a bullet to the head.

Gaetano knew he would be going with me and was already cutting across the lot. "Hey, Pops, ready to rock?"

His disrespect scalded me to my marrow. If he had called me Pops in front of Big Tommy Fortunato, he would have eaten half his teeth. But those days are just a speck in the rearview of my dying LeSabre.

"I'll drive," he said. "I'm afraid that bucket of bolts of yours will never make it."

I grabbed the handle on his garish yellow car. As I opened the door, I watched Little Tommy help his mother in from the garden. It was a tender moment that I didn't think the boy was capable of. *Uncle Ange,* I thought. He called me Uncle Ange for the first time in years. I watched until they disappeared under the shade of the veranda.

"Pops, you coming?"

I slid into the passenger seat. "What kind of car is this, other than a mark for every cop between here and Altoona?" I asked.

He laughed. "You're funny, Pops. It's a Camaro. Sweet ride, huh? They call it the Bumblebee."

"Yeah, sweet."

He squealed the tires as he pulled onto the main road. I glared at him and he eased off the gas.

"You have to be discreet in this business," I said. "We're not like the gangbangers. They roll into town with those Jap cars all jacked up with the big wheels and the music blaring. They want everyone to see them. That's not the way we operate. We work in the shadows. We get in, we get the job done, and we get out. If we do it right, nobody even knows we were there. Sometimes the poor son of a bitch we are going to see doesn't even know. Get yourself a boring car, brown, gray, something that mixes in with every other car on the street. That way, if the cops ask somebody what they saw, they don't remember the car. You drive this thing, they say, 'Yeah, I remember a car, it looked like a big damn bumblebee.'" This made Gaetano smile. "I'm serious, boy."

I leaned my seat back and inspected the dashboard. It looked like it belonged on a fighter jet. "Do you know where we're going?" I asked.

"It's over on the other side of Midland, somewhere along the river. I've been there once. I'll look it up when I get a little closer."

"Have you got a map?"

"A map? Pops, who uses maps? I got a GPS on my phone."

"See, that's exactly what I'm talking about. You've got to start listening to me. You shouldn't use a cell phone on the job. How many times have I told you that? If the FBI wants to track you, all they've got to do is get your cell-phone number. You can't leave an electronic record for them. No phones or credit cards. If you need gas, or something to eat, you pay cash, so no one knows you were there."

"I swear, Pops, I've never seen anyone who worries like you."

"You'd be wise to worry a little bit. It'll keep you alive. I'm supposed to be training you, but you don't listen. You got your own ideas and they're going to get you killed. You're careless, and in this business you can't be careless."

It started spitting rain. I slouched and looked out the window as raindrops beaded on the glass and raced past. I might as well have been talking to the wind. This kid, he was born careless. He would never make it to seventy-two.

Carlo never made it that far, but he had no one to blame but himself.

We were like brothers—Carlo, Big Tommy, and me. When Big Tommy's dad was head of the family, we were seen as the future of the organization. We weren't like these punks today. We had respect for the family. When Big Tommy took over, there was no one that he trusted more than Carlo and me. If he had a tough job to do, he handed it to us.

One day in the summer of 2008, Big Tommy called me into his office and said, "I got a job for you."

"Do you want Carlo in here for this?" I asked.

"No. It's a solo mission." He pointed to an index card on the corner of his desk. In order to maintain his distance from any dirty work, Big Tommy never uttered the name of the mark. The name was printed on the underside of the index card. I picked it up and a flush of heat consumed my face.

The name on the card was Carlo Russo.

"Can you do this?" he asked.

It felt like I was trying to chew a mouthful of steel wool. "Why?"

"Carlo . . ." His voice faded out. "Carlo has been playing double agent with the Varacalli family. They want to cut into my turf. He's been helping them. In exchange he gets a piece of the pie. You know, Angelo, I love Carlo like a brother, but I cannot tolerate this kind of disloyalty."

"Carlo?"

He nodded. "I'll ask you again, Angelo. Can you do this?"

"My loyalty is to you and the family, first and always."

"You're a good man. Take him to the cabin. Tell him we have a shipment coming in."

I thought my face would combust. "Okay," I said. "Consider it done."

I handed him the index card. Big Tommy put it in the ashtray and set it on fire with his cigar lighter. Just before I left the room, I turned and looked at the head of the Fortunato family. Where Big Tommy was concerned, I was largely a man of blind obedience. I rarely questioned him. But I had to ask, "You're sure about this, right, boss?"

"If I wasn't sure, his name wouldn't have been on that index card."

Big Tommy owned a hunting cabin on two hundred acres south of Buffalo. Periodically he would send us up there to make an exchange of prostitutes. It wasn't good to keep the same girls in a whorehouse for a long time. Some johns get tired of seeing the same talent, while others fall in love. Either way, it's not good for business. So periodically we would ship our hookers to Cleveland, the Cleveland girls would go to Buffalo, and the "Buffalo gals," as we called them, came to us. Carlo and I would meet our contacts with the Buffalo mob at the cabin and they would bring down the girls. Carlo liked this, because it usually meant an overnight in the cabin with the ladies.

I didn't waste any time. Carlo went into the bathroom to take a leak as soon as we got to the cabin. "When are they getting here?" he asked me from behind the closed door. I didn't answer. As he stepped out, still hitching up his pants, he was asking again. "Angelo, when are the girls—"

He was looking down the barrel of my Baby Glock. "There are no girls, Carlo. Get your hands up."

He slowly lifted his hands to shoulder height, frowning; his pants fell down around his ankles. "What the hell's this?"

"You know what this is."

"No, I don't. I swear."

"Big Tommy found out you've been burning the candle at both ends—working with the Varacallis."

"What? No, no. They wanted to talk to me, but I . . ."

"No more, Carlo. I'm sorry."

"No, Angelo, wait. Don't do it, for God's sake. Let me go. I'll go away, far away, and no one will ever hear from me again, I swear. You can tell Big Tommy you clipped me. He'll never know."

"I'll know." I pointed at his pants with the barrel of my pistol. "Pull your pants up. I don't want you to go out like that."

He started to cry. "Come on, Angelo, we've been friends forever."

His blubbering made me angry. How many times had I heard Carlo Russo tell a mark to take it like a man? "Is this how you want to go out, crying with your pants down around your ankles?"

He extended his right hand, tears running down his cheeks. "Please, Angelo, I beg—"

I put one right in his heart. A clean shot. He dropped on his back and was dead before he hit the floor. I took his 9-millimeter Beretta out of his suit jacket, then wrapped up his body in a paint tarp. I dragged him deep into the woods at the back of the property and spent the rest of the afternoon digging a deep grave in the sandy bottom of a dried creek bed. When I got back to town, I stopped at Undo's. I had the shrimp with linguine in a cream sauce and ordered a bottle of Chianti with two glasses.

The name of Carlo Russo was never again uttered in the presence of Big Tommy Fortunato.

Gaetano drove through Aliquippa, my old stomping grounds, and up into Monaca. "We're going to Midland. Why didn't you just cut across to Shippingport?" I asked.

He looked at his phone and tapped some buttons with his thumb. "It's not right in Midland. The GPS says this is the shortest route."

"You kids couldn't find your way to the crapper without looking at your CBS."

"GPS, Pops."

"Whatever."

We crossed the bridge over the Ohio River into Rochester, and another bridge over the Beaver River into the city of Beaver. As we were driving out of town on Route 68, I sat up straight in the seat and turned slightly toward Gaetano. "Little Tommy, he wants to make sure you've got the stones for this job. Are you ready to pull the trigger tonight?"

He smiled and nodded. "Oh, yeah. I'm ready. I was born ready, Pops."

This kid, I could have smacked him.

"Taking a man's life is no small thing, you know?"

"I want to do this. I'm ready."

"What are you carrying?"

"A Luger."

"A Luger? What are you, a member of Hitler's SS?" I retrieved the revolver that I had tucked into my waistband and held it out on my palm.

"What's that?"

"If you're going to be a pro, you need a pro's piece," I said. "Use this. It belonged to a great man—Carlo Russo."

Gaetano looked at me, then the pistol, then back at me. "Really? You're giving me Carlo Russo's gun?"

"Carlo never called it a gun. It was his 'piece.'"

He snatched it out of my hand. "Thanks, Pops." Gaetano examined the pistol as he drove, rolling it around in his hand. "I appreciate it. I'll make ol' Carlo proud." He drove with his knee while releasing the cylinder, checking to see each chamber loaded.

"It's ready to go," I said. "Remember, your first option is to put one in the back of his head. He can't fight back if he doesn't see you coming. Put it right behind the ear if you can. If not, fill his chest with lead—heart and lungs. Don't shoot him in the face."

"Why?"

"You shouldn't have to ask me that. It's disrespectful. Their relatives can't put them in an open casket if you shoot them in the face."

"All these years in the game, Pops, and you've never shot anyone in the face?"

"Not one time. I've taken out the lowest scum on earth, but a pro doesn't shoot them in the face. You don't do that to their families."

"Seems to me that shooting them in the face sends a message. It tells them you mean business."

"Sometime tonight, maybe for just two or three seconds, try to listen to one thing I tell you." I took a breath and rubbed my eyes with my fingertips. "So what's the story?"

"Same deal as usual. Some gangbangers from Youngstown are poaching on our turf again. Little Tommy's warned them. Tonight they figure out he's serious as a heart attack. This guy we're meeting thinks I want to score some heroin."

"Okay, remember, don't get careless and don't get cute. This ain't the movies. Don't be talkin' to him and makin' him beg for mercy. You're not playing for style points. Do the job and get out."

"I've got it. You're coming with me, right?"

"And what, hold your hand?"

"No, just be my backup."

"What happened to all that bravado? Five minutes ago you couldn't wait to clip this guy."

"Come on, Pops, it's my first time."

I groaned. "Fine."

Just outside of Glasgow we crossed over Little Beaver Creek and turned north onto Calcutta-Smith Ferry Road. We drove east, passed the Ohio-Pennsylvania line, and followed the road to the edge of Beaver Creek State Forest. He pulled onto a dirt road and said, "I think the meeting point is up here."

"You *think* it's up here?" I asked, my voice climbing. "We're coming out here to clip someone and you're not even sure where you're meeting him?"

He swallowed. "This is right," he said. "I remember now."

He drove a quarter mile into the heavy woods and pulled to the edge of the dirt path. "Your Bumblebee is going to get all muddy," I said.

"Let's get out," Gaetano said. "I don't want to be sitting in the car when he shows up."

"What if he brings company?" I asked.

"He won't."

We exited the car. He turned off the engine but left the headlights on.

"Wait by the car," I said. "Lean against the hood; look relaxed. You want him to let down his guard." I pointed to a thicket of trees. "I'll back you up from over there in the brush, out of sight."

I'd only taken two steps when I heard the click of the pistol hammer locking into place. Gaetano said, "That's far enough, Pops."

I turned to find him standing in the glow of the headlights, his arm extended, the pistol I had just handed him pointing at my forehead.

"Me?" I asked.

"You've been a bad boy, Pops. You've been talking to the feds."

"No, they've just been talking to me. They want me to flip, but I haven't told them anything."

"That's not what Little Tommy heard. He's still got some friends around the bureau from the old days. They told Little Tommy that you're going to sell out for a little house in the country."

"That's not true. Can't we talk about this?"

"Nothing to talk about, Pops. It's time for you to go see your buddy Carlo." He rolled his wrist, and the chrome plating on the revolver glinted in the beam of the headlights. "Ironic, ain't it, Pops? You're going to cash out on the wrong end of Carlo Russo's gun—I mean, his *piece*." He chuckled, but just for an instant before his upper lip curled and his eyes turned to slits. "I'm glad to get rid of your tired ass." He squeezed the trigger and the hammer fell. Snap. Nothing. He squeezed again. Snap. Nothing.

Gaetano looked down at the revolver and frowned. "What the . . ."

It took only a moment for him to realize what had occurred, but by then I had pulled Carlo's 9-millimeter Beretta out of my waistband and had a bead on him.

I had always figured that eventually someone would put a bullet behind my ear—I saw it as an acceptable risk of the profession. But not today. Not this young punk.

"Keep your hands up where I can see them, Junior." I took two steps closer. "You actually thought I would give a punk like you Carlo Russo's weapon." He looked down at the useless revolver. "Carlo never used a revolver, and I would never let you touch his piece. How many times have I told you that you were careless and it was going to get you killed? Too many, and now it has."

Before he could plead for his life, I emptied the magazine into his chest. It was overkill, so to speak, and the repercussion echoed through the forest. I rolled him over with my foot and pulled his wallet from his pants pocket. There was four hundred and twenty-two dollars inside, and I took it. Normally that is considered bad form in my business, but I didn't care. I fished through his pants pockets and found the keys to the Camaro. As I was about to walk away, his cell phone started to chime. I snatched it from a jacket pocket. On the white screen were the initials LTF—Little Tommy Fortunato.

I touched the green button on the screen and said, "Hi, Tommy."

He stammered for a minute. "Uncle Ange, hey, can I speak to Gaetano?"

"He can't talk right now, Tommy."

"Is he busy?"

"No, he ain't busy at all. He just can't talk."

There was a long pause on the other end. "Oh, okay, tell him to call me back when he can."

"Yeah, I don't think that's going to happen anytime soon."

"Why's that?"

"He wasn't as ready for this job as you thought. I told you he was careless."

"What happened?"

"You sleep tight tonight, Tommy."

He was still talking when I hit the red button.

For the first time in years I feel like I'm in charge, and that I matter again.

Little Tommy and Gaetano looked at me like I was a dinosaur, and maybe that played to my favor. You see, when you've been in the business as long as me, you know when something is going down. You feel it in your bones. That's why I filed down the firing pin on the revolver and made up the story about it being Carlo's. You don't live to be seventy-two in this business being careless. You've got to think ahead.

I squeeze behind the wheel of the Bumblebee and head back to the city. I have to admit, it's a pretty sweet ride. As I drive, I consider my options.

Maybe I'll take Special Agent Lawrence G. Braddock up on his offer. The damp winters here were starting to wear on me. Having a little place in Arizona might be nice.

Or maybe I'll go shoot Little Tommy Fortunato in the face.

I'll think about it a while.

In the meantime I'll use Gaetano's money to treat myself at Undo's, just like the old days. I'll get a corner booth, order the bucatini with clam sauce, a Chianti, and maybe a cannoli.

Contributors' Notes

Other Distinguished Mystery Stories of 2019

Contributors' Notes

Pam Blackwood grew up south of Greensboro, North Carolina, surrounded by extended family, a host of animals, and a child's haven of nine wooded acres to explore. She learned to love stories by listening to those her father told at the supper table on Saturday evenings. Now, somewhat tamed, she lives in the city limits with her husband, Taylor, and two black cats, Jem and Scout.

• The concepts in "Justice" are very personal to me. Having lost several loved ones over the years, I, like William, am unable to accept platitudes as comfort for the day-to-day heartbreak that comes with loss. The story was driven by my desire to let William find his way back, even while giving full expression to his bitterness and grief.

Jerry M. Burger is professor emeritus of psychology at Santa Clara University. His short stories have appeared in the *Bellevue Literary Review, Harpur Palate,* the *Briar Cliff Review,* and the *Potomac Review,* among other publications. His novel, *The Shadows of 1915,* examines the generational effects of the 1915 Armenian genocide.

• The seed for "Home Movie" came from a newspaper article I stumbled upon several years ago about the discovery of some pre-WWII movies. The films were of Jewish citizens taken in either Germany or Poland just before the rise of the Nazis. What I recall most from the article is the descriptions of how happy everyone seemed and how they had no idea that their world was about to change for the worse. This observation got me thinking about how photographs and home movies necessarily capture people and events in the middle of their stories and how differently we react to old pictures based on what those stories turn out to be.

James Lee Burke has published thirty-nine novels and two collections of short stories. He is the recipient of two Edgar Awards, the Mystery Writers of America Grand Master Award, and a Guggenhcim Fellowship. Three of his novels have been adapted for the screen, and a fourth is in production. He and his wife, Pearl, have lived for many years in western Montana.

• The first scene in my story is one I remember from the days after Pearl Harbor, when my mother and I pulled up to my grandfather's house. I remember the coldness, the dust, the broken windmill rattling in the wind, the bareness of the land, as though it had been stricken by an angry hand, the light that had been drained forever from the sky. Psychologists call this a world-destruction fantasy. However, this was no fantasy.

And neither were the deportees. In bad times, frightened people seek scapegoats. The desperate and the poor on our borders have no voice. A man in our White House demonizes them. I hope this story says something about the precipitous times in which we live. I also hope it says something about the goodness of Latino people and the holiness that I believe is characteristic of the many I have known and lived among.

Michael Cebula's fiction has appeared in a variety of publications, including *Ellery Queen Mystery Magazine, ThugLit, Midwestern Gothic, Mystery Weekly Magazine,* and the anthology *Murder Mayhem Short Stories.* His story "The Gunfighters" was selected as an honorable mention in *The Best American Mystery Stories 2019.* He lives in the Midwest with his wife, Sheryl, and his sons, Silas and Samuel.

• I can't write a short story until I know exactly what the first lines are, and once I put them down, they don't change. The opening lines of "Second Cousins" bounced around in my head for several months, but other projects got in the way before I could sit down and write them. Once I did, the rest of the story came fast. One of the things I find most fascinating about fiction—or real life, for that matter—are people who generally think of themselves as fundamentally good or normal discovering, to the contrary, exactly what they are capable of when life demands it. Hopefully "Second Cousins" explores a shade of that in an interesting and entertaining way.

The managing editor of *Alfred Hitchcock Mystery Magazine* under the editorship of Cathleen Jordan during the late 1980s, **Brian Cox** is now a newspaper editor in Detroit. He has received a handful of state and national press awards for his reporting and opinion writing. In 2017 his dramatic play *Clutter* made its world premiere at Theatre Nova in Ann Arbor, Michigan, and went on to earn two Wilde Awards, for best new script and best performance–original production. As the artistic director of PencilPoint TheatreWorks in southeast Michigan, Cox produces "Snapshots: Stories of Life," a live storytelling event in which people share true stories from their lives based on a personal photograph. He made his crossword puzzle debut when his puzzle "Knock-Knock" was published in the July 26, 2017, edition of the *New York Times*. He and his wife, Dana, have two children, Elijah and Annie.

• "The Surrogate Initiative" started out as a concept story after a particularly well-targeted advertisement came across my phone, prompting me to think, *Wow, they are getting disturbingly precise at figuring out my tastes and interests,* which led me to consider the idea that technology—AI in particular—cannot be far from being able to simulate an individual's decisionmaking process and accurately predict that person's judgments, and I started speculating what that might eventually look like. Jury duty struck me as a suitable environment to explore the question, and I became intrigued by the challenge of writing a science fiction legal thriller.

I ran the concept by a few lawyer friends of mine, and they seemed intrigued enough by the idea to buy me a beer and offer some insights, and I became involved in building the story out. I particularly enjoyed imagining Detroit in the not-too-distant future.

As the plot developed and the character of Cassandra Howard emerged, I sensed loneliness in her that I didn't understand, and it was through considering her loneliness that the special relationship with her father formed, which led me to this larger idea that the technological pursuit of digitally capturing our identities—our personhood—could result in an approximation of immortality, which, I realized with a forehead slap, I had read about years and years ago in a book by Frank J. Tipler called *The Physics of Immortality,* large swaths of which I hadn't understood but had nonetheless found fascinating.

Having lost my mother a few years ago, I know Cassandra's ache to have her father back, and I wonder how many of us who have felt that loss, if presented with the opportunity she has to resurrect her parent, would make the same choice at the end. The temptation and emotional reward would be too great for me, I fear.

Doug Crandell has received awards from the Sherwood Anderson Foundation, the Virginia Center for the Creative Arts, Kellogg Writers Series, Barnes & Noble Discover Great New Writers, and the Jentel Artist Residency. One of his stories appears in *Pushcart Prize 2017.* NPR's Glynn Washington chose Doug's story for the 2017 Page to Screen Award. A short story was awarded the 2017 Glimmer Train Family Matters Fiction Award, and stories are forthcoming in *Ellery Queen Mystery Magazine, The Sun,* and the *Saturday Evening Post.* Doug has been appointed as public service faculty at the Institute on Human Development and Disability at the University of Georgia. He is the author of four novels, two memoirs, and a true crime book about Santa Claus, Georgia.

• I grew up on farms in Indiana, places that were owned by landlords. My folks were called cash renters, a configuration that's similar to sharecropping. On one of those properties, nestled among corn and soybean fields, is a real water feature named Shanty Falls. As a kid I played there, and when we left the place for another, the falls stayed with me. Those types of geographies can follow a writer for a long time, and I was somewhat dismayed that I'd never used it as a backdrop for fiction before. That explains the inspiration for the setting.

I've had quite a few inquiries about the ending of the story, which I will attempt to explain here. When I was in college, my best friend since kindergarten had traveled to the campus to spend the weekend with me, and we found several parties to attend, all of which had cheap keg beer. My friend had always been a bit careless with his own safety, sometimes getting into fights. In a crowded house party, from across the room I could see he was flirting with someone's girlfriend, and the guy, someone we all knew liked to fight, decided to beat up my friend. People scattered, and I rushed to help while others pulled the guy off my best friend. When I got a good look at him and helped him to the car, it was clear he'd need stitches.

After he got almost a dozen stitches above his right eye and lip, I took him home to my rundown apartment. He was in pain but slept a lot. I found myself angry, with that kind of deep-down need for revenge. But I'm Quaker, and that provided a conundrum. I stewed. By 4 a.m. I found out where the guy lived and drove there, knocked on the door. His roommates roused him. I told the guy that my friend he'd beaten was in a coma, on life support. I told him the cops had asked me for names of others at the party. I told him that my friend's parents were bringing their lawyer, flying in from Chicago, arriving in the next hour. I told him he'd better run.

I'd struck him with lies, with fiction, with an invention. I made up a story in real life thirty years ago to get payback, then used the technique again as the closer for Shanty Falls. It feels true to me.

David Dean's short stories have appeared regularly in *Ellery Queen Mystery Magazine,* as well as numerous anthologies, since 1990. His stories have been nominated for the Shamus, Barry, and Derringer Awards, and "Ibrahim's Eyes" won the *EQMM* Readers Award for 2007, as did "The Duelist" for 2019. His story "Tomorrow's Dead" was a finalist for the Edgar for best short story of 2011. He is a retired chief of police in New Jersey and once served as a paratrooper with the 82nd Airborne Division. His novels, *The Thirteenth Child, Starvation Cay,* and *The Purple Robe,* are all available through Amazon.

• "The Duelist" is what's called historical fiction, and yes, I do get the irony. I have written but a few, and I only wrote those because the stories wouldn't have worked set in modern times. So, too, did "The Duelist" demand a historical context, because of its plot, its characters, and its language. In many ways the story is as much about language—what is being said, and how, as well as what is not said but lies beneath—as it is about the violence that serves to frame the story and provide its impetus.

What I can state is that the story is one about deception and truth, vengeance and justice, bravery and cowardice, love and loss. But it's mostly about bullying, and *that's* why I wrote it, though I didn't think of it at the time. It was only later that I recognized my motivation. Most of us have experienced being bullied or made afraid by someone at some time in our lives. I am no exception. In fact, looking back on my life, I suspect that being bullied had a lot to do with my choosing to be a police officer for twenty-five years. I wanted to protect people. I don't like bullies. My guess is that you don't either. If that's the case, "The Duelist" may satisfy you.

A former journalist, folksinger, and attorney, **Jeffery Deaver** is a number-one bestselling author whose novels have appeared on bestseller lists around the world, including the *New York Times,* the *Times* of London, Italy's *Corriere della Sera,* the *Sydney Morning Herald,* and the *Los Angeles Times.* His books are sold in 150 countries and have been translated into twenty-five languages. He has served two terms as the president of the Mystery Writers of America.

The author of forty-three novels, three collections of short stories, and a nonfiction law book, and a lyricist of a country-western album, he has received or been shortlisted for dozens of awards. His *The Bodies Left Behind* was named Novel of the Year by the International Thriller Writers association, and his Lincoln Rhyme thriller *The Broken Window* and a stand-alone, *Edge,* were also nominated for that prize. He has been awarded the Ian Fleming Steel Dagger and the Short Story Dagger from the British Crime Writers' Association and the Nero Award. He is a three-time recipient of the Ellery Queen Readers Award for Best Short Story of the Year and a winner of the British Thumping Good Read Award. *Solitude Creek* and *The Cold Moon* were both given the number-one ranking by *Kono Mystery Ga Sugoi!* in Japan. *The Cold Moon* was also named Book of the Year by the Mystery Writers Association of Japan.

Deaver has been honored with the Lifetime Achievement Award by the Bouchercon World Mystery Convention and the Raymond Chandler Lifetime Achievement Award in Italy. *The Strand Magazine* also has presented him with a Lifetime Achievement Award. Deaver has been nominated for eight Edgar Awards from the Mystery Writers of America, an Anthony, a Shamus, and a Gumshoe.

• I've always had an affection for reading short fiction, and I've learned much about writing from the work of Edgar Allan Poe, Joyce Carol Oates, Arthur Conan Doyle, and Ray Bradbury, among many others. I also

thoroughly enjoy writing short stories. I've always felt that all storytelling has as its most important goal emotionally engaging the audience to the greatest degree possible. I want to be *captivated* by art and entertainment, not merely intrigued or interested.

In long-form fiction this level of intensity is accomplished through creating complex, utterly real characters (good and bad) and intersecting, fast-paced plots. Without the luxury of length, however, how can short fiction achieve such emotional intensity?

"Security" is a perfect example of how I try to do just that: I grab readers with one device only: a shocking twist (or, ideally, two or three) at the end. I'm the illusionist, the sleight-of-hand artist, juggling props and displaying cards and keeping their eyes (in my case, minds) from seeing the truth —until, at the very end, it's *OMG, so* that's *what was going on!*

"Security" was part of an anthology called *Odd Partners,* in which we authors were asked to pair disparate protagonists, or antagonists, put them in a pressure cooker, and see what would happen. My story involves a streetwise woman security guard and a by-the-book law enforcer whose job is to protect an ambitious political candidate who doesn't make their job very easy, to put it mildly.

I spent about a month outlining the story (I outline everything I write), getting the pieces to come together—especially making sure the ending would be completely unexpected yet completely fair. Only after it was planned out did I write the prose. I pounded out "Security" in two or three days. I'd write more here, but I'm hesitant to, for fear I'd give away some of the surprises.

Besides, as any illusionist will tell you, one doesn't talk about a magic trick; one performs it. Enjoy!

John M. Floyd's short stories have appeared in *Alfred Hitchcock Mystery Magazine, Ellery Queen Mystery Magazine, The Strand Magazine,* the *Saturday Evening Post,* the 2015 and 2018 editions of *The Best American Mystery Stories,* and many other publications. A former air force captain and IBM systems engineer, he is also an Edgar nominee, a three-time Derringer Award winner, a recipient of the Edward D. Hoch Memorial Golden Derringer Award for Lifetime Achievement, and the author of eight books. He and his wife, Carolyn, live in Mississippi.

• If I recall, my first inspiration for "Rhonda and Clyde" came on a bitterly cold day. (We don't have many of those here in the South, thank God.) It probably put me in a *Fargo* frame of mind, because when I created Wyoming sheriff Marcie Ingalls that morning, the image of the movie character Marge Gunderson sort of jumped into my head, and it stayed there throughout the planning of the story. That choice of a protagonist

wasn't surprising; I've always liked stories about strong and smart women in law enforcement, and the way their colleagues (and the criminals) often make the mistake of underestimating them.

I also remember wanting to (1) give her a deputy she didn't particularly like and (2) make the villains a husband-wife team, maybe because I especially enjoy writing dialogue and I knew both those partnerships would give me a lot of opportunity for that. This line of thinking was a bit different for me, because I usually start with the plot and only then come up with the characters. In this case I created my players first and then dreamed up something for them to do, with some twists and reversals along the way. Anyhow, once I had all that in mind, I sat down and wrote the story in a couple of days' time—and it turned out to be one of my favorites.

Maybe an occasional cold snap isn't a bad thing . . .

Tom Franklin is the author of a collection of stories, *Poachers,* the title story of which won an Edgar Award. His novels include *Hell at the Breech, Smonk,* and *Crooked Letter, Crooked Letter,* which won the L.A. Times Book Prize for Mystery/Thriller, the UK's Gold Dagger for Best Novel, and the Willie Morris Prize for Southern Fiction. His most recent novel is *The Tilted World,* cowritten with his wife, Beth Ann Fennelly. He lives in Oxford, Mississippi, and teaches in the MFA Program at Ole Miss.

• I wrote this story because the great Lawrence Block asked me to, for his terrific anthology *From Sea to Stormy Sea.* Block had writers choose an American painter (from a list) and then select one of his or her paintings (from another list) and go from there. My painter was John Hull, and the painting is called *This Much I Know.* I'd not heard of this artist, but the picture he did was rather quiet, muted in color, depicting a small house and a couple of cars, bystanders, cops. It seemed like an "after" shot— something terrible had happened in that house, and I began wondering what the "before" was. The story came quickly after that.

Richard Helms is a retired forensic psychologist and college professor. He has been nominated six times for the Short Mystery Fiction Society's Derringer Award, winning it twice; five times for the Private Eye Writers of America Shamus Award; twice for the International Thriller Writers Thriller Award, with one win; and once for the Mystery Readers International Macavity Award. He is also a frequent contributor to *Ellery Queen Mystery Magazine,* along with other periodicals and anthologies, and has recently written three screenplays for independent filmmakers in North Carolina. A former member of the board of directors of Mystery Writers of America and the former president of the Southeast Regional

Chapter of MWA (SEMWA), he was presented with the SEMWA Magnolia
Award for service to the chapter in 2017. "See Humble and Die" is his first
appearance in *The Best American Mystery Stories*.

• I've lived in the South all my life. Though a greater portion of those
sixty-five years has been spent in cities like Charlotte, Charleston, and
Atlanta, I have always been fascinated by small towns. In fact, for twenty-
three years—until we downsized and moved back to Charlotte in 2016—
we lived in a town so small it had neither a police force nor a post office of
its own. Law enforcement was handled by the county Sheriff's Department,
and our mail arrived courtesy of a post office in a town ten miles away. We
were one step removed from being a 1950s-style rural route.

Living in a small town is a strange mix. On one hand, neighbors tend to
be closer and to support one another better than in a city. The downside
is the potential for simple arguments to turn into bitter, decades-long
blood feuds or, in the worst case, to erupt overnight in violent retribution.
Resentments simmer and run long and deep in places where you cannot
escape or hide from disputes.

My captivation with small-town life led me to devour Bill Crider's series
of Texas-based Sheriff Dan Rhodes novels. I finally met Bill at the Shamus
Awards in St. Louis several years back. We developed a casual friendship
that I dearly wish had been closer and of longer duration. Bill was gracious
enough to provide a cover blurb for one of my small-town Judd Wheeler
crime novels (*Older Than Goodbye*), and I am indebted to him for his
support. I last talked with Bill at Bouchercon in Toronto, only months
before he passed away. When I heard that Michael Bracken was editing
a book of Texas private eye stories, I endeavored to produce a story that
would make Bill proud. With the inclusion of "See Humble and Die" in
this collection, I hope that mission was accomplished.

Ryan David Jahn is the author of seven novels, including *Good Neighbors,*
which won the Crime Writers' Association John Creasey Dagger, and *The
Dispatcher,* which was named by the *Financial Times* as a top-ten crime novel
of the year. He lives with his wife, Jessica, and two daughters, Francine and
Matilda, in Louisville, Kentucky.

• My father killed himself in March 2004 while living in an RV park in
Bullhead City, Arizona. I hadn't talked to him in eight years, and don't
remember crying when I found out—don't remember feeling much
of anything at all. It was just information, like reading the obituary of
someone you've never met in the morning paper. A stranger died and
I was supposed to be torn up about it or something, but I wasn't. I got a
box of his things, including pictures he'd taken in Vietnam, his medals,
and letters he'd written to his own father. I read about his platoon taking

mortar fire; I read about a single leg lying in the dirt and how disconcerting it was to see it detached from a body.

An RV lifestyle catalogue dated February 2004 was in the box of his belongings I'd gotten. My father had circled a cabinet set, something he planned to buy for the RV he was living in if and when he got the money together. That made me cry. In February he'd had plans for the future— he was going to buy some new cabinets for his RV—but in March he was dead. I wondered if he'd saved some of the money.

My youngest daughter, Francine, likes to go hiking with me. We drive out to the woods and spend hours surrounded by trees, walking in relative silence. Sometimes we see a family of deer. Francine and I both freeze in those moments, and the deer freeze, and we all look at each other with dumb blank eyes, and in that instant—in that second before a distant twig snaps, breaking the spell—the world is absolutely perfect and beautiful. Take a picture and keep it forever. I'm not the most self-reflective person on earth, so I can't tell you why, but "All This Distant Beauty" is about the mental and emotional juxtaposition of those two things: my father's suicide sixteen years ago and an afternoon hike with my six-year-old daughter. Make of it what you will.

Sheila Kohler is the author of eleven novels, three volumes of short fiction, a memoir, and many essays. Her most recent novel is *Dreaming for Freud,* based on the Dora case, and *Open Secrets* will be published in July 2020. Her memoir, *Once We Were Sisters,* was published in 2017 in the United States, England, and Spain. She has won numerous prizes, including an O. Henry Award. Her work has been included in *The Best American Short Stories* and published in thirteen countries. She has taught at Columbia, Sarah Lawrence, Bennington, and Princeton. Her novel *Cracks* was made into a film directed by Jordan Scott, with Eva Green playing Miss G. You can find her blog at *Psychology Today* under "Dreaming for Freud."

• When Joyce Carol Oates, with her habitual generosity, asked me for a story for the anthology *Cutting Edge,* I sat down to write one for her, and "Miss Martin" appeared quite fast on the page, though I had to go back and revise somewhat, of course.

As so often with stories, there are some details from life: a house on Long Island with a loft above the dining room, which we built for grandchildren in the summer. Even the fall occurred to my poor husband, who went up the ladder that a workman had propped up carelessly against the wall and punctured a lung. I wanted to change the usual triangle here, with the "wicked stepmother" turning out in the end to be of help to my young protagonist. Here too, I have been a stepmother in life, and of course I do come from South Africa. I asked my husband, a psychiatrist, what a father could do that might merit punishment, and his response came fast: "Incest," he said.

Jake Lithua was forever corrupted at the age of five, when he discovered his father's Dungeons & Dragons Basic Set. Ever since, he has been interested in telling stories of heroism and courage, fantastical or real-world. His short story "The Most Powerful Weapon" was first published in *The Odds Are Against Us;* his novella "Trust" is included in *Ye Olde Magick Shoppe,* published in 2018. He lives far too close to Washington, D.C., for anyone's good.

• Ariya, or a character like her, has been bouncing around in my head for a long time. She began her conceptual life as a teenage American mercenary, a cold-blooded, traumatized survivor of war crimes who sticks out like a sore thumb among the relatively ordinary students at her boarding school. Then ISIS exploded onto the world scene in 2013 and 2014; with the savagery of their crimes, and especially their treatment of the Yazidis, it made sense to have the character who would become Ariya be a Yazidi herself, an enslaved child bride.

I don't remember why I chose the name Tristan for the American Green Beret. Maybe I had James Herriot's books floating around in the back of my head. But I like the idea of introducing Tristan, making it seem like he would be the white knight, and then pulling the rug out. Still, he plays an important role: he teaches Ariya that she is not just a victim, that she too can act. It is a lesson that we all can learn a little better, I think.

The anger that Tristan expresses at the Americans leaving is mine as well; in a sense, the story was motivated by my fury that we had abandoned people who had risked so much to ally with us and allowed ISIS to run rampant for over a year. Beating an ISIS mujahid to death in fiction doesn't accomplish much in the real world, but it certainly felt good.

After twenty-five years in federal law enforcement, **Rick McMahan** retired as a senior special agent with the Bureau of Alcohol, Tobacco, Firearms and Explosives (ATF) in 2017. Currently he is a law enforcement instructor for Kentucky's Department of Criminal Justice Training. Rick's short stories have appeared in various publications, including twice having the privilege of being published in Mystery Writers of America anthologies (*Death Do Us Part* and *Vengeance*). "Baddest Outlaws" appeared in *After Midnight,* an anthology by the Writers' Police Academy.

• The idea for "Baddest Outlaws" came from a real-life cop story told to me by my former coworker and friend Shawn Morman. Before becoming an ATF agent, Shawn was a Kentucky state trooper. Now, in Kentucky, Kentucky State Police is known as a no-nonsense agency enforcing the law in many remote counties. In some parts of the state officers are working where their nearest backup (if any) is a half hour away. KSP instills a distinct confidence and attitude, along with the sharply creased uniforms and polite conversation (No, ma'am, Yes, sir).

The way Shawn told the story was that when he started policing, several of the more experienced troopers warned him not to go on any call having to do with a certain family without several more officers (not just one!) as backup. Like a line from my story goes, when Kentucky state troopers leave their academy, they think they're ten feet tall and bulletproof. I wondered what kind of dangerous criminals would make them be so cautious. He said that the family, every last one of them, was combative with law enforcement. Then Morman told me that the family known for fighting police were all "little people." At that point I knew I had just found the nugget of a story that I needed to write.

I guess it's because Kentucky has had some memorable and colorful crime groups that I wanted to make the criminal family more than just a family of ne'er-do-wells. Marion County's Cornbread Mafia was a group of marijuana growers who instilled respect and fear among their own and other criminals. In fact, Johnny Boone ran the Cornbread Mafia with a very strict code of silence. During his first stint in prison, Boone had *omerta,* the Italian Mafia's word for its code of silence, tattooed across his back. Over fifty members of the Cornbread Mafia were prosecuted in federal court, and not a single one agreed to cooperate with the government and turn state's witness. Boone himself fled before trial and for several decades eluded police.

Another unique crime group was Drew Thornton's cocaine-smuggling crew, made up of ex-military members and ex-cops, all criminals, as chronicled in the book *The Bluegrass Conspiracy.* They flew cocaine from South America into the southeast United States. They claimed to be working for the CIA. Of course that was never proven and denied by the government, but they sure had a ton of weapons they moved around. They had connections to politicians in Kentucky, some rumored to be as high as the governor's office. As the crew became more brazen, law enforcement took notice and began investigating the group. As criminal investigations grew, the crew began to unravel. Several members went to prison, for everything from stealing classified government equipment to drug trafficking as well as murdering a Florida judge. However, Drew Thornton's end wasn't in a courtroom; rather, his demise played out like a scene from a bad spy movie. While flying back with a load of cocaine, his plane was being targeted by Customs aircraft, which he couldn't lose. In an attempt to get away, Drew put on a parachute and jumped. However, he had strapped several duffel bags of cocaine along with a silenced pistol to his body, overloading the chute. He plummeted to his death, and was discovered when a homeowner walked out to his driveway to get his morning paper. Before jumping from the plane, Thornton and his copilot had shuffled more duffel bags out along their route. One of those floating parachutes full of cocaine landed in the Smoky Mountains National Forest. A curious black bear got into the duffel bag, and before his heart exploded, the bear consumed several pounds of Colombian powder. The Cocaine Bear is stuffed and on display in a museum in Kentucky.

With such colorful (and, never forget, dangerous) criminal organizations in Kentucky's history, I wanted the Creeches to be just as unique. In deciding where to set the story, I used the imaginary Clement County, a place invented by my writing mentors Hal Blythe and Charlie Sweet. Many of their own mysteries, published under their pen name (Hal Charles), are set in Clement County, so I decided it would be as good a place as any for the Baddest Outlaws of Kentucky to call home.

Lisa Morton is a screenwriter, the author of nonfiction books, and an award-winning prose writer whose work was described by the American Library Association's *Readers' Advisory Guide to Horror* as "consistently dark, unsettling, and frightening." She is the author of four novels and 150 short stories, a six-time winner of the Bram Stoker Award, and a world-class Halloween expert. Her most recent books include *Weird Women: Classic Supernatural Fiction by Groundbreaking Female Writers 1852–1923* (coedited with Leslie S. Klinger) and *Calling the Spirits: A History of Seances*. Lisa lives in the San Fernando Valley and online at www.lisamorton.com.

• My grandfather loved to shoot anything with his 16mm movie camera (remember when we had cameras instead of phones?), and I inherited a box of these tiny reels of film that could have *anything* on them. I suspect most of them are probably pretty dull vacation footage with people I won't even recognize, so I've never paid to transfer them to DVD, but whenever I glance at that box, I always wonder, *What if . . .* ? What if there's something on there that he filmed by accident, or meant to destroy after he had the film developed? He was a lifelong resident of Indiana, so it's thoroughly unlikely that he photographed any Veronica Lake–ish movie stars (like the title character in my story). I think I prefer to let the movies remain unknown and instead imagine that they hold tantalizing mysteries.

John Sandford (pen name for John Camp) has written more than fifty thriller novels, all of which have appeared, in one form or another, on the *New York Times* bestseller list, including many that debuted at number one. A former newspaper reporter, Sandford won a Pulitzer Prize for feature writing in 1986 for stories about a farm family experiencing small farming's economic and financial crisis of the mid-1980s. In addition he has written nonfiction books on art (*The Eye and the Heart: The Watercolors of John Stuart Ingle*) and plastic surgery (*The Kindest Cut*). He lives in Santa Fe with his wife, the screenwriter Michele Cook, and their Belgian malinois, Willa.

• I don't write much short fiction, but when Lawrence Block approached me about doing a short story based on a famous painting, the idea greatly appealed to me. I'm an art history buff, the way some people are Civil War buffs, and have a special affection for American paintings of the first half of the twentieth century. I also play guitar, strictly as a hobby, and once considered writing a thriller based around L.A. pop music culture. My prospective title for the novel was "Girl with an Ax." Maybe I still will do that, but she showed up first in this short story. And there was another thing going on. Way back when, working as a reporter, I was also trying to write novels, without much initial success, Larry Block was well known for his how-to books on writing as well as his fiction. I was looking through one of them when I encountered something to the effect of "Throw away your first chapter." That was the only thing I ever got out of a how-to book, but it sort of changed my life. He was saying, in effect, don't go through a bunch of tedious scene-setting and character introductions—go with the story. I threw away my first chapter and was on my way as a fiction writer. I've always felt indebted to him for that, so when he asked . . .

dbschlosser is an award-winning fiction and nonfiction author and an award-winning editor. His fiction has appeared in university literary journals and online magazines. His nonfiction and journalism have run in business and trade publications, academic and scientific journals, and print and online news outlets. As a political, public relations, advertising, marketing, and content strategist, he has delighted and offended people in the *New York Times* and *Wall Street Journal* as well as on *Hard Copy* and *Inside Edition.* As a teacher, he has engaged high school debaters, university writers and communicators, continuing education mystery fans, and writers and editors at seminars and conferences. Kansan by birth, he turned Texan while earning degrees at Trinity University and the University of Texas. After living and working in nearly a dozen states, he, his lovely wife, Anne, and their dogs consider Seattle home.

• "Pretzel Logic" was inspired by Steely Dan's song of the same title. I am grateful to Brian Thornton for his invitation to submit a story to the anthologies of crime fiction inspired by the band's music, *Die Behind the Wheel* and *A Beast Without a Name,* which he curated and edited. The concept of pretzel logic appealed to my sense that no matter how irrational a person's behavior seems to observers, a rational human acts on motives I can understand if I peel enough layers off the onion. Part of the joy of storytelling is interpreting behavior and motivation through action. Part of the joy of Steely Dan's music is that it's open to so many different interpretations. The musicians who crafted the song claimed it's about time travel. That was not my interpretation. After living in cities challenged by race issues I'd associated with prior generations before encountering them in mine, I also was inspired by the concept of minstrelry in the southland. I've been illuminated by more than a few light-bulb moments in which I came to understand as rational what appeared initially to me irrational. I wanted to explore my fellow humans going about routines that seem counterintuitive, counterproductive, or antisocial but on deeper consideration make not just sense but perfect, tragic sense. I also have wanted to work into a story the location of the story's climax—one building in two states. That building exists in Kansas City, but I imagine this story's fictional metro area is more like Charlotte, which sprawls over the line between the Carolinas. I'm optimistic that Bax will enjoy more adventures there, and I hope that you will enjoy reading about them in the future.

Wallace Stroby is an award-winning journalist and the author of nine novels, four of which feature professional thief Crissa Stone, whom *Kirkus Reviews* called "crime fiction's best bad girl ever." His previous short story, "Night Run," was chosen for the 2017 edition of *The Best American Mystery Stories*. He has also written for *Esquire Japan*, BBC Radio 4, *Reader's Digest*, *Salon*, *Slant*, *Writer's Digest*, *Inside Jersey*, and other publications. A lifelong resident of the Jersey shore, he was an editor for thirteen years at the *Newark* (N.J.) *Star-Ledger*.

• Few books meant as much to me in my formative years as the novels of Lawrence Block. So I was happy to accept his invitation to contribute a short story to his 2019 anthology *At Home in the Dark*. The brief was simple—the stories could be in any genre, set anywhere and in any era, as long as they were at the "darker end of the spectrum." I chose to revisit my series character Crissa Stone, a blue-collar professional thief who'd previously appeared in four novels, the last being 2015's *The Devil's Share*. Fittingly for the anthology, I wanted the story to take place over the course of a single night, with Crissa trying to hold on to $100,000 in stolen drug money while its previous owners hunt her down across a barren New York City nightscape. So I'm grateful to Larry for both the invitation to contribute and the chance to bring Crissa out of retirement, if only briefly.

Robin Yocum watched his father come home from a West Virginia steel mill black with fly ash and soot and thought, *There's got to be an easier way to make a living.* When he discovered that writing required no heavy lifting and offered virtually zero chance of falling into a ladle of molten steel, he signed up. Yocum is proud of his Ohio River Valley roots and sets his fiction in eastern Ohio, near his boyhood home of Brilliant. A former award-winning crime reporter with the *Columbus Dispatch*, he has published two true-crime books and five novels. *A Brilliant Death* was a finalist for both the 2017 Edgar and the Silver Falchion Award for Best Adult Mystery. *Favorite Sons* was named the 2011 Book of the Year for Mystery/Suspense by USA Book News. Yocum is a proud graduate of Bowling Green State University, where he received a degree in journalism that prevented an untimely and fiery death in the steel mill.

• When I'm asked where I get the ideas for my stories, I offer this honest answer: I have no earthly idea. How does one explain imagination and the creative process? My brain is always pinballing with ideas.

With that said, I was no stranger to the presence of the mob while growing up in the Ohio River Valley. The Youngstown mob controlled the prostitution and gambling in Steubenville. It was the worst-kept secret ever. The whorehouses lined Water Street, and gambling was everywhere. Literally everywhere. I could get football spot sheets at my high school. I'm not even sure I knew they were illegal.

That's where my protagonist, Angelo, was born in my imagination. He was a product of a system that thrived in the Ohio Valley when the steel mills were at their zenith. My late father said that the reason the Ohio Valley economy boomed was because the 60,000 steelworkers who lived and worked there spent every dime they made. A portion of those paychecks went for prostitutes and gambling. But when the mills died, there was no money for playing the daily number or the spot sheets, and there was certainly not enough money for a turn with the girls on Water Street. With no profits to be had, the mob retreated from the valley.

When that happened, I remember wondering what became of the old guard, the low-level mobsters, bagmen, and enforcers who made their money protecting the prostitutes, collecting debts, and breaking bones. You know, doing mob stuff. Does the mob have a retirement plan or offer severance packages? I'm betting no.

As the story unfolds, that's where we find Angelo. He's an admitted dinosaur who has lost his usefulness to the family. The story explores my version of what happens when a longstanding member of the mob is no longer mission critical. I can't image it would be good.

Other Distinguished Mystery Stories of 2019

HANSEN, PAUL
    Tough Love. *New Ohio Review,* no. 25
HORROCKS, CAITLIN
    Teacher. *The Arkansas International,* no. 6
JANEWAY, JUDITH
    Get a Life. *Fault Lines,* ed. by Margaret Lucke, Sisters in Crime Northern California Chapter
JOHNSON, BOB
    The Continental Divide. *The Hudson Review,* Summer
KLEIN, DAVID
    Finch. *The Hudson Review,* Spring
KNOPF, CHRIS
    Catch and Release. *Down to the River,* ed. by Tim O'Mara, Down and Out
MCANDREW, TYLER
    Letters from Toby. *Epoch,* vol. 68, no. 1
MCFADDEN, DENNIS
    Cannibals in Canoes. *Antioch Review,* Summer
MONTGOMERY, SCOTT
    No One Owns the Blues. *The Eyes of Texas,* ed. by Michael Bracken, Down and Out
OATES, JOYCE CAROL
    Final Interview. *The Strand Magazine,* July–November
REED, ROBERT
    The Province of Saints. *The Magazine of Fantasy and Science Fiction,* January/February
ROSS, J. PAUL
    Gethsemane. *Antioch Review,* Summer
ROZAN, S. J.
    Cooking the Hounds. *Mystery Tribune,* Winter
THIELMAN, MARK
    Blind Spot. *Alfred Hitchcock Mystery Magazine,* May/June
WALKER, JOSEPH
    Bonus Round. *Alfred Hitchcock Mystery Magazine,* May/June
WILEY, MICHAEL
    Spray. *Ellery Queen Mystery Magazine,* March/April
ZELTSERMAN, DAVE
    Brother's Keeper. *Ellery Queen Mystery Magazine,* May/June

THE BEST AMERICAN SERIES®

FIRST, BEST, AND BEST-SELLING

The Best American Essays

The Best American Food Writing

The Best American Mystery Stories

The Best American Science and Nature Writing

The Best American Science Fiction and Fantasy

The Best American Short Stories

The Best American Sports Writing

The Best American Travel Writing

Available in print and e-book wherever books are sold.

Visit our website: hmhbooks.com/series/best-american